STOLEN BY THE BRATVA DEVIL

AN AGE GAP SECRET BABY FORCED MARRIAGE
CHRISTMAS MAFIA ROMANCE

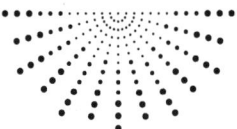

ALEXIS LEE

CONTENTS

PROLOGUE

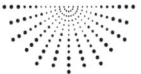

Kholod

The bullet grazed the brick wall inches from my cheek, spraying grit and razor-sharp snowflakes across my face like goddamn shrapnel. My gut wound burned like somebody'd jammed a red-hot poker right through me—every breath ripping fresh hell. Warm blood was leaking out fast, dragging the last scraps of heat from my body.

This filthy, cramped back alley in South District had turned into my personal slaughterhouse. The stench of rotting trash, gunsmoke, and fresh blood hung thick in the air, turning my stomach.

"Kieran... that son of a bitch..." I slumped against the slick, frozen wall, sucking in ragged breaths. My Beretta 92F was scorching hot in my grip, and three of those Irish pricks were already sprawled at my feet, leaking out their last. But there were more shadows out there. Dmitri was off handling that seized shipment at the docks—I'd sent him ahead. Right now, I was flying solo.

I'd fucked up bad. Never figured Kieran would have the balls to hit me on Christmas Eve, this close to my turf. Ballsy. Reckless. Suicidal.

Boots crunched on the snow at the alley mouth—slow, deliberate, like they were savoring the kill. Low Irish drawls cut through the night, mocking, cat-and-mouse bullshit. They were closing in, drawing out the fun of watching me, boss of the Morozov family, bleed out in this shithole gutter.

"Jingle bells, jingle bells, jingle all the way..." Church bells and carols drifted from somewhere distant, crisp and cheerful. To me, it sounded like a fucking dirge.

My vision was going fuzzy, ears ringing like a busted fire alarm. My trigger finger was numb from blood loss and the biting cold—dead weight.

I was saving my last round for myself.

Scuff—crunch—

A soft shuffle from deep in the alley. No copper tang of blood. Just a faint whiff of something sweet. No killer vibe.

Instinct kicked in. I wheeled around on pure adrenaline, gun leveled into the dark, voice a gravelly bark. "Who's there? Show yourself!" It didn't even sound like me—raw and wrecked.

A slim shadow flinched in the gloom.

"Out! Or I shoot!" I snarled it louder, though each word yanked at my gut like a knife twist.

The figure froze, then edged into the dim light, slow as hell.

Blood blurred my eyes; couldn't make out details. But the outline? Girl. Young.

"You need help?"

"No."

"But you're—"

"Beat it!" No time for some lost civilian stumbling into this mess. My focus had to stay on the real wolves at the mouth.

She didn't budge. Stepped closer instead.

"Hey! Over there! I heard something!"

"Morozov ain't getting far! The bastard's hit!"

My growl had drawn 'em. Footsteps pounded now, closing fast.

Game over. I yanked her into my chest, clamping a hand over her mouth.

We were mashed tight. Orange blossom—clean, sharp—cut through the alley's rot like a lifeline.

"Over there!"

"Sorry..." she whispered, hot against my palm. Then she shoved me back against the wall. Before I could blink, her arms hooked around my neck.

"Oh, baby, I hate to let you go!" she hollered, voice bright and loud as hell.

Next thing, her lips crashed into mine—cold, soft, electric.

I froze solid.

Whizzing bullets. Shouts. Carolers. The fire in my gut. All of it? Gone. Just her mouth on mine, clumsy and sweet, that orange scent wrapping around my skull.

Her kiss was green as hell—awkward, just pressing close. She trembled against me, maybe from the freeze, maybe fear. Long lashes brushed my skin like feathers.

To sell it, she flicked her tongue in tentative, tracing my lips. Hesitant. Teasing.

Me—a guy who ran empires, crushed throats without blinking—reduced to this. Letting some stranger call the shots. The thrill hit like lightning, mixing with the raw edge of death. My blood fired up, body betraying me in the worst goddamn way. I nearly groaned right there.

She felt it, stiffened to pull back. But fuck that—my arms locked, dragging her deeper. I took over, sucking her tongue, pinning her head so she couldn't squirm free. My palm slid to her neck—cool silk under my fingers. She gasped into my mouth, a soft whimper that lit me up worse.

Christ, I was rock-hard, throbbing. If not for the hole in my belly, I'd have her pinned and screaming under me right then.

"...Shit, it's just some horny couple making out! Damn it!" A gravelly voice from the mouth, pissed-off and fading.

"Nah, let's bounce. Check elsewhere. He can't have gone far!"

The crunch of boots receded into the night.

She'd saved my ass.

The realization slammed me like a gut punch. Her smarts. Her guts. How long had that kiss dragged on? Seconds? An eternity? When she finally broke free, we were both heaving, fogging the air between us.

"...They're gone," she murmured.

"You..." I started, but agony clawed my stomach again. I grunted, knees buckling. She caught me, steadying my weight like it was nothing.

"You're bleeding bad! You need a hospital—now!" Her fingers flew over her phone.

"Hello? Hello? Is this emergency services? I'm at... South District, near the narrow alley behind Seventh Street. Someone's been shot."

She clicked off, slung my arm over her slim shoulders without a word. "Hang on. Ambulance is coming."

She was tiny, no muscle to her, but she hauled me anyway—dragging us toward the glow at the mouth. Her warmth seeped through her coat, soft curves pressing close against the snow's bite.

Every step was torture. Pure fire.

We hit the mouth just as sirens wailed closer, cutting the dark.

She exhaled sharp, shifting to prop me better. Minutes later, medics swarmed—stretcher out, prying me off her, dumping me on the gurney.

My hand brushed something cold, metallic. With my last gasp, I snatched it.

A bracelet.

They wheeled me into the rig. Door swinging shut. I twisted for one look—her face, anything—but bang. It sealed, muffling the world.

"Find her..." The vow burned in my brain as black spots swallowed me whole.

Whoever you are. Wherever you run.

You're mine.

CHAPTER ONE

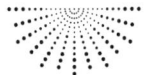

Noelle

"He looks like a breathing iceberg," Isabella whispered in my ear, her breath warm against my earlobe, carrying the scent of her expensive perfume.

I jolted back to reality, realizing I'd been staring at the man at the altar far too long.

The organ's solemn notes echoed through the towering dome of the Cathedral Basilica of Saints Peter and Paul, creating an almost sacred harmony with the silent snow drifting outside on this peaceful Christmas Eve. Yet my heart felt as though an invisible hand was squeezing it tight, beating frantically and heavily.

This dark green velvet gown was the result of Mother Sofia's entire afternoon of careful selection. She had knelt before me, smoothing every wrinkle in the skirt like a devout believer.

"Perfect! Noelle. I knew it. The dark green makes your skin look porcelain-white while maintaining dignity. A man of Kholod's stature will certainly appreciate this understated elegance."

She looked up at me, studying my face with an almost fevered gleam in her eyes. As she spoke, her well-manicured hands pressed firmly against an imperceptible wrinkle in my dress.

In the mirror, I looked like a stranger wrapped in finery. The velvet shimmered under the lights, its body-hugging cut creating unfamiliar curves—this dress was beautiful like an exquisite cage.

"Mother," I finally spoke, my voice hoarse, "why do you keep mentioning Kholod? It's his wedding today, not mine."

I couldn't understand why, ever since learning about this wedding, Kholod's name had become her gospel. From hairstyle to accessories, every requirement she had for me was judged by the ultimate standard of "Mr. Kholod will like this."

Mother stood without answering my question. Moving behind me, she began arranging loose strands at the back of my head, her fingertips cold and unyielding.

"What do you know? Noelle, do you think this is just some ordinary wedding? This is an opportunity! A once-in-a-lifetime opportunity!"

"Opportunity?" I met her gaze in the mirror. "To catch some wealthy man?"

She let out a sharp laugh, as if she'd heard the world's greatest joke. She spun me around, gripping my shoulders tightly, forcing me to look directly at her. "Noelle Bellucci, can you be realistic for once? Look at this house! Look at that café downstairs with nothing but flies for customers! Look at me bowing and scraping to debt collectors on the phone every day!"

Her voice began to tremble, deep exhaustion and despair showing through her flawless makeup. "Your father left us more than just the Bellucci name—he left us a complete disaster! Those people who used to grovel before us are now waiting to watch us fall, waiting to devour us alive! The money we owe—we could sell the house twice and it wouldn't cover our debts!"

I fell silent. These words cut like dull blades, repeatedly slicing through nerves already numb. This was our reality—a sinking quagmire I was powerless to change.

"So," I asked quietly, "I should be packaged like merchandise and sent to a party to be sold to the highest bidder?"

"What else?!" Mother's voice shot up. "Keep clinging to those unrealistic photo albums and blogs, daydreaming about traveling the world? Noelle, dreams don't fill stomachs! They don't pay debts!"

She took a deep breath, seeming to summon every ounce of strength to calm herself. She adjusted my collar again, her tone softer but filled with suffocating desperation.

"Listen, sweetheart. Today, every elite in Philadelphia will be there —Kholod's friends, his business partners, all men at the pinnacle of power. You don't need to do anything except be seen." She cupped my face as if admiring a work of art.

"Look at you, Noelle. How beautiful you are! Do you know how much I've invested in cultivating you? Just appear there, flash an appropriate smile, and someone will notice you. That will be our only lifeline."

"So you're simply using his wedding to find me a buyer."

Mother's face went ashen, her expression deeply conflicted. She lowered her head and fastened a delicate diamond necklace around my neck. The cold touch made me shudder.

"Noelle," she finally said, her voice weary and raspy, "don't blame me."

"Darling, relax." Isabella gently patted my hand, drawing me from the memory. Her voice carried undisguised envy. "Look, that's Kholod —a name everyone on the East Coast knows. Wealth, power... everything he possesses is legendary. I wonder which fortunate woman could make him willing to enter marriage."

A wave of bitterness swept through me. I quickly suppressed this unnecessary emotion, telling myself it had nothing to do with me.

"Honestly, Noelle, I truly feel sorry for you. With your pretty face, if you'd come to your senses earlier, you might be the one standing at that altar."

"Don't talk nonsense." I lowered my eyes. "The Morozov family would be delighted to see us in debt."

I pulled out my phone from my purse and browsed my travel social media account.

I retrieved my phone and scrolled through that carefully maintained travel account—Norway's fjords, Tuscan sunshine, bustling

7

Southeast Asian markets. These photos were all collected from others' videos and documentaries, constructing a dream completely unrelated to the Bellucci family's decline and Mother's increasingly urgent pressure.

I sighed silently and stuffed the phone back into my pocket, as if this could hide away that freedom-seeking part of myself as well.

When I looked up, my gaze involuntarily returned to the altar. Kholod Morozov. Even at this distance, standing in silence, he radiated suffocating dominance. I couldn't make out his features clearly, only catching his stern profile and those eyes that occasionally glanced toward the priest—cold and sharp as premium amber.

"The ceremony's beginning," Isabella whispered excitedly in my ear.

The priest approached the altar, solemn Latin prayers echoing through the church. The organ music swelled, and everyone held their breath, watching that heavy oak door.

One minute.

Five minutes.

Ten minutes.

The door remained firmly shut.

"Where's the bride?"

"She didn't... run off, did she?"

"Run? Could she even escape Philadelphia? Does she have a death wish?"

"Look at Kholod's expression... I'd rather go winter swimming in the Delaware River."

"I bet a hundred dollars we'll hear gunshots within ten minutes."

Whispers rose and fell like a flock of disturbed crows, circling beneath the church's ornate dome, making the air thin and tense.

In the front row, Anastasia Morozov maintained her dignified posture, but a shadow flickered in her usually commanding eyes. Beside her, Anya made no effort to hide her irritation, glancing at her diamond-studded watch and leaning toward her mother to complain. "How much longer do we wait? What on earth is Kholod doing?"

"My God! What's happening?" Isabella exclaimed.

I didn't answer, my gaze unconsciously locked on the man at the altar. He stood motionless as a mountain, as if the surrounding commotion had nothing to do with him. But I could sense the air around him crystallizing into ice, about to transform into a blizzard.

The priest cleared his throat awkwardly, attempting to continue the proceedings, but his voice was drowned in the growing murmur of voices.

Then Kholod suddenly turned around.

Time seemed to freeze.

Those amber eyes swept like a falcon's gaze across the restless crowd, past the ornate decorations and flickering candlelight, locking onto me with deadly precision.

A chill crept up my spine. I looked toward my mother's direction—she sat in the front side section, hands tightly clasped.

What was Kholod gonna do?

Before the thought could fully form, he was already moving. Not toward the side door to search for his missing bride, but striding down the altar steps with long strides, across the red-carpeted aisle, straight toward me!

Shocked gasps erupted around us. Isabella drew in a sharp breath.

He moved with frightening speed, his black formal coat billowing behind him like a cold wind. In an instant, his towering figure loomed over me, his shadow completely engulfing me.

He seized my wrist violently.

"Ah!" I cried out in pain.

"Mr. Morozov! You..." Isabella's voice became shrill with shock.

He completely ignored her.

"Stand up."

"Let go of me!" I struggled, but his left arm locked around my waist like an iron vice. Terror flooded through me, yet the scorching heat from his palm through the fabric sent an inexplicable tremor of excitement through me.

Every eye in the church was fixed on us.

"Kholod, you've lost your mind! This is your wedding!" I tried to pry his fingers loose, my nails leaving scratches on his hand, but he showed no reaction.

Half-forcing me forward, I stumbled past the front rows. I whipped around to look at Mother—Sofia Bellucci.

She turned her face away, lips trembling, avoiding my gaze.

In that moment, my heart plunged into an icy abyss.

She knew. She had always known.

My last hope extinguished. I stopped struggling. The so-called "attending an important wedding," the so-called "seeking opportunities for the family"—it had all been a conspiracy against me from the very beginning.

I was the sacrificial offering.

Kholod half-carried, half-dragged me to the front of the altar, positioning me before the panic-stricken priest. He seized my right hand and raised it, our fingers forced to intertwine intimately, exposed under everyone's stare.

He turned toward the priest, toward the hall full of guests, his voice cold as a blade, cutting through every corner of the church.

"Continue the ceremony." He paused, his gaze sweeping over faces filled with shock or terror before finally settling back on my pallid face, the corner of his mouth curving into an almost cruel smile.

"My bride is Miss Noelle Bellucci."

CHAPTER TWO

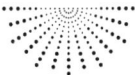

Kholod

The car was thick with the bitter aftertaste of cigars mixed with leather—a perfect match for my mood. Outside, Philadelphia's streets blurred past in the falling snow, everything fading to gray and white. The convoy moved silently toward the Cathedral Basilica of Saints Peter and Paul, the place that would soon become my battlefield.

Three years had dulled most details of that winter attack—washed away by blood and time. I only remembered the bone-cutting cold, and that single thread of orange blossom scent cutting through the ice and snow.

I survived. Kieran and his crew? I damn near wiped them off the map. People come and go, but this bracelet—it was the only proof that snowy night ever happened.

I had Dmitri tear through every connection, searching Philadelphia and beyond for the bracelet's owner. The trail twisted and turned, finally pointing to the crumbling Bellucci family. To a woman named Noelle Bellucci.

When Dmitri dropped her photo on my desk, something between pure joy and deeper obsession seized me instantly.

The girl in the picture had soft, flowing hair and clear brown eyes like a forest stream. She wasn't smiling—just staring at the camera with distant defiance in her expression.

She was beautiful. And those pure eyes? They matched the kindness I remembered from that beam of light.

I went to see her myself, bracelet in hand. The Bellucci house was a shabby old place, worn thin but still pretending to have class. Her mother Sofia's careful, almost groveling attitude made my skin crawl.

"I want to see Noelle."

"Yes, yes, she'll be right down." Sofia's smile turned even more desperate to please.

When she walked into the living room wearing simple home clothes, irritation flickering across her face at being disturbed, my heart did something it hadn't done in three years—it forgot how to beat steady.

"Is this yours?"

After she sat down, I pushed the bracelet toward her.

She picked it up, studied it carefully, confusion filling her eyes. After turning it over and over, she set it down and gave me a vague answer. "Maybe... I can't remember."

Can't remember?

Those words hit me like ice water, dousing the fire that had been burning in my chest. How dare she forget? That bracelet was the only thing I'd managed to grab in all that darkness and blood!

I crushed down the violence that surged up, leaned forward, locked my eyes on hers, and said exactly what I'd come to say—the obsession that had eaten at me for three years. "Noelle Bellucci, marry me."

She jerked like she'd been stung, her beautiful eyes wide with disbelief.

"Do you know what you're saying?"

"I know exactly what I'm saying."

"No way." She refused flat out, her expression complicated.

"Why?"

"Kholod Morozov, you have the nerve to ask me why? You should know better than anyone."

"I don't understand. Spell it out."

"Between us..." She took a deep breath. "Marriage is impossible."

"We're both single. Why is it impossible?"

"How can you say something so shameless?"

"Marry me, and the Morozov family will handle Bellucci's debts."

The air seemed to freeze for a few seconds.

"You think you can buy me?" Noelle shot to her feet, her chair scraping harshly, flames in her eyes ready to burn me alive.

"It's what you deserve."

She laughed bitterly. "So to you, I'm no different from a diamond in a jewelry store?"

"I'm just solving a problem."

"Solving a problem?" She pointed at me, furious. "You're solving YOUR problem! You never once considered me!"

Something exploded in my chest. "Noelle, don't test my patience!"

"Patience? Let me tell you something, Kholod Morozov—even if every man on earth dropped dead, I still wouldn't marry you!"

I laughed. Pure rage.

Perfect. She'd not only forgotten, she'd rejected me in the most brutal way possible. The urge to destroy everything screamed through my veins. I wanted to wrap my hands around her delicate neck, force her to tell me what gave her the right to forget, what gave her the right to refuse—but looking at her pale, stubborn face, I did nothing.

I stood up, looking down at her, and left the bracelet on the table.

"You'll remember. You have to remember."

Back in the car, I only said one thing to Dmitri.

"Dig."

The investigation results landed on my desk fast. Turns out she was convinced her father's death was my fault—absolutely ridiculous. Old Bellucci gambled himself into debt, got cornered by loan sharks, and jumped off a building. Now, somehow, that blood was on my hands?

I never planned to explain. Morozovs don't justify themselves to anyone.

If she was dead set on calling me a killer, then fine. I'd be exactly what she wanted. I'd make her spend her whole life paying for this debt she'd stuck me with.

But her resistance was fiercer than I'd expected. I decided to give her time, let her see reality—accepting me was her only choice.

I had her watched, officially for protection, really to see what she actually cared about.

She locked herself in her room all day, curtains drawn tight, like she was hiding from the whole world. The few times she fought with Sofia, it was always over stupid shit—table manners or posture. Every gift I sent came back untouched with the same message: "Tell your boss to give it up," sometimes with a few curses thrown in.

It drove me fucking crazy. I could control billions in shipping routes, make the entire East Coast underworld bow down, but I couldn't read this woman's mind.

I'd just finished handling dock business and should've gone straight back to the office, but when the car passed near her place, I changed my mind.

"Go to the Bellucci house."

The driver hesitated but quickly turned around. I waited outside her building for ages, hoping to hear her voice—even if she was fighting. Then she walked out of the apartment building wearing a perfectly tailored black cocktail dress that showed off her slender neck and smooth shoulders. She had light makeup on, her long hair swept up in an elegant twist, walking in thin heels.

She'd never dressed like that for me. Not even when her mother forced her to see me last time.

"Follow her." My voice came out colder than I'd intended.

The car tailed her taxi all the way to Rittenhouse Square. I watched her walk into Parc, and five minutes later, I followed.

I spotted her immediately.

Across from her sat some guy in his forties, receding hairline, custom suit that couldn't hide his gut. He had this sleazy smile plastered on his face, one hand holding his drink, the other creeping toward her.

A blind date. She was on a fucking blind date.

I took a corner table, ordered whiskey, but my eyes never left them.

"Noelle, you're more stunning every time I see you." The guy's voice was slick enough to make me sick. "I heard the Bellucci family's having some troubles? Don't worry, I've got pull at the commerce association. These things are nothing."

Noelle kept her eyes down and said quietly, "Thank you, Mr. Williams."

Her submission felt wrong. Foreign.

"Call me Oliver." The man's grin got more disgusting. "We'll be family soon enough, won't we?"

He reached out and covered her hand where it rested on the table.

I gripped my glass tighter.

Noelle tensed but didn't pull away. Instead, she gave him this sweet, obedient smile and nodded.

I'd imagined her looking shy and compliant in my arms countless times. Now she was giving that look to someone else—some piece of trash I could crush without thinking. The glass almost cracked in my hand.

"I understand your situation," Oliver got bolder, stroking the back of her hand. "Marry me, and you won't have to worry about anything. I'm older, sure, but I'll take good care of you."

"You're too kind." Her voice was barely audible.

Oliver was clearly encouraged. He stood up and moved to her side. "Come on, let's drink to celebrate meeting each other."

His hand landed on her shoulder, fingers rubbing her bare skin.

My sanity was hanging by a thread.

Noelle's eyelashes fluttered, but she still picked up her glass.

"Good girl," Oliver whispered in her ear. "Want to see my new apartment tonight? Amazing view..."

His other hand slid toward her waist.

Noelle finally shifted away, her voice tight with nerves. "Mr. Williams, please don't..."

"What's the problem? We're getting married." Oliver, emboldened by alcohol, grabbed her arm and tried to pull her up. "Come on, you need someone to take care of you. I'll keep you comfortable for life."

"No, I'm not ready..." Noelle started struggling, but he was obviously stronger.

"Stop playing games." Oliver lost his patience and yanked her to her feet. "I've seen plenty like you. Who are you trying to impress?"

Noelle went white as a sheet. "Let go of me!"

I set down my glass and stood up.

"Let go of me!" Her cry drew stares from around the room.

Oliver got pissed and started dragging her toward the door. "Ungrateful bitch! You should be honored I'm interested!"

I crossed the room and grabbed Oliver by the collar.

"What the fuck—" His curse died in his throat the second he saw my face.

I smashed my fist into his nose. He went flying, crashed into the next table, sent dishes shattering everywhere.

The restaurant erupted in chaos.

I turned to Noelle. She was holding her bruised wrist, looking at me with complicated eyes.

"Come with me."

"I don't need your fake concern."

"Noelle, don't make me get rough in here. You know what that bastard was trying to do to you."

"Of course I know."

"Then are you really that desperate?" I grabbed her arm and pulled her close. "Will you spread your legs for just anyone?"

"Kholod Morozov, yes, I'm exactly that desperate. Now you should understand—I'd rather marry scum like him than you." She didn't even flinch, like she was admitting to every accusation I'd thrown at her.

"Do you know what you're saying?"

"I know exactly what I'm saying." She laughed coldly. "So a woman like me could never be worthy of the great Mr. Morozov. Please, just leave me alone."

She broke free and headed for the door.

I stood there, watching her walk away.

She'd forgotten me. She'd rejected me. She'd rather marry any random piece of trash.

This was betrayal.

All my so-called patience and careful planning became a joke in that moment.

Three days later.

"Boss," Dmitri reported. "Kieran O'Connell's been getting bold at the docks. The cops raided our Kensington warehouse last night, took a whole shipment. Evidence points to him—looks like he's trying to use the police to hit us, expand his territory."

A starving dog living off my scraps, and he has the balls to bare his teeth.

"Handle it." The words came out flat, emotionless. "Clean."

"Understood." Dmitri nodded, then continued. "Also, like you ordered, everyone who was pressuring the Bellucci family has backed off. Sofia's on board, too."

I smiled coldly. That greedy woman had agreed almost without hesitation.

Fine. Saved me the trouble.

The car stopped at the church's side entrance. The snow was heavier now, falling thick and covering the building in solemn white.

I didn't get out immediately. The window reflected my blurred image—hard features, expressionless, eyes holding three years of obsession and absolute determination.

Dmitri opened my door. Cold air rushed in.

"Everything's ready?" I straightened my cuffs.

"Yes, boss. Everyone inside is ours." Dmitri said quietly. "The priest knows what to do."

I stepped out, my shoes crunching through the snow.

I should've stopped caring whether she was willing, or whether she hated me.

I'd been searching for three years. Waiting for three years. This light that had wandered into my dark world—since it had lit my way once, it had to stay forever.

Whether through love or hate.

CHAPTER THREE

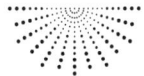

Noelle

The drive from the church to Gladwyn Manor felt like a never-ending funeral. I sat in the back seat, with a full person's width between me and Kholod.

I didn't look at him, my gaze fixed on the window, watching the snow-covered scenery blur past as Philadelphia's lights were swallowed by thickening darkness and encroaching forest—as if I were being swallowed too.

"Cold?" Kholod broke the silence, his voice low and resonant in the sealed confines of the car.

I didn't answer.

He chuckled softly. "Playing deaf, huh?"

"I'm just not sure what to say to the man who kidnapped me."

His tone turned playful. "Noelle, we're legally married now. This is me bringing you home."

I finally turned to him, locking eyes with those sharp amber irises that pierced the dim light. "Your home is no different from a prison to me."

He narrowed his eyes, leaning forward slightly, an oppressive weight crashing over me. "You really despise the idea of marrying me that much?"

"You've ruined my life."

"I've given you the Morozov name, the position every woman in Philadelphia dreams of—and that's ruining you?"

I took a deep breath, forcing down the surging emotions. "To me, it's just another form of captivity."

Kholod reached out suddenly, pinching my chin between his thumb and forefinger, forcing me to face him. "Noelle, if I truly wanted to cage you, you wouldn't even have the chance to speak."

His fingers were cool, but his grip was firm enough to make my jaw throb. I tried to pull away; he only tightened it.

"Let go," I gritted out.

"Keep up the stubborn act," he leaned in closer, his breath—a mix of cigar and mint—brushing my face. "I want to see how long you can hold out."

The car entered a private estate surrounded by dense forest, finally pulling up in front of a villa. Villa? It looked more like a fortress, with its dark gray stone, black steel accents, and vast expanses of bullet-proof glass.

Kholod got out first, opened my door, and extended his hand.

I stared at that long, knuckled hand but didn't take it. Instead, I steadied myself on the doorframe and stood.

He withdrew it, a flicker of displeasure crossing his eyes, but he said nothing and turned toward the villa.

New home. New cage.

The wedding dinner—if you could even call it that.

The long table was draped in pristine white linen, with silverware gleaming coldly under the crystal chandeliers. Anastasia still wore her tailored black suit from the ceremony, the soft luster of pearls at her neck failing to soften the aloofness on her face. She appraised me openly, her gaze sharp enough to cut through flesh, as if dissecting the very essence of my soul.

Anya was more blunt. She barely looked up, only glancing over while toying with her phone, her lips curled in an unmasked sneer colder than the wind howling outside.

"Sit," Anastasia said at last. Kholod strode to the head of the table, and a servant guided me to the seat on his left. A maid quietly arranged my place settings and poured the red wine.

The entire meal unfolded in silence, broken only by the faint clink of knives and forks against fine porcelain. I sat with my back ramrod straight, grateful for once for the etiquette lessons Sofia had drilled into me. In that moment, they were my only armor, preventing me from faltering in such hostile territory.

I cut into my food mechanically but couldn't bring myself to swallow a single bite.

"Coming from Bellucci stock, handling this is already impressive," Anya said suddenly, eyeing me with mock pity. "Noelle, have you ever used cutlery this elaborate? Need me to teach you?"

My fingers tightened around the knife and fork, nails biting into my palm. I looked up and offered her the faintest of smiles. "Thanks for the offer, Anya. But I figure as long as the knife cuts and the fork lifts the food, I'm set. After all, no matter how fancy the tools, they're still just for eating, right?"

Anya faltered, her face flushing with irritation. She opened her mouth to retort, but Anastasia, at the head of the table, lightly tapped her fork against her plate.

"Silence during meals. That's the house rule."

Anya pouted, shooting me a venomous glare, but fell silent.

That stifling wedding dinner finally came to an end, and a maid escorted me to the master bedroom.

The room was enormous, done in a classic European style, but the palette was oppressive—dark wood furniture, deep green velvet curtains, and massive floor-to-ceiling windows overlooking a snow-blanketed forest. The only remotely bright element was a brand-new vanity tucked around the corner, jarringly modern amid the aged pieces.

The maid opened a door to reveal a bathroom nearly as large as my old bedroom. Another maid stood ready with towels and fresh clothes.

"Madam, please bathe."

I allowed them to remove my gown and stepped into the tub. Warm water infused with lavender oil enveloped me, but it only heightened the sense of suffocation.

He'd investigated me. Thoroughly.

Three years ago, on that Christmas Eve, it was me who pulled him back from the brink of death.

I'd never forget that night. Snow swirling everywhere, I'd left the church mass and taken a shortcut home. In that dimly lit alley, I spotted him—face pale as death, eyes bloodshot. High brows, deep-set eyes, a sharp nose like a mountain ridge, thin lips pressed tight, jawline resolute. Snowflakes clung to his thick lashes. He slumped against the wall, his tall, imposing frame appearing uncharacteristically fragile.

I kissed him. Saved him, too. No denying it—at first sight, his stunning looks had captivated me.

I searched for him afterward, but he vanished without a trace. I dismissed it as a chance encounter.

Until I saw that stern profile in the financial news, paired with the name "Morozov." My heart plummeted.

The man I'd saved was the king of Philadelphia's underworld.

Worse still, less than six months into his rule, my father died. Suicide.

In those final months, I watched our family disintegrate, saw the light fade from his eyes.

Only later did I learn that Kholod Morozov was the architect of our ruin. He'd lumped my family in with his enemies.

The man I'd saved had killed my father.

How bitterly ironic.

So when he appeared with that bracelet, proposing marriage, I was stunned by his audacity.

I thought my outright rejection would deter him.

I was wrong.

He didn't relent. Instead, he began stalking me, a persistent shadow infiltrating every corner of my life.

That's why I agreed to the blind date my mother arranged, enduring the man's repulsive stares and touches.

Between him and me, my father's death would always loom.

Even if I'd saved him. Even if he'd married me now. Even if my heart still raced uncontrollably every time I saw him.

I hated him. Hated myself even more for it.

"Madam?" The maid's gentle voice interrupted. "The water's getting cold."

I opened my eyes, feeling tears slide down my cheeks, mingling indistinguishably with the bathwater.

Once the bath was over, I slipped into the silk nightgown they'd prepared—though I despised the feel of silk against my skin; it always left me chilled. I asked the maid to fetch a robe to drape over it, finally feeling some warmth.

The maids bowed and withdrew, leaving me alone in the room.

I sat on the edge of the bed, staring at this unfamiliar, opulent cage. I knew what was coming next.

I was his lawful wife now. Tonight was our wedding night.

I drew in a deep breath, forcing myself to stay calm.

No matter what, I had to find a way to escape. I couldn't remain by my father's killer's side.

"What are you thinking about?" Kholod pushed the door open, carrying in a rush of cold air and the heavy scent of cigar smoke. He said nothing more, just approached from behind, his towering shadow engulfing me completely.

"When I can leave," I replied without turning, my voice as flat and lifeless as stagnant water.

He let out a low laugh. "Noelle, you still don't understand. The moment you set foot here, leaving became impossible."

I turned to face him, meeting those amber eyes that gleamed unnervingly in the dim light.

"Why?" I demanded, my heart aching, but my composure held firm.

"Why me? Philadelphia is full of women desperate to marry you. Why choose me?"

"Because you're destined to be mine." He advanced step by step, his gaze turning predatory. "What you did the first time we met—do I need to remind you?"

"I don't know what you're talking about." I averted my face, hiding the panic in my eyes.

"Don't know?" He seized my chin abruptly, forcing me to look at him. "Then why did you react so intensely to that bracelet?"

"Because you used some sketchy bracelet to blackmail me into marriage!" I wrenched free from his grasp and stood. "Kholod Morozov, who do you think you are? You believe money and power let you do whatever you damn well please?"

"I'm your husband."

"A man who used threats and family debts to force me? You call that a husband?"

"Whether I qualify isn't for you to decide." He narrowed his eyes, closing in steadily. "I offered you a choice. You squandered it."

"Choice?" I retreated until my back hit the wall. "That was a threat! It was kidnapping!"

"So what?" He was right in front of me now, hands planted on either side of my body, caging me in. "The outcome is the same. You're my wife. That's a fact."

"I'll never acknowledge this marriage!" His presence was suffocating, but I lifted my chin defiantly. "I hate you!"

"Hate me?" He leaned down, his hot breath fanning my face. "Good. Hate is a bond too."

"You're a psychopath! A control freak! A stalker!" I couldn't contain my emotions any longer; they erupted. "What am I to you? Your pet?"

"Pet?" Kholod laughed, a smile I'd never seen before—cruel and exhilarated.

"No, Noelle, pets are for pampering." He leaned in closer, hands still braced, trapping me. "You..."

He bent to my ear, his voice a devilish whisper. "You're for taming."

"Who the hell do you think you are, trampling my dignity like this?!" His words ignited a fury in me, and I struggled more fiercely.

"Dignity?" He straightened, towering over me. "We don't need that useless crap between us."

He lowered his head to kiss me; I jerked my face away. The scorching kiss landed on my cheek, the cigar scent making me shudder.

"Let go!" I shoved him with all my strength.

My resistance seemed to set him ablaze. He abandoned the kiss, instead yanking me away from the wall like an object and hurling me toward the massive bed.

Caught off guard, I fell backward, crashing onto the mattress that sank like quicksand.

Before I could recover, he was on top of me, his massive frame pinning me down.

Rip—

The fragile silk of the nightgown tore apart in his hands. Cold air enveloped my exposed skin, making me shiver uncontrollably.

"You bastard!" I raised my hand to strike him, but he caught my wrist effortlessly and pinned it above my head.

He forced his knee between my thighs, hands braced on either side of me, his amber eyes churning with raw, undisguised desire.

Even enduring this brutal treatment, even with fear and hatred raging inside me.

But as my gaze drifted over his face, vivid with lust and devastatingly handsome, a forbidden thrill stirred deep within me.

I must be insane.

How could I feel this way for my father's killer?

Kholod's hands began to roam, rough and demanding, mapping the curves of my body as if he owned every inch. His fingers trailed down my sides, teasing the remnants of my torn nightgown before stripping it away entirely, leaving me bare and vulnerable beneath him. The air crackled with electric tension, and I despised how my skin tingled under his touch, betraying my resolve.

He smirked, that cruel glint lingering in his eyes, as he captured my lips in a punishing kiss. I resisted, biting back, but he only deepened it, his tongue claiming my mouth with the taste of cigar smoke and unyielding dominance. One hand cupped my breast, his thumb circling the nipple until it peaked, sending unwelcome sparks of pleasure shooting through me. "Fuck, you're so responsive," he growled against my lips, pulling back to drag biting kisses down my neck, leaving stinging marks that blurred the line between pain and arousal.

His other hand ventured lower, slipping between my thighs, fingers brushing my core. I gasped, my body arching involuntarily. He let out a dark chuckle, pressing a finger inside, probing. "Not so unwilling after all, huh? Look at you, already dripping wet for me." His voice was rough, triumphant. "Why is that, Noelle? You claim to hate me, but your body's screaming for more."

I whimpered, loathing the truth he exposed, the slick evidence of my arousal. He added a second finger, pumping slowly, stretching me with deliberate thrusts that made my hips buck against my will. The foreplay was merciless; he scissored his fingers, curling them to stroke that sensitive spot inside, making stars explode behind my eyelids. His mouth descended on my breast, sucking hard, teeth grazing the taut peak while his thumb worked relentless circles over my clit, coiling the tension until I was panting, my thighs quivering uncontrollably.

But he wasn't satisfied yet. He withdrew briefly, reaching for the nightstand drawer—always one step ahead, the bastard. He pulled out a sleek vibrator, high-end silicone with multiple settings, switching it on to a low hum that filled the room. "Gonna open you up properly," he rasped, positioning it at my entrance, teasing before easing it in inch by inch, the vibrations rippling through my core like shockwaves.

I moaned, clenching around the intrusion, the fullness both foreign and intoxicating. "Look at that," he murmured, his voice thick with smug satisfaction as he observed my every twitch. "So fucking tight... shit, you're a virgin, aren't you? This virgin pussy's been waiting for me all along." He twisted the toy deeper, cranking up the intensity, his free hand holding my hip steady as I writhed beneath him. "God, that gets me hard. Knowing I'm the first to take you like this. See how it's gripping? It's begging for me, Noelle. You've been saving yourself for this moment, haven't you?"

His filthy, possessive words only heightened the ache, making me even wetter. He thrust the vibrator in and out, building me toward the edge with ruthless precision, until I was a writhing mess of desperate pleas and gasps, the boundaries between hatred and desire dissolving into haze. "Please..." I didn't even know what I was begging for anymore.

At last, he discarded the toy, stripping off his clothes in a frenzy— shirt torn open, pants shoved down, revealing his thick, throbbing cock, veins pulsing, tip slick with precum. He aligned himself, rubbing the head against my soaked folds. "Ready for the real thing?" he taunted, then pushed in slowly, inch by agonizing inch.

I bit back a cry of pain as he stretched me, the burn intense, my body resisting the invasion. But even through the discomfort, something primal shifted—my hips rose instinctively, welcoming him deeper, my walls clenching around him. "Fuck, so damn tight," he groaned, holding still for a moment to let me adjust, though not for long.

My nails dug into his back, raking down his spine, leaving angry red trails. He grinned, savage and delighted. "Yeah, that's it—mark me. Show me how much you crave this." His thrusts intensified, slamming harder and deeper, the bedframe creaking under the force. The wet slap of skin against skin echoed through the room, mingling with my moans and his guttural grunts. He adjusted his angle, hitting that perfect spot with every punishing stroke, driving me toward oblivion.

Sweat-slicked bodies moved in frantic rhythm, the air thick with the musk of sex and lingering cigar. I hated him, but God, the way he filled me, claimed me—it was all-consuming. His mouth returned to my neck, sucking dark bruises, murmuring filthy endearments. "Take every inch, Noelle. This pussy belongs to me now."

The ferocity mounted, emotions tangling in a storm of hate, lust, and vengeance. But suddenly, my breath caught, a familiar constriction gripping my chest. Asthma. Damn it, not now. My vision darkened at the edges, breathing turning shallow and labored, my face paling to a sickly blue as panic flooded in. Desperately, I reached for the nightstand, fumbling blindly for my inhaler.

Kholod didn't notice at first, too lost in the heat, driving into me with deep, relentless thrusts. But then he felt my body tense, heard the wheezing rasp. "Noelle?" He pulled back, eyes widening in alarm as he saw me gasping, hand scrambling. He snatched the inhaler from the drawer—somehow knowing exactly where it was—and pressed it into my trembling fingers.

I grabbed it frantically, inhaling deeply like my life depended on it, the medicated mist surging into my lungs. It triggered a violent coughing fit, tears and sweat streaming down my face in a chaotic mess. I looked utterly wrecked, gasping and shuddering in the aftermath.

A flicker of something like heartache crossed his eyes, perhaps even remorse. He leaned down, gently brushing soaked strands from my forehead, his voice uncharacteristically soft. "Breathe, Noelle. Slow and easy. I've got you." His thumb stroked my cheek tenderly as I coughed and gradually steadied my breaths.

Once the attack passed, my breathing normalizing, he shifted, still buried inside me, hard and insistent. "We can continue now."

I lashed out instinctively, my foot kicking up and connecting with his groin—not enough to seriously injure, but enough to make him grunt in pain. "You bastard!"

He winced but let out a dark, rumbling laugh. "Feisty as ever. Looks like you're eager for more." Brushing off my protest, he resumed his movements, but gentler this time—slow, languid thrusts that stoked a different kind of flame. His hands caressed rather than restrained, lips grazing mine in unexpectedly soft kisses. The tenderness was disorienting, clashing with everything I knew of him.

We built toward climax together, unhurried, until ecstasy crashed over us—me tightening around him in waves, him spilling deep inside with a low groan. As he collapsed beside me, he drew me into his arms, whispering against my ear. "You can't die. In my world, you don't have that privilege."

CHAPTER FOUR

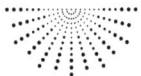

Noelle

Kholod Morozov... a demon.

Every inch of my body ached as if it had been crushed. I gritted my teeth, cursing him a thousand times over in my mind.

The bed beside me was empty, bearing only the impression of where he had lain. The air still carried that scent of cedar and tobacco, silently reminding me of every moment from last night.

I had actually been beneath my father's killer...

I squeezed my eyes shut, refusing to recall how my body had betrayed me. Those shivers when he touched me, the uncontrolled moans—all of it filled me with deep self-loathing.

A maid slipped into the room soundlessly. Seeing I was awake, she bowed her head respectfully. "Ma'am, hot water is ready. A bath will help you feel better."

With her support, I endured the soreness and made my way to the bathroom. When the warm water enveloped my body, my tense muscles finally began to relax. That's when a familiar fragrance drifted over—sweet with a hint of bitterness.

My eyes snapped open. I watched the maid dripping essential oil into the tub. There was no mistake—that scent dissolving into the water was my favorite from home. An obscure Italian artisan brand that almost no one knew about.

This couldn't be a coincidence!

That devil of a man had inflicted the cruelest violence upon me, then turned around and offered this barely perceptible "consideration" in the most bone-chilling way. Did he know every detail about me?

After the bath, much of the physical pain had eased. The maid dressed me in an understated cotton dress—simple in design but exquisite in cut and fabric, soft against my skin. She tried to cover the marks on my neck with makeup. I refused.

"Don't bother. Leave it."

The maid hesitated, then nodded respectfully. Under her guidance, I made my way to the dining room.

Two people were already seated at the table. Anastasia was elegantly sipping tea, dressed in a dark purple high-necked dress, her hair pinned back without a strand out of place. Even at home, she maintained an impeccable appearance. Anya was lazily flipping through a French fashion magazine, her red-painted nails casually skimming the pages.

The head chair sat empty, announcing the master's absence.

When I entered, both women glanced up. Their gazes felt like cold probes, first lingering for a second on the marks around my neck. Something unreadable flashed in Anastasia's eyes. Then she nodded slightly, indicating I should sit.

I quietly took the seat across from Anastasia, trying to ignore their scrutinizing stares.

A maid served my breakfast. Delicate china, fresh fruit, and what looked like appetizing Eggs Benedict. But I had no appetite.

"Looks like you didn't sleep well last night?" Anya looked up, her expression loaded with meaning.

I returned a distant smile. "New environments take getting used to."

"Getting used to?" She laughed lightly. "Becoming part of the Morozov family is about more than just getting a good night's sleep."

"Anya." Anastasia set down her teacup, her voice calm but warning.

Anya shrugged and returned to her magazine.

"However, Noelle," Anastasia turned to me, the sound of porcelain clinking crisp, "now that you're part of this family, you should follow the rules. For instance, you shouldn't keep your elders waiting."

My grip tightened on my silverware until my knuckles went white. This was clearly another power play.

Anya let out a timely snort, finally lifting her eyes from the magazine to look me up and down like I was some cheap knockoff.

"Mother, don't be too demanding." Anya sneered. "The fact that she can even learn these manners is impressive enough, isn't it?"

The words hit like a barbed whip. They were deliberately reminding me of my "background."

I took a deep breath, suppressing my anger. "You're right, I was thoughtless. I just didn't sleep well last night and got up late. Besides, Kholod didn't tell me the meal times."

I deftly redirected the blame back to the real person in control.

Sure enough, both Anastasia's and Anya's expressions froze momentarily, as if they'd been choked. Anastasia lifted her teacup, taking another sip to cover her reaction, and said nothing more. Anya pursed her lips and returned her attention to the magazine, but her page-turning had taken on a distinctly irritated edge.

Breakfast ended in an almost suffocating silence. I ate small bites, everything tasting like sawdust.

Back in the bedroom, I rubbed my lower back and collapsed onto the sofa, closing my eyes to rest.

"Ma'am, Mr. Morozov instructed that you rest well today. Call us if you need anything," the maid said respectfully before withdrawing.

I was alone in the room.

That afternoon, I curled up on the sofa by the fireplace with my laptop. This was my only remaining connection to my former self.

I began updating my long-neglected travel blog, describing Iceland's glaciers and aurora, pouring my longing for freedom into every word. This was my only remaining mental escape.

I was so absorbed in writing that I completely missed the movement behind me.

Until a strong hand with prominent knuckles reached over my shoulder and slammed my laptop shut with a sharp "snap!"

"Ah!" I screamed, my heart nearly jumping out of my throat. I spun around to find Kholod Morozov's cold face right in front of me. I had no idea when he'd entered, moving like a silent predator.

"Not bad writing." He picked up my laptop, his tone unreadable as his long fingers skillfully navigated the trackpad, scrolling through page after page of my yearning and descriptions of the free world. His gaze examined them like evidence of a crime.

"Give it back!" The humiliation of having my privacy so brutally violated made me explode with rage. I stood to grab the laptop back.

But he easily pressed me back down onto the sofa with one hand, his massive strength pinning me in place. His body heat seeped through the thin fabric, carrying a dangerous sense of oppression.

"Seems you still have energy for useless thoughts." He looked down at me, eyes ice-cold. "Wasn't I thorough enough last night?"

His words made my cheeks burn.

"Give me back my laptop!" I struggled, trying to push his hand away, but it was like an ant trying to topple a tree.

"Disobedience requires punishment." He made his cold declaration, producing a pair of icy handcuffs from somewhere. Under my horrified gaze, he clicked them efficiently around my wrists, securing me to the sofa's heavy wooden armrest.

The cold metal pressed against my skin. I was completely immobilized.

"What are you doing?!"

He didn't answer, just stepped back with the laptop. His fingers moved across the trackpad, clicking into the blog's backend.

"No—" I sensed what he was about to do and screamed in despair.

But it was too late.

His index finger pressed the red "Delete Account" button without hesitation.

A popup appeared: "Are you sure you want to delete this account? This action cannot be undone."

He didn't hesitate for even a second. He clicked "Confirm."

On the screen, a small loading circle spun for a few moments. Then my blog—years of work, all my dreams, all my spiritual refuge— instantly became a blank page. All the words, all the photos, all my heart and soul... vanished in that moment.

I stared at the blank page in shock, my mind equally blank. I forgot even how to cry. It wasn't just a blog—it was the only breathing space I'd secretly carved out for myself in a suffocating life bound by family obligations and my mother's demands. It was my entire imagination of what another life could be.

Now it was gone. Effortlessly erased by him.

Kholod closed the laptop with a dull thud, shattering my last illusion. He picked up my phone from the coffee table, unlocking it skillfully—he even knew my passcode!

He moved in front of me, leaning down close to my ear. His hot breath against my skin brought no warmth, only cold that penetrated to my bones. His voice, like Siberian wind carrying ice shards, carved each word clearly into my eardrums.

"I'm taking away these useless things."

He paused, savoring the broken light in my eyes before continuing his verdict.

"From now on, your world can only have me in it. You will never escape me."

He straightened up, taking my phone and laptop with him. He didn't even unlock my handcuffs, just gave me one last look with those all-controlling eyes, then turned and left the bedroom as silently as he'd entered.

In the room, only I remained—handcuffed to the sofa, powerless to struggle.

The fireplace flames still danced, crackling softly, but they could no longer drive away the bone-deep cold surrounding me.

I looked out the window at that endless snow-covered forest. It had once symbolized freedom and vastness. Now it looked more like a massive, natural prison.

He didn't just want to imprison my body—he wanted to completely destroy all my longing for the outside world, to break the wings of my thoughts.

Tears finally fell, delayed but inevitable. But colder than the tears was the growing clarity in my heart—this battle would be far more brutal and hopeless than I had ever imagined.

CHAPTER FIVE

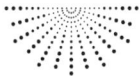

Kholod

"Boss, Sofia Bellucci's here. Says she wants to see the missus."

I raised an eyebrow. That cold-hearted bitch who'd pawn off her own daughter without blinking, all for the family hustle. Showing up now? Right on cue. I was itching to watch what kind of bullshit performance this so-called "loving" mom had lined up.

"Let her in," I said into the intercom, eyes glued to the monitor. "Take her to Noelle."

On the screen, Noelle was curled up on the couch by the fireplace, knees hugged tight to her chest. Hadn't moved an inch in three damn days. Not since I'd shut down that pathetic little blog of hers myself.

Her eyes were blank. Face like stone. Didn't give a shit about the fancy spreads on the table, the marble floors, or the maids tiptoeing around with their polite bullshit. Nothing.

This zombie act? It pissed me off way more than her yelling or fighting back. I'd take her screaming in my face, those pretty brown eyes blazing at me. At least that meant she felt something. At least it meant I could still get under her skin.

Through the hidden cams and mics, I watched clear as day as Sofia got led in. Fake-ass smile plastered on her face, all cautious and sweet.

"Oh, my sweet Noelle..." She hustled over to the couch, arms out for a hug like she gave a damn.

Noelle's body went rigid—just a twitch, but I caught it. She turned her head away, dodging the embrace. Her voice came out flat, scraped raw. "Mom."

Sofia's smile slipped for a split second, that awkward flash, but she slapped it back on like nothing. Sat down, grabbed Noelle's hand, and launched into the same tired crap. "Mr. Morozov's a big shot, be a good girl, keep the husband happy."

I snorted, took a pull from my vodka. Lame as hell. Trying to school her daughter on sucking up to men, like that'd buy her a comfy spot in this high-society cage? What a joke.

Noelle's worth wasn't in playing nice with anybody. It was in her—just her. That goddamn light she carried.

I was about to kill the feed when Sofia made this little move that froze me solid.

She was yapping away, but one hand "accidentally" patted Noelle's wool skirt pocket. And in that split-second lift-off? She slipped something black and flat right in there. Quick as a snake.

My glass hung in midair.

The balls on her. How the fuck did she know Noelle was cut off from the world? Who gave her that burner phone to smuggle in?

One answer hit me like a brick: Noelle.

Had to be her. She'd pulled off this three-day corpse routine to drop my guard, reached out somehow, and roped Mom in to play delivery girl.

Well played. Really clever.

I set the glass down. The cold burn slid down my throat, but it lit a fire in my chest that scorched everything else away. Thought I'd clipped her wings, and she'd stay put. Bullshit. She was still scheming to bolt—right under my nose, with this amateur-hour con.

Dmitri ghosted into the study doorway without a sound. "Boss?"

"Get the car ready." I stood, straightened my cuffs, kept my voice even. "Taking Noelle out shopping. Something she'll like."

Dmitri's eyes flickered—surprise, but he didn't push. Just nodded. "Yes, sir."

By the time I hit the bedroom, Sofia was long gone. But her cheap-ass perfume lingered like a bad memory.

I stepped up to Noelle, my shadow swallowing her whole.

"Bored in here?" My tone was calm. Too calm.

She lifted her head slowly, eyes still dead, just staring through me like I was a ghost.

"Get yourself together. You're allowed to go out." I watched her face close—every twitch, every micro-shift.

There it was: a quick spark deep in those eyes. Shock. Maybe a hint of panic. Gone in a blink, buried under the blank mask again.

"Don't wanna?" I prodded.

She hung there for a beat, then mumbled, "Whatever you say."

Downtown was a zoo—horns blaring, crowds shoving. Noelle stepped out of the car all stiff and jumpy, yanking her coat tight around her. Eyes darting everywhere, like she was hunting or hiding from something.

Dmitri and I hung back in a plain black sedan, one-way glass giving us the full show. She paused at a stall hawking handmade pottery, fingers tracing the rim of some iris-flower mug. Lost in it, almost.

"Want me closer, boss?" Dmitri murmured.

"Nah." I lit a cigar, the smoke hazing up the window. "Let her finish the act."

Didn't take long. This tall guy in a brown leather jacket strolled up —built like a linebacker. Made a beeline for Noelle.

Lorenzo Conti. Son of some washed-up Bellucci crew guy. Noelle's old playground buddy. Small-time hack running a hole-in-the-wall gallery, calling himself an "artist."

He snagged her arm, face all lit up like a kid on Christmas, yapping something heated. Yanked her toward a quiet alley off the main drag.

Too far for audio. All I could see was Noelle twisting away, shaking her head, face twisted in worry and pleading. But the prick wouldn't let go—clamped on like a vice, even tried reeling her in closer. Looked for all the world like a pair of star-crossed lovers fighting the man. That unnatural flush on her cheeks, the fire in her eyes? It was like pouring gas on the rage boiling in my gut.

"Boss, you need me to—" Dmitri's hand twitched toward his piece, eyes narrowing to slits.

"No." I shut him down, voice flat as ice. But my knuckles were white around the cigar, squeezing till it nearly snapped. "Snap every photo. Every angle. Every goddamn touch. Dig up everything on this Lorenzo prick."

I dragged deep on the smoke, let the bitter bite fill my lungs, choke down the urge to storm out there and rip the bastard apart.

"I'll make sure he learns," I ground out, eyes locked on those two tangled shadows in the alley. "What happens when you eye my woman."

That night, I rolled into the villa without flipping a light. The bedroom glowed just from the fireplace—flames dancing shadows across the velvet duvet.

Noelle was fresh from the shower, in this silk slip that hugged her just right. She hopped up when I walked in, fingers twisting the hem like it was a lifeline.

"How was your afternoon?"

She met my gaze, that wariness flashing quickly. "Fine. Just wandered the market."

"Wandered?" I echoed, stepping closer. "Pick up anything good?"

She froze—didn't see that curveball coming. "Uh, just browsed some crafts."

"Oh yeah?" I closed the gap, towering over her. "Where's your haul? I don't see any."

Her face drained white. "I didn't buy anything. Just looked."

"Looked." I nodded slowly. "For two hours? What the hell were you doing out there?"

"I... just killing time. Taking in the sights..."

"Sights?" My voice cracked up, and I slammed my palm on the nightstand—boom echoing like a gunshot. She jumped a foot, whole body locking up. "Noelle, I'm giving you one shot. Tell me straight—who'd you meet today?"

"I... I didn't meet anybody..."

"Still lying to my face!" I snatched up the stack of photos, flung 'em across the bed like confetti from hell. "Then what's this crap?!"

They fanned out right in her line of sight. Her skin went ghost-pale.

"Now," I advanced, slow and steady, "one more time. Who'd you see?"

"It... it was Lorenzo..." The words clawed out of her throat. "But I didn't set it up! He just... showed up..."

"Just showed up?" I barked a laugh, bitter as bile. "You expect me to swallow that? How'd he know you'd be there? Know your schedule?"

"I don't know!" Her voice cracked, tears bubbling up. "I swear, I don't!"

"And the phone?" I cut in, eyes narrowing to knives. "That burner your mom shoved in your pocket—you think I missed that shit?"

She turned to stone. Color bled out of her face till she looked like death.

"You called him. Didn't you?" I pressed, relentless. "Set up the time, the spot. Right under my nose, pulling off some reunion bullshit. Noelle, you really think I'm that stupid?"

"No!" She jerked her head up, tears spilling hot and fast. "I didn't! I never even touched the damn phone! It was Mom... she must've told him..."

"Sofia?" I latched onto the slip. "How the fuck would your mom know your plans? Unless you spilled."

"I didn't!" She was frantic now, words tumbling. "I just mentioned wanting to get out, stretch my legs. I never thought..."

"Noelle, make it believable. A mom just 'happens' to tip off her daughter's ex about her day?"

"He's not my ex!" It came out a shout. "We never... there was nothing! Ever!"

I scooped up a photo—his meaty hand clamped on her arm, bodies damn near glued.

"Then explain this."

She stared at it, eyes swimming. "He wanted to get me out... said he'd save me, take me away. But I said no! I fought him off the whole time, Kholod—I told him to back off! You gotta believe me..."

"Believing you means buying that 'no' required getting that close? Letting him manhandle you like that? Looking all fired up and flushed?"

"I was pissed! Telling him not to be an idiot!" She was rambling, reaching for me, desperate. "Kholod, please, just listen..."

I swatted her hand away, the fury in my chest roaring to life. "Shut it. I'm done with your lies."

I unbuckled my belt, the heavy croc leather whispering through the loops. The buckle clinked, dull and final.

Her eyes locked on it—pure terror flooding in. She scrambled back till her legs hit the bedframe, voice breaking. "Kholod... what are you doing? Don't... don't hit me..."

Hit her? Like some street thug with a temper? Nah. That was too cheap for what she deserved.

I snagged her wrists, looped the belt tight around 'em, and lashed her to the brass bedpost. Cold metal bit into her skin.

She thrashed, pointless—like a moth in a web, just tangling deeper.

"Kholod... please... let me explain..." Desperation choked her words.

I leaned in close, noses brushing, breaths clashing—hers shaky, mine a frozen storm. "You need to remember who owns you."

Tears streaked her cheeks, soaking the pillow.

But in my head? One thought hammered away.

I'd erase every trace of anyone else on her.

She was mine.

Only mine.

I ripped her silk nightgown open with a savage yank, the fabric tearing like a scream in the quiet room. Threads snapped and fluttered to the floor, exposing her pale skin to the flickering firelight. Noelle turned her face away in humiliation, tears sliding silently down her cheeks, but I wasn't having that. I grabbed her chin, forcing her head back, making her eyes meet mine. "Look at me," I growled, my voice low and dangerous. "Watch how I claim you, how I mark your body and soul with my brand. You're mine, Noelle. Every goddamn inch."

She whimpered, her bound hands straining against the leather belt tied to the bedpost, but I didn't give her a second to breathe. My mouth crashed down on hers, bruising, demanding, my tongue forcing its way in like I owned her—which I fucking did. Her body arched under me, half resistance, half something darker that made my blood boil hotter than hell. I trailed rough kisses down her neck, nipping at her collarbone, feeling her pulse hammer against my lips like a war drum. Her breaths came in short, ragged gasps, and I could smell her fear mixed with that faint, intoxicating scent that was all her —sweet, floral, and utterly addictive.

The fire in me built, uncontrollable, a raging inferno that demanded release. I lowered my head, my gaze locking on the trembling peak of her breast. It was perfect, pink and begging for my attention, heaving with every shaky inhale. I leaned in, gentle at first, like a kiss, my lips closing around that sensitive bud, sucking softly, my tongue flicking over it in slow, deliberate circles. She let out a moan she couldn't hold back, her body betraying her completely, hips twitching involuntarily against mine. That sound—it drove me wild, a raw, needy whimper that sent a jolt straight to my cock. The moment I felt her quiver under my touch, her nipple hardening in my mouth, my eyes darkened with primal hunger. I opened my mouth wider and bit down hard on the tender flesh just beside the tip, my teeth sinking into her soft skin like it was mine to ruin.

Noelle screamed, a sharp, piercing cry that echoed off the walls, raw and desperate. Her body bowed up violently, arching like a bowstring pulled taut, straining against the belt that yanked her back down with a merciless snap. I didn't let go, biting deeper, savoring the way her flesh gave under my teeth until the metallic tang of blood filled my mouth, sweet and rusty, a coppery rush that made my dick throb. Finally, I pulled back, licking my lips clean, watching the red imprint bloom on her breast like a fresh brand, angry and vivid against her pale skin. I leaned in close, my breath hot against her ear, my voice a low, menacing whisper. "Remember this lesson, Noelle? Now you've got my mark on you. It's permanent. You'll never wash it away, no matter how hard you try."

She collapsed against the mattress, her chest heaving in uneven gasps, eyes staring blankly at the ceiling, like she'd checked out entirely, her spirit shattered into a thousand pieces. But then she shifted, turning her head slowly, those brown eyes fixing on me with an icy, almost eerie calm that sent a chill down my spine. Her lips curved into the faintest smirk, a ghost of a challenge, like she was mocking me silently. Like she was saying, Is that all you've got, Kholod Morozov? Your punishment ends here? Just a bite and some empty threats?

That look—it pissed me off to no end, but damn if it didn't make me laugh, a dark, bitter sound that rumbled from my chest like thunder. This woman, so fucking defiant, even now, even after everything. It ignited something feral in me, a beast that clawed its way to the surface. I surged forward, grabbing her thighs with bruising force and prying them apart, pinning them down with my weight so she couldn't move an inch. "You think that's it?" I snarled, my face inches from hers, my breath mingling with her tear-stained one. "Let me show you what my real punishment looks like, you insolent little thing."

My hand slid between her legs, fingers brushing her core, feeling the heat radiating from her. She was warm, but not wet enough—not slick and ready like I wanted her to be, begging for it. I smirked, rubbing her slowly, teasing the folds with deliberate strokes, parting them to expose her fully. "Look at you, all tied up and still acting tough. But your body's honest, isn't it? Gonna get you dripping for me, you little tease. Feel that? That's me owning this pretty pussy." I dipped a finger inside, curling it just right, pumping in and out while my thumb circled her clit in tight, insistent loops. "Come on, Noelle, get wet for your husband. You know you want this cock—admit it, you dirty girl. Imagine how good it'll feel when I stretch you wide, filling you up until you can't think straight." She ignored me, biting her lip hard, refusing to react, her eyes defiant, but I could feel her starting to slicken under my touch, her body betraying her stubborn pride. Stubborn as hell, but it only made me harder.

Patience snapped like a brittle twig. I yanked my pants open, freeing myself, hard and throbbing, veins pulsing with need. Without warning, I positioned at her entrance and thrust in deep, burying myself to the hilt in one brutal stroke that made her gasp sharply. Her walls clenched around me like a vice, hot and tight, gripping me like she never wanted to let go. "Fuck, that's tight," I groaned, starting to move, pounding into her with relentless force. "You submit yet, Noelle? Gonna be a good girl from now on? Or do I have to fuck the defiance out of you, you sneaky little bitch? Admit it—you love being my fucktoy, don't you?"

She just rolled her eyes, giving me that white-hot glare, like she was above it all, untouchable even as I claimed her. Oh, that fueled me, stoking the flames higher. I reached down, finding that swollen nub with my fingers, pinching it hard, rubbing relentlessly in rough circles that made her squirm. She cried out, a sharp moan escaping despite herself, her voice breaking the air like shattered glass. "There we go," I taunted, grinning wickedly. "See? That's how you behave. Moan for me like the good slut you are. Your pussy's weeping for more—listen to how wet you are." Her body jerked, and as another whimper slipped from her lips, raw and involuntary, I leaned in and bit her shoulder, teeth clamping down on the curve, hard enough to bruise, the salt of her skin exploding on my tongue. She yelped, the sound mixing with her gasps, her hips bucking up involuntarily, pulling me deeper.

I switched up the rhythm, pulling out slow, teasing the tip just at her entrance, letting her feel the emptiness, building the frustration until she was clenching around nothing. Then, I slammed back in deep—nine shallow thrusts, quick and teasing, barely grazing her depths, making her whine in frustration, followed by one hard, punishing plunge that made her whole body shake, hitting that sweet spot inside her that had her walls fluttering wildly. "Say it," I demanded, repeating the pattern, slow and torturous, then that deep hit that buried me balls-deep. "Tell me you've learned your lesson. Say you'll never pull that shit again, you disobedient whore." She bit her lip harder, trying to hold out, her breaths coming in frantic pants, but I pinched her clit again, twisting just enough to send electric sparks through her nerves, pushing her closer to the edge.

Another moan tore from her throat, louder this time, a desperate keen that filled the room, and I struck, biting down on her collarbone, sucking the skin between my teeth, leaving a dark hickey that would bloom purple and remind her for days. "Fuck, Kholod!" she gasped, her voice breaking, trembling with the strain. I kept up the rhythm, fast shallow pumps now alternating with slow, grinding deep ones, hitting that spot inside her over and over, the wet sounds of our bodies echoing obscenely. Her breaths turned to pants, her bound hands twisting in the belt, nails digging into her palms. "Say it, Noelle. Beg me to let you come. Admit you're mine and you'll behave, or I'll edge you all fucking night."

She arched again, a desperate whine escaping, her body trembling on the brink, and I bit her other shoulder mid-moan, the taste of her skin addictive, her cry vibrating through me like a drug. "Okay... I... I've learned," she finally choked out, tears streaming down her flushed cheeks. "I won't do it again. Please, Kholod... just... let me come... I'm yours..."

That was music to my ears, a sweet surrender that made my cock twitch inside her. I sped up, thrusting harder, faster, the bed creaking under us like it might break. Her body tightened, coiling like a spring, walls pulsing around me in rhythmic squeezes, and I felt her shatter, her climax ripping through her with a scream that echoed in the room, her juices soaking us both. I didn't stop, riding her through it, drawing out every shudder, every pulse, until she was a trembling, boneless mess beneath me, gasping for air.

But I wasn't done. Not by a long shot. The fire in my veins demanded more—I needed to own her completely, to drown out any thought of escape or that bastard Lorenzo, to etch myself into every fiber of her being. I untied the belt from the bedpost but left her wrists bound together, flipping her onto her stomach with effortless strength. She gasped, face pressed into the pillow, ass up in the air, vulnerable and exposed. "What are you—" she started, her voice muffled and breathless, but I cut her off with a sharp slap to her thigh, the crack resounding, making her yelp and her skin bloom red.

"Shut up and take it," I muttered, my voice gravelly with lust, positioning behind her. My hands gripped her hips, fingers digging in hard enough to leave crescent marks, bruising her creamy flesh, and I thrust back in, deeper from this angle, filling her completely, stretching her to her limits. She moaned into the fabric, muffled but raw, a guttural sound that spurred me on. I set a punishing pace, each slam forward jolting her body, the slap of skin on skin filling the air like rhythmic thunder. "This is what happens when you test me," I growled, leaning over her, my chest pressing against her back, trapping her under my weight. "You think you can sneak around? Plot with your little friends? I'll fuck that idea right out of your head, make you forget anyone but me."

She twisted, trying to look back, her bound hands fumbling uselessly, but I pushed her head down, holding her in place with a firm grip on her hair, yanking just enough to sting. My free hand snaked around, finding her clit again, rubbing in tight, insistent circles that had her squirming, her ass pushing back against me despite herself. "Feel that? That's me owning you. Every. Damn. Inch. Your pussy's mine to use, to fill, to ruin." A fresh moan bubbled up from her, high and needy, and I bit the nape of her neck, teeth grazing that sensitive spot, sucking hard as she cried out, leaving another mark that would peek out from her collars, a secret brand for the world to wonder about.

I varied the speed—slow, deliberate drags out, letting her feel the emptiness, the ache of my absence, then quick, brutal thrusts that bottomed out, grinding against her cervix. "Beg for more," I demanded, my voice rough, edged with dominance. "Tell me you love being my dirty secret, my personal fuckdoll." She hesitated, her body betraying her with involuntary clenches, but another pinch to her clit broke her resolve. "Please... more... I love it," she whispered, voice hoarse and broken, laced with shame and desire.

Satisfied, I ramped it up, pounding relentlessly, the heat building between us like a furnace. As her moans grew frantic, climbing higher, more desperate, I bit her earlobe, tugging sharply, then trailed down to her shoulder blade, nipping sharply each time she gasped, marking her with a trail of bites that would ache tomorrow. Her second orgasm hit like a tidal wave, clenching around me so tight it pulled my own release from me, waves of pleasure crashing over us. I groaned, spilling inside her, marking her from the inside out, hot and possessive.

We collapsed in a tangle of limbs, breaths heaving like we'd run a marathon. I rolled off, pulling her against me, her bound hands trapped between us, her body still trembling in aftershocks. She was spent, eyes half-closed, sweat-slicked skin glowing in the firelight, but I could see the fire still simmering in those brown depths—a spark of defiance that hadn't been fully extinguished. Good. I'd tamed her for now, broken her just enough to remember, but I knew this dance wasn't over. She was mine, body and soul, and I'd remind her every damn night if I had to, with bites, thrusts, and unrelenting possession until she craved it as much as I did.

CHAPTER SIX

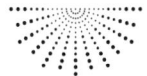

Noelle

"Ma'am, it's time to wake up."

The maid's gentle voice pulled me from unconsciousness. I opened my eyes to curtains already drawn, sunlight streaming in with the snow outside, the brightness stabbing at my eyes.

Everything hurt. My wrists bore dark purple marks where he'd gripped them, my fingers too stiff to move properly. The bite on my chest burned, a constant reminder of last night's humiliation. I lay curled on the chaise lounge, staring out at the monotonous snow within these high walls, feeling like a caged bird.

"Ma'am?" The maid called again, worry creeping into her voice.

"I heard you." My voice came out hoarse, barely recognizable. "Draw me a bath."

She hesitated, then nodded and headed toward the bathroom.

The sheets beside me were cold. Kholod had been gone for hours. He was like a storm—devastating everything in his path, then vanishing without a trace, leaving only wreckage behind.

I struggled to sit up, every movement pulling at my wounds. Walking to the mirror, I stared at the stranger looking back—pale face, lifeless eyes, neck and collarbone covered in telltale marks.

And that bite on my chest, already scabbing but still horrific to look at.

I reached out to touch it gently. Sharp pain made me gasp.

Kholod Morozov.

What exactly do you need to do to me before you'll let me go?

Lunch was brought by Darya—I'd only learned the name of this maid who'd been with me since entering the manor today. That afternoon, I sat by the bedroom window, flipping through a geography magazine—Kholod's only allowance for mental escape after shutting down my blog.

Suddenly, a knock at the door. "Ma'am, please come to the living room."

I opened the door, confused. Daniel waited respectfully outside.

I followed him downstairs, hearing a maid say, "This way, please."

In the living room, several men and women in elegant suits directed assistants carrying gift boxes branded with luxury logos—Chanel, Dior, Hermès, Van Cleef & Arpels...

"Mrs. Morozov, hello." A woman who looked like a manager approached with a perfect smile. "Mr. Morozov ordered this season's complete collection for you. Are you available for fittings now?"

I stared at those towering boxes, nausea rising from my stomach.

This was compensation, wasn't it? His way of gilding brutality with money.

"No need." My voice was cold. "Just leave them there."

"But ma'am..." The manager looked troubled. "Mr. Morozov specifically requested we ensure every piece fits properly..."

"I said no." I cut her off, turning to leave.

Just then, Anastasia emerged from the study. She glanced at the items in the living room, her expression unreadable.

"Take these to her bedroom," she told the butler, her voice calm but brooking no argument.

I stood halfway up the stairs, watching them begin moving everything, emotions churning inside me.

Anastasia looked up at me, her gaze loaded with meaning—assessing, evaluating.

Anya returned from outside, saw the scene, jealousy flashing in her eyes before turning to mockery.

"Wow," she deliberately raised her voice, "looks like someone's really good at pleasing my brother. So many gifts—your methods are impressive."

"Anya." Anastasia's voice carried a warning.

"I'm just stating facts." Anya shrugged, walking to the pile of boxes and casually opening a Hermès one. "Birkin, and Himalayan too. Noelle, you're really lucky."

I ignored her and headed upstairs.

"Noelle." Anastasia suddenly called out.

I turned and nodded. "Yes?"

"Men express affection in ways that can be... difficult to accept," her expression was inscrutable, "but you must learn to value it."

"Yes, thank you for the guidance." I curtsied politely, not taking her words to heart at all.

Back in the bedroom, the jewelry had been properly arranged in the vanity's jewelry cabinet, and Darya was directing several maids in organizing the clothes. Looking at them, I felt only deep revulsion.

Did he think this could erase everything? That money could buy my compliance?

I sat on the bed's edge, picking up the new phone Kholod had given me—strictly limited functions, contacts containing only a few people, including my mother and Isabella, whom I'd added myself.

As I stared at the phone, it suddenly rang.

Sofia.

I hesitated for a few seconds, then finally answered.

"Noelle!" My mother's voice came through, barely containing her urgency. "You finally answered! You haven't been returning my messages, I thought..."

"I'm fine, Mother." I cut her off, my voice weary.

"Good." She sighed with relief, then immediately shifted topics. "Noelle, I heard the Morozov family has a big dock project. Could you mention it to Kholod, get us involved? Even just a small piece..."

I closed my eyes, helplessness washing over me.

"Mother..."

"I know it's difficult, but Noelle, you're a Morozov now. You need to learn to use that position." Her voice carried natural expectation. "All that education you received—wasn't it for this day? Did you learn what I taught you last time? You need to learn to please your husband, make him..."

"Enough." I interrupted, suppressed anger in my voice. "Mom, I'm not your tool for profit."

"What are you saying?" Her voice rose. "I'm your mother! This is for your own good, for our family! Noelle, you have to understand—only Kholod can save us now..."

"Then go beg him yourself. Don't go through me."

"Noelle!"

I hung up.

The phone immediately rang again. I hit decline.

She called again.

I turned it off.

The room fell silent again. Sitting on the bed's edge, I felt like a doll being torn apart from all directions.

Kholod wanted me to be the perfect wife.

Mother wanted me to save the family.

But no one asked who I wanted to be.

I stood and wandered aimlessly around the room, entering the walk-in closet to look at those luxurious things. They lay there quietly, like elegant shackles.

I didn't want to touch any of them.

For the next three days, I barely left my room.

Anastasia didn't mention learning rules again, as if she'd forgotten I existed. Anya rarely appeared either. When we occasionally met at meals, she'd just glance at me without much conversation. I welcomed the peace.

At night, I curled up on the sofa by the bedroom fireplace, reading my geography magazine. This issue focused on Northern Europe, with extensive coverage of Norway's fjords.

I stared at those photos, imagining myself standing in that pure landscape, breathing cold, free air.

If I could escape this place...

If I could regain freedom...

Just as I lost myself in fantasy, the door suddenly burst open.

I startled, the magazine sliding to the floor.

Kholod stood in the doorway, still wearing his outdoor coat, carrying the chill and cigar scent with him.

He was back.

His gaze swept the room before settling on me.

"What are you wearing?" His voice was calm, yet sent chills through me.

I looked down at myself—still that plain cotton dress, simple and modest, though it clashed completely with this luxurious manor.

"Is there a problem?" I asked back.

He didn't answer, walking straight into the closet. Moments later, he emerged carrying a deep blue silk nightgown embroidered with delicate lace.

"Put this on." He tossed the dress beside me.

I picked it up but didn't move.

"I said, put it on," he repeated, impatience creeping into his voice.

"I don't like silk," I said calmly. "It's slippery and cold."

"I don't care what you like." He stepped closer, his eyes turning dangerous. "I only care whether you obey."

"What if I don't?" I looked up, meeting his gaze.

I didn't know why I had the courage.

Maybe it was these days of suppression and humiliation that made me unable to continue submitting.

Maybe it was Mother's call that made me realize—if I didn't fight for myself, I'd forever remain just someone else's tool.

He narrowed his eyes, dangerous energy radiating from him.

The next second, he grabbed my arm violently, yanking me up and slamming me against the wall.

"You're challenging me?" His voice was low, suppressing rage.

"I'm just expressing my opinion." I gritted my teeth, though my arm ached from his grip. "I'm your wife, not your doll."

"Wife?" He laughed coldly. "Noelle, get this straight—everything you have now, including the clothes on your back, I gave you. Think about your crumbling family. What makes you think you can negotiate with me?"

His words were like a knife, stabbing straight into my heart.

"Yes, the Bellucci family is declining, I have no right to negotiate," my voice began shaking, "but that doesn't mean you can treat me like property!"

"Property?" He gripped my chin, forcing me to look at him. "You're worth much more than property."

Before the words finished, his other hand grabbed my collar.

"Rip—"

The fabric tore from neckline to hem, exposing my undergarments.

"You're insane!" I struggled hard but couldn't budge him an inch.

He remained unmoved, watching me with almost glacial eyes. "Remember, you're mine. Everything about you, from your hair to your toes, only I get to adorn."

He picked up the dress, roughly pulling it over me.

The icy touch made me shudder all over.

"Kholod Morozov, what gives you the right to treat me this way?!" I finally couldn't help shouting, tears bursting forth. "Who do you think you are?!"

My challenge seemed to ignite his long-suppressed fury.

He backed me into the corner step by step, his overwhelming presence making it hard to breathe.

"What gives me the right?" He repeated my words, dangerous light flashing in his eyes. "Because you're a Morozov now. Because your reunion with Lorenzo made me the laughingstock of all Philadelphia."

"There's nothing between us!" I was practically screaming. "I've explained this countless times!"

"Explain?" He sneered, leaning closer. "Your explanations are worthless against evidence."

He suddenly kissed me, teeth biting down hard on my lower lip, the taste of blood filling my mouth.

I tried to resist, but he pinned me down completely.

In the struggle, my bra was torn open, exposing my chest to his view.

Kholod's movements suddenly stopped.

He stared at the bite mark near my nipple, something complex flashing in his eyes before being replaced by deeper fury.

"It's healing," he said quietly, as if talking to himself. "Soon it'll be gone."

He released me, walking to the nightstand and pulling open a drawer.

I leaned against the wall, panting, dread rising in my heart.

He pulled out a small box. Inside was a tattoo kit—needles, ink, disinfectant.

"What are you doing?" Terror filled me as I edged toward the door —I wanted to run.

He didn't answer, catching up in a few steps and dragging me back to the sofa, using his knee to pin my legs so I couldn't move.

"No!" I fought desperately. "Kholod! You can't..."

"I can." He cut me off, taking out a disinfectant wipe to clean the wound on my chest. "This mark will fade, but I can give you one that never will."

"Please..." My voice broke with tears. "Don't do this..."

He ignored me completely.

The moment the cold needle pierced my skin, sharp pain shot through the already sensitive area.

"Ah—Kholod! Let me go!"

"Quiet." He said coldly. "This is just the beginning."

Tears blurred my vision. I could feel the needle puncturing my skin over and over, each stab accompanied by excruciating pain. I couldn't help crying out in agony, so he simply sealed my mouth with a kiss.

He was carving his name into my body.

Time felt endless.

When the final needle pierced, I was trembling from crying, breathless from his kiss.

Kholod set down the needle, gently wiping the red, swollen skin with a cotton ball. His fingers and the cold cotton inevitably brushed over the tip, the tingling and pain causing another shudder.

I looked down, and where the bite mark had been, two clear Cyrillic letters were now branded: "H.M."

Kholod Morozov.

"This," he caressed that patch of skin, his voice full of satisfaction, "will never fade."

I closed my eyes, tears falling silently.

He'd won.

In the cruelest way possible, he'd completely made me his possession.

That night, Kholod sat by the bed for a long time, quietly watching me.

I curled up on the other side, my back to him.

"Does it still hurt?" he suddenly asked.

I didn't answer.

After a long while, he stood and walked to the door.

"Rest now," he said. "Starting tomorrow, Mother will teach you proper behavior. Don't disappoint me again."

The sound of the door closing was especially harsh in the silent room.

I turned over, staring at the ceiling.

My hand unconsciously touched that red, swollen patch of skin on my chest.

I finally understood deeply—he'd carved a mark on my body that could never be erased.

Outside, snow began falling again. This winter seemed like it would never end.

CHAPTER SEVEN

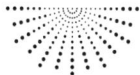

Kholod

"Boss, Lorenzo Conti has been sent back to the Bellucci family."
Dmitri stood in the study, delivering his report. "Our men showed
restraint—three broken ribs, fractured right wrist."

"What's the Belluccis' reaction?" I didn't look up from the files in
my hands.

"Sofia Bellucci went ballistic, blamed Lorenzo for acting on his
own. According to our sources, there's serious upheaval inside the
family. Some think Lorenzo was defending family honor, others think
he's a hothead who nearly destroyed their last hope."

I set down the files and leaned back in my chair, fingers drumming
against the armrest.

"He destroyed himself." My voice was ice. "Arrogant fool."

"There's something else. Those competitors who've been pressuring the Bellucci businesses—they're getting restless again. Seems
they didn't take your warning seriously."

"Who's pulling the strings?"

"We suspect Kieran. That old fox has been quiet lately, and those
families all have murky connections to him."

Kieran.

My fingers stopped drumming. My gaze turned cold.

"Teach those families a lesson. Make them understand—Morozov warnings are only given once."

"Understood." Dmitri nodded. "How far should we go?"

"Bankrupt them." My tone was casual. "But no blood. Now's not the time to deal with cops."

"Yes, boss," Dmitri responded. "And Sofia Bellucci..."

"Warn her," I cut him off. "Keep Lorenzo in line. If he shows his face around here again, next time won't be just a few broken ribs."

"Understood."

Dmitri turned to leave. I stopped him.

"Wait."

"Boss?"

"The gifts," I asked. "Were they delivered?"

He paused, then understood. "All delivered. Every piece you personally selected."

"Did she..." I hesitated. "Did she wear them?"

Dmitri's expression shifted slightly. "According to Darya, the missus only wore the blue dress. Everything else remains untouched in the walk-in closet."

My fingers resumed their drumming, faster and harder than before.

"Fine." I waved him away.

Alone in the study, I stood and walked to the floor-to-ceiling windows, gazing at the snow-covered forest beyond.

What the hell does this woman want?

Jewelry? She refuses it.

Designer clothes? She won't wear them.

Money? She won't touch it.

I'd given her everything women dream of, and she acted like it didn't exist.

This silent rejection irritated me more than any fierce resistance could.

I was used to solving problems with money and power. But with Noelle, none of it worked.

Freedom?

That was the one thing I couldn't give her right now.

I decided to find answers myself.

The surveillance showed her in the library, so I went there quietly.

This library had been my father's favorite place. Dark oak shelves stretched from floor to ceiling, housing over ten thousand books. Fire danced in the hearth, adding warmth to the massive space.

There she was—curled on the carpet by the window, back against the bookshelf, a heavy art book spread across her knees.

I recognized it—Iceland: The Land of Ice and Fire, something I'd had shipped from New York last week.

She was sketching in a drawing pad, copying glaciers and aurora from the book with charcoal.

Her expression was focused and peaceful, as if her soul had already flown to that distant world.

Sunlight bathed her, casting a soft glow across her profile. Her fingers holding the charcoal were delicate but steady, each stroke revealing her hunger for freedom.

I held my breath.

This scene reminded me of years ago—a little girl from a family I'd had executed for conspiring with Kieran against me.

She'd had that same look of longing.

But that girl had died by my gun, the light in her eyes extinguished in an instant.

At the time, I'd felt something like regret.

I'd built my life on rules, on control. Such yearning had no place in my world. Yet here it was again, shining in my wife's eyes—she was using charcoal to build a spiritual realm I couldn't touch.

Did I really want to snuff out that light completely? Just thinking about it sent needle-sharp pain through my chest.

But I couldn't let her go either. Maybe when she finally learned obedience, I could let her taste freedom again.

I watched too intently, unconsciously stepping forward.

"Click—"

My shoe hit the wooden floor at the carpet's edge.

In the silence, the sound was jarring.

Worse, when I tried to adjust my position, I bumped the side table.

The crystal vase on top wobbled—

"Crash!"

It shattered.

Noelle spun around, startled. Her brown eyes met mine before I could hide my emotions.

Her body tensed instantly. All that peace shattered, replaced by wariness.

"Don't you make any sound when you walk?"

Annoyance and embarrassment surged through me. Kholod Morozov exposed by a damn vase—ridiculous.

I lifted my chin, adopting an arrogant pose to mask my earlier lapse, and walked slowly toward her.

My shoes crunched on crystal fragments.

"Just a vase," I crouched down and picked up a sharp shard, playing with it between my fingers. "Tomorrow I can buy you a hundred more."

"Some things, once broken, can't be bought back with any amount of money." She closed her sketchbook, clutching it to her chest like protecting some precious treasure.

Her words sent an inexplicable thrill through me.

She was still fighting. Even if only with words.

I dropped to a crouch in front of her, one hand braced against the bookshelf beside her, trapping her between myself and the books.

"Is that so?" My gaze moved from the shard in my hand to the sketchbook pressed against her chest.

"But some things are just temporarily out of reach. Doesn't mean they'll never be seen."

She tried to hide the sketchbook, but I'd already pulled it free.

I flipped it open. The pages showed her landscapes—Iceland's glaciers, Norway's fjords, Scotland's highlands...

Every stroke was meticulous, full of heart.

"You're talented." I meant it, my fingertip lightly tracing the aurora lines she'd drawn.

The slight callus on my finger rasped against the paper.

I could feel her body trembling slightly at my touch.

"You want to go here?" I leaned closer, my breath almost touching her lips. "Iceland?"

She turned her face away, silent.

"Beg me," I whispered in her ear. "Maybe I'll take you."

She whipped her head around, fury blazing in her eyes. "In your dreams."

"Dreams?" I laughed coldly. "Noelle, you need to understand something. From now on, every landscape you see requires my permission."

"You're insane."

"Maybe," I admitted. "But that doesn't matter. What matters is you're my wife. And my wife shouldn't spend her days fantasizing about escape."

"I wasn't—"

I didn't let her finish.

One hand gripped the back of her head, the other caught her chin, forcing her face toward mine as I kissed her hard.

She struggled, pushing against my chest.

I didn't budge.

This kiss carried punishment and a possessiveness I couldn't explain.

I needed her to understand—she belonged to me.

Her body, her soul, even her dreams belonged to me.

Finally, I released her.

She gasped for air, tears pooling in her eyes.

"I hate you." Her voice shook.

"I know." I stood, looking down at her. "But that doesn't matter."

I left the library, leaving her sitting there alone.

An hour before dinner, I had the maid deliver a black silk gown to Noelle.

It was custom-made for her in Paris last week. From the moment I got it, I'd imagined how she'd look wearing it. Tonight, I wanted her at the dinner table in that dress.

Thirty minutes later, I entered her room.

The dress lay untouched on the sofa. She still wore her plain casual clothes, standing at the window watching the snow.

My fury ignited instantly.

"Seems you didn't hear what I said."

She turned, that stubborn expression still on her face.

I approached step by step. She backed up until her back hit the window frame.

I reached out, fingertips catching the hem of her casual dress. "Your drawings today were beautiful. But Noelle, beauty needs the right frame."

I released her hem, instead gripping her chin and forcing her to look up at me.

"Under my roof, you're part of me. Your image reflects my taste."

"What if your taste conflicts with my comfort?"

I stared into her eyes, that defiant fire burning bright. This woman always found new ways to challenge me.

"Then your body learns to accommodate my taste. Noelle, every time you obey makes the air under this roof more pleasant. Every time you resist—even over something small like a dress—makes things very troublesome."

I locked eyes with her, making sure she understood my meaning.

"And I hate trouble. Now put it on."

I released her and walked to the door.

At the threshold, I stopped without turning around.

"You have ten minutes. If you're not changed by then, I'll help you change—my way."

I left the room and closed the door.

Leaning against the wall outside, I lit a cigarette.

She'd change. I was certain.

At dinner, I waited at the head of the table.

The door opened. Noelle walked in.

She wore the black silk gown.

The dress perfectly outlined her figure—slender waist, flowing curves. The high slit revealed glimpses of her long legs as she moved.

She'd pinned her hair up simply, exposing the lines of her neck and collarbone.

My breath caught slightly. She was beautiful. So beautiful I wanted to hide her away where no one else could see.

She sat in the chair to my left, graceful but cold-eyed.

I could feel the resistance radiating from her, but I didn't care. She'd put it on. She'd obeyed. It was a good start.

Mother and Anya had already taken their seats. Mother gave Noelle an appraising look, a flicker of satisfaction crossing her features.

Dinner proceeded in silence. I cut my steak, but my gaze kept drifting to Noelle.

She ate little, her movements mechanical, as if eating was just an obligation.

Then Mother spoke suddenly.

"Noelle, you know Kholod smoothed over some troubles for your family's business, don't you?"

I set down my knife and fork, looking at Mother. Why bring this up?

Noelle froze, too, surprise flashing in her eyes when she looked at me.

I met her gaze expressionlessly, saying nothing.

She lowered her eyes, answering quietly. "I didn't know. But I imagine it wasn't for me—it was for the Morozov family's reputation."

Her response surprised me. I'd expected gratitude, at least a thank you. But she didn't, maintaining that distance and coldness.

Mother said nothing more, but something stirred restlessly in my chest.

For the family's reputation? Maybe. But when she was so quick to distance herself, irritation still flared within me.

CHAPTER EIGHT

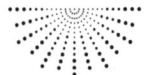

Noelle

"Noelle! That's wonderful! You did absolutely perfectly!"

Sofia's voice crackled through the receiver, barely containing her excitement. "You know what? Those families that have been crushing our business—they're all going under! Their cash flow has dried up completely, and now they're scrambling to file for bankruptcy!"

I gripped the phone, leaning against the bedroom window, watching the snow drift down outside.

"Is that so?"

"Of course it's true!" Sofia's tone grew even more animated. "And that dock property that used to be ours? Now people are actually willing to negotiate! Noelle, this is all your doing!"

"My doing?" I gave a bitter laugh. "Mom, I haven't done anything."

"You married Kholod Morozov—that's everything!" Her voice carried that familiar note of certainty. "Noelle, you need to keep this up. Make Kholod treasure you more, make him dependent on you. You understand what I'm saying?"

I closed my eyes as a wave of revulsion washed over me.

"Mom, I'm tired."

"Tired of what?" She suddenly raised her voice. "Noelle, you need to push harder! Are you pregnant yet? If you could give Kholod a son, then our family would truly—"

"Enough." I cut her off sharply. "Mom, I have things to do. I'm hanging up."

"Noelle! You—"

I ended the call abruptly.

Mom claimed the family's turnaround was all thanks to Kholod. That brutal, twisted man—why would he help the Belluccis?

I recalled Anastasia's words at dinner, remembered Kholod's impassive face. Was he really doing this for me? Or for the Morozov family's reputation? Regardless, he had indeed helped my family. At least Mother would believe I was being useful. For the time being, I probably wouldn't receive any more of those suffocating calls urging me to please my husband.

I could have some peace.

At that thought, a flicker of gratitude stirred within me. I couldn't help but recall our moments together since I'd entered this manor—his sudden appearance in the library, those burning amber eyes when he bent to kiss me, his dangerous, invasive presence when he whispered in my ear, the tremor-inducing sensation of his calloused fingertips tracing my skin...

My pulse quickened.

Damn it.

How could I feel this way about him?

Father's face suddenly surfaced in my mind. I remembered clearly how the Bellucci family had crumbled step by step under pressure, remembered Father's increasingly gaunt features, his desperate expression during those late-night threatening phone calls, Mother collapsing with grief at his funeral...

This man was my enemy! How could I feel grateful? How could I experience even a moment's flutter of attraction? He had destroyed my family first, and now he appeared like some kind of savior. What was this? Charity? Or another form of humiliation?

I curled up on the window seat, wrapping myself in the silk throw. Outside, the snow fell more heavily as evening descended.

I sank into deep confusion and inner turmoil.

A few days later, in the afternoon, I was taking tea with Anastasia and Anya in the sun-drenched conservatory.

This was one of my least favorite daily rituals. The glass conservatory was flooded with light, expensive tropical plants flourished luxuriantly, and floral fragrances drifted through the air—it should have been pleasant, but their presence made it suffocating.

Anastasia sat elegantly in a wicker chair, silently perusing a Russian book. Anya lazily scrolled through her phone, occasionally glancing up at me with calculating eyes. I sat across from them, mechanically raising my teacup to my lips while tasting nothing.

In this stifling silence, a maid entered.

"Madam," she addressed Anastasia respectfully, "a Miss Isabella Vance is here requesting to see Mrs. Noelle."

I froze. Isabella? What could bring her here?

Anastasia looked up, her brow creasing slightly, clearly displeased by this unexpected visitor.

"Show her in," she said coolly.

Moments later, Isabella clicked into the room on high heels. She wore a cream cashmere coat over a pink dress, her makeup flawless and her smile radiantly sweet.

"Mrs. Morozov, hello!" She approached Anastasia with enthusiasm, offering a slight curtsy. "I do hope you'll forgive my unannounced visit. I simply missed Noelle terribly and had to see how she's settling in."

Anastasia merely inclined her head without speaking.

Isabella turned to Anya next. "Miss Anya, what a pleasure to see you again! When I spotted you at Paris Fashion Week, that Dior creation you wore was absolutely divine! I can still picture it perfectly!"

Anya snorted softly, setting down her phone. "Miss Vance certainly has a remarkable memory."

"Oh, not at all." Isabella seemed utterly oblivious to the sarcasm, her smile growing even brighter. "Being able to remember beautiful things is truly a gift."

Finally, she moved to my side, grasping my hands firmly and studying me intently.

"Noelle! You've lost weight!" Her voice brimmed with concern. "Just look at you—you're so pale. Haven't you been eating properly? Or perhaps..."

She let the words hang meaningfully, her gaze sweeping deliberately over my neck—where Kholod's marks had faded to pale purple bruises.

I gently squeezed her hands in reassurance. "I'm perfectly fine, Isabella."

"Miss Vance is quite fascinating," Anya interjected suddenly, her voice pitched just so. "Our family's new missus has barely settled in, and here you are, already paying social calls."

Isabella's smile flickered momentarily but recovered swiftly.

She turned to Anya with wide, innocent eyes. "Oh, Miss Anya, you've misunderstood completely. Noelle is my dearest friend—now that she's finally found happiness in marriage, I want to ensure she's thriving."

She linked her arm through mine affectionately. "Isn't that right, Noelle? You know how much I worry about you."

"Yes, absolutely! I know how much you care!" I clasped her hand, laughing as I leaned into her warmth.

She shifted smoothly, addressing Anastasia with an even sweeter expression. "You see, I've always maintained that marrying into the Morozov family is every woman's dream! Speaking of dreams, Mrs. Anastasia, the way you've curated this manor is simply exquisite— your taste is beyond compare. These tropical specimens must be specially air-freighted from South America, surely? What extraordinary attention to detail."

Anastasia set aside her book, regarding Isabella with an unreadable expression.

"Miss Vance, you have expertise in horticulture?"

"Oh, I wouldn't presume to claim expertise—merely some modest appreciation," Isabella replied with becoming humility. "Though I have heard tell that the Morozov family maintains an even more magnificent estate in Saint Petersburg, featuring a Winter Garden that's considered a masterpiece. I would be absolutely enchanted to experience such artistry someday."

"I'm afraid you'd find yourself disappointed," Anastasia replied flatly. "That estate doesn't receive visitors."

"Naturally, I was merely making conversation." Isabella smiled with perfect grace.

She turned back to me. "Noelle, would you mind showing me around the manor? I'm positively bursting with curiosity!"

I glanced toward Anastasia, awaiting her permission.

The elderly woman remained silent for several moments before finally nodding. "Go. Don't dawdle—return before dinner."

I escorted Isabella from the conservatory, conducting a tour of the manor grounds.

Throughout our walk, she maintained a steady stream of admiring exclamations.

"This library is absolutely magnificent!"

"That fireplace must be worth a fortune!"

"Noelle, you're incredibly fortunate!"

I responded absently, my thoughts elsewhere.

When we reached the greenhouse, Isabella suddenly halted and drew me to a secluded bench.

"Noelle," her voice took on a serious tone, "are you... truly all right?"

"What do you mean?" I looked at her with confusion.

"I mean..." she hesitated, "living with Kholod—have you adjusted to it?"

"Well enough." I preferred not to elaborate.

"I heard..." she dropped her voice conspiratorially, "I heard something happened to Lorenzo."

My entire body went rigid.

"What... what happened to him?"

"Oh, darling." Isabella sighed heavily. "From what I understand, he suffered several broken ribs and a fractured hand. All because..."

She gazed at me with pointed significance.

"Because of what?" I pressed urgently.

"Because he tried to rescue you." Isabella gripped my hands tightly. "Noelle, I know perfectly well there was nothing between you and Lorenzo, but Kholod sees things differently. He was furious, which is why he..."

"I see." I interrupted, my voice trembling slightly.

"Noelle, you must be extraordinarily careful." Isabella's eyes filled with genuine worry. "A man of Kholod's stature and temperament... you absolutely cannot risk provoking his anger again. I'm desperately concerned for your safety."

"I haven't provoked him." I protested weakly.

"Of course you haven't, darling." She patted my hands soothingly. "But sometimes, even when you've done absolutely nothing, these men will imagine slights. It's their nature—they're intensely possessive creatures."

She leaned closer, her voice dropping to barely a whisper. "Noelle, you must learn compliance. I know it's difficult, but for your family's sake, and to make your own existence more bearable, you need to be accommodating. Please?"

I gazed into her sincere eyes, feeling genuinely moved. In this moment, she seemed to be the only person who truly cared about my well-being.

"I understand. Thank you, Isabella."

"We're friends, after all!" She brightened considerably. "Oh, regarding your wardrobe... while what you're wearing is lovely, it doesn't quite reflect your current position. Perhaps I could help you select some pieces? I know several exceptional designer ateliers..."

"That's not necessary." I declined politely. "Kholod has already provided extensively for me."

"Wonderful, then." She nodded approvingly. "Still, Noelle, you really should consider evolving your style. Men are such visual creatures—you want Kholod to feel that you're making an effort for him. That's how you earn better treatment."

I remained silent, simply nodding in acknowledgment.

We continued chatting about inconsequential matters—new handbag collections, shoes, upcoming social events...

Before departing, Isabella embraced me warmly.

Just as she began to pull away, she whispered almost inaudibly in my ear. "Darling, stay obedient and compliant—that's how you survive and thrive."

Then she released me, turning with practiced elegance to glide away.

I remained standing there, watching her silhouette vanish down the corridor.

At dinner, Kholod failed to appear. Only Anastasia, Anya, and I sat at the long table. The atmosphere remained as oppressive as ever. I mechanically cut the food on my plate while Isabella's words echoed relentlessly in my mind.

Suddenly, Anya set down her cutlery with a sharp clink and fixed me with a piercing stare.

"Keep your distance from that woman." Her voice was ice-cold, her gaze razor-sharp.

I startled, looking up at her in bewilderment.

"Excuse me?"

"Isabella Vance." Anya articulated each syllable with cutting precision. "Stay away from her. Right now, you're her most promising ladder for social advancement."

This unexpected warning left me completely off-balance. I glanced toward Anastasia, but she appeared entirely unsurprised and gave a slight, knowing nod.

My heart plummeted. They were warning me. But about what exactly? Were they alerting me to Isabella's hidden agenda? Or were they mocking me—suggesting that as the daughter of a fallen family, I was cut from the same cloth as social climbers like Isabella?

I kept my expression carefully neutral, simply lowering my gaze and murmuring quietly, "Okay, I understand. Thank you for the warning."

Anya's frown deepened, clearly taken aback by my subdued response.

"Do you truly get what I'm telling you?" she pressed.

"I do." I met her gaze with a polite smile. "I'll be appropriately cautious."

"You—" Anya started to continue, but Anastasia's voice cut through sharply.

"That's enough, Anya." She set down her wine glass with finality. "Maintain your composure."

Anya shot me one last resentful glare but fell silent.

Dinner concluded in heavy silence. I rose to excuse myself.

"Noelle." Anastasia's voice stopped me in my tracks.

I paused and turned back to face her.

She sipped her after-dinner wine with deliberate leisure, her voice calm yet carrying unmistakable authority. "Anya's words may be harsh, but you would be wise to heed them carefully."

She raised her eyes—those penetrating amber orbs so remarkably similar to Kholod's—meeting mine with newfound seriousness. "In this household, learning to distinguish genuine sentiment from calculated manipulation is your most essential survival skill."

"Yes, I understand completely."

Returning to my bedroom, I slumped against the closed door and released a long, shuddering breath. What an absolutely wretched day.

I drifted to the window, gazing out at the impenetrable darkness of the forest beyond. Snow continued its relentless descent, flake by flake, silently shrouding the world in white. Much like my existence—buried beneath accumulating layers of constraint and expectation.

I recalled Isabella's parting whisper, "Stay obedient and compliant."

Submission.

Appeasement.

This was the universal expectation placed upon me.

I was suddenly overwhelmed by profound exhaustion and desolation. What exactly was my role in this house? Wife? Tool? Or merely some disposable ornament?

I curled up on the window seat, cocooning myself in the cashmere throw. Outside, the snowfall intensified, as though intent on burying the entire world beneath its weight. And here I sat, trapped in this gilded cage, watching those crystalline fragments cascade helplessly downward. I had lost not only my freedom—it seemed my final shreds of dignity and autonomous identity were being systematically stripped away as well. How would I endure the endless days stretching ahead?

The thought sent bone-deep cold coursing through me.

CHAPTER NINE

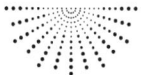

Kholod

"Boss, Miss Vance has left."

"I know." I didn't look up, just stared at the surveillance feed on my computer screen. "What did they talk about?"

"Mostly women's stuff. Clothes, bags, makeup—that sort of thing. But..."

"Speak."

"Miss Vance mentioned Lorenzo Conti. She told Mrs. Morozov that Lorenzo got hurt trying to save her. And she advised Mrs. Morozov to behave and not anger you anymore."

My fingers froze.

Lorenzo. That name was like nails on a chalkboard.

"Keep watching her," I said coldly. "And check Isabella's movements too."

"Yes, boss."

After Dmitri left, I pulled up Noelle's phone records.

The phone I'd given her—every call and text automatically backed up to my servers.

I'd expected to find evidence of her carrying on with Lorenzo Conti, or plotting with the Bellucci family.

Instead, the records showed nothing but spam, ads, and communications with Sofia and Isabella.

Isabella's messages were all trivial nonsense—"Isn't this new Chanel gorgeous?" "Want to get spa treatments next week?" "I saw these shoes that would be perfect for you"...

Boring as hell.

But Sofia's texts piqued my interest.

The latest one came this afternoon. "Noelle, I know you're struggling right now, but you have to hold on. The family needs you. Kholod is a good man—he's helped us so much. You need to repay him properly, understand?"

Good man?

I snorted.

Sofia Bellucci was definitely a practical woman.

I scrolled up to find more of the same—

"Have you figured out how to get Kholod to help us again? It would be great if we could get that dock property back."

"Noelle, you need to learn to use your position. You're the lady of the Morozov house—that's your advantage!"

"Any signs of pregnancy? Are those methods I taught you working?"

...

Every message coached Noelle on how to use me, please me, and exploit me for the family.

I leaned back in my chair and lit a cigar.

I wanted her to come begging.

Better yet, I wanted her to walk into my study of her own accord. Her movements might be clumsy, inexperienced, but just imagining her trying to please me with that not-quite-tamed body and those eyes. Those clear eyes looking up at me, whispering "please"—

I could picture the entire scene.

Under my gaze, she'd reach out with trembling hands, tentatively trying to unbutton my shirt. She'd be so nervous she'd fumble helplessly, the button slipping from her fingers again and again. Her eyes would redden with frustration, but she still couldn't manage that first button.

I'd watch coldly, offering no help.

Would she give up on the button and rise on her toes, clumsily pressing her tear-salted lips to mine?

Or would she go further?

She'd wear that stubborn expression as she slowly sank to her knees beside my chair. Tear stains would still mark her face, eyes red-rimmed, like a little beast forced into submission.

I'd raise my hand, spreading it before her. She'd resist at first, but eventually extend her warm tongue to lightly trace my cold palm.

No, that wouldn't be enough.

I'd make her pull down my zipper, take me in her mouth, submit to me completely.

That would be more exquisite than mere physical conquest—crushing her pride utterly, making her offer everything willingly.

The thought intoxicated and excited me more than any liquor, making my lower body tighten, hard and aching.

But none of it happened. Nothing.

She was like a stone, giving no response, never asking me for anything. She'd rather wear plain clothes every day, hold books about distant landscapes, rather sit in her room staring into space than bow her head in submission.

I scrolled through the records again. Noelle's replies to Sofia were brief—"okay," "fine," "Yeah"—utterly dismissive.

She'd even hung up on her mother several times.

I felt like I'd thrown a powerful punch into soft cotton, the rebound filling me with frustration.

Why couldn't she just be like other women—content to enjoy all this, or at least like a proper commodity, knowing how to please her buyer?

She simply couldn't.

At dinner time, I didn't return to the manor. An important meeting detained me, but all evening, those business terms and profit distributions couldn't capture my thoughts.

Noelle's face kept surfacing in my mind. What was she doing? Would she feel relieved that I wasn't there? These thoughts were maddening. When had I started caring so much about a woman's thoughts?

By the time the meeting ended, it was late. I drove back to the manor, snow-covered driveways gleaming coldly under the headlights.

I pushed open the master bedroom door. Noelle was curled up on the sofa by the window, a book in her lap, but she clearly wasn't reading. Her gaze was fixed blankly outside, looking forlorn.

I stood in the doorway watching her for a while, then approached silently.

She didn't notice. I stopped behind her, close enough to smell the fresh orange blossom scent in her hair.

"Your friend left." I broke the silence.

Her body stiffened, but she didn't turn around.

"You won't even let me see female friends?" Her voice was calm, but she deliberately emphasized "female."

My lips curved slightly.

"This isn't about gender, Noelle." I leaned down. "Male or female, your heart shouldn't belong to anyone else."

"Then where should it belong?" She finally turned, those eyes looking straight at me. "With you?"

Her question caught me off guard.

"Of course." I quickly recovered, my fingers lightly stroking her nape.

Her skin was warm and smooth. The moment I touched her, she trembled as if shocked. This pleased me—at least her body still remembered my touch, remembered who was in control.

"You're shaking."

"Your hands are cold." She turned away.

"Liar. Are you afraid of me, or... anticipating me?"

"You're overthinking it."

"Am I?" My fingers traced down her neckline, stopping at her collarbone. "Then why is your heart racing?"

She didn't answer, just stood up abruptly, putting distance between us.

"If there's nothing else, I'd like to rest."

"There is something." I straightened, adjusting my cuffs. "Come with me."

"Where?" she asked warily.

"My study." I walked toward the door. "Now."

Noelle stood in the study doorway, not entering, her body tense as a drawn bow.

"Come in. Close the door." I walked to my desk and opened a drawer.

She hesitated for a few seconds, then complied.

I took out a velvet jewelry box and placed it on the desk.

"Come here."

She approached slowly, her gaze falling on the box.

I opened it. A platinum necklace—twisted thorn vines encrusted with diamonds, with a holly berry carved from ruby hanging at the center, blazing brilliantly in the firelight.

"Beautiful, isn't it?" I lifted the necklace, diamonds flowing between my fingers.

"Yes, it's beautiful." Her voice was soft. "But I don't need it."

"I'm not asking for your opinion." I met her eyes. "Put it on."

"I don't want to."

"This is an order, Noelle."

"And if I refuse?"

I stared at her for several seconds, then smiled.

"You won't."

I moved behind her, wrapped the necklace around her throat, and fastened it.

"Look." I embraced her from behind, turning us toward the floor-to-ceiling window.

The glass reflected our image. The beige dress complemented the twisted thorns at her neck, the blood-red ruby flickering with her breathing, startlingly beautiful.

I stood behind her, chin resting on her head, arms around her waist.

"How beautiful," I whispered in her ear, breath washing over her earlobe.

I could feel her breathing quicken.

My hands began wandering over her body, sliding from her waist to her stomach, then slowly upward until I cupped that fullness.

I played with the delicate sensation in my palm, fingertips lingering lightly around the peak. I caressed the textured skin where my name was etched, feeling her body's uncontrollable trembling in my arms.

She didn't pull away. Good.

I lowered my head and kissed her neck.

"The most beautiful collar can't change the fact that this is a cage."

My movements stopped abruptly.

"What did you say?" I released her, moving to face her, wanting to see her expression clearly.

She looked up, those eyes clear and calm.

"I said," she spoke deliberately, "the most beautiful collar can't change the fact that this is a cage. Kholod, you can possess my body, control my actions, and put the world's most expensive necklace on me. But none of that changes the fact—"

She reached up, touching the necklace at her throat.

"I am your prisoner. And you are my jailer."

Her words were like ice water, instantly extinguishing all my desire.

In its place came rage.

This woman—she could always maintain that damned clarity at the most crucial moments.

"You really know how to kill the mood."

"I'm just stating facts."

Fury churned in my chest. I wanted to tear her apart, destroy that clarity, see her collapse and beg beneath me.

But I didn't.

Because doing so would only prove she was right—prove I really was just a savage who could only assert dominance through violence.

I took a deep breath, forcing myself to calm down.

"Get out." I turned away from her, voice ice-cold. "Now. Get out of my study immediately."

She didn't move. Just looked at me calmly.

"What are you waiting for?" I raised my voice. "I told you to get out!"

"Can I take off the necklace?"

"No. You have to wear it."

"But—"

"Get out!" I spun around and roared.

She straightened her spine and walked toward the door.

At the doorway, she stopped without turning back, just said softly:

"Good night, Kholod."

Damn. Damn woman.

I slammed my fist on the desk, scattering papers everywhere.

I walked to the liquor cabinet, poured myself a vodka, and knocked it back hard.

CHAPTER TEN

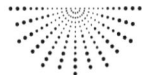

Kholod

Two in the afternoon. I glanced at my watch.

"Boss, the Eastern European arms dealer accepted our terms and ended the meeting early."

"Good." I kept it brief. "Cancel everything else today."

As our convoy pulled into the manor grounds, movement behind the greenhouse glass caught my eye. I stepped out and headed straight there. The moment I pushed open the door, warm air laced with tea fragrance enveloped me.

Sunlight streamed through the glass panels, casting dappled shadows across the floor. Noelle and Isabella Vance sat side by side on the sofa near the fireplace. Noelle held a thick fashion magazine while Isabella pointed excitedly at some page.

What surprised me most was Noelle—her head tilted slightly, lips curved in the kind of relaxed smile I'd never seen before.

My brow furrowed deeply. An inexplicable irritation churned in my chest. I'd never liked outsiders roaming freely through this place.

They sensed my arrival.

"Mr. Morozov!" Isabella practically sprang to her feet, face lighting up with delight. "You're back! What perfect timing!"

Noelle's smile vanished as if someone had flipped a switch. In its place came the familiar coldness and wariness I knew so well. She rose slowly, closing the magazine and letting it hang at her side.

"Miss Vance." I nodded curtly, but kept my eyes locked on Noelle. "When are you leaving?"

The air froze.

"I... I was just about to say goodbye," she struggled to maintain that sweet tone. "Just came to see Noelle. Haven't seen her in ages—I missed her so much..."

"Kholod! Isabella is my friend. How could you treat her like this?" Noelle stepped protectively in front of Isabella, fire blazing in her eyes.

Friend? In this world, true friends were rarer than roses in the Arctic. And the way she defended this so-called "friend" particularly grated on me.

"Noelle," Isabella quickly grasped her arm, "it's fine. Mr. Morozov is probably tired."

Then she turned back to Noelle, patting her shoulder reassuringly. "Oh, didn't you have something to give me?"

Noelle clearly froze, her brow creasing. "What?"

"That necklace you mentioned!" Isabella reminded her. "You said it would suit me perfectly and wanted to give it to me. It's in your room, remember?"

Noelle caught on quickly. "Oh! Right, how silly of me—I nearly forgot. I'll go get it right now."

She shot me a look brimming with displeasure, then glanced worriedly at Isabella, as if ensuring I wouldn't mistreat her friend.

Only after receiving Isabella's reassuring nod did she turn and leave the greenhouse.

Once her footsteps faded, only the two of us remained.

Isabella stood there awkwardly, fingers twisting the fabric of her skirt.

"Mr. Morozov," she began softly, obvious nervousness in her voice, "I'm sorry. I just... I was so worried about Noelle."

I walked to the tea service and poured myself a cup. The liquid cascaded down, creating ripples in the porcelain.

"She's here. There's nothing to worry about."

"I know." Isabella nodded hastily. "This is certainly the safest place. It's just... Noelle has such a stubborn nature. I worry she can't adapt to the Morozov family's way of life. After all, the difference between the Morozov and Bellucci families..."

She stopped mid-sentence, as if realizing she'd said something inappropriate.

I offered no response, simply lifted my teacup and sipped slowly.

"Actually, Noelle is wonderful," she continued cautiously. "Kind and intelligent, just a bit headstrong. With some patience, she'll make an excellent wife. We grew up together—I know her so well..."

"I have no interest in hearing this." I cut her off.

I didn't need to learn about Noelle from someone else.

Isabella choked on my abrupt interruption, embarrassment flickering across her features. She opened her mouth as if to speak, then thought better of it.

"Then... Mr. Morozov," she asked carefully, "may I tidy up my things first?"

I gestured toward the scattered items on the tea table.

Isabella exhaled in relief and crouched down to collect her belongings.

She picked up her phone first, then her lipstick, movements somewhat frantic. When she reached for her handbag, she seemed to lose her balance, toppling forward.

The bag hit the floor, its clasp springing open and spilling contents everywhere.

Compact mirror, keys, business cards, and—

A bracelet.

Platinum chain adorned with emerald-carved Christmas holly leaves and ruby berries.

My breath caught.

Isabella frantically dropped to her knees, desperately trying to gather everything, her movements rushed and panicked.

"Wait." My voice sliced through the silence.

She froze, looking up with terror in her eyes.

"Mr. Morozov..."

"That bracelet. Let me see it."

"This... this is just..."

"Give it to me."

Isabella picked up the bracelet with trembling hands and offered it to me.

I took it, examining every detail between my fingers.

The scratches on the chain, the gem cuts, the clasp workmanship—everything matched my memories perfectly.

My finger traced to a particular spot—near the clasp, where an incredibly fine welding mark caught the light.

Years ago, this bracelet had been broken. I'd sent it for repair, and the craftsman used the most exquisite technique to mend the break. But even the finest craftsmanship leaves traces. And here, in the exact same location on this bracelet, the telltale welding mark stared back at me.

My heart felt crushed by an invisible fist, breath stopping entirely.

"Where did this bracelet come from?" My voice came out hoarse.

Isabella trembled from head to toe.

"It was... Noelle gave it to me..."

"When?"

"Before the wedding... I saw it at her place and took it back..."

I seized her wrist. "This was originally yours?"

"Yes... I'd had it for years, wore it almost daily... then it disappeared..."

"When did you lose it?"

"Three years ago, in winter... around Christmas..."

My breathing grew labored.

"Three years ago," I spoke each word deliberately, "did you save someone in South District?"

Isabella's eyes went wide suddenly.

"Was... was that you?" Her voice broke. "So that person was you..."

"Continue."

"That day I attended mass at the church... on my way home, I saw someone covered in blood in an alley..." She wiped away tears. "I was terrified, but I went over anyway..."

"Then what?"

Her face flushed crimson. "I heard people coming... got so nervous, and I... leaned in very close..." Her voice grew smaller. "I don't know what came over me... maybe I was too frightened..."

I remembered that night. That inexperienced kiss.

If that girl was her, why was she so embarrassed about that kiss? Shame? Or perhaps... mortification at having done such a thing with a complete stranger?

"What happened after that?"

"Then I called an ambulance," she continued through her sobs. "After they carried you away, I ran home... only discovered the bracelet was missing when I got there..."

"Why didn't you come forward all these years?"

"I was terrified!" She nearly shouted. "You were covered in blood— I was afraid those people would hurt me... Later when I heard someone was searching for the bracelet's owner, I became even more frightened that it was for revenge... By the time you'd identified Noelle, I didn't dare speak up..."

Tears streamed down her cheeks. "I was afraid you wouldn't believe me... and besides, you'd already married her... I was afraid of destroying your happiness..."

I stared at her, studying her tear-streaked face.

Every detail aligned with that night in my memory.

The alley.

The injury.

The ambulance.

The lost bracelet.

So Noelle knew I was searching for Isabella. But she hadn't told me the truth. She was gambling—gambling that I would believe it was her.

"Go home for now." My voice turned glacial. "This requires investigation."

"I understand..." She nodded through her tears. "But please don't blame Noelle—she truly is a good person..."

I silenced her words. I pulled out my phone and pressed the intercom.

"Dmitri."

Moments later, Dmitri appeared in the doorway.

"Escort Miss Vance home."

"Yes, boss."

Isabella hastily gathered her belongings, cast me one final pleading glance, and followed Dmitri out.

The greenhouse fell silent once more. Only the crackling of logs in the fireplace and my increasingly heavy breathing remained.

I stood there, clutching the bracelet tightly, its metal coldness biting into my palm.

I pulled out my phone and called Dmitri again.

"Deploy every resource we have. I want every detail about that Christmas Eve three years ago. Every person who might have been near that alley, every possible witness, every potential lead."

"Boss, you..."

"Focus on Isabella Vance," I interrupted. "Her family background, everywhere she went three years ago, her social circles. Find the brand of this bracelet and all records of who might have purchased this particular batch back then."

I paused, my voice growing even colder.

"I want the truth. At any cost."

"Understood, boss. I'll oversee this personally."

I ended the call and collapsed onto the sofa, elbows on my knees, face buried deep in my hands.

Over the following days, I conducted business as usual—handling affairs, chairing meetings, making decisions. But everyone noticed something was amiss. Mother hesitated multiple times during dinner, clearly wanting to speak. Anya became unusually subdued.

Only Noelle remained unchanged. She sat at my left during meals, quietly eating, occasionally glancing up with wary, puzzled looks.

I still found myself uncontrollably watching the surveillance monitors, observing her every movement throughout the manor. She read books, painted, and strolled through the gardens. Sometimes she would pause at the walk-in closet entrance, gazing at those mountains of luxury items, then turn and walk away.

She hadn't touched a single piece.

If she truly was some fortune-hunting fraud, why did she show such disdain for all of this? The thought made me agitated, even brought an unfamiliar flicker of panic.

If she wasn't that girl, then everything I'd forced upon her...

On the third evening, Dmitri finally returned.

When he entered the study, his expression was as somber as if attending a funeral.

He carried a thin manila folder.

"Boss." His voice was subdued.

"Report." I leaned back in my chair, fingers drumming lightly on the armrest.

He placed the folder before me. "We located Isabella Vance's former nanny. She testified that three years ago, Miss Isabella did indeed possess a Christmas holly bracelet. She treasured it dearly, wearing it almost constantly. But after that Christmas Eve, the bracelet vanished. Miss Isabella wept over its loss for quite some time."

My fingers stilled.

"The bracelet originated from a small artisan shop where young women would commission custom pieces. The proprietor confirmed the pickup signature belonged to Isabella herself."

He extracted a photograph. "We also found several shopkeepers who operated in that alley vicinity back then. One grocery store owner recalled seeing a distraught young woman that night. When shown Isabella's old photograph, he indicated she looked familiar."

My fist clenched tightly.

"Additionally, hospital archives confirm that the day after you were admitted to emergency care, someone did visit. The nurses' station registry bears the signature: Isabella Vance."

Every piece of evidence pointed to one person—Isabella Vance.

"That's enough." My voice sounded hollow. "Leave."

"Boss..." Dmitri hesitated.

"Leave."

"Yes, sir."

He turned and departed, gently closing the door behind him.

I sat alone in the encroaching darkness.

Snow began falling outside once again. I opened the folder, turning each page methodically. Nanny testimony, jewelry store receipts, shopkeeper identification photos, hospital record photo-copies. They formed an unbroken chain, all pointing toward the same inescapable conclusion—the person who had saved me was Isabella Vance, not Noelle Bellucci.

I closed my eyes, and Noelle's face materialized in my mind. Her revulsion upon first meeting me, her resolute rejection of my proposal, her struggles in the church, her complete indifference to every gift. That damnable, unyielding pride of hers.

In this moment, everything acquired a new interpretation.

Not character traits. Not some nonexistent family vendetta. Simply the guilty conscience of an impostor.

A woman who knew she wasn't that person, yet went along with the deception, hoping to climb into high society, but too cowardly to actively confess the truth.

Rage erupted like a volcanic explosion. The fury of being deceived, of being made a fool, nearly obliterated my rationality. I surged to my feet, snatched up the bracelet and that damning stack of evidence, and strode from the study, heading directly for the master bedroom.

I would confront her face to face. I would look into her eyes and hear her confess with her own lips. I wanted to see just how long this woman could maintain her charade.

I threw open the door. Noelle had just emerged from her bath, damp hair cascading over her shoulders as she sat at the vanity, staring blankly at her reflection in the mirror.

At the sound, she whirled around in alarm. Seeing my expression, bewilderment flashed in her eyes, quickly replaced by wariness. She instinctively rose and stepped backward.

"Kholod... you..."

I gave her no time to react, advancing step by step until I stood directly before her.

I withdrew the bracelet from my pocket, spread it across my palm, and held it before her eyes. My gaze locked onto hers, determined not to miss the slightest flicker of change.

Suppressing the rage roiling within me, I asked with deceptive calm, each word precisely articulated, "Noelle. I'm asking you one final time. This bracelet... is it truly yours or not?"

CHAPTER ELEVEN

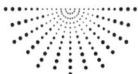

Noelle

Kholod's voice was eerily calm, yet every word sliced like a blade of ice.

I stared at the bracelet in his hand, my mind a whirlwind of confusion.

That style of bracelet—it must have been one of the pieces my mother bought for me back then. But the exact design? I couldn't remember it at all.

Growing up, Mother had loaded me up with countless pieces of jewelry, clothes, and bags—all to help me snag a spot in some rich family. She called them "necessary investments," essentials for fitting into high society. I'd never cared; they were just extensions of her own ambitions.

"I told you," I lifted my head, meeting those amber eyes burning with rage, "I really don't remember."

"Don't remember?" He sneered. "Or too scared to admit it?"

"Kholod! What the hell are you obsessing over?" I raised my voice. "I've had tons of jewelry my whole life—similar bracelets alone, at least half a dozen. How could I possibly remember every single one?!"

"Then why not just deny it outright?" He stepped closer, his gaze dangerous. "The first time I showed up with this bracelet, why didn't you flat-out say 'that's not mine'?"

"I never admitted it!" I backed up until my back hit the dresser. "You decided that all on your own!"

He held the bracelet right in my face, his voice dripping with sarcasm. "Noelle Bellucci, you think I'd buy that bullshit?"

I finally exploded. "Kholod Morozov, you've been talking to yourself from the start! You showed up with that bracelet, insisting I'm your savior! I said I don't remember, but you had to pin it on me!"

"So you just went along with it?" His eyes darkened, turning sinister. "Let me think you were the one?"

"Went along with what?!" I practically yelled. "I've been rejecting you the whole time! I said I wouldn't marry you! You threatened me, used my family's debts to force me! This is all your doing!"

"And the bracelet?" He grabbed my shoulders hard enough to nearly make me yelp in pain. "Why'd it end up with Isabella?"

Isabella? What did she tell him?

"I..."

"You what?" He pressed. "Spit it out! Did you know all along that bracelet wasn't yours?!"

"I don't know!" I struggled to shake off his grip. "I really don't!"

"Still lying!" His voice turned frantic, shoving me toward the bed. "Noelle, how long are you gonna keep this act up?!"

I stumbled back, my calf hitting the bedframe, and I lost my balance, crashing onto the mattress.

Before I could react, he was on me, pinning me down.

"Let me go!" I shoved at his chest. "Kholod, what the fuck's wrong with you?!"

"Wrong with me?" He laughed coldly, grabbing my wrists with one hand and slamming them above my head. "I'm just realizing I've been a joke from the start!"

"You are a joke!" I fired back in fury. "A joke who latches onto a bracelet and calls someone his savior! A stalker who watches people like a creep! An arrogant—"

"Enough!"

His roar made my ears ring.

The next second, I heard fabric ripping.

The sound tore through the air.

My nightgown split open, cold air hitting my skin, and I shivered uncontrollably.

"Kholod! You psycho! Let me go!" I thrashed wildly.

He pinned my legs with his knee, holding me still.

His gaze dropped to my chest—those two Cyrillic tattoos, stark under the light.

"Look at this," he said, his fingers roughly grinding over the skin. I gasped in pain. "Where do you think you're running to? Noelle, you've been mine for a while now."

"I'm not yours!" I glared at him, tears welling up. "You forced me!"

"Not?" He smirked. "Then what's this? Just decoration?"

His fingers pressed hard on the tattoo, then circled around, brushing the tip of my breast accidentally. A tingle shot through me, and I stifled a moan.

"Kholod..." I clenched my teeth. "Why not go after Isabella? She's your real savior, so why get worked up over me?"

I regretted it the instant it left my mouth.

He froze, his whole body rigid. Rage exploded in his eyes like a volcano.

"Looks like," his voice dropped low and terrifying, each word dragged from his throat, "I need to show you why in a way you'll understand."

He leaned down and bit hard into the tattoo on my chest.

"Ah—!" Pain ripped a scream from me.

I tried to break free, but he held me down like iron.

He lifted his head, those amber eyes now dark as an abyss.

"Don't even think about shoving me off to someone else," he growled, his breath hot against my skin. He bent lower, his tongue flicking out to lick the tattoo, slow and deliberate. The bite mark throbbed, a sharp pain mingling with an itchy numbness that spread like wildfire through my body. It hurt, but the sensation twisted into something else—my skin flushing, heat pooling between my legs as my nipples hardened in the cool air. I bit my lip hard, trying to hold back, but a soft whimper escaped anyway, my hips shifting involuntarily.

"See? You're such a slut," Kholod murmured, his voice laced with mockery as he watched my body react. "I barely touch you, and you're already soaking wet, squirming like you can't get enough."

Fury surged through me like a storm. How dare he talk to me like that? I kicked out hard, my foot connecting with his crotch by accident. He grunted in pain, but instead of pulling away, he snatched my ankle in a vise-like grip, his fingers digging in.

"So eager to please," he said with a twisted grin, his eyes gleaming with dark amusement. "Guess I need to find a way to make you behave."

He yanked my hands higher, binding them securely to the headboard with silk ties—tight and unyielding, cutting off any chance of escape. Then he reached into the nightstand drawer, pulling out two metal cuffs. He snapped them around my ankles, spreading my legs wide apart and chaining each one to the bedposts at the foot of the bed. With a rough, deliberate tug, he stripped away the tattered remnants of my nightgown, along with my underwear, leaving me completely naked and exposed, every inch of my body on display.

I was splayed open, vulnerable and humiliated, shame burning through me like acid alongside the raw anger. My core ached from the earlier teasing, and now with my legs forced apart, I felt utterly powerless. "If you can't handle this, just kill me!" I spat, my voice trembling with rage and defiance.

He chuckled darkly, the sound low and menacing. "Oh, I'll kill you —but not like that. I'll fuck the life out of you instead, make you scream until you can't anymore."

Before I could even process his words, he grabbed something else from the drawer—a small, sleek vibrating ball. He held it up for me to see, his smirk widening, then, without ceremony, he pushed it deep inside me, the cool intrusion making me gasp and arch against the restraints. He flicked on the remote, and it buzzed to life, sending intense vibrations rippling through my core, hitting every sensitive spot with relentless precision.

He stepped back, arms crossed, just watching me like I was his personal entertainment. The vibrations built quickly, mercilessly, my body responding against my will—hips bucking, muscles clenching as waves of pleasure crashed over me. I twitched and writhed, the cuffs rattling, drawing closer and closer to the edge, my breath coming in desperate pants. I was right there, teetering on the brink of release— then he stopped it. Completely. The sudden absence left me hanging, frustrated, and aching.

"Now," he said, leaning in close, his face inches from mine, "do you want to die?"

I glared at him through the haze of denied pleasure, my body screaming for more. Anger boiled over, mixed with this infuriating annoyance—I hated him for edging me like this, for leaving me so close yet so unsatisfied. It was torture, and the frustration only fueled my rage. "Just strangle me, you bastard! End it!"

That clearly pissed him off. His eyes narrowed to slits, fury flashing in those amber depths. Without a word, he hit the remote again, cranking the intensity higher this time. The egg thrummed back to life inside me, vibrating fiercely, pushing me right back toward the peak even faster. My body betrayed me completely, trembling and arching, sweat beading on my skin as the pleasure built to an unbearable crescendo. I was gasping, moaning despite myself, muscles clenching tight, so damn close— and he killed it again, leaving me whimpering in agonized frustration.

"Still want to die?" he repeated, his voice edged with barely contained anger, hovering over me like a predator.

This time, I couldn't take it anymore. The repeated denial had set every nerve on fire, my body a throbbing mess of need. The ache was too much, the frustration twisting into desperate longing. "Please... just kill me," I whispered, my voice breaking, tears of humiliation stinging my eyes.

"How?" he demanded, his tone rough and insistent, leaning closer, his breath hot on my neck.

"Fuck me to death," I begged, the words tumbling out in a rush of desperation. "Please, Kholod—fuck me until I'm dead."

He grinned, triumphant and predatory. "That's more like it, you needy little thing."

He stripped off his clothes quickly, his cock already hard and throbbing, veins pulsing with anticipation. Without warning, he positioned himself between my spread legs and slammed into me, burying himself to the hilt in one brutal thrust. I cried out at the sudden stretch, the fullness overwhelming, filling every inch of me. He didn't hold back, pounding into me with raw force, each thrust deep and punishing, claiming me completely.

"Look at you, taking my cock like the whore you are," he growled, one hand pinching my nipple hard, twisting it until I yelped. "Begging for it after all that attitude. You're mine, Noelle—say it, you filthy slut."

I moaned, the words choked out between gasps. "Yours..."

"Not good enough." He thrust harder, his pace brutal, his free hand sliding down to rub my clit in rough circles, amplifying the sensations until I was seeing stars. The vibrating egg still hummed faintly inside me, syncing with his movements, driving me insane with overstimulation. "Admit it—you're just a needy little slut, spreading your legs for the man who owns you. You love being fucked like this, don't you? Begging for my dick like a bitch in heat."

Humiliation burned through me, twisting with the building ecstasy, but I couldn't deny how my body responded, clenching around him greedily. "Yes... fuck, yes," I gasped, hating myself for the admission, for how wet and eager I was.

He laughed low and dirty, his hips snapping forward with vicious intensity. "That's right. No one else gets to touch this tight pussy. It's mine to ruin, mine to fill whenever I want." He leaned in, biting down on my neck hard enough to leave another mark, sucking on the skin as he drove deeper, the bed creaking loudly under the force. Sweat slicked our bodies, his grunts mixing with my desperate whimpers and moans. He shifted his angle slightly, hitting that perfect spot inside me over and over, making sparks explode behind my eyes, building the pressure to an excruciating level.

I was lost in it, my body coiling tighter and tighter, the earlier denials making this climax build like a raging storm. Every thrust sent jolts of pleasure-pain through me, my bound limbs straining against the cuffs. "Kholod... please..."

"Beg for it, slut," he commanded, slowing just enough to tease, his cock dragging torturously in and out. "Tell me how bad you need to come all over my cock, how much you love being my fucktoy."

"I need it—fuck, I need to come! Please, Kholod, make me come!" The words spilled out, shameful and raw, my voice breaking on the plea.

He sped up immediately, relentless and unforgiving, his fingers digging into my hips as he fucked me harder, deeper. "Come for me, then. Show me you're my dirty little wife, clenching around me like the whore you are."

The orgasm hit like a freight train, ripping through me with shattering force, my walls clenching around him in spasms as I screamed his name, my body convulsing against the restraints. Waves of ecstasy crashed over me, leaving me shaking and breathless, but he didn't stop —he pounded through it, extending the pleasure until I was oversensitive, whimpering and begging incoherently for mercy.

Finally, he tensed above me, his thrusts erratic as he chased his own release. With a guttural groan, he buried himself deep one last time, spilling hot and thick inside me. As he came, he leaned down, whispering in my ear, his voice hoarse and cruel. "Remember, if you're not my savior, then to me, you're no different from those women who trade their bodies for favors. Be good, Noelle. Obey."

I lay there, spent and trembling, his words sinking into me like venom, the weight of his possession crushing. He pulled out slowly, leaving me bound and exposed, my body still humming from the intensity, slick with sweat and evidence of our encounter. The humiliation burned deep, but so did the twisted satisfaction, leaving me conflicted and raw.

CHAPTER TWELVE

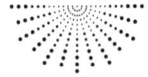

Noelle

"Noelle, come out for a walk!"

Isabella's cheerful voice drifted through the door, accompanied by gentle knocking. I lay on the master bedroom bed, staring at the ceiling, having lost count of how many days it had been.

Ever since that night, Kholod had moved out of the master bedroom, as if he couldn't bear to see me anymore. He was the one who'd dragged me here, yet this whole situation felt like some twisted joke.

"Noelle? Are you there?" Isabella knocked again.

I took a deep breath and sat up.

"Come in."

The door opened, and Isabella peeked her head in, wearing a sweet smile. She was dressed in a pale pink cashmere dress, her makeup flawless, practically glowing.

"Such beautiful weather—don't waste it cooped up in here." She sat on the bed's edge and took my hand. "You look pale. You need some fresh air."

Isabella was staying here at Kholod's invitation. He'd said the manor was too quiet, that she could stay as long as she wanted. Of

STOLEN BY THE BRATVA DEVIL

course. In his mind, she was now the savior. The whole thing was absurd, but I should blame Kholod, not her.

"Come on!" Isabella pulled me to my feet without waiting for an answer. "Stop moping around—you'll make yourself sick."

"Fine." I finally got up, threw on thick clothes, and followed Isabella outside.

Light snow dusted the garden, flakes settling gently on the trimmed hedges. I pulled my coat tighter as we walked side by side down the freshly de-iced path.

"You know what? Yesterday I saw this gorgeous new Valentino gown," Isabella said excitedly. "The cut was absolutely perfect! It would look stunning on you. Should we order one?"

"No, thanks," I declined. "You know my closet's already overflowing."

"But those are all Kholod's picks, right?" She blinked at me. "A woman needs her own style. Can't just let men choose everything."

I didn't respond. She was right. But I had zero interest in those dresses.

"This manor is absolutely stunning!" Isabella looked around. "I couldn't sleep last night—I kept thinking how living here must feel like a dream!"

"It's okay. I don't find it particularly beautiful." Very typical Kholod style—cold and monotonous.

"I completely disagree." She laughed. "You can tell everything here was carefully designed. Look at how those trees are shaped! Noelle, you're so lucky!"

Just then, Kholod appeared from another path. He wore a charcoal coat with the collar turned up, making his face look even more severe.

Seeing us, he paused for a moment, then walked straight over.

"Kholod!" Isabella brightened. "You're back!"

He nodded, his gaze sweeping past my face.

"Taking a walk?"

"Yes!" Isabella smiled. "Noelle's been shut up in her room all day, so I dragged her out for some air."

"Mm-hmm." Kholod made a sound of acknowledgment, then naturally positioned himself between us. "I was just heading to check the greenhouse. Join me."

His placement cleverly separated us. I walked on his left, Isabella on his right.

"Oh, Kholod," Isabella's voice came from his other side, "did you hear about last week's auction at the Philadelphia Museum of Art? They sold an authentic Monet for an absolutely shocking price!"

"Yes, I know." Kholod's voice sounded gentler than usual. "A Japanese collector bought it."

"My God! You know all the details!" Isabella marveled. "Are you into art?"

"I dabble. The family has some pieces—feel free to look anytime."

"I'm so jealous!" Isabella's voice filled with longing. "I've always dreamed of having my own collection room filled with art from around the world."

"Pick whatever you like and take it."

"Really? That's wonderful..."

Without realizing it, I'd fallen a step behind. Their conversation flowed so naturally, so smoothly—as if they were the couple and I was just an unnecessary observer.

"Do you ski?" Isabella continued. "I heard the slopes in the Alps are incredible!"

"Been a few times. St. Moritz has excellent snow quality."

"Amazing! I've always wanted to go but never found the time..."

"You should check it out sometime." His tone carried encouragement—the kind of warmth he'd never shown me.

"Noelle, do you ski?" Isabella suddenly turned to me.

I snapped back to attention. "No."

"That's such a shame!" she said regretfully. "Skiing is so much fun! Right, Kholod?"

"Yeah," Kholod responded. "Though not everyone's suited for that kind of sport."

I bit my lip and kept walking with my head down.

"Oh, that reminds me!" Isabella suddenly perked up. "Kholod, didn't a new French restaurant open in Philadelphia? I heard the chef came from Paris—Michelin three-star!"

"Le Jardin? Went last week. Food was excellent."

"I can never get a reservation! That's the Morozov influence for you!"

Every word stung. Art, skiing, Michelin stars—these weren't topics I couldn't discuss, but I'd never been interested. I preferred natural landscapes and handicrafts. When I'd chat with Isabella about these things before, she'd always find me boring.

Kholod even smiled—making him look less harsh but utterly foreign to me.

"...there's this Children's Art Foundation organizing a charity auction soon. I've been invited to help," I heard as I tuned back in.

"Is that so?" Kholod sounded interested.

"Yes!" Isabella nodded. "But it's my first time doing something like this. I'm a bit nervous..."

"Need help?"

"Would you really?" Isabella looked at him with delight.

"Tell me what you need."

"I..." Isabella seemed embarrassed. "I was thinking, if we could have a really significant piece as the finale..."

"I'll have Dmitri arrange it."

Isabella's eyes lit up with excitement. "Kholod, thank you so much!"

He agreed so readily. Yet when I'd wanted to go out shopping, he'd insisted on having me watched.

"By the way, Kholod," Isabella continued, "have you been to Iceland?"

"A few times," Kholod said. "Mainly for business."

"Noelle always talks about wanting to go there. It must be beautiful, especially the northern lights."

"The winters are long, but it's definitely worth seeing."

He was discussing Iceland with her. My dream destination. The place I'd mentioned repeatedly in my photo albums and blog posts.

My fingers clenched tight.

"Noelle, what's wrong?" Isabella noticed my reaction. "You look pale."

"I'm fine." I forced a smile. "Just tired."

"Let's head back then." She said thoughtfully.

"No need." I stopped walking. "You two go to the greenhouse. I want to be alone for a bit."

I turned and walked back.

"Noelle—" Isabella called after me.

"Let her go." Kholod's voice carried over, calm and cold.

I paused for a moment, then quickened my pace.

I wandered aimlessly through the garden as the snow grew heavier, covering our earlier footprints. Only when my hands and feet went numb did I decide to return.

Passing the greenhouse, I couldn't help but glance inside. They were still there, sitting on the sofa at a proper distance. Isabella was saying something with a smile. Kholod leaned in slightly, listening, a rare gentle curve to his lips.

This was a Kholod I'd never seen—relaxed, warm, even enjoying himself.

My heart twisted painfully. I turned and hurried away, snowflakes hitting my face like ice.

Dinner time.

I still sat to Kholod's left, with Isabella beside me. She kept the conversation lively.

"Mrs. Anastasia, today's roast duck was absolutely delicious!" she said brightly. "The spice blend was ingenious."

"That's the chef's credit," Anastasia replied coolly.

"You're too modest!" Isabella continued. "I heard this is a traditional Russian dish, but the preparation is very intricate. Getting to taste something so authentic is truly an honor!"

She then turned to Kholod. "Kholod, thank you so much for the necklace you sent this afternoon. It's absolutely stunning."

"It's nothing." Kholod's tone was flat.

"Maybe to you it's nothing," Isabella's eyes filled with gratitude, "but for those children, it's a chance to change their lives. Mr. Morozov, your charitable heart is truly admirable."

Kholod didn't speak, just smiled faintly—that same gentle expression again.

I'd seen that necklace—countless diamonds linked together, sparkling brilliantly in the greenhouse sunlight, the center stone as large as a dove's egg. For Isabella, he was willing to donate jewelry worth over a hundred million. My heart churned with conflicted feelings.

"Noelle cares about charity too, don't you?" Isabella suddenly asked me.

All eyes turned to me.

I looked up with a polite smile. "Of course."

"See!" she told Kholod with a laugh. "Noelle thinks it's wonderful too! You must come help me at the auction, Noelle!"

"She won't be going." Kholod suddenly spoke, his voice calm but final.

Isabella blinked. "Why not?"

"She's not suited for those kinds of events."

Was he making decisions for me? Or did he simply not want to bring me?

"Oh, I see." Isabella looked disappointed, then turned to me. "Well, Noelle, you rest up. We'll do the next event together."

I forced a smile. "Sure."

Dinner continued.

Isabella and Kholod chatted from charity auctions to Philadelphia social circle gossip. Their conversation buzzed around me, but I couldn't absorb a single word.

After dinner, I stood to return to my room.

"Noelle, wait," Anya called out.

I turned around.

She approached and lowered her voice. "Whatever's happening between you and Kholod, don't let Isabella come to this house anymore."

I froze, hurt welling up.

"But... I didn't invite her this time."

"What?" Anya frowned.

"Kholod invited her to stay," my voice carried bitterness. "Said she could stay as long as she wanted."

Anya's face changed.

Just then, Anastasia walked over.

"What's wrong?" she asked.

"Mother," Anya turned to her, "did you know Kholod invited Isabella to stay?"

Anastasia looked stunned, her expression complex.

"I didn't know." She looked at me. "Noelle, what happened?"

"That's what Isabella told me."

She fell silent for a moment.

"It seems," her voice was quiet, "Kholod is more confused than I thought."

She turned to me, her gaze serious. "Noelle, listen. Even though I'm not satisfied with you—your background, your family... none of it appeals to me. But compared to Isabella Vance, I'd rather accept you."

Her words shocked me.

"But Kholod..." my voice caught.

"Kholod is my son," Anastasia said, "but this is between you two. I won't interfere. Just remember your position—you're the lady of this house. That position is yours. Whatever happens, don't forget that."

I stayed silent. She sighed. "Go on, get some rest."

I nodded and headed upstairs.

Back in the master bedroom, I closed the door and leaned against it.

Kholod was gentle with Isabella, patient, even smiled.

With me...

I walked to the mirror and started unbuttoning my shirt to change into pajamas, then saw the tattoo again.

H.M.

Kholod Morozov.

He'd carved his name into my skin, claiming ownership. Yet now, he wouldn't even look at me.

I rebuttoned my shirt and walked to the window. Snow kept falling, flake after flake, seeming endless. I should be happy—if he wasn't coming for me, I wouldn't have to endure that torment. If he focused on Isabella, I could have peace. Wasn't this what I wanted?

I sat on the bed. This had been our marriage bed, where he'd tormented me, possessed me, left countless marks. I lay down and buried my face in the pillow. It still carried his scent—cedar and tobacco, a faint reminder that he'd once slept here.

So this cruel, domineering man could be normal with others, even pleasant. That hurt more than any humiliation.

A sense of loss washed over me, as if something that had belonged to me—even though it was full of pain and hatred—was being casually taken away.

CHAPTER THIRTEEN

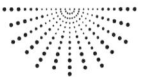

Kholod

"Boss, are you really going to meet Kieran tonight?"

Dmitri's voice carried a rare note of concern.

"He reached out first. Not showing would make me look guilty." I leaned back in my chair, rubbing my temples. "Station men around the club. Keep them ready."

"Understood."

I lit a cigar and took a deep drag.

Everything had been pissing me off lately. Isabella had been staying at the manor for weeks now. Truth was, being around her felt a hell of a lot easier than dealing with Noelle. She spoke softly, knew how to read the room. She'd adjust to whatever I wanted—when I was working, she'd sit quietly nearby, not like Noelle, who always watched me with those wary, hostile eyes.

She didn't talk back, didn't fight me, didn't say things that cut deep. With her, I didn't have to stay on edge constantly. Didn't have to worry about what would set me off next, didn't have to see that stubborn defiance in her eyes that made me both furious and... something else I couldn't ignore.

I crushed the cigar and stood up. Maybe forcing Noelle to stay was a mistake from the start. Isabella was better suited for me—she was my real savior. Gentle, kind, obedient. And Noelle... just a beautiful lie. A damn fraud.

So why did thinking that make my chest ache with a dull pain I couldn't name? I shook my head, pushing the thoughts away. Get it together, Kholod Morozov. What the hell are you thinking?

Lunch was uncomfortably quiet.

Isabella broke the silence first. "Kholod, this beef is incredible. I heard you had it specially prepared?"

"Yeah," I grunted.

"It's amazing! I'm so lucky to get to try it!"

"Good."

"Noelle, did you go to the garden today? You should keep up with your exercise!"

Noelle looked up, voice flat. "No. I'm not feeling well."

"Oh, you should rest then!" Isabella said with genuine concern.

She turned back with a sigh. "Speaking of beef, Noelle, do you remember those wagyu steaks we used to love? I still miss that taste sometimes. I remember it was Lorenzo who..."

She stopped dead.

The air froze. My grip tightened on the silverware. Why the hell was she bringing up that name?

Noelle's face changed, voice tense. "Why are you suddenly talking about him?"

"Oh, I ran into him a few days ago," Isabella said, looking worried. "He looked terrible—completely worn down. I heard that ever since what happened last time, he's been really depressed..."

Enough.

I slammed my silverware down. The crash echoed through the dining room.

Everyone jumped.

"Looks like you two really do have deep feelings for each other," I turned to Noelle, voice dripping with sarcasm. "Even your good friend here is so worried about him."

Noelle set down her utensils, fire blazing in her eyes. "Kholod, I'm telling you for the last time—I have nothing to do with him."

"Nothing?" I laughed coldly. "Then explain why Isabella cares so much about him. How did she 'run into' him? Why is she telling you about his condition?"

"How the hell should I know?" Her voice rose. "Why don't you ask Isabella?"

"I'm asking you!" I stood, leaning over the table to loom over her. "Noelle Bellucci, are you still thinking about him? Still secretly in contact?"

"You're insane!" She shot up too, eyes blazing. "You've got me locked up in here—I can't even leave! How could I contact him?!"

"You'd find a way! Through your mother, through Isabella..."

"Enough!"

Mother set down her fork, fixing me with a stern look.

"Shouting at the dinner table—is this how the Morozov family behaves, Kholod?"

She paused, glancing at Isabella.

"We have a guest. Do you want her to see us make fools of ourselves?"

I clenched my jaw, forcing down the rage.

Anastasia turned to Noelle, her tone slightly softer. "Noelle, go to your room."

Noelle took a deep breath, nodded, and left. Her back was straight but couldn't hide the loneliness.

I watched her go, and the anger only burned hotter—made worse by my mother's apparent "favoritism." This woman was already influencing everyone around me.

"Kholod, come to my study after dinner." Mother's order.

"Yes." I sat back down, forcing myself to appear calm.

The rest of dinner passed in silence. Only the sound of silverware on china echoed through the massive dining room.

I went to Mother's study. She was focused on trimming a pine bonsai, scissors cutting away excess branches with surgical precision, filling the room with a solemn atmosphere.

"Sit." She didn't look up.

I took the chair across from her, waiting. Mother rarely interfered with my personal business. But when she did, it was because I'd made a mistake she considered serious.

"You've been spending a lot of time with Isabella lately." She finally set down the scissors, her flat tone carrying weight.

"She's easy to be around," I answered honestly.

"Easy?" Mother trimmed another unnecessary branch, a hint of mockery in her voice.

"Kholod, you need to learn the difference between a warhorse that can help you conquer new territory and a canary that only sings pretty songs."

I frowned. "What do you mean?"

She put down the scissors and turned around, eyes sharp enough to see straight through any pretense.

"Kholod, whatever old grudges you're carrying, whoever you think your real savior is—you need to remember one thing."

She sat across from me, hands folded elegantly but with undeniable authority.

"You married Noelle Bellucci. You announced in front of all of Philadelphia—hell, all of American high society—that she's your wife. The future mother of the Morozov heir."

"So?"

"So," her voice deepened, "the Morozovs need stability. Her stability is the family's stability. If her position wavers, the Morozovs waver. Do you understand?"

"But she's a fraud." I shot back. "She pretended to be my savior."

"So what?" Mother's counter-question caught me off guard. "Did you really marry her just because of that bracelet?"

"Of course."

"Then why didn't you divorce her immediately and marry Isabella the moment you discovered the truth?"

I opened my mouth but found myself speechless.

"You have feelings for Noelle." Mother continued. "She means more to you than just a savior."

"I..."

"As for Isabella, yes, she's gentle and obedient. But she's not your wife, and she's too perfect to be real. As head of this family, you need someone who'll stand beside you in a crisis, not a nod-along that tells you what you want to hear."

"My son," Mother's voice softened, "don't let emotions become a blade your enemies can turn against you."

She waved her hand dismissively. "Go. Think carefully about what I've said."

I stood and left the study. Mother's words echoed in my head, but I didn't want to listen, didn't want to admit that Noelle had already become more than an obsession.

The next day was surprisingly clear. The snow had stopped, sunlight sparkled on the snow-covered garden, making everything look bright and clean. Isabella suggested we take a walk together. I agreed.

We strolled along the garden paths.

"Kholod," she looked up at me with a radiant smile, "what beautiful weather today!"

"Yeah," I responded.

"I've always wanted to ask," she continued, "why do you support charity work so much?"

"Just feels like the right thing to do."

"You're so kind!" Her eyes were full of admiration. "Not cold like people say..."

I didn't respond. I was cold. She just hadn't seen that side yet.

When we reached a path covered with smooth pebbles, Isabella's foot suddenly slipped.

"Ah—" She cried out, losing her balance, falling toward me.

I instinctively reached out to steady her.

My palm pressed against her wrist. I could clearly feel her skin— soft, slightly cool.

But instead of stirring any romantic thoughts, the touch filled me with inexplicable revulsion. Like touching something fundamentally incompatible with my nature—a physical, instinctive rejection.

"Thank you, Kholod." Isabella steadied herself against my arm, a shy blush coloring her cheeks.

She didn't let go immediately. Instead, she gripped tighter. Skin against skin, her warmth spreading to me, making that discomfort even more pronounced.

I smoothly withdrew my arm. "The path is slippery. Be careful."

"I will." She smiled.

We continued walking, but I deliberately maintained distance. I didn't want to touch her again.

That evening, I was in my study handling paperwork.

A gentle knock on the door.

"Come in."

Isabella entered, carrying documents.

She wore a tight white dress that accentuated her slim waist and curves. The air filled with an overpowering orange blossom scent— sickeningly sweet and cloying.

Noelle wore the same fragrance, but hers was always light and pleasant.

Why was I thinking about her again? I refocused on my visitor.

Isabella walked to my side, placing the documents on the desk. "Kholod, this is the preliminary plan for the charity auction. Could you take a look?"

"Leave it there." I didn't look up. "I'll review it tomorrow."

"But..." She leaned down, moving closer. "There are some details I'd like to confirm with you now..."

Her perfume grew even stronger, almost suffocating. I frowned and leaned back slightly.

"Like this," she pointed to a line in the proposal, her body almost pressed against my arm, "do you think this price point is appropriate?"

I glanced briefly. "It's fine."

"What about this?" As she turned the page, her hand deliberately covered mine.

Instantly, intense nausea surged through me. I jerked my hand away and stood abruptly, the chair scraping loudly against the floor.

"Kholod?" Isabella looked at me in surprise. "What's wrong?"

I wasn't sure if it was the overly cloying perfume or the temperature of her skin—so different from Noelle's—that made me feel sick. I only knew that every cell in my body was rejecting this contact.

But it hadn't been like this before.

In that alley, her scent, her lips and skin—I'd wanted to absorb them into my very being. If I truly found her repulsive, why had I spent three years searching?

Maybe her perfume really was just too strong tonight.

"I just remembered I have a meeting." I straightened my cuffs, avoiding her gaze. "Dmitri will take you home."

"Home?" Isabella froze. "But... didn't you say..."

"Your family contacted me," I pressed the intercom. "It's been two months. Your mother is worried."

"But I..."

"Dmitri," I spoke into the phone. "Take Miss Vance home. Now."

"Yes, boss."

Isabella's smile completely froze.

She opened her mouth to say something, then fell silent under my cold stare.

"Well... alright then." She forced a smile. "I won't disturb you any longer."

She turned and left the study, her posture rigid.

After the door closed, I collapsed into my chair, taking a deep breath. Isabella was gentle and understanding—so why did my body instinctively reject her?

I closed my eyes, and another figure appeared unbidden in my mind.

Noelle.

Her cold eyes, stubborn expression, soft body... Damn it. I grabbed my coat. I needed some fresh air.

That evening, I met Kieran as planned.

This man who'd once nearly killed me now had gray hair and a face full of wrinkles. But those eyes were still cunning and ruthless.

"Morozov," he blew out a smoke ring, grinning with dark amusement. "Rare to see you honor an invitation."

"Cut to the chase. What do you want?"

"Straight to business." Kieran laughed. "I want to talk about the dock operations. You're eating the meat—how about letting us have some of the soup?"

"The docks belong to the Morozovs." My voice was ice-cold. "You want soup? Depends on whether you've earned it."

After some verbal sparring, he barely managed to trade a piece of real estate for scraps of port business.

Kieran shook his head. "Still so domineering. But..." He looked at me meaningfully. "Even the strongest fortress can fall to termites from within. Watch out for fires in your own backyard."

"What's that supposed to mean?"

"Nothing much." Kieran's grin turned more sinister. "Just heard... your household has been quite lively lately. New bride, female house-guest... you're a lucky man indeed."

He knew about what was happening at the manor. Who had told him? My fists clenched, knuckles turning white.

"Kieran," my voice was cold as winter, "mind your own damn business."

"I wouldn't dare meddle in Morozov affairs." He spread his hands mockingly. "Just offering some friendly advice to an old friend— sometimes the most dangerous enemy isn't outside your walls, but lying right beside you in bed."

He stood up, brushing off nonexistent dust from his jacket.

"That's all for today. Think over the dock proposal. As for your domestic situation..." He shook his head with feigned regret, then closed the door and left. But his words had lodged themselves in my mind.

"The most dangerous enemy lies beside you in bed."

What was he implying? Noelle? Or...

I pulled out my phone and called Dmitri.

"Run background checks on everyone in the manor. Maids, butler, cook... everyone."

"Boss, you suspect..."

"Someone's been leaking information. Kieran knows too much."

"Understood."

"And Isabella Vance," I paused, "check all her movements and contacts. I want results within three days."

"Yes, boss."

I hung up and sank into the sofa, closing my eyes. Right now, I didn't know who I could trust.

Noelle? Isabella? Mother?

CHAPTER FOURTEEN

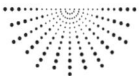

Noelle

"Ma'am, Miss Vance left last night," Darya whispered as she brushed my hair.

"So suddenly?" I was taken aback.

"Boss's orders. We don't know the specifics."

I fell silent. Kholod's thoughts were always impossible to read.

After she finished my hair, braiding it into a simple fishtail, Darya led the maids out. I settled into the window-side chaise with a book.

The geography magazine fell open to Norway's fjords, but I couldn't absorb a single word.

Since Isabella's visit, Kholod barely set foot in the master bedroom. I didn't bother asking where he went—perhaps while she was here, they spent their time in her room discussing topics that held no interest for me.

Now she was gone. I should have felt relief—no more witnessing their nauseating interactions, no more enduring that gnawing sense of being replaced. Yet the heaviness in my chest refused to lift.

I closed the magazine and gazed at the melting snow outside. Those cold touches, those possessive kisses—they both terrified and...

I shook my head, banishing the tangled thoughts, and headed to the library for geography atlases.

Knock knock. Someone at the door.

"Come in."

"Ma'am, Mr. Dmitri has a message," Darya said, entering with a curtsy.

I set down my book and looked up. "Go ahead."

"The boss says in three days, the Morozov family is hosting a charity gala at the Kinmel Performing Arts Center. You're required to attend."

I blinked. "Me?"

"Yes, ma'am. The boss specifically emphasized that this gala is crucial for the family's image. All of Philadelphia's most important political and business leaders will attend. As lady of the house, your presence is mandatory."

Mandatory. Always mandatory.

"I understand. Anything else?"

"A styling team will handle all preparations. Materials and gowns will be delivered shortly. You needn't concern yourself with the details."

"Fine."

After Darya left, I tried to continue reading but couldn't concentrate. I imagined walking arm-in-arm with Kholod, playing the devoted couple under spotlights—such was my "duty."

The guest materials arrived promptly. Staring at the thick portfolio, my head began to throb. Though I'd navigated similar events before, the Bellucci family's network paled in comparison to the Morozovs' labyrinthine complexity.

I had Darya move everything to the conservatory—this kind of work required a pleasant environment.

Settling into my chair, I forced myself to memorize those unfamiliar faces and backgrounds. It felt like those nights cramming financial terminology for my CFA exam.

I was untangling the relationships between several Morozov branch family wives when the sharp click of heels approached rapidly.

Anya appeared in the doorway. She wore a crisp black pantsuit with a long coat that accentuated her already imposing height. She took the chair across from me with little ceremony.

"Mother sent me to highlight the key figures you need to focus on, so you don't stand there like a wooden post, unable to distinguish anyone, and disgrace the Morozov name."

I was accustomed to her blunt arrogance. This directness was actually easier to navigate.

"Thank you for coming," I said with a smile and nod.

Anya seemed pleased with my compliance. She extracted a page from my files. The photograph showed a middle-aged man with a genial smile and immaculately styled hair.

"Richard Joels, city planning committee," she said, tapping the photo with her fingertip. "He adores discussing family and charity in public, cultivating his devoted family man image. But never mention his 'private art collection apartment' in the university district—especially don't inquire about that apartment manager who's the same age as his daughter. With hypocrites like this, simply smile and praise his sense of social responsibility."

I committed this to memory, impressed by her surgical insight. This wasn't mere gossip—it was precise character assessment.

She flipped several pages, indicating a heavily bejeweled woman with an exaggerated smile. "Victoria Harrington. Her husband's shipping company is angling for a piece of our business." Anya's red lips curved slightly. "She's currently obsessed with collecting nineteenth-century French fans, particularly those with scandalous histories. You don't need expertise—just comment 'there must be a fascinating story behind such exquisite craftsmanship' when she shows off, then listen. She'll consider you a kindred spirit, even if you find those tales utterly vulgar."

"And this one..." Anya's pace quickened, but I kept up effortlessly. Seeing that I not only retained the essential points but could extrapolate with pertinent questions, approval flickered in her eyes.

Perhaps weary from her explanations, she leaned back and studied me while sipping her tea. "That's sufficient for today. You're better than I anticipated."

"I appreciate the compliment."

She looked mildly surprised, then lapsed into brief silence. As I continued organizing my files, she spoke abruptly. "Isabella's gone—finally some peace. Kholod, he..." She hesitated, then concluded tersely, "Just keep your head down, avoid trouble, and you'll manage."

I glanced up in surprise. I hadn't expected such words from her. Her expression was uncomfortable, a flicker of pity crossing her eyes as she regarded me.

She pitied me.

"I will," I answered calmly.

"See that you do." She rose and departed hastily.

I watched her retreat, the oppression in my chest intensifying until I could barely breathe. I quickly reached for my inhaler but still felt something constricting my throat. Pity... How pathetic had I become in their eyes? I couldn't suppress a bitter laugh. That was precisely what I needed least.

On the afternoon of the gala, the entire master bedroom was commandeered by the styling team.

I sat at the vanity, surrendering to their ministrations. The woman in the mirror gradually transformed into a stranger—flawless makeup, an elegant chignon, every detail perfect yet utterly artificial.

"Ma'am, the gown has arrived."

Darya and the maids carefully presented an enormous gift box.

When the dress was revealed, the entire room seemed to illuminate.

Ice-blue satin shimmered under the lights, the hem scattered with delicate crystals. The strapless design sculpted the shoulders and décolletage, the fitted bodice hugged every curve, while the skirt cascaded into an elegant mermaid silhouette.

"This is Valentino haute couture from this season—only three exist worldwide," a stylist murmured reverently.

I stared at the dress, my emotions in turmoil. Kholod never

appeared in person, yet he wielded this method to craft me into an exhibition piece.

After donning the gown, I stood transfixed before the mirror. The woman reflected back was breathtakingly beautiful. The ice-blue fabric rendered my skin luminously pale, while the sapphire necklace at my throat blazed with brilliance—far surpassing the one he'd given Isabella in both size and clarity.

The stylists chorused their praise, yet that flawless Mrs. Morozov in the mirror felt like a complete stranger.

When our convoy arrived at the arts center, media and guests had already assembled. Kholod emerged first, his black tuxedo lending his features a stern cast. He turned and extended his hand. I drew a steadying breath and placed mine in his palm.

His hand was warm, gripping mine with measured pressure as he assisted me from the vehicle. Camera flashes erupted like a tempest, shutters clicking incessantly.

"Mrs. Morozov! Over here!"

"What are your thoughts on tonight's charitable focus?"

Kholod's arm encircled my waist, creating a barrier against the eager press. I maintained a gracious smile, acknowledging them with subtle nods while remaining silent. Under countless scrutinizing gazes, we entered the opulent ballroom.

Crystal chandeliers cascaded light, champagne fountains sparkled, strings wafted through the air. Every guest wore formal attire and practiced smiles.

"Kholod!" A middle-aged man in navy approached us. "You made it!"

"Mayor Williams," Kholod acknowledged with a nod.

"This must be your lovely wife?" The mayor's attention shifted to me. "I've heard wonderful things. Mrs. Morozov, you look absolutely luminous tonight."

"You're very kind," I replied with a smile.

For the following half hour, I circulated on Kholod's arm among Philadelphia's elite—mayors, congressmen, entrepreneurs, socialites— exchanging the same tedious pleasantries. I functioned as an elegant accessory adorning his arm, smiling and responding at precisely the right moments.

"Noelle!"

A familiar voice rang out.

I turned to see Isabella approaching in a rose-colored gown, her face radiant with joy.

"You look absolutely stunning! Magnificent tonight!" She clasped my hands. "That dress is perfection on you!"

"Thank you," I replied courteously. "You look lovely as well."

"Kholod," she addressed him, eyes bright with anticipation, "thank you for the invitation. I'm truly honored."

Kholod merely offered a cool nod. "Sure."

Watching them, bitterness rose in my throat once more. So he had invited her. Of course. She was organizing a charity auction—this gala would provide excellent research material. How considerate of him.

The orchestra struck up a waltz. The ambient lighting dimmed, leaving only the spotlight illuminating the dance floor. Guests instinctively withdrew, every eye focused on the center.

Tradition dictated that the evening's first dance belonged to the host and hostess. I gathered my skirts, preparing to step forward. Kholod released my hand and strode toward the dance floor.

His steps never faltered. He walked past me entirely.

Kholod approached Isabella and, before the assembled crowd, extended his hand with practiced elegance.

"May I have this dance?"

His voice carried distinctly through the hushed ballroom. Isabella colored prettily, casting an uncertain glance my way before placing her hand in his. "The honor would be mine."

Kholod guided her to the spotlight's center. There, they began to dance. I remained frozen in place, sensation draining from my limbs. Every gaze in the room shifted from the dancing pair to me—probing, pitying, savoring the spectacle.

"Mrs. Morozov appears rather displeased."

"What's this about? Barely six months married?"

"I heard Miss Vance is actually the one who..."

Whispers cascaded from every direction like a swarm of needles piercing my skin. Heat flooded my cheeks while my chest felt crushed beneath an enormous weight, each breath a struggle. I had become a publicly exposed joke, my dignity ground to powder before this audience.

"Mrs. Morozov, are you quite well?" some lady inquired with false solicitude.

"Perfectly fine."

"Your gown is exquisite," another woman observed, studying my expression, "though Mr. Kholod and Miss Vance do appear rather... intimate?"

"They're friends."

"Friends?" Her smile turned knowing. "How enlightening."

I'd endured enough.

"Please excuse me a moment."

I pivoted, lifting my skirts, and navigated through the crowd with as much grace as I could summon. Each step brought the sensation of burning stares boring into my back. I reached a secluded corner of the hall, pressed myself against the wall, and drew a shuddering breath.

Damn you, Kholod Morozov.

"Care for a drink?"

A man's voice materialized beside me.

I looked up to find a man of perhaps forty standing nearby. He wore a rumpled gray suit, his hair slicked back with excessive precision, but his eyes held an unfocused quality, and alcohol fumes emanated from him.

"No, thank you."

"Don't be so standoffish," he said, edging closer with a smile. "Standing here all alone must be terribly lonely."

I frowned and shifted away. "I'd prefer to be left alone, if you don't mind."

"I'm James Thompson, vice president of the Real Estate Association..."

I attempted to leave, but he extended his arm, blocking my path.

"No need to rush off," he said. His gaze began traveling over my body with increasing boldness. "That dress is absolutely stunning... and this figure, my God..."

My pulse quickened alarmingly.

"Please move aside."

He suddenly planted his clammy hand on my waist. "I merely want to chat. Don't be so unfriendly..."

"Get your hand off me!" I tried to push him away.

The restrictive gown hampered my movements—any forceful action risked the straps slipping from my shoulders.

"Keep your voice down," he breathed against my face, reeking of alcohol. "Everyone's watching Kholod and Miss Vance dance. No one's paying attention over here. Come now, let's get better acquainted..."

His hand began sliding lower, attempting to tug at my dress.

"I said let go of me!" I tried to kick him but found myself trapped by the mermaid silhouette.

His hands grew increasingly aggressive. I felt the side zipper being pulled apart, desperation and terror washing over me in waves. Just as I prepared to scream—

"Get away from her."

The voice cut through the air like ice. Before the man could react, powerful hands seized him and hurled him backward, sending him stumbling across the floor.

Kholod stood before me. Those amber eyes burned with a fury more terrible than anything I'd ever witnessed.

"Mr-Mr. Morozov..." James Thompson's intoxication evaporated instantly. Recognizing who I was, his face drained of all color. "I-I was only... I—"

"Only what?" Kholod advanced with predatory grace, his voice dropping to a menacing whisper. "Only eager to die?"

"I... I'd had too much to drink... I didn't realize..."

Before he could finish, Kholod's hand shot out and seized his wrist.

Crack.

The bone snapped with surgical precision. As agonized screams filled the air, the ballroom plunged into absolute silence.

"Kholod!" Isabella's voice pierced the quiet as she hurried over, gathering her skirts, panic etched across her features. "What's happened? You..."

Kholod didn't spare her so much as a glance. He turned, those blazing amber eyes locking onto mine with laser intensity. I pressed against the wall, trembling uncontrollably—whether from my earlier ordeal or his current expression, I couldn't say.

He crossed the distance between us in swift strides.

"Can you walk?"

I managed a nod.

Without another word, he bent and swept me into his arms—one hand behind my knees, the other supporting my shoulders.

"Kholod..."

"Be quiet."

He held me securely and strode through the parting crowd without a backward glance. Every guest stepped aside as whispers erupted anew, but he seemed utterly oblivious.

Dmitri waited with the car. Kholod settled me into the passenger seat before taking the wheel himself. As we pulled away from the arts center, silence enveloped the interior. I huddled against my seat, gaze downcast, that revolting touch still lingering at my waist.

Veins pulsed visibly at his temples, mirrored by the tension in his white-knuckled grip on the steering wheel.

After an interminable stretch, he asked quietly, "Are you hurt?"

I hesitated, then shook my head.

"Good."

That unexpectedly gentle tone stirred something nameless in my chest. The car gathered speed through the darkness.

CHAPTER FIFTEEN

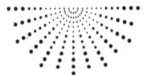

Kholod

The steering wheel creaked under my grip.

I floored the accelerator, and the engine let out a deep growl. Outside the window, Philadelphia's lights blurred into streaks—streetlamps, neon signs, buildings whipping by in twisted lines.

Damn it.

I glanced at the passenger seat from the corner of my eye.

Noelle huddled in her ice-blue gown, the skirt fanning out like wilted petals. Her face was pale as death, hands clutching the seatbelt, silent as a fragile porcelain doll. But the images flashing in my head made my temples throb—that greasy hand on her waist, those hungry eyes devouring her body, the ripped skirt...

"Fuck," I snarled through gritted teeth.

Noelle flinched but didn't look at me, just turned her face to the window. A wave of killing rage nearly swallowed my sanity whole. I almost wanted to pull my gun and blow that bastard away. But snapping his wrist was a better fit—I'd make him remember in agony what happens when you touch Kholod Morozov's property.

That restraint only pissed me off more. I hated this feeling, hated how she could make me lose control so easily.

"Kholod, you're driving too fast," Noelle said, her voice shaky.

"Shut up."

She went quiet. The car filled with the engine's roar and the tires screeching against the road. I told myself the fury was just because my possession had gotten tainted.

Yeah, that's it.

She was my wife, her body marked with my imprint, she belonged to me. That scum daring to touch her was a direct challenge to my authority. Getting this mad was only natural.

But deep down, a voice howled. It wasn't just possession—it was fear. Fear of losing her.

"No," I muttered.

"What?" Noelle turned to look at me.

"Nothing," I said, staring dead ahead at the road. "Don't talk."

The car barreled through the manor gates, speeding down the driveway, and I pulled straight into the garage. I slammed on the brakes, tires squealing on the concrete, the whole car shuddering to a halt.

Noelle's body jerked forward from the inertia, the seatbelt yanking her back with a pained yelp.

I killed the engine. Hit the button. The heavy garage door rumbled down, sealing us in with a low mechanical hum. Metal hit the ground with a booming thud, cutting off the outside world completely.

The garage lights blazed bright, bouncing off the polished concrete in harsh white glares. The place was dead silent except for our ragged breaths.

I turned to her. Those brown eyes, bright and fierce under the lights, burned like wildfire, ready to consume everything.

"You must be pretty pleased with yourself, huh?"

My voice scraped out from deep in my throat, hoarse and unfamiliar.

Noelle froze, confusion flickering in her eyes. "What?"

"I said," I leaned over, bracing against the seat to trap her in that tiny space, "are you pleased with yourself?"

"Kholod, I don't know what you're talking about."

"Putting on that vulnerable act in front of my people, getting everyone to pity you, all those wives whispering, the men eyeing you with sympathy—"

"I didn't!"

"Making me lose it like a damn fool!" My roar echoed in the car.

Noelle's face went even paler, pressing back against the door, fear finally breaking through in her eyes.

"I didn't do anything," she said, voice trembling. "It was that man, he—"

"So you just stood there waiting to get groped?" I sneered. "Noelle, you could've screamed, fought harder, you could've—"

"I'm wearing the dress you picked!" She broke, tears streaming down. "This damn mermaid dress! I couldn't even lift my legs! Kholod Morozov, tell me how the hell I was supposed to fight?!"

Her words hit like a bucket of ice water. I stared at her red-rimmed eyes, the tears streaking her cheeks. Damn.

"And," she choked out, "you left me alone there! You invited Isabella to the opening dance right in front of everyone! You made me the joke of the whole ballroom!"

Every word stabbed like a knife straight to my chest.

"So now it's my fault?" She wiped at her tears, voice dripping with sarcasm. "What do you want? Me to just take the humiliation? Or lie back and let you have your way? Tell me, what the fuck do you want?!"

"I want you to shut up."

I crushed my lips against hers. She struggled hard, but I reclined the seat flat, pinning her under me. I found the zipper at her waist, yanked it down, and shoved my hand inside, rough over her skin.

"Mmm... let go... Kholod... you!"

She fought, but my kiss muffled her words into nonsense.

I didn't say a thing, just worked on stripping her dress, easing off her lips to let her breathe.

She gasped and looked at me. "What the hell's wrong with you?!"

"Nothing's wrong."

I leaned down, my fingers hooking the delicate crystal clasp by her zipper.

"I just want you to understand one thing."

"No—"

"You're mine."

With a tug, the dress slipped from her chest, exposing her breasts and the pasties covering them. I ripped those off and tossed them aside, staring at the tattoo near her nipple with my name etched in. The rage strangely calmed—that mark made her mine.

"Kholod Morozov! You bastard! Pervert! You—"

I dipped my head and sealed her curses with another kiss.

She thrashed wildly, trying to bite me. I bit her lower lip instead, grinding my teeth until I tasted blood.

"You like biting so much?" she gasped, eyes blazing with fury.

"Yeah," I admitted. "Especially you."

I yanked the dress off, leaving her in that tiny thong and those long legs bare under the garage lights. Every inch of her skin glowed, exposed and flawless. The seatbelt still held her down, trapping her across the chest and stomach—god, the sight made me want to make her scream.

"Look at this," my fingertips traced the tattoo. "You can't escape."

"I know," she said, suddenly calm. "I've known for a while."

That dead submission pissed me off more than fighting.

"Don't look at me like that."

"Then how?" she shot back. "Like Isabella, all adoring? Like some socialite, envious? Kholod, what do you really want?"

"I want your eyes only on me."

The words hung there, stunning us both.

Noelle stared.

"What?"

"Shut up." I clamped my hand over her mouth, cutting off any questions. No chance for her to push.

My other hand roamed her body, tracing those familiar curves. Damn, I knew this body too well. Every spot that made her shiver, every angle that drew out moans, every rhythm that broke her—I had it all memorized, and I was addicted.

Being this close, pressed against her, only fueled the fire. God knows how these past couple months had tormented me with this need. Good thing she was right here, under me now.

"Kholod—" She mumbled broken syllables against my palm.

"Shh." I nipped her earlobe. "No talking."

My fingers slid between her thighs, dipping into her warmth. She was already starting to get wet there, slick and inviting. I smirked against her skin.

"Looks like you enjoy this in the car, too, huh? Your body's not lying."

She tried to snap back, but I brushed that sensitive spot, and her words melted into fragmented moans. She got even wetter, her hips twitching involuntarily. "Bet you were thinking about this the whole drive, sweetheart. Soaking for me already? That's my girl."

Seeing her somewhat compliant now, I pulled my hand from her mouth. I stripped off my own clothes quickly—no words needed. Grabbing her waist, I positioned myself and thrust in deep, no preamble.

Noelle screamed, her body arching up against the seatbelt.

I didn't give her a second to adjust. I started pounding into her, wild and relentless. Every thrust drove deep and brutal, like I was nailing her to the damn car seat. I needed to erase that bastard's filthy gaze from her skin, wash away every trace. This was me reclaiming absolute ownership of her body. She'd remember whose she was—mine, only mine.

"Kholod, slow down... please," she gasped, nails digging into my shoulders.

"Can't slow down," I growled, not breaking rhythm. "You won't remember if I do."

"You're insane," she whimpered, but her body clenched around me.

"All because of you," I shot back, leaning in to sink my teeth into her shoulder, marking her fresh. I licked down her neck, then lower, trailing my tongue over her waist—the same spot that scum had touched. "Fucking hate that he put his hands here. Gonna make sure you feel only me."

She moaned, twisting under me, but I kept up the pace, sucking and biting along her side, erasing any memory of him with my mouth. "Tell me you hate it too. Say it."

"I... I hate it," she breathed, eyes squeezing shut as I thrust harder.

"Good girl." I grabbed her hips tighter, pulling her into each slam. "Now open your eyes. Look at me."

She didn't, just turned her head away, stubborn as hell.

"Open them," I demanded, slowing my thrusts just a bit, teasing.

Her eyes fluttered open, defiant and fiery.

I eased the pace even more, rolling my hips slowly and deeply. "You feeling good? Tell me."

She bit her lip, jaw clenched, refusing to answer.

"No answer? Fine, I'll stop." I started pulling out, inch by inch.

Her eyes widened in panic. "You bastard—"

I stopped completely, hovering at her entrance, not moving.

Noelle broke, wrapping her legs around me desperately, pulling me back. "Don't stop... please, Kholod, don't."

I grinned, thrusting back in shallow. "So, is it good? You like it?"

Tears welled up, spilling over. "Yes... it's good. So good."

Satisfied, I ramped up the speed, pounding harder. "Only I get to touch you like this? Only I make you feel this way?"

"Yes," she cried, voice breaking with sobs. "Only you... only you can make me like this."

I felt her walls starting to spasm around me, clenching tight. I leaned close to her ear, whispering hot. "Scream for me, Noelle. I love hearing you lose it."

She shattered then, her body convulsing as the orgasm hit her hard. Her cries echoed in the garage, raw and unrestrained, just like I wanted. I didn't let up, driving through it, chasing my own release while she trembled beneath me.

CHAPTER SIXTEEN

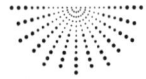

Noelle

He wasn't stopping.

Kholod's scorching breath burned against my neck as his hands traced every inch of my skin with deliberate possession. The garage lights blazed so bright I could barely keep my eyes open, and there he was, pinning me down, amber eyes churning with emotions I couldn't decipher.

"Kholod..." My voice came out hoarse. "Enough..."

"Not enough." He lowered his head, pressing a kiss to my collar-bone. "Not even close."

I tried to push him away, but my body betrayed me with its trembling. That man's touch still clung to my waist like something vile, but when Kholod's fingers covered the spot, the nausea began to fade. His touch was rough, demanding—yet somehow it cleansed every trace of disgust from my body.

"You're distracted?" He bit gently at my chest, pulling me back to reality.

"Mmm... Kholod..."

"Look at me." His command was absolute, one hand cupping my face, forcing our eyes to meet. "Noelle, look at me."

"What the hell are you thinking about?" He frowned.

"Nothing."

"Liar." His fingers slid to my waist, pressing exactly where I'd been grabbed. "Still thinking about that piece of trash?"

"No—"

"Then why are you so tense?" His lips brushed my ear. "Relax, Noelle. I'm the only one who gets to touch you."

That possessive declaration brought an absurd sense of safety. I should hate him—he'd destroyed my family, humiliated me in front of everyone. But he'd also saved me, snapped that man's wrist, carried me away, claimed me in the most insane way possible.

"Kholod..." I heard my voice shake. "You..."

"Hmm?" He looked up, eyes burning into mine.

I bit my lip, not knowing what to say, not even knowing what I wanted to say.

He seemed to read my confusion, lips quirking up. "Don't talk."

His kiss came again, impossibly gentle this time. Tongues dancing, exploring, until I melted completely in his arms.

Damn it. Kholod Morozov always knew how to control me.

When his fingers slipped inside again, I couldn't hold back a broken moan.

"See?" he whispered against my ear, voice rough as gravel. "Your body's still hungry."

"Shut up..."

"Why?" He grabbed my hand, making me feel how wet I was. "Don't you like it?"

"I... ah—"

He guided my fingers, finding that spot that made me lose all control, rubbing in maddening circles. My back arched involuntarily, nails digging into his skin.

"Noelle, who makes you feel like this?"

"You do..."

"Louder."

"Kholod!" I practically screamed it, tears threatening to fall. "You... it's you..."

"Good." His satisfied chuckle rumbled through me as he pushed deep inside.

"Ah—!" This angle was deeper, practically nailing me to the seat.

"Remember this feeling," he moved with brutal rhythm, whispering in my ear. "Remember who gives it to you."

I couldn't respond, could only ride the waves he created. The car filled with gasps and the sound of flesh against flesh, shame and pleasure twisted together.

Watching this untouchable man lose control because of me, go mad because of me—something deep inside me thrilled at being needed.

He needed me. Not the savior, not some marriage pawn, but Noelle Bellucci herself. The thought both terrified and exhilarated me.

"Kholod... I... I can't..."

"Hold on a little longer." He pressed his forehead to mine, sweat dripping.

"No... really..."

"Together." His order was final as his hand found where we were joined, fingers working that sensitive spot.

When he touched the most sensitive place, climax crashed over me like a tidal wave. I screamed, feeling him follow moments after.

For a long time, only our ragged breathing filled the garage.

He pushed himself up, studying my face.

"Noelle..." he started, voice unusually hesitant.

"Don't talk." I turned away. "I don't want to hear it."

He fell silent for a few seconds, then said nothing, just lifted me up and fixed my clothes.

The expensive ice-blue dress was wrinkled beyond repair, but he patiently helped me back into it.

"Can you walk?"

I nodded, then immediately stumbled when I tried to stand.

He caught me instantly, then swept me up without a word.

"Put me down—"

"Shut up."

I finally gave up struggling, letting him carry me through the garden back to the master bedroom.

He set me on the bed and headed for the bathroom. Soon, water was running.

"Go shower." He emerged. "I've drawn you a bath."

I didn't move.

"Noelle." He approached the bed. "Don't make me say it twice."

"I can't walk!" I glared at him.

He paused, then simply carried me to the bathtub. Warm water lapped over my body, orange blossom oil filling the air. Kholod sat on the edge, watching me.

"Aren't you leaving?" I asked.

"No. I need to make sure you don't pass out in there."

"I'm not that fragile."

"Really? Who couldn't walk just now?"

My face burned red. "That's your fault—"

"How? Tell me, Noelle. Because I was too rough?"

"Kholod Morozov!"

"I'm listening." His grin widened.

I splashed water at his face.

He froze, then wiped the droplets away, eyes turning dangerous.

I woke up the next afternoon.

Opening my eyes, I found myself in clean pajamas—my favorite fabric. Thank God, he'd finally stopped forcing me into those flimsy dresses. The other side of the bed was empty but still warm. Kholod had actually slept here last night.

I sat up, my whole body aching. Last night's memories flooded back, making me cover my face with my hands.

"Madam, you're awake?" Darya entered with a tray. "The boss ordered lunch prepared for you."

I lowered my hands, looking at her. "Where's Kholod?"

"The boss went out for an important meeting."

I nodded silently.

Sensing my mood, Darya asked gently, "Are you alright?"

"I'm fine. Thank you, I'd like to be alone for a while."

After she left, the room fell quiet again. Looking at the eggs, steak, and fruit on the tray, I couldn't help wondering—was this man who drew baths and prepared thoughtful meals really Kholod?

I shook my head, pushing away the confusing thoughts.

After lunch, I got up to wash. The woman in the mirror looked flushed, her neck and collarbone marked with intimate bruises. I touched those red marks, remembering how he'd looked claiming me last night. Damn it. I was thinking about him again.

A knock interrupted my thoughts. Darya announced, "Madam, Mrs. Anastasia requests your presence in the study."

I paused. "Now?"

"Yes. She's waiting for you in the study."

I straightened my clothes and followed Darya to Anastasia's study.

The door was ajar. I knocked.

"Come in." Her voice called out.

I pushed inside. Anastasia sat behind her desk with several thick ledgers spread before her. She looked up, something appraising in her gaze.

"Sit." She indicated the chair across from her.

I sat down, waiting for her to speak.

"I heard about last night." She closed the ledger. "Kholod did right. That trash got what he deserved."

I said nothing.

"You don't need to feel guilty or ashamed." She continued. "In our world, only the weak get bullied. And you, Noelle, you're the lady of the Morozov house. No one will dare treat you like that again."

"Thank you," I said quietly.

"That's not why I called you here." She stood and walked to the bookshelf, retrieving a set of keys from a drawer. "Follow me."

I followed her through corridors to a concealed door. Keys turned, and we descended stairs to a metal door. After entering a code, it slowly opened.

When the lights came on, I froze completely.

The massive climate-controlled vault gleamed with Faberge eggs, diamond tiaras, antique paintings, and exquisite jewelry—every piece priceless.

"This is the Morozov family collection, inherited from Imperial Russia," Anastasia spoke slowly. "Never displayed publicly."

I stared at the artwork, speechless.

"I need to update the insurance inventory," she turned to me. "Someone needs to carefully catalog every piece. Anya lacks patience and constantly makes mistakes. Now you'll take over."

"Me?" I looked at her in surprise. "But..."

"This is a very important task." She cut me off. "If you do well, you'll have preliminary authority over Morozov family assets. If you don't..."

She didn't finish, but the meaning was clear.

"I understand." I took a deep breath. "I'll do my best."

"Good." She nodded. "Starting tomorrow, you'll work here every afternoon. I'll assign someone to assist you."

The following days, I immersed myself completely in the artwork. Each piece carried history, and I carefully recorded their provenance and value. Anastasia often checked my progress, occasionally sharing stories behind the pieces.

This afternoon, I was cataloging jewelry. Anastasia came to check again, watching me record an ornate necklace, then suddenly asked, "Do you know its background?"

"Not yet, I'm still documenting the materials."

"This necklace once belonged to a Grand Duke."

"Oh?" I looked up.

"He was incredibly powerful. Owned entire provinces, wealth beyond measure. Even the Tsar showed him deference." She paused, eyes distant. "But he had one fatal weakness—gambling."

My hand trembled slightly.

"He lost everything at the card table. Land, wealth, including this necklace." Her voice was soft. "What finally destroyed him wasn't battlefield enemies, but his most trusted friend at the gambling table. That man didn't just take his fortune—he framed his business rival for his death."

She gave me a meaningful look. "A clichéd story that keeps repeating."

I didn't understand why Anastasia was telling me this.

Seeing my confusion, Anastasia seemed to understand, adding, "Noelle, truth is often different from what appears on the surface. Don't trust what others say without solid evidence. Now, we need to pick up the pace."

After she left, I kept pondering the story. What other truths didn't I know?

That evening, I sat alone in my room, flipping through a fashion magazine. Looking at the jewelry, I couldn't help thinking of Kholod.

He loved giving me these things, which often left me feeling helpless. I'd be happier if he just let me go shopping than receiving limited edition Chanel perfume.

I found myself thinking about Kholod's actions last night, the things he'd said. If only he weren't my father's killer!

Wait. Father?

Anastasia's story suddenly became crystal clear in my mind, especially that phrase "framed his business rival for the death." The story Anastasia told suddenly echoed in my head, especially that line about "framing his biggest business rival for the death."

Could it be? No! This was impossible! Everyone knew Morozov drove my father to death, that their pressure left him with no choice but suicide. The Morozov family's pressure cornered my father, leading to his suicide jump. Everyone in our circle knew this.

I knew Father gambled, but... that story kept replaying in my mind. What if father's death had nothing to do with Kholod? What if someone exploited Father's weakness and framed Kholod? I knew father was a gambler, but... that story kept playing over and over in my head. What if father's death wasn't because of Kholod?

What if someone else exploited Father's weakness, then framed Kholod?

My whole body shook. If Kholod didn't kill my father, then all this hatred I've carried for so long...

I squeezed my eyes shut, afraid to think any further.

CHAPTER SEVENTEEN

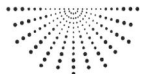

Kholod

"Boss, the dock accounts have been verified."

Dmitri's voice crackled through the intercom, but I was staring at the surveillance feed on my computer screen, not hearing a word.

"Boss?"

"Yeah, got it." I snapped back to attention. "Proceed as planned."

"Yes, sir. Also, regarding Miss Isabella Vance, we've transferred the funds as you instructed. Future requests will be accommodated within reason, but she won't be allowed near the manor again."

"Good."

I cut the intercom and turned back to the screen.

In the collection room, Noelle was wearing white gloves, carefully polishing a gilded religious icon. Her movements were gentle and deliberate, like she was handling something precious and fragile. Soft light hit her face from the side, outlining her delicate profile—the slight upturn of her lashes, her straight nose, those lips I knew all too well.

Damn it. I was actually wondering what it would feel like if she touched me with that same gentle care...

I rubbed my temples, forcing myself to turn to the pile of documents. But within three minutes, my eyes drifted back to the screen.

How many times today? Ten? Twenty?

Ever since that night in the garage, everything had spiraled out of control.

I'd thought completely possessing her would calm this restlessness. Instead, it was the opposite—that loss of control hadn't brought satisfaction, but worked like an addictive drug, making me crave her even more.

Not just her body.

Everything about her.

The slight furrow in her brow when she read quietly, her focused expression while painting, her occasional soft smile, even the defiance in her eyes when she looked at me coldly—it all hooked into every nerve I had.

I was finding it harder and harder to bear moments when I couldn't see her.

On screen, Mother walked into the collection room. She stopped beside Noelle, saying something. Though there was no sound, I could see Noelle listening intently, nodding occasionally.

Then Mother did something that surprised me—she reached out and lightly patted Noelle's shoulder.

Brief, gentle, but significant.

Mother rarely showed such warmth. She was a woman who kept her emotions deeply buried, maintaining severity even with Anya and me.

But now, she'd actually initiated physical contact with Noelle.

That iron-willed woman, whom even I had to respect, was showing approval instead of scrutiny when facing Noelle.

What kind of power did this woman have?

How did she do it?

I stared at that slender figure on screen, feeling something churn and expand in my chest, almost breaking through my ribs.

Just watching her through surveillance wasn't enough anymore. I needed to be closer.

I needed—

"Fuck." I cursed under my breath, slammed the computer shut, and stormed out of the study.

Over the next few days, I prowled my own manor like a stalker.

I knew her daily routine. Two fixed hours in the collection room each afternoon, curled up by the library fireplace reading travel magazines in the evening, and helped Mother prune those prized roses in the greenhouse when weather permitted.

I tracked all her movements.

Then, like a ghost, I'd hide in shadows, secretly watching her.

It was sick, I knew. But I couldn't control myself.

This afternoon, I stood in the shadowed colonnade outside the greenhouse, watching the two figures inside. Mother was pruning a blooming red rose while Noelle handed her tools. Sunlight streamed through the glass dome, casting her in a soft halo. She wore a simple beige sweater dress, hair loosely pinned up, exposing her slender neck.

"This branch is too dense, it'll affect airflow," Mother said, efficiently cutting off a half-opened bud.

Noelle caught the rose, placing it in the bamboo basket beside her. "Isn't it a shame to cut such a beautiful flower?"

"Keeping it would be the real shame." Mother didn't look up. "Sometimes sacrificing things that seem beautiful makes the whole more perfect. It's the art of balance."

"I understand."

"You're smart, Noelle." Mother set down her shears, turning to look at her. "Much smarter than I expected."

Noelle seemed a bit embarrassed. "You're too kind."

"I never say empty words. Your work in the collection room has been excellent—the ledgers are organized perfectly. Even I can't find fault."

"Thank you for giving me this opportunity."

"This isn't an opportunity. It's what you've earned. You proved your abilities."

I leaned against the stone pillar, watching this woman who held her own before Mother, my heartbeat gradually accelerating.

She'd actually won Mother's approval.

"Kholod, he..." Noelle hesitated before continuing, "he's been acting strange lately. He..."

Mother looked at her, eyes deep and knowing.

"The more he acts like this, the more it shows he cares."

Noelle was clearly stunned. "Cares?"

"Someone who doesn't care won't waste energy tormenting another person. Kholod's been like this since childhood. The more he cares about something, the more clumsily he handles it."

"But—"

"Don't overthink it." Mother patted her hand gently. "Keep doing what you're doing. Time will give you answers."

I turned and silently left the colonnade.

Mother's words echoed in my head.

"The more he cares about something, the more clumsily he handles it."

She was right.

Damn it, she was always right.

That evening, I entered the library.

Noelle would come at this time—she did every day, without fail.

I'd hidden in advance in the decorative alcove by the wall. Originally, it housed a marble statue, but I'd had it removed a few days ago. Now it could accommodate a grown man.

This was absurd.

The head of the Morozov family, hiding in his own library to spy on his wife.

But I couldn't help myself.

Sure enough, the library door opened shortly after.

Noelle walked in carrying several heavy art books, heading straight for the sofa by the fireplace. She sat down and opened a book about Norwegian fjords, firelight dancing across her face.

I held my breath, watching. From this angle, I could clearly see her lowered lashes, her nose tip reddened by the fire, and her fingertips gently caressing the pages—tender as if touching treasure.

What was she thinking? Imagining standing before those fjords? Or planning her escape?

That thought tightened my chest.

No. She'd never escape.

She belonged to me.

Just then, Noelle suddenly stood and walked toward the bookshelves.

My heartbeat instantly accelerated.

Damn, what book did she want?

She stopped before the tall bookshelf, looking up at a book on the highest shelf.

She glanced around, then wheeled over a ladder from the corner. The sound of rolling wheels grew closer. I pressed against the alcove wall, not daring to breathe.

She slowly climbed the ladder, reaching for that book about Finland. Now she was less than a meter away, the orange blossom scent from her hair hitting me full force. Firelight illuminated the fine hairs at her nape, her soft breathing audible as she stretched on tiptoe.

Every muscle in my body tensed.

Her fingertips had just touched the book spine—

"Ah—!"

The ladder suddenly slipped sideways.

Noelle lost her balance, falling backward as the book tumbled from her grasp, hitting the floor with a heavy thud.

I lunged out almost on instinct.

I caught her waist, using my body to break her fall. But my momentum was too strong, combined with her falling weight, and we both crashed heavily onto the carpet.

She groaned, her entire body pressed against mine.

My back ached from the impact, but I didn't care. My arms wrapped tightly around her, like I'd recovered lost treasure.

She was soft and warm all over, carrying that maddening scent.

The softness of her chest pressed against me, her waist and curves outlined perfectly in my hands. Her startled breath brushed my neck.

Finally touching her. Like a desert traveler taking his first sip of water.

But it wasn't nearly enough. I wanted more.

"Kholod?" She pushed herself up, eyes wide with shock. "Why are you here?"

"I..."

How to explain? That I'd been hiding in an alcove spying on her for half an hour?

"I was just passing by." I heard myself say stiffly. "Heard the noise and came in."

"Passing by the library?" Her eyes were full of suspicion. "Darya says you only ever work in your study."

Damn Darya.

"People change." I forced authority into my voice.

Noelle clearly didn't believe me, but she didn't press. She tried to get up from on top of me, palms braced against my chest. That insignificant pressure froze my entire body. Her palms were so soft— even through my shirt, I could feel their warmth, setting my chest ablaze.

I wanted to grab that hand. Press it against my chest. Instead, I pulled her back down, pressing her against me again.

"What are you doing?" She tensed.

"Making sure you're not hurt." I tightened my hold.

"I'm fine! Let go—"

"Don't move. Let me check."

I flipped us over, pinning her beneath me, cupping her face in my hands.

Her cheeks were flushed from the fall, eyes misty with unshed tears, lips slightly parted like a silent invitation. Just like that night in the garage—trembling, crying, finally surrendering beneath me.

My desire was already iron-hard. And I intended to follow it.

"Don't move. I need to make sure you're not hurt."

I stroked her soft cheek, sliding my hand to her nape, fingers threading through her silky hair, gently kneading. "Did you hit your head?"

"No. Can you let me go now?" Noelle still tried to struggle.

"Good." I slid slowly down her arm, gripping her wrist. "What about here? Did you twist anything?"

"No!" Noelle shook her head, trying to pull her hand back.

I held her wrist firm, turning it over, thumb drawing circles on her tender palm. Her helpless position made the beast inside me even more restless.

"That's good." I released her wrist, my palm following her waist's curve upward. "When you fell, did you hit your ribs?"

Her whole body went rigid, sucking in a sharp breath.

"Don't..." Noelle finally broke, her voice catching with tears.

"Why?" I stopped moving, lips almost touching her ear. "Does it hurt?"

My fingertips traced the edge of her bra, and she went taut as a drawn bowstring.

I dropped the pretense, covering that softness completely with my palm. I listened with satisfaction to her broken whimper.

"Seems fine here too." I increased the pressure of my massage.

Noelle completely gave up resistance, eyes squeezed shut, letting me do as I pleased.

I moved to her flat stomach, then her thigh. "What about here?" My palm settled on her inner thigh, that most sensitive, vulnerable place.

She snapped her eyes open, pupils flooded with panic and silent pleading.

"Don't... not here..."

"Not here? Our examination is finished."

I leaned to her ear. "Looks like you're perfectly fine everywhere."

The fire in Noelle's eyes blazed brighter. "Kholod! You pervert!"

"Yes, I am." This wasn't the first time she'd called me a pervert. I looked at her flushed eyes and moist lips, leaning down to kiss her roughly.

"Boss."

Dmitri's voice came from the doorway—calm, controlled, but like ice water over my head.

I immediately released Noelle. Dmitri hadn't entered.

"Sorry to interrupt, but the documents you requested are ready and need your personal review and signature."

"Wait in my study."

"Yes. Also, Miss Isabella Vance called wanting to thank you in person for your generous support."

I waved irritably. "Unnecessary. Decline all such requests going forward."

"Understood."

I looked down at Noelle beneath me, her eyes sparkling with mockery.

"Boss, time to get to work."

I reached out, thumb lightly brushing her lower lip.

"You can't escape."

"Psycho!" She turned her face away, voice thick with embarrassed anger.

I smiled, standing up to look down at her.

"Maybe," I admitted. "But you're what made me sick."

With that, I turned and left the library.

In the hallway, I leaned against the wall, slowly exhaling.

My fingertips still held the feel of her skin, her scent still lingering on my lips.

Not enough. Nowhere near enough.

But I had to restrain myself. I needed to handle those damn documents first.

Then...

I looked at the library's closed door, my gaze turning dark.

Reason was screaming: She's a liar. She impersonated your savior. She deceived you.

But my body was roaring: She's yours. She can only ever be yours.

Instinct shrieked: She's different. This woman is different from everyone else.

I closed my eyes, taking a deep breath.

Then opened them and made a decision.

Fuck the savior.

Fuck the truth.

Fuck everything.

Whoever she was, she could only belong to me.

Back in my study, Dmitri had already arranged the documents neatly on my desk.

I sat down and picked up my pen, but my mind was full of her soft body and warm breath.

"Boss?" Dmitri called my attention back. "Are you alright?"

"Fine," I said expressionlessly. "Get to business."

"About Isabella Vance—"

"I said to avoid meeting requests going forward." I cut him off. "Give her money, give her resources. That's it."

Dmitri was quiet for a moment. "Boss, with respect, Miss Vance is the one who actually saved you. Treating her this way seems..."

"Dmitri, my personal affairs don't require your input."

"Yes, sir."

CHAPTER EIGHTEEN

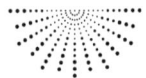

Noelle

Morning came with Kholod at the bedroom door, carrying a massive dress box.

"Get dressed. There's a gala tonight."

I set down my book, eyeing the box with its high-end designer logo suspiciously. "What's the occasion?"

"Isabella's charity auction." He stepped inside, placing the box on the bed. "Seven tonight. Philadelphia Museum of Art."

Isabella's auction? I froze. Wasn't this the same event he'd said I wasn't "suitable" for?

"Didn't you say I wasn't suitable for that kind of thing?" I stared at him, trying to read something in his expression.

Kholod paused, his Adam's apple bobbing slightly. "I changed my mind." He turned away, pretending to study the wall art, his voice sounding awkward. "She's your friend, after all."

"So you changed your mind for me?"

"Don't flatter yourself." He unbuttoned his cuffs and rolled up his sleeves, exposing strong forearms. "I just figured the lady of the Morozov house shouldn't miss public events. Don't want people thinking I'm hiding you."

The explanation sounded reasonable, but something felt off.

"What about Isabella?" I couldn't help asking. "You two now..."

"Isabella is just...Isabella." He finally faced me. "There won't be anything deeper between me and her. Happy?"

His tone was impatient, but his eyes flickered with nervousness, like he was waiting for my reaction.

"Just curious."

"Curious?" He moved closer, bracing his hands on either side of me. "Or jealous?"

My cheeks burned. "Kholod Morozov, don't be so full of yourself!"

"No?" That wicked smile tugged at his lips. "Then why are you blushing?"

"I'm just... hot!"

"Hot?" He leaned closer, breath warming my face. "Noelle, your ears turn red when you lie."

"I'm not lying!"

His finger touched my earlobe gently. "Look. Burning up."

I shoved him away, jumping to my feet, glaring at him fiercely. "Did you come here just to mess with me?"

"No." He straightened his shirt. "I brought you a dress and wanted to make sure you'll dress properly."

"Of course I will. I won't embarrass the Morozovs."

"Good." He headed for the door, turning back at the threshold. "Styling team arrives at five. Don't keep me waiting too long."

"Fine."

After the door closed, I sat back on the bed, staring at the dress box. My heart was racing and erratic. Today's Kholod was too unusual —actually changing his mind for me, testing my reactions...

No, who cares if he's acting strange!

I covered my face with my hands. Noelle, what the hell are you thinking?

At five sharp, the styling team arrived. They redid my makeup and curled my hair into soft waves, pinning it to one side to expose my neck and ear.

"Time for the dress, ma'am."

I stood as they lifted the gown from the box and couldn't help but gasp.

Deep crimson velvet flowed with rich luster under the lights. The plunging V-neck extended to my chest, sleeveless and figure-hugging, with a high slit that climbed nearly to my thigh.

This dress was far too sexy.

"This is really for tonight?" I hesitated.

"Yes, ma'am," Darya replied. "The boss chose it himself."

I bit my lip but finally let them help me into it.

The dress fit perfectly, clinging to every curve. The velvet was soft and smooth against my skin, but made me feel wrapped in some kind of dangerous temptation.

"The zipper's in back, ma'am. Let me help you."

"You can all leave."

Kholod's voice suddenly came from the doorway. I turned around in shock. He was leaning against the doorframe, those amber eyes fixed directly on me. More precisely, on my reflection in the mirror wearing the half-zipped dress.

"Yes, boss." Darya and the stylists quickly packed up and filed out, thoughtfully closing the door.

Only the two of us remained in the room.

"Turn around," he commanded.

"What?"

"Turn around." He walked in, voice low. "I'll zip you up."

My heart instantly accelerated.

"I can do it myself—"

"Noelle." He cut me off. "Turn around."

I bit my lip and obeyed.

Through the mirror, I could see him move behind me, his long fingers gripping the zipper pull.

"Lift your hair."

I swept my long hair to one side as instructed.

He began pulling slowly upward, the metal teeth catching one by one with soft whispers. His knuckles occasionally brushed against my bare spine. Every touch sent shivers through me.

"Could you go a bit faster..." My voice trembled involuntarily.

"Why rush?" He whispered in my ear, warm breath fanning my neck. "I'm enjoying this process."

"You..."

"Such smooth skin." His voice dropped even lower, carrying dangerous implications. "Makes me reluctant to let go."

The zipper finally reached the top, but his hands didn't leave. Instead, they slid along my shoulders toward my arms, settling at my waist. In the mirror, his gaze was dark and intense.

"I knew red would be perfect on you."

We looked incredibly intimate in the reflection, his tall frame nearly enveloping me. The image was heart-stopping.

"I still need to put on jewelry..." I said softly.

"No rush." His arms tightened, pulling me against him. "We have time."

"You're beautiful," he sighed near my ear. "So beautiful I want to hide you away where no one else can see."

His words made my heart pound like a drum.

"We still have to go to the gala..."

"The gala can wait."

Before I could finish speaking, his kiss descended, commanding and possessive, as if declaring that in this moment I belonged only to him.

After what felt like an eternity, he finally released me and pulled out a jewelry box from his pocket. Inside was a set of ruby jewelry—necklace, earrings, bracelet—each stone full and rich, gleaming like blood under the lights.

"Turn around."

I turned, and he fastened the necklace around my neck. The cool gems touched my skin as his fingertips lightly brushed my nape.

"Perfect." He stepped back to admire me. "You'll be the center of attention tonight."

"I don't want to be too conspicuous."

"But I do." His thumb gently traced my jaw. "Let's go."

He offered his arm, and we walked out together.

The convoy arrived at the Philadelphia Museum of Art, the neoclassical building blazing with lights in the night.

Kholod helped me from the car, and once I was steady, he wrapped an arm around my waist, protecting me at his side as we entered the museum's grand hall together.

"Kholod!"

Isabella's voice rang out.

She wore pure white tonight with a silver wrap, her makeup exquisite and her smile sweet. She walked straight toward Kholod with a radiant smile, arms slightly open in preparation for an embrace. But Kholod sidestepped, avoiding her gesture. Her movement froze mid-air, smile stiffening.

"Isabella. Congratulations, tonight's event is very well organized." Kholod's tone was polite but distant, completely different from his relaxed manner during their manor garden stroll.

"Thank you." Isabella awkwardly lowered her arms. "It's also thanks to your support. Without the Polaris Tear, tonight wouldn't have gotten so much attention..."

"It was nothing." Kholod cut her off.

His arm around my waist tightened slightly, as if making a statement. Isabella bit her lip, her gaze shifting from Kholod's face to mine.

"Noelle, I thought you wouldn't come." She hugged me gently.

"You're tonight's star. Go for it."

"I will." She nodded. "I won't keep you two any longer—I need to greet other guests."

She turned and hurried away, her departure seeming rather hasty. I looked up at Kholod, puzzled—they'd clearly gotten along well before, so why the sudden coldness?

"What are you looking at?" He looked down, meeting my scrutinizing gaze.

"Nothing. Just think you're treating Isabella differently than before."

"Am I?" he asked back, tone casual.

"Before you seemed..."

"It's in the past." He interrupted me, guiding me deeper into the hall with his arm around my waist. "Focus on the present. Come on, the auction's about to start."

The auction was held in the museum's main hall. Kholod and I sat in the front row VIP section, surrounded by Philadelphia's most powerful faces.

Isabella took the stage as host. She performed admirably, her voice melodious, making each auction item sound captivating. Guests bid frequently, the atmosphere lively.

"Next is tonight's featured item—the Polaris Tear diamond necklace, generously donated by Mr. Morozov. All proceeds will go toward children's arts education..."

Under the spotlights, the necklace was dazzling. Bidding calls rose and fell, prices climbing rapidly. I glanced at Kholod—he sat expressionless, fingers tapping the armrest lightly, as if completely disconnected from it all.

"Sold!"

The gavel fell to thunderous applause. Isabella's eyes glistened with tears as she bowed deeply. "Thank you all for your generosity! Special thanks to Mr. Morozov!"

She looked toward us, eyes full of gratitude. Kholod merely applauded politely, expression calm.

After the auction came the cocktail reception, with elegant music and servers weaving through the crowd. Kholod went to speak with political figures while I stood alone in the lounge area with champagne.

"Noelle."

Isabella suddenly appeared, grabbing my hand. I nearly spilled my drink.

"What's wrong?"

"I need to tell you something." Her voice was somewhat choked, eyes already rimmed with red.

"You're crying? What happened?"

"Nothing..." She wiped her eyes with the back of her hand. "I just... Noelle, I'm sorry..."

"Why apologize? The auction was a great success."

"Not for that." She took a deep breath, tears falling. "For what happened at the last party... I never expected Kholod to invite me to dance. I was so shocked, didn't know how to refuse... I never meant to steal your spotlight, much less replace you."

"Isabella..."

"Now everyone outside is saying I'm his mistress, that I want to climb up the social ladder... But I really don't! Noelle, I just wanted to help you, never thought it would turn out like this..."

She cried pitifully. Looking at her, complex emotions surged through me. Although Anastasia and Anya had both warned me to stay away from her, saying she had ulterior motives, Isabella was still my childhood friend.

She was the one who came to see me when I first married into the Morozov family, comforting me. During my loneliest times, she chatted with me and kept me from going insane. And I knew what it felt like to be publicly humiliated, what it was like to become the focus of everyone's gossip. In some ways, we were both victims of Kholod Morozov's unpredictable moods.

"This isn't your fault." I patted her hand gently. "I never blamed you."

"Really?" She looked up, eyes full of hope.

"Really," I said earnestly. "Kholod is just like that—he does everything on a whim."

"But..."

"Don't overthink it." I put my arm around her. "We're still friends. Rumors always pass eventually."

"Noelle..." She gripped my hand tightly, tears flowing again. "Only you truly understand me..."

"Stop crying." I handed her a handkerchief. "You're tonight's star—you can't let others see you cry."

She took the handkerchief and wiped her tears forcefully, trying to calm her emotions. We shifted to discussing fashion, and the atmosphere gradually became more relaxed.

Just as we were getting into our conversation, a large hand settled on my waist. Kholod had appeared behind me at some point.

"What are you two chatting about so happily?" His gaze moved between Isabella and me.

"Nothing much, just casual conversation," I said.

"Kholod!" Isabella immediately straightened up, her smile carrying a hint of nervousness. "I still need to greet other guests, so I'll excuse myself."

She left almost like she was escaping.

Kholod stared at her retreating figure for a few seconds, then looked back at me.

"She was crying again?"

"How did you know?"

"Her eyes are swollen." He said flatly. "What about?"

"She..." I hesitated. "She apologized to me about last time. Said the rumors outside are troubling her."

Kholod's brow furrowed slightly. "Those rumors—I'll have them handled. Come on, there are some people who want to meet you."

The next hour and a half was like a social marathon. Kholod led me through various circles, introducing me to every important figure. "This is my wife, Noelle."

Each time, his hand rested on my waist or he stood within half a step of me, using body language to announce to everyone—this woman belongs to him.

Unlike last time, compliments flowed like a tide. I smiled and responded appropriately, making polite but meaningless social conversation.

Kholod remained by my side throughout, never straying more than three feet away.

The gossip-loving Mrs. Anderson approached with champagne. "Mr. Morozov! Mrs. Morozov! You two are such a perfect match tonight!"

"Mrs. Anderson, good evening." I nodded politely.

"I was just chatting with some ladies, and everyone was praising you!" She looked at me, eyes sparkling with curiosity. "They said you're not only exceptionally beautiful but also very cultured and refined. By the way..."

She lowered her voice, pretending to be mysterious. "I saw Miss Vance talking with you earlier? Your relationship with her... with all the rumors flying around outside, I wonder what the truth is..."

I was hesitating on how to respond when Kholod's cold voice cut in.

"Miss Vance is dedicated to charity, and the Morozov family appreciates this spirit and provides support." His sharp gaze swept toward Mrs. Anderson. "As for our relationship, I consider her a little sister."

Mrs. Anderson was clearly surprised, too. "Oh! So that's how it is! I guess I was overthinking..."

"My wife is only Noelle." He tightened his arm, pulling me closer. "I hope everyone understands this clearly."

His voice wasn't loud, but every word was firm and authoritative.

Mrs. Anderson's face paled somewhat. "Of... of course, I understand completely. Mr. Morozov, I absolutely didn't mean anything else..."

"I hope so," Kholod said indifferently, then led me away.

By ten o'clock, the reception was winding down. When we said goodbye to Isabella, her smile was especially radiant.

"Thank you both for coming." Her gaze focused mainly on me. "Noelle, let's get together again sometime."

"Sounds good."

"If you need anything in the future, you can contact Dmitri." Kholod suddenly said. "The family will continue supporting your charitable work."

"Thank you, Kholod!"

He nodded without speaking and led me toward the exit.

In the car, I couldn't help asking, "Why were you so cold to Isabella?"

"I was just treating a sister appropriately." He fastened my seatbelt for me. "Being too close easily causes misunderstandings. Noelle, I don't want anyone to get the wrong idea. You are my wife."

He was emphasizing this point again. Over and over, as if convincing others, but also as if convincing himself.

150

I leaned back in my seat, watching the passing night scenery through the window, recalling everything about tonight. From the moment we entered, he deliberately distanced himself from Isabella while keeping me closely protected at his side, announcing my status to the entire world.

This change puzzled me. Saying I wasn't moved would be a lie, but with the cause of my father's death still unclear, I couldn't let this brief warmth deceive me. I had experienced his cruelty and unpredictability too deeply—this might just be another, more sophisticated game.

I couldn't see through him. This sudden protection made me more uneasy than any previous torment.

CHAPTER NINETEEN

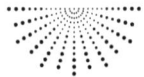

Noelle

"Noelle! It's been forever! How have you been?" Isabella's cheerful voice came through the phone.

"Not bad." I tucked the phone between my ear and shoulder, continuing to cross-check the catalog numbers. "How about you?"

"Crazy busy! So much follow-up from the auction. But I'm finally done. Are you free the day after tomorrow? Let's go shopping and have some tea! It's been way too long since we had a proper chat."

"Shopping? Where?"

"There are some lovely boutiques that opened on Ninth Street. I want to check them out. Then we can go to Rittenhouse—you'll absolutely love their pastries!"

That was Philadelphia's most exclusive tea room, elegant and refined, a favorite haunt of society ladies.

"Sounds lovely." I set down my pen. "But I need to ask Kholod first..."

"Ugh..." Her tone carried a hint of annoyance. "It's just tea. He won't say no, will he?"

"You know his temper."

"Fine, fine. Ask him then." Isabella laughed. "Oh, I have a little surprise for you too! You'll find out when we meet!"

"A surprise? What kind?"

"It wouldn't be a surprise if I told you!" She sounded mysterious. "Remember to dress up! Love you!"

After hanging up, I felt a long-lost sense of lightness.

Honestly, things had been peaceful lately, but also monotonous. Every day was either organizing antiques in the collection room or reading and painting in the library. Occasionally, I'd have tea with Anastasia, listening to her family stories.

Kholod had indeed moved back to the master bedroom, but he kept his distance. Aside from occasional kisses, he hadn't overstepped. During the day, he handled family business, and at night, he'd just lie quietly beside me, reading documents.

A chance to get out and see friends was more than welcome.

At dinner, I gathered my courage.

"Kholod."

He cut his steak and looked up at me.

Anastasia and Anya also paused, their eyes on me.

"I... Isabella asked me out the day after tomorrow." I tried to keep my tone light and casual. "She wants to go shopping and have tea. May I go?"

Kholod set down his knife and fork, wiping his mouth with his napkin. He didn't answer immediately.

The dining room fell so quiet you could hear the wood crackling in the fireplace.

Anya raised an eyebrow, surprise flickering in her eyes.

Anastasia lifted her wine glass, her gaze moving between Kholod and me.

"Just the two of you?" Kholod finally spoke.

"Yes." I nodded. "She said she wants to catch up."

He fell silent for a moment, his fingertips drumming the table. "What time?"

"Leave at ten, back around four or five."

He studied me, his amber eyes unfathomable. "Fine."

"Really?" I was surprised. "You're okay with it?"

"Since she invited you, go ahead." He picked up his cutlery again, his movements deliberately casual.

I could hardly believe my ears.

"Thank you," I said sincerely.

"But," he suddenly looked up, his expression serious, "you need to be back by seven."

"Okay."

"Noelle, if you're not back by seven, I'll come get you myself."

"Got it." I found it amusing. "I'll be back on time."

He continued eating, satisfied.

Anya leaned back in her chair, teasing. "Noelle, what kind of spell did you cast on Kholod?"

"Anya." Warning laced Anastasia's voice.

"Okay, okay, I'll stop." Anya made a zipping motion across her lips.

I kept my head down, feeling my cheeks burn.

Standing in the walk-in closet, I finally chose a light pink knit dress paired with a cream coat—simple, elegant, yet refined.

"Madam, you seem to be in wonderful spirits today." Darya smiled as she adjusted my collar.

"Probably because I get to go out."

"The boss is waiting downstairs. He says he'll drive you personally."

I picked up my purse, my heart racing inexplicably.

Kholod stood in the foyer wearing a charcoal casual suit, less intimidating than usual. When he saw me coming downstairs, he looked up, his gaze sliding from my face to my hem and back again.

"That dress suits you perfectly."

"Thank you." I walked over to him. "You don't need to drive me. Dmitri could—"

"I'll take you." He cut me off, extending his hand. "Let's go."

I placed my hand in his palm, my fingers enveloped by his warmth.

We walked out of the villa side by side. The understated black sedan waited in the courtyard.

He opened the passenger door for me, waited until I was settled, then closed it and walked around to the driver's seat. The engine purred to life, and the car slowly pulled out of the manor.

"Have fun," he said suddenly. "Buy whatever catches your eye."

"Okay."

Outside the window, early spring Philadelphia showed new green on the branches, the sky clear and bright. The car soon stopped in front of Rittenhouse Palm Pavilion.

"Go on."

I unbuckled my seatbelt and opened the door.

"Noelle." He called my name again.

"What?"

"Keep your phone on," he said. "Call me if anything happens."

"Okay."

"I'm serious." He stared at me. "Anything at all."

"I know." I smiled. "Kholod, you're unusually talkative today."

He was momentarily speechless, just watching me intently.

After getting out and walking a few steps, I couldn't help but look back. He hadn't left yet, watching me through the window. I waved at him. He nodded, then finally started the engine and drove away.

"Good afternoon, do you have a reservation?" A uniformed server smiled politely.

"My friend is already inside," I said. "Isabella."

"This way, please." The server nodded immediately.

He led me through the dining area to a quiet booth by the window. Through the large floor-to-ceiling windows, I could see the fountain and greenery of Rittenhouse Square. Sunlight streamed in, warm and inviting.

Isabella was already there. When she saw me, she immediately stood up and waved.

"Noelle! Over here!"

She wore a light blue dress today, her long hair cascading over her shoulders, makeup subtle, looking gentle and sweet.

I hurried over, and she opened her arms for an enthusiastic hug.

"You're finally free!" She released me and pulled me to sit across from her. "Let me look at you—wow, that dress is gorgeous! Pink is absolutely perfect on you! Makes your skin look porcelain!"

"Thank you." I sat down across from her.

"Here, I already ordered tea. Their Earl Grey is divine, and their scones with clotted cream and jam are to die for!"

A server brought tea service and a tiered stand. The three-level silver stand was laden with exquisite treats—finger sandwiches, macarons, fruit tarts, chocolate mousse... Each looked like a work of art.

"It looks incredible." I marveled.

"Right!" Isabella smiled proudly. "I told you this place was worth it. Try this smoked salmon sandwich—it's heavenly!"

The fresh salmon with cucumber and cream cheese had complex, rich flavors. It really was delicious.

"How is it?" She looked at me expectantly.

"Divine!" I nodded. "Isabella, you always pick the most wonderful places."

"Of course!" She poured me tea. "I heard you're helping Mrs. Anastasia organize her collection?"

I nodded. "The family has some Imperial Russian pieces that need re-cataloging."

"Sounds so sophisticated! What kind of things?"

"Faberge eggs, antique jewelry, paintings..." I said. "Each piece is priceless."

"My God!" She gasped. "Aren't you nervous handling all that?"

"At first," I admitted. "I'm used to it now. Every piece has its own story. It's fascinating."

"You're incredible." She said sincerely. "If she's trusting you with something so important, she must truly believe in you."

"Perhaps."

We chatted while enjoying the tea service, the atmosphere light and pleasant.

"Oh, did you see Valentino's show last week?" Isabella said excitedly. "That feathered gown collection was absolutely stunning!"

"I did." I smiled. "But I think it's too dramatic for everyday wear."

"Oh come on, gowns are supposed to be dramatic!" she said. "Those simple everyday pieces are so dull."

"But I like simple."

"Your taste..." She shook her head helplessly. "You could be so much more dazzling."

"Dazzling isn't always wise," I said honestly. "I prefer to keep things low-key."

"Speaking of keeping things quiet," she lowered her voice, eyes sparkling with gossip, "the O'Connell heiress broke up with her fiancé!"

"What happened? I thought they were blissfully happy?"

"Turns out he was cheating! Guess what? She threw her engagement ring right in his face and stormed out!"

"Good for her!"

"Exactly! That's how you deal with cheating bastards!"

We chatted about more society gossip and fashion, time flying by in pleasant conversation.

Checking my watch, it was almost three. "Weren't we going shopping? Should we head out now?"

"Don't rush!" Isabella grabbed my hand. "I haven't given you your surprise yet!"

"Oh, right!" I remembered. "What's the surprise?"

"Guess!"

"I haven't a clue." I laughed. "Just tell me."

"Okay, okay." She set down her teacup, smiling mysteriously. "Get ready for your surprise."

She waved toward a corner of the restaurant.

I followed her gaze—

My smile froze.

Lorenzo was walking over with an enormous bouquet of red roses.

No. This couldn't be happening.

He looked gaunt, his cheeks hollow, eyes sunken. What terrified me most was the obsessive gleam burning in his eyes.

"Surprise!" Isabella beamed innocently, completely oblivious to my horrified expression. "I know you two had a misunderstanding. Lorenzo's been so worried about you, wanting to clear the air. As your mutual friend, I thought I should help you work this out!"

She sounded so reasonable, so well-meaning, yet it sent chills down my spine.

"Isabella..." I shot to my feet, the chair scraping harshly. "This... this isn't a good idea..."

"Why not?" She grabbed my hand, preventing me from leaving, eyes full of confusion. "Noelle, don't be nervous. Lorenzo just wants to talk. He means no harm. You two used to get along so well, didn't you?"

"Things are different now..."

"It's fine! You two chat, I'll pop to the ladies' room."

"Isabella!" I tried to call her back and stand to follow her, but my wrist was seized.

"Noelle."

Lorenzo set the roses heavily on the table, petals scattering. His eyes never left me, filled with long-suppressed emotion.

"You look so much better." His voice was hoarse and trembling. "I've been worried sick about you... thinking about you every single day... wondering if you're all right..."

"Lorenzo, I'm fine." I tried to keep my voice steady, taking a step back. "You don't need to worry. Your injuries... are they healing?"

"Injuries?" He laughed bitterly. "That's nothing. Nothing compared to what you've endured."

"I haven't endured anything..."

"You're still defending him!" He suddenly grew agitated. "You're clearly being held prisoner! Tormented! Why are you still protecting him?"

Other patrons began to stare. Those gazes felt like needles in my back.

"Lorenzo, please calm down." I lowered my voice. "This is a public place..."

"I don't give a damn!" He stepped closer. "Noelle, I came here today to take you away!"

"What?" I was stunned. "Lorenzo, do you hear yourself?"

"I'm perfectly lucid!" His eyes grew more frenzied. "I'll take you away from here! Away from Philadelphia! Somewhere he'll never find you!"

"You've lost your mind!"

"I've never been more clear-headed!" He came around the table, closing in. "That Russian bastard can't give you happiness! He'll only imprison you, torture you, treat you like his possession!"

"Lorenzo, listen to me—"

"No! This time, you listen to me!" He cut me off, advancing. "I've arranged everything! Car's waiting at the back exit, documents are ready! If you're willing, we can leave this instant! New York, Canada, anywhere!"

"I won't go with you!"

"That monster has brainwashed you!" He was nearly shouting. "Are you going to let him cage you forever?"

The whispers around us grew louder.

"What's this about a mark?"

"Isn't that Mrs. Morozov?"

Shame and fury churned in my chest.

"Lorenzo!" I hissed through gritted teeth. "Shut up!"

"I won't!" His voice rose higher. "I want everyone to know what kind of monster Kholod Morozov is! He abuses you, he—"

"Enough!"

I raised my hand and slapped him hard across the face.

The sharp sound rang through the restaurant.

Everyone froze.

Lorenzo clutched his cheek, staring at me in disbelief.

"You... you slapped me..."

"Yes!" Tears finally spilled over. "What happens between Kholod and me is none of your damn business!"

"But—"

"No buts!" I wiped my tears away. "What gives you the right to think I need saving?"

His voice was anguished. "Noelle, I know! I know everything! Aunt Sofia forced you! The Bellucci debts forced you! You don't love him—"

"So what? This is my choice!"

"That's martyrdom!"

"Call it whatever you like!" I took a shaky breath. "Lorenzo, now please leave."

"I'm not leaving!" He lunged forward, yanking me closer. "Noelle, come with me! I'll protect you! Give you freedom! I'll—"

"Let go of me!" I struggled fiercely. "Lorenzo, release me!"

"Never!" He gripped tighter. "Noelle, please, come with me..."

Customers around us rose from their seats, some snapping photos with their phones, others murmuring, and someone had summoned the restaurant manager.

I could feel the pain shooting through my wrist, feel the sweat from his palms.

"Isabella! Isabella!" I searched frantically for her, desperate for help. But she was nowhere to be found.

"Stop calling for her!" Lorenzo grabbed me with both hands now. "Come with me! Right now!"

I fought desperately. "Lorenzo, this will only make things worse for me!"

His strength was frightening. "I'm saving you!"

"Let me go!"

"Come with me!"

We grappled like this before everyone's eyes.

I remembered Kholod's parting words, but my purse had tumbled onto the seat, my phone trapped inside, completely beyond reach.

"Lorenzo!" I screamed with every ounce of strength. "If you don't let go, I'm calling the police!"

"Police?" He sneered. "You think the cops dare interfere with Morozov business? Noelle, don't be naive! In Philadelphia, only I can protect you!"

His hands began sliding toward my waist, attempting to lift me bodily.

"Don't you dare touch me!"

"Noelle, don't be frightened, I won't hurt you..."

"Sir!" The restaurant manager finally arrived. "Please stop this! You're disturbing our other guests!"

"Back off!" Lorenzo roared. "This is private business!"

The manager was cowed by his aggression, hesitating and retreating. I looked around desperately—the other patrons merely gawked, no one stepping forward to help.

The pain in my wrist intensified.

Lorenzo's arm was already encircling my waist, preparing to carry me off by force.

CHAPTER TWENTY

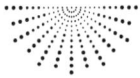

Kholod

"So, Mr. Morozov, regarding the shipping route for this cargo, I suggest..."

Harrison's voice echoed through the private room, but I wasn't hearing a damn word. Through the gaps in the blinds, my eyes tracked the figure in the hall below.

Noelle.

She sat in a window booth, sunlight spilling across her, the pale pink dress making her look soft and sweet. Isabella sat across from her, both laughing at something. Seeing her smile like that, my tense nerves relaxed slightly.

Good. She really was just enjoying tea. After dropping her off this morning, Harrison had called for this last-minute meeting—perfect timing to check on her safety before picking her up tonight.

"Mr. Morozov?" Harrison's voice pulled me back. "Do you think this plan will work?"

"It's fine." I turned to the shipping chart on the table. "But you need to guarantee no customs issues during transport."

"You can count on that." Harrison nodded. "I have reliable connections at customs..."

He kept explaining details, but my attention drifted back to the window. Noelle picked up a pastry, taking delicate little bites. Watching her focused expression, my mouth curved slightly upward.

Bringing her out was the right call.

"So we have a deal?" Harrison asked.

"Yeah, that works." I nodded. "The lawyers will send the contract tomorrow."

"Excellent!" Harrison stood, extending his hand. "It's an honor working with the Morozovs."

I shook his hand.

After seeing Harrison out, I returned to the window for one last look before leaving.

Suddenly, commotion erupted below. I frowned, looking down, and froze solid.

Lorenzo Conti. That persistent bastard was walking toward Noelle with a massive bouquet of red roses.

How the hell was he here? How did he know Noelle was here?

My eyes swept the hall—Isabella was gone. Where the fuck had she gone?

Lorenzo reached the table, slamming down the flowers. I watched him grab Noelle's wrist, both of them struggling as nearby customers turned to stare. He was saying something frantically, gripping harder, almost pulling her into his arms.

And Noelle—she clearly wasn't kicking the bastard where it counted.

Burning rage shot straight to my head. She'd lied to me again. Never stopped lying!

Having tea? Clearing her head? All bullshit! Her real purpose was meeting Lorenzo Conti! Even Isabella was being used—pretending it was a casual hangout when it was really a secret rendezvous with her old lover!

All my restraint these past days, my attempts to start fresh—it was all a fucking joke!

"Fuck!"

I slammed my fist into the window frame, the blinds shaking violently.

I spun around and stormed out of the room.

I descended the stairs one step at a time, fury climbing with each step. Waiters in the hallway scrambled out of my way, terror written across their faces.

I knew exactly how terrifying I looked right now.

Bloodlust pounded through my veins.

I hit the last few steps and entered the hall. The chattering stopped dead. Everyone turned to stare. I walked straight toward that booth, each step heavy, my shoes striking marble with dull thuds.

The crowd parted automatically. I could see Lorenzo still gripping Noelle's wrist, his other arm tight around her waist, trying to pull her away. Her cheeks were flushed, her struggles seeming weak—more like she was melting into her lover's embrace.

My vision turned blood red.

"Let go of her."

My voice wasn't loud, but it cut clearly through the entire hall.

Lorenzo went rigid, slowly turning his head. When he saw it was me, all color drained from his face.

"Kholod..." His voice shook, but he still held Noelle tight. "What are you doing here..."

"What am I doing?" I stepped closer. "Looks like the last lesson didn't sink in deep enough."

"I just wanted to talk to Noelle..."

"Talk?" I stopped in front of him, looking down. "By holding her like that?"

"I wasn't—"

"Shut up."

I grabbed his collar hard.

"Kholod!" Noelle cried out. "Don't—"

I ignored her. Her protests only stoked my rage higher.

I jerked hard, sending Lorenzo crashing to the floor.

He hit the marble with a sickening thud.

Since he was still gripping Noelle, she got dragged down too, crying out in pain.

"Noelle!" Lorenzo struggled to help her up.

I stomped on his outstretched hand.

The sound of breaking bone cut sharp through the air.

"Ahhhhh!"

Lorenzo's scream shattered the hall's silence.

"Kholod!" Noelle tried to get up. "Stop! You'll kill him!"

"So what?" I pulled brass knuckles from my pocket, sliding them onto my right hand with deliberate slowness. "Killing him would make my day."

"No!" She lunged forward, trying to grab my arm.

I shoved her back with my free hand.

She fell backward, eyes full of terror.

Perfect. Let her be afraid. Let her see what betrayal costs.

I bent down, grabbed Lorenzo's collar, and hauled him up from the floor.

"Kholod... please..." His face twisted with pain. "I... I just wanted to save her..."

"Save her?" I laughed coldly. "What the fuck gives you the right to save her?"

"Because she's miserable!" he shouted. "This is all because of you!"

Before he finished speaking, my fist connected with his face. The metal edges of the brass knuckles tore through flesh from his right eyebrow to his left jaw.

Blood sprayed out, staining his white shirt and splashing across my hand.

"Ahhhhh!"

His screams grew more desperate.

"Kholod!" Noelle begged through tears. "Stop hitting him!"

I wasn't listening.

Another punch.

Right to his nose.

"Crack."

Bone shattered.

Lorenzo tried to fight back, swinging wildly.

Pathetic.

I easily caught his fist and twisted hard.

"Snap!"

Another bone broke.

"Ahhhhh!"

He collapsed, curling into a ball as blood poured from his wounds, spreading across the floor in a horrifying red pool.

Still not enough.

Not nearly enough.

I pulled out the folding knife I always carried and flicked it open with a sharp "click."

Cold steel glinted.

"No!" Noelle threw herself at me, grabbing my arm. "Kholod! Please! Don't kill him!"

"Let go."

"I won't!" Tears streamed down her face. "It's all my fault... punish me instead... don't kill him..."

"Your fault?" I turned to look at her. "Noelle, finally admitting it?"

"I..."

"Admitting you planned all this? Admitting you used Isabella to set up this meeting so you could see him?"

"No!" She shook her head frantically. "I really didn't know he was coming! Isabella said she had a surprise for me... I thought..."

"You thought what?" I cut her off. "You thought I'd believe that?"

"It's true!" she cried. "Kholod, I'm not lying..."

"Enough."

I shook off her hands and crouched down, grabbing Lorenzo's arm. He was barely conscious, only managing weak moans.

The knife tip pierced his skin, blood seeping out. I began carving, one slow, deep cut at a time, forming letters.

"Ahhhhh!"

His screams echoed through the hall. Customers covered their mouths in horror, some diving under tables.

Blood ran down his arm, pooling on the floor.

P. U. N. K.

Four letters.

Punk.

"This is what happens when you touch my property," I whispered in his ear, voice cold as ice. "Remember this lesson, Lorenzo Conti. Next time, I won't just carve letters in your arm."

I released him. He convulsed in the pool of blood.

"Dmitri." I stood up, shaking blood off my hands.

"Yes, boss."

He walked in with two bodyguards—I'd had them waiting outside.

"Send him back to the Belluccis," I said coldly. "Tell Sofia that next time, there won't be a body to send back."

"Understood."

Dmitri and the guards lifted the moaning Lorenzo. Blood traced a long streak across the floor as they dragged him.

"Noelle..." Lorenzo called weakly. "Noelle... don't... don't trust him... he's a monster..."

"Get him out." I waved impatiently.

The guards covered his mouth and dragged him away.

The hall fell into deathly silence.

Everyone stood frozen like statues, not daring to make a sound.

I turned around. Noelle knelt on the floor, hands covering her face, shoulders shaking violently from crying. Her dress had spread around her, the pink fabric stained with blood.

I walked over and crouched down.

"Look at me."

She shook her head, covering her face tighter.

"Noelle." My voice turned colder. "I said look at me."

She still wouldn't obey. I lost patience, prying her hands away and gripping her chin, forcing her to look up. Tears streaked her face, eyes swollen red, lips white from biting them.

"Open your eyes," I commanded.

"I..."

"Open them!"

She opened her eyes, trembling, those brown eyes filled with fear and despair.

"Look closely." I pointed toward the exit where Dmitri was directing the guards dragging Lorenzo out. "That's what happens to him."

Lorenzo was still struggling, still calling her name.

"That's the price for touching you," I whispered in her ear. "That's what happens when someone tries to take you away."

"Kholod..." Her voice shook. "Please believe me... I really didn't know he was coming..."

"Believe you?" I laughed coldly. "Noelle, how many chances have I given you?"

"This time really wasn't me..."

"Enough." I cut her off, releasing her chin and standing up. "I don't want to hear any more lies."

I looked down at her.

She knelt there, trembling all over, like a frightened little animal. The customers around us were still watching, eyes full of curiosity and gossip. I stripped off my suit jacket and threw it over her.

"Put it on."

She stared at me blankly.

"I said put it on!" I snarled. "Or do you want everyone to see you like this?"

She finally snapped out of it, trembling as she pulled on the jacket.

I bent down, pulled her up from the floor, and threw her over my shoulder. Everyone stepped aside—no one dared stop me.

Under countless stares and whispers, I carried her out. Now I just wanted to get her back somewhere I had complete control, where I could get to the bottom of exactly how many more lies she was hiding.

CHAPTER TWENTY-ONE

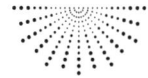

Noelle

"Get in the car."

Kholod's voice cut like a Siberian gale, icy and unrelenting.

I hadn't even recovered from the bloody chaos at the tea room when he hoisted me over his shoulder, rough as hell, and shoved me into a black SUV. The door slammed shut with a bang, sealing off the outside world.

Through the window, I caught sight of Lorenzo being dragged away by a couple of guys in the opposite direction. His face was a mangled mess, the gash from his brow to his jaw deep enough to expose bone, looking gruesome under the streetlights.

"Lorenzo—" I tried to shove the door open.

A hand clamped down on my shoulder, pinning me back into the seat.

"Don't move." Kholod's tone was flat, emotionless.

"He's going to die!" I struggled against it. "Please, at least take him to a hospital—"

"None of your business," Kholod said it stone-faced, then pulled out a black strip of cloth and tied it over my eyes.

"No—"

Everything plunged into darkness. The car roared to life, engine growling low.

I slumped against the seat, fists clenched in my skirt, nails digging in like they might tear through the fabric. It was all over. Isabella's meticulously planned "surprise," Lorenzo's obsession, Kholod's rage—it all twisted together, obliterating my last shred of hope.

The drive stretched on forever, winding through endless turns. I felt the car descend a slope, the air growing colder, heavier, more oppressive.

Finally, it stopped.

The door yanked open, and I was hauled out, my feet hitting cold, hard ground. Someone gripped my arm, guiding me forward, my heels echoing in the vast emptiness like an ominous countdown.

"That's enough." Kholod's voice broke in.

The blindfold came off, and blinding white light forced me to squint.

It was a basement. Concrete walls, smooth and frigid, with embedded LED strips casting a harsh, unforgiving glow. A dark gray leather sofa dominated the center, while a metal table and chairs huddled in the corner.

The worst part was the suffocating silence. Thick soundproofing isolated us completely from the world above.

Kholod lounged on the sofa, legs crossed, cigar smoke curling lazily from his fingers. Those amber eyes gleamed through the haze, piercing and intense.

"Everyone out," he ordered Dmitri.

"Yes, boss."

The heavy metal door thudded shut with a resounding boom, sealing us in.

Now, it was just him and me.

"Come here."

I stood frozen, my legs heavy as lead.

"I said, come here."

I gritted my teeth and stepped toward him. Each click of my heels echoed sharply, like a timer ticking down to my doom.

I stopped three paces away.

He flicked his cigar, ash crumbling to the floor.

"You'd better spill everything." He sounded like he was interrogating a condemned prisoner.

I drew in a deep breath, forcing myself to stay calm. "I already told you, Isabella said it was a surprise! I had no idea Lorenzo would show up. Kholod, why won't you believe me?"

"Believe you?" He cut me off, then laughed.

That laugh was ice-cold, devoid of any warmth.

"Noelle Bellucci, you really think I'm that stupid?" He rose to his feet, advancing step by step. "Hand-delivering your old flame as a surprise? You think I'm blind?"

"He's not my old flame!"

"Oh?" He sneered, now right in my face, seizing my chin with a grip so tight I could barely breathe. "Then why did Isabella arrange the meeting?"

"I don't know!" I twisted, trying to break free. "I really don't!"

"Still lying!" Fury ignited in his eyes. "You think using Isabella as a shield will make me buy it?"

"I'm not lying!" Tears welled up in my eyes. "She just invited me for tea—how could I have known—"

"Enough." He released me, stepping back, his gaze a turbulent mix of disappointment and rage. "I'm done listening to your lies."

"Kholod, I really didn't—" I reached for his arm.

He swung his hand sharply, shoving me away. I stumbled back into the cold wall.

"You know what I hate most?" He closed in, trapping me between the wall and his body. "Being played for a fool. And you, Noelle, you've tested my limits over and over again."

"I didn't—"

"Shut up!" His roar echoed deafeningly in the sealed space.

I flinched, tears finally spilling down my cheeks.

He stared at me for a moment, then seized my wrist and flung me onto the sofa.

Before I could react, he was on top of me, one knee pressing into the sofa's edge, his massive frame completely overshadowing mine.

"No—"

His palm clamped over my mouth, rough and unyielding.

"I don't want to hear another word." His voice was hoarse, eyes blazing with wild fire. "Every damn thing from your mouth is a lie. If that's all it's good for, keep it shut."

I thrashed my head, struggling desperately.

The sound of fabric tearing pierced the air. He hiked up my skirt, hooked the edge of my panties, and ripped them off in one brutal yank.

No hesitation—he unbuckled his belt, yanked down his zipper.

He thrust into me without warning, raw and brutal, no preparation whatsoever. Pain exploded through me, white-hot and excruciating, like I was being ripped apart from the inside. I wanted to scream, but his hand muffled it into desperate whimpers, my body arching in agony as he drove deep, his movements heavy and merciless.

"Why'd you betray me?" he growled, slamming harder with each accusation, his hips pounding against mine. "Is it better with Lorenzo? Does he get you this fucking excited?" Another savage thrust. "Which of your words are even true, Noelle?"

I shook my head frantically, tears streaming, but he didn't let up, his weight pinning me down, every brutal motion sending shockwaves of pain tearing through my core.

Finally, he pulled his hand away from my mouth.

I gasped, words spilling out in broken fragments. "I didn't—I swear, Kholod, it wasn't like that—"

He silenced me by ripping my bra down in one vicious tug, exposing my breasts. His hands clamped onto them, kneading roughly, fingers digging in deep. "You're just a lying bitch," he snarled, twisting harder as he kept pumping into me, the friction building despite the lingering ache.

I was furious, desperate, and then—my asthma flared up. I wheezed, my chest tightening, air escaping me. He reached into his pocket, yanked out an inhaler, and shoved it into my mouth mid-thrust, not slowing his rhythm for a second. "Breathe," he barked, forcing the puff as he rammed in deeper.

Relief flooded in quickly, but so did something else. With each punishing stroke, my body started to betray me—growing slick, heat building despite the pain. I felt the shift from pure torment to a twisted blend.

He noticed immediately. "Even like this, you're getting off?" he taunted, his voice thick with mockery. "Look at you, soaking wet already. What a slut."

Shame burned through me; I wanted to vanish, to crawl into some dark hole. "It's not—it's not like that," I choked out, but my hips bucked involuntarily.

"Then why are you getting wetter?" He accelerated, thrusts turning frantic and punishing. His fingers latched onto the tattoo on my chest —the mark claiming me as his—and pinched it hard, grinding down. Pain flared, but so did a dark jolt of pleasure, forcing a gasp from my lips.

I couldn't hold it back; a moan escaped, low and unwilling.

"Only I can make you like this," he hissed, staking his claim, his grip tightening as he drove in deeper, faster.

I hated his roughness, hated how he refused to believe me. But worse, I hated my own body—how it responded, craving more under his assault, pleasure sneaking in amid the hurt.

His pace turned feral, hips slamming with wild intensity. Pain and ecstasy blurred together; I couldn't tell if I was sobbing or moaning anymore, my voice breaking in the heavy air.

"Is this what you wanted from Lorenzo?" he demanded, pounding relentlessly. "Would you be this wet and slutty under him?"

My body went limp from the onslaught, every nerve alight, and suddenly, a bitter laugh escaped me. "Are you... jealous?" I managed, my voice shaky but defiant.

"Shut your mouth," he snapped, but I saw the flicker in his eyes.

"You're jealous," I pressed on, even as he kept going. "Not mad about betrayal—you're losing it over Lorenzo. You think I still want him!"

"I said shut up!"

"Kholod, admit it—you care. You're jealous as hell."

"You fucking—shut up!" His hand shot to my throat, squeezing, then he crushed his mouth against mine in a brutal kiss, silencing everything. He bit down hard on my lower lip, drawing blood, the metallic tang spreading through our mouths as he devoured me, his hips never faltering.

In that savage hold, something snapped inside me—a wild, reckless spark. My body was already yielding to him, syncing with every thrust. Why fight it anymore? If I couldn't escape, why not dive in? Let the Morozov boss serve me for a change. What the hell.

When he broke the kiss, I reached up, wrapping my arms around his neck. "Kholod Morozov, if you want me this bad, then fuck me harder."

He froze for a split second, eyes widening, then surged back with manic fury, pounding into me like a tempest unleashed.

I met him thrust for thrust, rolling my hips to match his rhythm, chasing the blistering high. Pleasure built relentlessly, overwhelming everything, and I screamed for more—"Harder, Kholod! Don't stop!"—letting it consume me. No point in resisting; I'd sink into it, own the chaos, revel in the surrender on my own terms.

He growled low, his hands roaming possessively—pinching my nipples until they throbbed, slapping my ass as he drove deeper, the sofa creaking under the force. Sweat slicked our skin, his breath scorching my neck as he bit down again, marking me fresh. I clawed at his back, nails raking red lines, urging him on. The initial pain twisted into something electric, every rough grab and slap of flesh making me clench tighter, grow wetter.

"Is this what you need?" he rasped, flipping me onto my stomach without withdrawing, yanking my hips up to take me from behind. His fingers tangled in my hair, pulling my head back as he slammed in, the new angle hitting spots that made stars explode behind my eyes. I pushed back against him, moaning loudly, the sound bouncing off the soundproof walls.

"Yes—fuck, yes!" I cried, no holding back now. My body trembled, racing toward the edge, his cock filling me utterly, stretching me with each punishing stroke. He reached around, his fingers finding my clit, rubbing firm circles that left me gasping, the dual assault shoving me higher.

"You're mine," he snarled, thrusting so hard it shook me to my core. "Say it—no one else gets this."

"Yours," I gasped, not thinking, just feeling the wave crest. But deep down, that twisted thrill surged: I was using him too, turning his rage into my ecstasy, wielding the pleasure like a blade.

He ramped up the pace, relentless, one hand spanning my waist to hold me steady, the other teasing my breasts, rolling my nipples until they ached with delicious torment. I felt him thicken inside me, teetering on the brink, but he held back, prolonging it, making me beg.

"Please—Kholod, more!" My voice cracked, body arching as orgasm tore through me, clenching around him in shuddering waves. He followed seconds later, groaning deeply as he spilled into me, hips jerking with raw force.

We collapsed in a heap, breaths ragged, his weight pressing me into the cushions. But even in the afterglow, that dark edge persisted —I'd surrendered, but on my terms, stealing a sliver of control amid the storm.

He pulled out slowly, leaving me empty and sore, yet strangely sated. Rolling me over, he pinned me with a possessive stare. "Don't think this changes anything."

I smirked through the haze. "Oh, it does." Because now I knew: his jealousy was my leverage. If he wanted to own me, I'd make him earn it, every brutal inch.

The room hung heavy with our mingled scents, the air thick with the aftermath. My asthma stayed at bay, but my pulse thundered, alive in a way I'd never known. Kholod traced the tattoo again, gentler this time, like an undeniable claim. I didn't pull away; I leaned into it, letting the heat linger.

We weren't done—not even close. He dragged me up, kissing me again, slower but no less fierce, hands mapping every curve like they were his territory. I bit back, our bodies pressing close. Round two ignited fast, his fingers dipping between my thighs, finding me still slick and ready.

"Fuck, you're insatiable," he muttered, hunger replacing anger.

"Only for you," I whispered, half-truth, half-taunt, as he pushed me back down, spreading my legs wide. He entered me again, slower at first, building a deliberate rhythm, each thrust drawing out moans I couldn't stifle.

The earlier pain melted into pure bliss, my nails digging into his shoulders as he rocked deeper, hitting that perfect spot repeatedly. Sweat beaded on his forehead, dripping onto me, mingling with mine. I wrapped my legs around him, pulling him closer, our breaths syncing in the dim light.

"Tell me you want this," he demanded, voice rough, hips grinding slow and hard.

"I want it—fuck, I need it," I admitted, the words tumbling free as pleasure coiled tight once more.

He grinned darkly, accelerating, one hand bracing on the sofa arm for leverage, the other stroking my clit with firm precision. I shattered first, crying out his name, body convulsing around him. He chased his release, thrusts turning erratic, finally burying himself deep with a guttural moan.

Exhaustion washed over us, but satisfaction hummed like a dangerous high. In this sealed prison, I'd rewritten the script—from victim to willing tempest. Kholod might believe he owned me, but I'd just carved out a piece of him too.

We lay tangled, his heartbeat pounding against mine. For a fleeting moment, silence reigned, broken only by our slowing breaths. Then he shifted, pulling me close, almost tender. But I knew the truth: this was merely the calm before the next storm. More fury awaited, and I'd face it head-on, reveling in the wreckage.

CHAPTER TWENTY-TWO

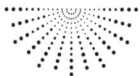

Kholod

I turned off the shower, water droplets falling from my fingertips. Noelle slumped against me, eyes closed, lashes still damp with water. Her whole body was limp and helpless—without my support, she would have collapsed to the floor.

Wet hair clung to her flushed cheeks, her skin still flushed from passion, covered in red marks—neck, shoulders, chest, waist... all my doing.

Damn. I'd thought I'd feel satisfied after venting, that I'd enjoy the revenge. But all that remained in my chest was a hollow emptiness, as if I'd lost something precious.

"Noelle?" I called softly.

No response. I lifted her chin. Her eyes remained closed, breathing steady—she'd fallen asleep from sheer exhaustion.

Understandable. After today's shock and what had just happened, she'd reached her breaking point.

I bent down and lifted her into my arms. She was so light it made my chest constrict. She'd been eating properly these past weeks, but still hadn't put on much weight. Walking out of the shower, I grabbed a clean towel from the nearby rack and wrapped her entirely in it.

She stirred slightly in my arms, letting out a sleepy murmur.

"It hurts..."

Just two words, but it cut through me like a dull blade.

I pushed open the bathroom door. Darya was waiting outside.

"Have the doctor stand by... get Emily," I said. "Prepare ointment and painkillers."

"Yes, boss."

"Also," I paused, "prepare warm milk and easily digestible food. Bring it when she wakes."

"Yes."

Carrying her through the corridor from bathroom to bedroom, her head rested against my shoulder, warm breath brushing my neck. The sensation was contradictory—moments ago I'd been brutal with her, yet now I was handling her with utmost care, terrified of causing more pain.

I laid her gently on the bed. She curled up, brow furrowed, clearly still in pain. Her lips were swollen and torn from my bites, finger marks vivid on her neck—stark reminders of how much force I'd used.

"Shit." I cursed myself under my breath.

A knock at the door.

"Boss, the doctor's here."

"Come in."

Emily entered with her medical bag. Seeing Noelle on the bed, sympathy flickered across her face.

"Boss, I need to examine Mrs. Morozov's injuries."

"Go ahead." I stood and walked to the window.

Behind me came the sounds of the medical kit opening, Emily quietly asking Darya to assist, and Noelle's pained whimpers when her injuries were touched. Each sound pierced my heart.

"Boss, Mrs. Morozov's external injuries aren't severe—mainly bruising and abrasions. I've applied medication. However..."

"What?"

"Mrs. Morozov's very weak," Emily chose her words carefully. "She needs proper rest. For at least a week, she shouldn't engage in any... strenuous activities." The final words were barely whispered.

"Understood. You may go."

"Yes." Emily packed up and left.

Darya was about to leave as well when I stopped her.

"Have the kitchen prepare more nourishing broths. What are her preferences?"

Darya considered this. "Mrs. Morozov seems to prefer light flavors —nothing too oily or heavily spiced."

"Then keep it light." I paused. "Also, bring up all her travel magazines."

"Yes."

After the door closed, I returned to sit beside the bed. I reached out to smooth her furrowed brow, but my fingers froze just before making contact.

What right did I have to touch her? I'd just treated her like a beast. Even if she'd eventually surrendered and responded, it was only because I'd forced her to.

"I'm sorry."

The words felt foreign on my tongue.

Kholod Morozov never apologized.

But now, seeing her body marked and wounded because of me, the words emerged unbidden.

What good were apologies? Could they erase the marks on her body? Could they undo what I'd just done to her?

No.

I stood and walked toward the door.

"Rest well," I told her sleeping form, then turned and left.

"Boss, he's downstairs." Dmitri waited at the entrance to the underground passage.

"What's his condition?"

"Still alive."

"Lead the way."

We descended the narrow spiral staircase, the air growing

progressively colder and damper, thick with the mingled scents of blood and disinfectant.

This was the manor's deepest basement, prepared for special circumstances, buried so far underground that even a nuclear blast couldn't reach it. At the end stood a massive steel door.

Dmitri pushed it open. The metallic tang of blood hit me immediately.

Lorenzo hung suspended by chains in the center of the room, toes barely grazing the ground. His clothes had been torn to shreds, revealing a torso covered in wounds—whip marks, burns, knife cuts, layered upon layer.

His face was even worse—swollen eye sockets, shattered nose, lips beaten nearly to pulp.

He hung his head, breathing barely perceptible.

"Is he conscious?"

"Intermittently," Dmitri reported. "We administered adrenaline, but he won't last much longer."

I approached him and lifted his chin.

His eyes opened to mere slits, pupils dilated and unfocused.

"Lorenzo Conti," my voice echoed in the empty chamber. "I'm going to ask you several questions. Answer truthfully, and I'll grant you a quick death."

His lips moved, producing indistinct sounds. "...kill me..."

"I will. But first," I released his chin, "tell me who orchestrated today's events."

"...don't know..."

"Don't know?" I picked up pliers from the nearby table. "Perhaps you need more encouragement."

I clamped the pliers around his right index fingernail and yanked hard.

"AHHHHH—!!!"

His screams filled the room as he convulsed violently, chains clanking.

"I'll ask again. Who arranged it?"

"It was... Isabella..." he babbled deliriously. "She said... Noelle wanted to see me... said she had a surprise for me..."

My hand froze.

"What did you say?"

"It was... Isabella..." he repeated incoherently.

"Speak clearly." I leaned in closer.

"She... called five days ago... said Noelle missed me... told me to come to Rittenhouse..." His words came in broken gasps. "She said... everything was arranged..."

"And then?"

"I went... wanted to take her away... but she kept refusing... begging me not to do anything stupid..."

I suddenly recalled the scene at the restaurant—Noelle had indeed been struggling, looking terrified, constantly trying to push him away...

"But Isabella said..." he mumbled, "she said Noelle was refusing with her words... but really wanted to see me... said women always say the opposite of what they mean..."

Fuck.

The pliers clattered to the floor.

Dmitri approached me. "Boss?"

"Have the doctor treat his wounds," I turned and strode out. "Don't let him die. I still have use for him."

"Yes."

Racing through the corridor, I went straight to my study and yanked out the stack of investigation reports on Isabella from the drawer.

I flipped through page after page. Nanny testimonies, jewelry store records, hospital documentation, shopkeeper identifications—every piece of evidence was flawlessly airtight.

Too flawless.

I suddenly remembered that after my meeting with Kieran, I'd ordered Dmitri to increase surveillance and intelligence gathering around the manor perimeter. Isabella's visits had been so frequent, and after each one, something unpleasant invariably occurred between Noelle and me. Especially this "surprise" she'd arranged—it had nearly obliterated Noelle's last foothold in my heart.

Then there were Mother's and Anya's warnings—stay away from that woman. She was too perfect, perfect to the point of being unreal.

Yet the evidence before me indicated she was my savior. Someone who'd extended help in my hour of need should harbor good intentions.

But what if... she wasn't that person at all?

"Damn it!" I slammed my fist on the desk.

I grabbed the phone and dialed Dmitri.

"Reinvestigate Isabella Vance. Bypass all witnesses she provided, avoid any leads that could have been compromised. Start from the beginning—where exactly was she that Christmas Eve three years ago?"

"But the previous investigation..."

"Do it over!" I bit out. "Check if she has any connections to Kieran."

"...Yes."

"One more thing," I took a deep breath, "obtain the original recording of that emergency call from three years ago from the hospital. Whatever it takes, I want only the original."

"Understood. I'll arrange it immediately."

After hanging up, I collapsed into my chair. If Isabella truly was lying... if everything Noelle had said was the truth... then what I'd just done to her...

"Boss, Isabella Vance is here."

The following evening, Dmitri's voice crackled through the intercom. I hadn't intended to see her, but considering that both Noelle and Lorenzo had mentioned her name, I decided to hear what she had to say.

"Have her wait in the sitting room."

After straightening my shirt, I entered the sitting room. Isabella sat on the sofa, clutching a handkerchief, eyes red-rimmed—she'd clearly been crying.

Upon seeing me, she immediately rose.

"Kholod!" Her voice was thick with tears. "I heard about... Lorenzo, he..."

"Sit." I settled into the single chair across from her, tone neutral.

She bit her lower lip and sat back down, fingers twisting the handkerchief anxiously.

"How is Lorenzo?" she asked tentatively. "Is he... is he still alive?"

"He's alive." I studied her intently. "You're concerned about him?"

"I'm just... worried." She shook her head frantically. "After all, it was my fault... I caused this..."

"Your fault?" I arched an eyebrow.

"It's all my fault!" She suddenly broke into sobs, tears streaming down her face. "I only wanted to help Noelle and Lorenzo resolve their misunderstanding... I never imagined he'd be so reckless..."

She wept, her entire body trembling.

"I truly just wanted to help... I thought if they met and talked things through, Lorenzo would finally give up, and Noelle could live peacefully... but I never expected it would turn out like this..."

"So you orchestrated all of this?" My voice was barely above a whisper.

"Yes..." She cried harder. "I know I was wrong, Kholod... I was too naive..."

"Why did you do it?"

"I thought it was just a misunderstanding," she looked up at me through tear-filled eyes. "Lorenzo kept asking about Noelle... I thought if they met once and cleared the air, he could move on... and Noelle could finally be free of him..."

"How did you contact Lorenzo?"

"He'd approached me before," she dabbed at her tears. "Asked how Noelle was doing... I felt sorry for him and shared a few details... Later he kept pestering me, so I thought... perhaps if they met once and settled things..."

"So you arranged that encounter?"

"Yes..." She hung her head. "I truly... truly only meant to help... Kholod, I swear I had no ulterior motives... I know Noelle is your wife, I absolutely... absolutely never intended to create problems between you..."

She wept pitifully, her tears and trembling appearing genuine.

"Did Noelle know about this?"

"No!" She immediately shook her head. "I didn't tell her! I only said I had a surprise for her... I never thought Lorenzo would be so impulsive..."

She stood and approached me, then dropped to her knees.

"Kholod, please forgive me," she sobbed. "I can apologize to Noelle personally... please don't blame her for my mistake... this is entirely my responsibility..."

I looked down at her kneeling form—face streaked with tears, voice trembling, remorse seemingly authentic. I still wanted to believe she was well-intentioned. After all, without her, there would be no Morozov left in this world.

"Stand up."

"Kholod..."

"Get up and sit down." My tone softened slightly.

She slowly rose and perched nervously on the edge of the sofa, still sniffling quietly.

"This matter..." I remained silent for a moment. "I'll get to the bottom of it."

"I can do anything to make amends..."

"That's not necessary." I cut her off. "But don't see Noelle for the time being."

Her face paled. "Am I no longer worthy of being her friend?"

"No," I said. "It's just that the situation is complicated right now. We'll see when things settle."

"I understand..." She kept her head down. "Is Noelle... is she all right?"

The question made my chest tighten.

"She's fine." I lied.

"That's good..." Isabella looked relieved. "Kholod, if... if there's anything you need me to do, please let me know. I owe Noelle an apology, and I owe you one as well..."

"If you truly want to make amends," I said, "then stay away from her. At least for now."

"I understand."

"Dmitri will escort you home. If you need anything in the future, have him relay it to me."

"All right... thank you, Kholod..."

She turned to leave, but glanced back at me when she reached the door.

"Kholod, I really am... so very sorry..."

"I know. Go."

After the door closed, I sank back into the sofa.

Every detail about her told me she was innocent, that she'd simply done wrong with good intentions.

I rubbed my temples. Perhaps I really was being overly suspicious. Maybe she truly was just too naive, underestimating Lorenzo's obsession.

"Boss." Dmitri had returned.

"What is it?"

"Before Miss Vance left," he handed me an envelope and a note, "she asked me to give you these."

The note bore Isabella's elegant but slightly shaky handwriting.

"Kholod,

I'm truly sorry. I know no amount of apologies can compensate for my mistake. If possible, please give the letter to Noelle. I'll always be her friend. Whatever happens, I hope she can find happiness.

—Isabella"

I stared at the note for a long time.

"Boss?" Dmitri interrupted my thoughts. "About the reinvestigation..."

"Continue the search." I placed the note on the table. "Don't overlook any leads."

"But Lorenzo's testimony..."

"Testimony can be fabricated," I said. "But some things can't be faked. Go check that emergency call recording. That's where we'll find the truth."

185

"Understood."

After he left, I stood and walked to the window. Night had fallen over the manor, shrouding everything in darkness except for the light still glowing in the master bedroom. Noelle should be awake by now.

I wanted to see her, yet couldn't bear to face the hatred and despair that might be in her eyes.

I lit a cigarette and took a deep drag.

CHAPTER TWENTY-THREE

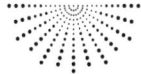

Kholod

I flipped through the investigation file in front of me, feeling like a dull knife was carving into my chest over and over.

It was Isabella who contacted Lorenzo, and Noelle had no clue. I'd let my emotions blind me, hadn't even checked her call logs.

"Fuck." I slammed the file shut.

"Boss?" Dmitri waited for orders.

"Send Lorenzo Conti back to the Bellucci family." My voice stayed eerily calm. "One last warning to Sofia. Next time, we won't even bother returning a body."

"Got it." He nodded and slipped out, closing the door softly.

I'd fucking wronged her. I lit a cigar and downed a big gulp of vodka, but it wasn't strong enough to burn away the guilt gnawing at me.

I'd let anger override reason again.

Late at night.

I stood outside the master bedroom door, hand hovering over the knob, frozen.

A faint light seeped through the crack—she always left the bedside lamp on before sleep.

I took a deep breath and turned the knob gently.

The door opened silently. I squeezed in sideways, moving like a thief.

On the bed, Noelle lay on her side, blanket only up to her waist. I stood there, watching her like some creep, borrowing the dim light. Her lashes were long, casting shadows on her cheeks. Her breathing was steady and soft. Her lips pursed slightly, like she was arguing with someone in her dreams.

Lost in the sight, I didn't notice her body twitch suddenly.

Her brow furrowed, and a tiny whimper escaped her lips.

She was having a nightmare.

"No... don't..." Her voice was faint, laced with fear.

My heart clenched hard. What was she dreaming? The shit I'd put her through? Or something worse?

She curled up, hands instinctively guarding her chest—right where my name was etched.

"I'm not... I didn't..." she murmured, voice thick with despair.

I almost reached out to wake her, but my hand froze mid-air. What right did I have to comfort her? I'd caused these nightmares myself.

After a while, her breathing evened out, and she sank back into sleep.

I exhaled slowly, pulled out the ointment, and gently lifted the blanket. Every bruise on her was proof of my brutality.

I twisted open the tube, squeezed some onto my fingers. The scent of mint and herbs filled the air. I leaned in, applying it feather-light to the worst mark on her arm. My fingertips circled her skin, tracing every ridge of the wound.

This was my doing.

I hiked up her nightgown hem. The bruise on her waist glared in the dimness. I gritted my teeth and kept going.

Spreading her legs, the finger marks on her inner thighs screamed my asshole moves; shifting her panties aside, the swelling at her core hadn't faded.

"I'm sorry," I whispered, my voice hoarse and foreign. "I'm sorry..."

After tending every spot, I capped the ointment and tucked her back in. But I couldn't leave, just sat on the edge, staring at her peaceful face.

If only time could rewind...

I shook my head. No ifs. I'd use what time I had left to make up for the irreparable damage.

* * *

"MADAM'S TEMPERATURE, pulse, and weight logs. Medical team assessment shows good recovery in bodily functions."

I scanned the report data, fingers lingering on "appetite improved" and "sleep stable." I waved Dmitri off, and he vanished quietly.

When the study door knocked softly, I wasn't surprised. Monitors showed she'd paced outside for five minutes. She pushed in, looking decent.

"What is it?"

"I want to go out for a bit."

I didn't want to allow it, but thinking of her stuck in bed for four full days because of me, guilt hit hard.

"Fine."

Her eyes lit up with disbelief, like a shooting star in the night.

"I'll allow one outing per week," I added, watching joy bloom on her face. "But Dmitri's men will tail you the whole time. I'll know your route, who you meet, and how long you stay." I locked eyes. "No contacting anyone on the list, including Isabella."

"I get it! I promise!" She bounced out like a little bird, light on her feet.

I called Dmitri right away. "Set up guards. She picks time and place. Allow bookstores, galleries, public spots. Give her the restricted list."

"Surveillance level?" Dmitri confirmed.

"Keep distance. No intervention unless she tries the list or bolts. Log places, times, purchases. Keep her safe."

"Understood."

* * *

"Target entered downtown Oak Street bookstore."

"Lingered in travel books section for forty-seven minutes."

"Bought a photography book and coffee. Read in the cafe area."

"No unusual contacts. Mood: calm, slightly happy."

...

The reports popped up on my phone, crisp and straightforward, detailing her perfectly normal path. The more innocent it seemed, the more guilt ate at me like ants.

A week later, I'd planned to tail her myself. But just as I geared up, the docks had an issue. A shipment got held by customs—I had to handle it personally.

I drove there, wondering where she'd go. By the time I sorted the mess, it was evening. In the car, I called Dmitri.

"What'd the madam do today?"

"She hit a downtown art supply store, bought charcoal pencils and a sketchbook," Dmitri said. "Then sat in a cafe for an hour, seemed like she was drawing."

"That's it?"

"She lingered outside a jewelry store for a while."

"Which one?"

"Lumiere Fine Jewelry on Walnut Street. Small place, handmade designs."

"What'd she buy?"

"Nothing," Dmitri continued. "Clerk said she eyed a necklace in pre-sale, available in a month. She stared a long time, then left."

"What kind?"

"I had a photo taken."

Seconds later, my phone pinged with an image.

It was a sleek, unique necklace—thin white gold chain with a small compass pendant. The compass looked antique with aged finish, but directions marked in colored gems.

"Clerk said it's the designer's limited edition, only ten made.

Theme's 'Pathfinder.' She read the card forever, got down when told about the wait."

"Good. Keep on her."

"Will do."

I hung up and dialed another number.

"Get me Lumiere Fine Jewelry's owner. Tell him Morozov wants the 'Pathfinder' necklace reserved. I need the finished piece tonight."

"Boss, they said it takes—"

"Morozov doesn't wait." I cut in. "Price is no issue. But tonight, that necklace is mine."

"Yes, boss."

By ten p.m., a velvet jewelry box arrived. I opened it; "Pathfinder" gleamed softly under the light.

I stared at the compass directions—which one pointed to her heart's desire?

I snapped it shut, checked the time—nearly eleven. She should be asleep. Box in hand, I slipped out of the study. The hallway was silent, just my footsteps echoing. I treaded light, keeping my shoes quiet.

At the master door, I breathed deep and pushed it open gently. Bedside lamp glowed. Noelle lay on her side, shoulders rising and falling—she was out.

I crept in, shut the door without a sound. Tiptoed to the bed. Moonlight filtered through the curtains, dappling the carpet. I bent down, placed the box on the nightstand as quietly as possible.

Just as I straightened up—

She stirred. My heart stopped.

Was she awake?

I froze. Noelle rolled over, facing me, eyes still shut.

Just light sleep.

I exhaled, turning to go—

"Who's there?!"

Her eyes snapped open, voice full of terror, on the verge of screaming.

"It's me." I leaned in quick, hand over her mouth. Her eyes widened, then flashed with rage once she recognized me.

She thrashed wildly, hands shoving my chest, legs kicking under the covers.

"Mmph—! Mmph—!" She tried to speak, but I held firm.

"Don't scream, it's me," I hissed low. "I'll let go if you stay quiet."

She glared, no sign of backing down. When her knee jammed into me, I grunted and released.

"Kholod Morozov!" She sat up, voice shaking with fury. "What the hell are you doing sneaking in here in the middle of the night? Playing thief?"

"I didn't sneak in. I have a key."

She grabbed a pillow and hurled it at me. "Get out!"

It hit my face, soft and harmless.

"Let me explain—"

"Fine, explain! Better make it clear why you're creeping around like a burglar?" Her eyes blazed in the light. "And why you're standing by my bed watching me sleep!"

"I..."

Shit, how to explain? Say I was dropping off a gift? This late? Who'd buy that?

She was still catching her breath, pounding her chest, even grabbing her inhaler for a hard puff.

I yanked her into my arms instead.

She fought hard, nightgown slipping off her shoulder. Maybe it was the midnight hush or her feeble pushes, but it felt like an illicit thrill.

I turned her face and kissed deeply. She stiffened at first, resisting, but as it deepened, her shoving hands weakened. My palm pressed her lower back, pulling her close; through the thin fabric, I felt every curve.

Damn, I was hard. Aching hard.

I released her lips, our breaths mingling hot and ragged. Noelle pulled back slightly, her chest heaving, eyes dazed but determined. "That's enough," she whispered, voice shaky, like she was trying to convince herself.

Enough? Hell no. This forbidden game was just getting started. I

192

smirked against her skin, my hand sliding under the hem of her night-gown, palm pressing against the soft flesh of her inner thigh. She tensed, instinctively trying to clamp her legs shut, but I wedged them apart with more force, my fingers stroking upward, teasing the heat building there.

"Look at us," I murmured, voice low and gravelly. "Doesn't this feel like we're sneaking around? Like a dirty little affair?"

Her body jolted, a shiver running through her. She stammered, words failing her—"I... you..."—but the way she trembled, the slick warmth pooling between her thighs, betrayed her. She liked it. Her hips shifted just a fraction, pressing into my touch, her excitement obvious in the way her breath hitched and her core clenched around nothing.

Seeing her give in like that fired me up. I leaned in close to her ear, my lips brushing the shell. "I want a taste of Mrs. Morozov," I growled, fingers dipping higher, circling her entrance. "Let me check how ready you are for me. Bet you're dripping already, aren't you? All wet and eager for this stranger in your bed."

Her reaction was instant—her nipples pebbled hard against the fabric, her thighs quivered, and a fresh rush of arousal coated my fingers as I teased her folds. She gasped, arching slightly, her body betraying her thrill even as her hands clutched at my shirt. But then she fired back, voice breathy and defiant: "Fine, show me how you stack up against my husband. Think you can do better than that controlling bastard?"

Her words hit like a spark to gasoline. I growled low, spinning her around in my arms, pinning her from behind. One arm banded across her waist like iron, holding her tight against me, while my other hand roamed freely, sliding down her belly and back between her legs from this new angle. I pressed my palm against her nape, keeping her facing forward, not letting her turn to see me. "You asked for it," I muttered, voice rough with need.

With a swift tug, I yanked off her nightgown, the last barrier gone. Moonlight spilled over her, highlighting every perfect curve—her breasts full and heaving, the dip of her waist, the swell of her hips. She was breathtaking, exposed and vulnerable. "Mrs. Morozov, you're fucking addictive," I rasped, grinding against her ass to let her feel how hard she made me. "Can't get enough of this body."

I fumbled with my belt, shoving my pants down just enough. Gripping her hips, I positioned myself and thrust into her from behind in one deep stroke, burying myself to the hilt.

She cried out sharply, the sound piercing the quiet room. I clamped a hand over her mouth immediately, leaning over her, my body covering hers. "Shh, not so loud," I hissed in her ear, voice strained. "You scream like that, and someone hears? We're both fucked. Keep it down, or this little affair ends before it starts."

Her walls clenched around me like a vise, hot and soaked, pulling me in deeper. It took everything not to lose it right there. I started moving, slow at first, building rhythm. I hooked one of her legs over my arm, lifting it to open her up more. In this position, I could thrust hard while my free hand worked her clit, rubbing circles that made her shake beneath me. She whimpered brokenly, body trembling, her muffled moans vibrating against my palm.

I leaned in, breath hot against her ear. "Who do you like better? Me or that asshole Kholod?" My voice was hoarse, thrusts picking up pace.

"You," she gasped when I eased my hand off her mouth just enough.

"Liar," I snarled, slamming into her harder, the bed creaking under us. "Who is it really?"

"Kholod," she moaned, fingers digging into the sheets.

I drove deeper, relentless. "Wrong. Who am I?"

"You! Kholod, you bastard!" she screamed, voice cracking.

That did it. I pushed her fully onto the bed, face down, ass up, grabbing her waist and hauling her back against me. I pounded faster, harder, the slap of skin echoing in the room. She begged, "Slower... please, it's too much," but I bit down on her shoulder, marking her with my teeth. "Can't wait," I growled. "Been dying for this forbidden fuck all night."

I flipped her onto her side, still buried deep, one leg draped over mine for leverage. My hand roamed her breasts, pinching nipples until she arched and whined. "Imagine your husband walking in," I taunted, thrusting at an angle that hit her sweet spot. "Seeing you like this, creaming around a stranger's cock. Bet that turns you on more."

She shuddered, inner muscles fluttering, a telltale sign she was close. "Yes... god, yes," she admitted, voice wrecked. Her hands reached back, clawing at my thigh, urging me on. I obliged, sliding a finger alongside where we joined, feeling how stretched she was, how slick and desperate. The wet sounds filled the air, obscene and intoxicating.

I pulled out briefly, just to tease, rubbing my length against her entrance. "Beg for it, Mrs. Morozov. Tell your lover what you need."

"Please... fuck me," she whispered, hips bucking. "Harder. Like you own me."

Grinning darkly, I slammed back in, the side-rear position letting me control every inch. I wrapped an arm around her throat—not choking, just holding her in place—as I rutted into her. Sweat slicked our skin; her breaths came in pants, matching my grunts. I nipped at her earlobe. "You're mine tonight. Forget that prick of a husband. This pussy's clenching like it knows who it wants."

Her body tensed, orgasm crashing over her—she bit her lip to stifle the cry, walls pulsing rhythmically around me, milking every thrust. It pushed me over the edge; I buried my face in her neck, groaning low as I spilled inside her, hips jerking erratically.

But I wasn't done. The game wasn't over. I rolled us so she was on her back, me hovering above, still half-hard inside her. "Round two," I murmured, kissing down her body. My tongue traced the bruises I'd caused earlier, now mixed with fresh marks from our frenzy. She squirmed, oversensitive, but her fingers tangled in my hair, pulling me lower.

I spread her thighs wide, settling between them. "Let's see how you taste after that." My mouth descended, lapping at her soaked folds, savoring the mix of us. She bucked, moaning softly, the thrill of secrecy making it hotter. "Quiet, remember? Or the whole house knows you're cheating."

Her hands fisted the sheets as I sucked on her clit, fingers curling inside her to hit that spot again. She came undone fast, thighs clamping around my head, body arching off the bed. I didn't let up, drawing it out until she was a trembling mess.

Finally, I crawled back up, pulling her into my arms. We lay there, breaths syncing, the room heavy with the scent of sex. "Admit it," I whispered, nuzzling her neck. "You love this sneaky shit."

She turned, eyes gleaming with post-climax haze. "Maybe. But don't think this changes anything with... him."

I chuckled darkly. "Oh, it does. Because next time, we'll make it even riskier." My hand slipped between her legs again, stroking lazily. The night stretched on, our bodies entwined in this twisted play, the lines between game and reality blurring with every touch, every whispered taunt. She melted under me again and again, the stolen passion burning hotter than any legitimate claim. By dawn, we'd exhausted ourselves, collapsing in a tangle of limbs, the compass necklace forgotten on the nightstand—but its direction? Pointing straight to her, always her.

CHAPTER TWENTY-FOUR

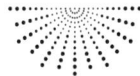

Noelle

In the darkness, I could feel every inch of my skin burning.

Kholod's weight finally lifted from me as he lay down beside me. Only our ragged breathing filled the room. My thoughts were spinning—I'd thought there was an intruder, but instead he'd claimed me in that primal way. Though it had been thrilling. The kind of thrill I actually enjoyed.

"You..." I gasped, catching sight of a box that had appeared on the nightstand.

A velvet jewelry box, gleaming softly in the moonlight.

It took me a few seconds to process what I was seeing. So all his sneaking around had been about delivering this?

I couldn't help but laugh, the sound sharp in the silence.

"What's so funny?" Kholod turned toward me, amber eyes boring into mine through the darkness.

"Nothing." I reached for the box, fingertips brushing the soft velvet. "Just never expected the great boss of the Morozov family to deliver gifts like some common thief."

His breathing hitched.

I opened the box to reveal the necklace I'd admired that afternoon. Dmitri must have told him.

"Didn't they say I had to wait a month?" I lifted the necklace, examining it with delight.

"Morozovs don't wait." His voice carried smug satisfaction.

"So bossy!"

"Whatever you want, I'll give you." The intensity in his gaze made my heart skip.

"Couldn't you just give me a gift like a normal person? Why snuck in and tried to slip away?"

"I wasn't trying to slip away." His voice was strained.

"Really?" I turned to face him, lips curving into a teasing smile. "Are you being actually shy?"

"Shut up." His warning carried no real threat.

"Seriously though." I sat up, clutching the sheet as it slipped. "I thought we had a real burglar. And you just went ahead and..."

I didn't finish, but the implication was clear.

I couldn't make out Kholod's expression in the moonlight, but I could feel his predatory stare fixed on where the sheet had fallen.

"It's late. We should sleep!" I quickly wrapped myself tighter.

"Noelle..."

"What?"

"Nothing."

He lay back down beside me, closing his eyes.

I studied his profile. Normal people just hand over gifts with a simple "this is for you." Not him—midnight room invasion, then distracted me in a weird way when caught.

The thought made me laugh again, shoulders shaking.

"Enough laughing." Kholod suddenly rolled over, pinning me again.

"No." I reached up, fingertip tracing his tense jawline. "You know what? You look even more like a pervert right now."

His breath was hot against my face, rapid and scorching. I could see fury blazing in his eyes, but strangely, I felt no fear.

"Whatever." He ground out the words.

He rolled to the far side of the bed, one arm behind his head, glaring at the ceiling.

"Kholod," I called softly. "Thank you for the gift."

The next morning, Kholod was already gone when I woke. The sheets still held his warmth and scent, proving that last night's madness hadn't been a dream.

I sat up, the necklace sliding down to my collarbone. I touched the small pendant, my lips curving involuntarily. After washing up and heading downstairs, only Anastasia and Anya were in the dining room. Kholod was obviously already handling business.

"Morning." I greeted them politely.

Anastasia looked up, her gaze lingering briefly on my throat. "Lovely necklace."

"Thank you." I sat across from her as a maid immediately served my breakfast.

Anya glanced at me. "From Kholod? He's certainly attentive to you."

"He's attentive to all his family."

Anya fell silent, and the dining room grew quiet. I started thinking about next weekend's Philadelphia Art Association gathering at Fairmont Park. I'd wanted to go since receiving the invitation, but considering Kholod's restricted list—if any banned individuals attended, would he still allow me to go?

Anxiety gnawed at me.

Go to his study and ask directly? "Kholod, I received an invitation. May I go?"—that felt too much like begging, likely earning only cold rejection or worse, that scrutinizing silence that would make me feel like a child making unreasonable demands.

Frustrated, I decided to head to the library for some peace. Perhaps I could find answers among the books, or at least temporarily forget this dilemma.

As I walked through the corridor connecting the main house to the west wing, Dmitri's familiar tall figure appeared ahead, coming from the direction of Kholod's study with a tablet in hand. We approached each other.

"Ma'am." He gave his usual expressionless nod.

"Dmitri." I nodded back, not slowing, planning to walk straight past.

But as we passed each other, he spoke in that steady, emotionless tone—casually, yet somehow deliberately. "Ma'am, regarding next week's Fairmont Park arrangements, security details have been preliminarily drafted. I'll have a car waiting for you at ten AM."

I stopped dead in my tracks, my heart clenching before racing. I spun around to face him.

Dmitri had also stopped, turning back with the same impassive expression, as if he'd merely commented on the weather.

"What did you say?"

Meeting my shocked stare, Dmitri explained. "The invitation was received and logged three days ago. When the boss reviewed this week's schedule this morning, he saw this appointment and raised no objections, instructing me to prepare your security detail in advance."

Raised no objections.

Kholod had seen the invitation. He knew I'd be attending a public event with countless strangers, and he'd permitted it.

Joy and disbelief washed away my earlier anxiety. I struggled to maintain composure, but felt my fingertips tingling.

"I... I see." I kept my voice steady. "Thank you, Dmitri."

"Just doing my job." He nodded again, then turned and walked away with measured steps.

I stood there, watching him disappear around the corner, motionless for a long time. Sunlight streamed through the tall stained glass windows, casting brilliant patterns on the floor. I reached up, touching the small pendant again—the cool metal seemed to carry warmth now.

Sunday brought exceptional sunshine. Walking into Fairmont Park with my art supplies, even the air felt sweet.

About a dozen easels were already set up on the grass, people in various casual clothes gathered in small groups discussing composition and lighting, filled with pure love for art.

"Hey! Are you new?" A cheerful female voice called from behind.

I turned to see a girl in paint-splattered denim overalls waving at me. She had fluffy golden curls and blue paint smudges on her cheeks, her smile radiant.

"I'm Zoe Harper." She approached, extending her hand without hesitation—fingers also covered in colorful paint. "And you?"

"Noelle." I shook her hand, feeling the warmth and roughness of palms clearly marked by years of holding brushes.

"Noelle who?" She tilted her head.

I hesitated. "Noelle Morozov."

"Cool! You're the legendary Mrs. Morozov?"

"Hardly that dramatic." I laughed.

She shrugged, clearly unconcerned about family backgrounds. "Come on, let's paint those cherry trees. The light's amazing—I want to try impressionist brushwork today."

Just like that, she pulled me toward a grove of cherry blossoms. We painted quietly for a while. Spring breeze stirred the petals, sending them floating like pink snow. Sunlight filtered through leaves, casting dappled shadows on the grass. We chatted while painting.

"Oh," Zoe pulled out her phone, "let's exchange contacts? When the association has more events, I'll invite you. Or you could visit my gallery—I'll treat you to coffee."

I hesitated, then gave her my number. Zoe quickly typed on her phone, then mine chimed.

"Done!" she said with satisfaction. "I'll call you whenever I discover interesting places. Philadelphia has so many fascinating corners that high society people never explore—those places hold the city's real soul."

"I'm looking forward to it."

As the sun began setting, the gathering wound down.

"See you later, Noelle." Zoe gave me a warm hug. "Remember to smile, okay?"

"I will." I hugged her back. "See you later, Zoe."

On the ride home, I sat in the car watching Philadelphia's streetscape. Dmitri's car followed like a silent shadow. But right now, I didn't mind. I touched the necklace, then checked Zoe's message.

"Had such a great time today! Looking forward to seeing you again! [heart emoji]"

The next evening, a deep blue velvet gown was delivered to my room. Elegantly cut with a perfectly designed neckline, paired with silver heels and a simple diamond bracelet.

Another dinner party, but this one was different—this was a gambling night.

When I came downstairs with my hair arranged, Kholod was already waiting in the hall. He wore his signature black three-piece suit, diamond cufflinks glinting under the lights.

"Ready?" he asked.

"Yes."

He extended his hand, palm up—a gentleman's invitation. I placed my hand in his warm, firm grip.

As our car pulled away from the manor, I spotted a familiar figure at the gate—Isabella.

She wore a flowing lavender chiffon dress, clutching a delicate handbag. Seeing our car, she immediately looked panicked and waved at us.

Kholod frowned, signaling the driver to stop.

As the window lowered, Isabella bent down, eyes slightly red. "Kholod, sorry to bother you... I wanted to return that bracelet, but you seem to be heading out..."

"What I give away is yours to keep." I knew the bracelet—Kholod had given it to Isabella specifically.

Isabella bit her lip, voice trembling. "It's too valuable. I feel uneasy keeping it. And..."

Tears welled in her eyes. "My family's all traveling, leaving me alone. Noelle knows I've always been afraid of the dark..."

Tears finally spilled over, glistening under the lights.

I sat in the back seat, emotions conflicted. Isabella had indeed been timid since childhood, always seeking my company when her parents were away. But since the Lorenzo incident, I'd felt an inexplicable distance from her.

"You don't have to return it," Kholod said curtly. "We're not available tonight. I'll have someone send you home."

"But..." Isabella turned to me, eyes pleading. "Noelle, I'm really scared of being alone. You know that... Could I..."

She didn't finish, but her meaning was clear. She wanted to come with us.

Honestly, I didn't want to agree at all. Tonight's gambling event was already making me nervous enough with Kholod bringing me along. Adding Isabella would only complicate things further.

But seeing her tear-streaked face, remembering our childhood together and how she'd kept me company through difficult times, my heart softened.

"Kholod," I spoke up quietly. "Let Isabella come along. One more person won't hurt."

Kholod turned to look at me, amber eyes boring into mine as if checking whether I was serious.

"You're sure?"

"Yes," I nodded. "Consider it helping her out. She really is afraid of being alone."

He was silent for several seconds, those eyes studying me as if trying to read my thoughts. Finally, he nodded. "Get in."

Isabella's face immediately lit up with gratitude. She quickly opened the door, sitting beside me and gripping my hand tightly. "Thank you, Noelle. I knew you wouldn't abandon me."

Her hand was warm and soft, holding tight. I managed a smile, saying nothing. The car restarted, heading toward Chestnut Hill.

Throughout the ride, Isabella chatted with Kholod. Her voice was sweet and gentle, topics ranging from recent museum exhibitions to Philadelphia social circle gossip, every word perfectly pitched— neither fawning nor creating awkward silences.

"I heard tonight's game includes Philadelphia's top business leaders," she said with curiosity and nervous undertones. "Kholod, will I embarrass you? I don't understand anything..."

"You won't," Kholod said flatly. "Just stay to the side."

"That's a relief." Isabella sighed, then turned to me. "Noelle, are you nervous? I'm super nervous—I've never been to anything like this."

"I'm fine."

Actually, I was very nervous, but didn't want to show it in front of her.

The car traveled down a long tree-lined drive, finally stopping before a brightly lit classical manor. Kholod helped me out as usual, with Isabella naturally following behind as the three of us walked toward the manor.

Doormen respectfully opened the entrance, revealing low conversation and elegant classical music inside. The hall was vast, luxuriously but tastefully decorated. Several tables covered in deep green felt occupied the center, surrounded by well-dressed men and women.

"Mr. Kholod." A middle-aged man in a charcoal suit approached with a beaming smile. "Your presence truly honors us."

"Peterson." Kholod nodded coolly, tone businesslike.

"And this is..." Peterson's gaze fell on me with the appraising look of someone evaluating merchandise, making me uncomfortable.

"My wife, Noelle." Kholod's arm tightened, pulling me closer to his side.

"Mrs. Morozov is truly beautiful." Peterson offered pleasantries, then looked at Isabella. "And this is..."

"My friend," I answered before Kholod could.

Peterson smiled, gesturing us forward. "The game will begin shortly, Mr. Kholod. Your seat is at table three. Follow me."

We followed him across the hall. I could feel countless gazes on us —specifically on me. Those looks held curiosity, assessment, scrutiny, making me feel exposed.

At table three, Kholod sat down with Isabella and me behind him.

"Stay close to me. Don't act rashly. Just watch."

He pushed a stack of platinum-edged ivory chips toward me—each worth a fortune, the total enough to change an ordinary person's life. I quietly accepted them.

The game was classic showhand. The opponent was Karl Winterlaub, a middle-aged man who'd inherited railroad wealth and radiated arrogance from his fingertips. He had significant port trade disputes with Kholod. The stakes were staggering, each betting round like a small merger. Kholod remained impassive, but I knew he hated losing, especially in front of potential business rivals.

After several hands, I noticed an extremely subtle habit of Winterlaub's. Whenever his hole card was an ace—especially when he needed it to complete a strong hand—his right ring finger would unconsciously tap once against the soft felt table edge, with consistent rhythm.

This movement was so hidden it was nearly imperceptible. Without the compulsive attention to detail I'd developed from living in oppressive environments, it would be impossible to detect. Was he using this to signal hidden accomplices in the game? Or was it merely an unconscious tell revealing his inner state?

Another crucial hand was dealt. Kholod's face-up cards looked good, but Winterlaub's visible cards were equally strong. The air grew tense. When Winterlaub's turn came, he pushed forward an eye-watering stack of chips with a confident smirk.

Just as he completed this action and lowered his hand, that ring finger tapped once more against the table edge.

My heart skipped a beat.

Kholod was about to call. Just as his fingers nearly touched his chips, I raised my champagne glass, pretending to sip, while my other hand, hidden beneath the table, quickly and discreetly traced a clear "A" in Kholod's palm with my fingertip.

His body went imperceptibly rigid for an instant. He didn't turn to look at me, showed no expression change, didn't even alter his breathing rhythm. But his hand stopped, then casually withdrew.

"Mr. Winterlaub," Kholod's voice remained steady but carried an icy smile, "You're really on fire today. Why don't we make it more interesting?" Instead of calling, he pushed forward chips worth nearly double the current pot—a massive raise.

This was an extremely risky move, completely inconsistent with his previous playing style. Winterlaub's confidence immediately cracked, staring at Kholod in disbelief, panic flickering in his eyes. He hesitated, then, after long consideration, folded with a grim expression.

Kholod didn't even show his hole cards, simply collecting all the chips on the table. He didn't need to reveal his hand—his action had declared everything. Winterlaub's rhythm was shattered, his confidence seemingly crumbling with it.

In the following hands, Kholod moved like a precise predator, tightening his grip. Eventually, Winterlaub not only lost all his liquid assets but signed a promissory note devastating enough to cripple his core industries.

When the game ended, we moved to the banquet hall. Soft lighting, flowing jazz, elegant socializing. But the looks directed at me were completely different now. Probing, surprised, even slightly awed.

Several powerful-looking men approached Kholod with their drinks.

"Brilliant reversal, Kholod." A gray-haired elder said meaningfully, his gaze falling on me like a searchlight. "Your wife has very sharp eyes. Mr. Morozov certainly keeps talented people close."

Kholod remained noncommittal, slightly shifting to shelter me in his shadow, his arm wrapping around my waist with undeniable possession.

I stood quietly beside him, enduring those stares, champagne bubbles rising steadily in my glass. I knew my unconscious action had not only helped Kholod win the game, but had also dropped a small but significant stone into this lake of power.

CHAPTER TWENTY-FIVE

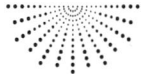

Kholod

I cradled my wine glass, ostensibly discussing port transportation deals with Peterson, but my attention was locked entirely on Noelle at my side.

She was in that deep blue velvet gown, the strapless design exposing her rounded shoulders and toned arms. The tailoring was impeccable, accentuating her slender waist and elegant curves. She stood there like a finely sculpted work of art.

That's exactly why those men's eyes swarmed over her like flies, unapologetic and blatant.

I noticed the old oil magnate, his stare practically glued to Noelle's bare collarbone. And that young banker lounging by the bar, eyeing her profile with a lecherous smirk.

My fingers clenched, the rim of the glass biting into my palm.

I wanted to carve those eyes right out.

"Mrs. Morozov has real talent," Williams remarked, his gaze lingering on Noelle. "I've been navigating these circles for decades and missed that sly fox's cheating entirely. But you caught it in an instant."

My arm tightened around her instinctively, pulling her even closer to my side.

"You're too kind," Noelle replied evenly.

"You're a pro at spotting casino sleight of hand—not something you pick up casually. Looks like we'll need you at every one of these from here on out." Williams gave me a pointed glance.

I'd been reluctant to bring Noelle along, but the hosts had specifically invited her, and after the Lorenzo fallout, we had to mend the family's reputation. I knew my world meant she couldn't avoid these events, but fury still churned in my chest.

She was exceptional. No question. She despised the wheeling and dealing, the ostentatious jewels, but her composure never faltered in any setting. That's precisely why I wanted to stash her away, out of sight from anyone else.

I was on the verge of tearing into the idiot when Isabella beat me to it.

"Oh, you're so insightful! Noelle's incredible!" Her voice dripped with sweetness, her eyes wide with awe. "I was just sitting there, totally lost and panicking. But Noelle saw through it right away."

She cozied up to Noelle, linking their arms with a radiant smile. "You must've been around this stuff since you were little, huh? Unlike me—I was clueless, just sat there and looked pretty. If I had even half your brains, every guy here would be head over heels for me!"

The moment Isabella's words landed, my rage peaked. I had no idea if Noelle had been exposed to this world as a kid—and if she had, so what? But her sharpness was pulling in those repulsive stares.

I started resenting her for drawing attention. Hell, it even dredged up thoughts of her deadbeat gambler father—why the hell had she learned any of it? Did she enjoy those men's leering? Was she trying to manipulate them somehow?

The ideas collided in my mind, and I found myself questioning if she was calculating—even though, deep down, I knew she wasn't.

"Kholod?"

Sensing my prolonged silence, she called my name softly, her voice laced with hesitation and worry.

I avoided her gaze, turning to Isabella instead and softening my tone slightly. "It's late. Let's get you home."

"What?" Isabella paused, then shifted to a remorseful expression. "I'm sorry—did I mess up? I just meant Noelle's so talented... I blurt things out without thinking. If I overstepped—"

Her eyes welled up, tears glistening as if she might burst into sobs.

"It's not about you," I interrupted. "Let's go."

Noelle abruptly clutched my sleeve. "Kholod, I—"

"We'll discuss it at home," I snapped, shrugging her off, my voice like steel.

At that point, anger had devoured my rationality. Nothing was getting through.

I didn't let Dmitri drive on the way back; I took the wheel myself, racing toward the manor. Isabella rode shotgun, occasionally glancing back at Noelle with unspoken words hovering on her lips.

Through the rearview mirror, I glimpsed Noelle. She slumped against the seat, eyes shut, her dress's hem creased, the skin of her shoulders gleaming a pale white under the passing streetlights.

Those men's gazes... My grip on the steering wheel turned vise-like.

We reached Isabella's street quickly. I stopped at her door and motioned for her to exit.

"Thanks for dropping me off, Kholod." Before leaving, she turned to Noelle once more. "Goodnight, Noelle. I... I'm truly sorry."

Noelle opened her eyes and managed a weak smile. "Goodnight, Isabella."

The door clicked shut, leaving just the two of us in the confined space.

I revved the engine, accelerating even faster than before.

"Kholod." Her voice floated from the back seat, weary and imploring. "I only noticed the cheating by chance. I was just trying to help you—"

"Help me?" I scoffed, whipping around to face her. "You take me for a fool, Noelle?"

"I didn't—"

"Your family runs underground casinos. You expect me to believe you don't know the ropes? It was all just a 'coincidence'?" My volume escalated. "Parading your skills in front of all those men—you thrilled? Reveling in how they undress you with their eyes?"

The accusation spilled out, and in the mirror, her face drained of color, tears shimmering in her eyes. Her lips parted, but no words came. The sight pierced me—I knew I shouldn't have gone there.

"Noelle, I didn't..."

"Stop the car!"

"Noelle, it's too late out..."

"Stop! Let me out!"

She unfastened her seatbelt, fumbling for the door handle, her glare burning with fury. Fearing she'd escalate, I decelerated and pulled into a scenic overlook on the Benjamin Franklin Bridge.

Noelle flung the door open, darted out nimbly, and slammed it behind her before striding away.

I bolted from the car, catching up and seizing her wrist.

"Noelle, hear me out—"

She spun around. "Fine! Yeah, I love their attention! I crave everyone staring! I picked it up from my dad—are you satisfied?"

I knew it was all bluster, but her words dredged up those clingy stares again. All I wanted was to shield her, keep her hidden from the world.

I hauled her by the waist into my embrace.

"Kholod, cut the crazy!" She thrashed, even attempting a kick.

I locked her in place; escape was impossible, so she sank her teeth into my shoulder. The bite was mild—like a kitten's scratch—and her soft, supple body writhing against mine only ignited a fiercer hunger to consume her completely.

"Kholod, you lunatic, what the fuck? I try to help and I'm the villain? I—"

I silenced her relentless chatter with a kiss, ensnaring her tongue—the source of all that aggravating fire—and sucking fiercely. She attempted to evade, but I held firm. In retaliation, she bit down on my tongue. I recoiled from the sting—damn, she was bite-happy tonight. My heart, my flesh.

"Calmed down?" I asked.

She said nothing, averting her face, though the fight had ebbed from her.

I drew her nearer, her form melding against mine. I was achingly hard. Noelle clearly felt it. She went rigid, her irritation morphing into incredulity.

"Kholod, you... seriously, even now?" A flush bloomed on her cheeks, tempting me to nip. And I did just that.

Noelle seethed, squirming wildly in my hold, shoving at my chest. In the tussle, her strapless dress slipped lower, revealing a tantalizing glimpse of cleavage.

Desire overwhelmed me. I hoisted her up, striding two paces to the bridge's railing and pinning her against it.

"Kholod! We're in public! Don't—"

I claimed her mouth, reducing her objections to muffled whimpers.

I tugged her zipper down, giving a sharp pull, and the bodice dropped to her waist. Clever design—no bra needed. Her creamy breasts sprang free, the tattoo of my name boldly etched on her skin.

A chill breeze swept by, her nipples pebbling into stiff points. I released her lips, lowering my head to nip and lave them.

Her delicate moans only hardened me further.

"See this?" I murmured, tracing the tattoo with my tongue. "You're branded with my mark, yet you dare entertain thoughts of other men —a whole crowd of them."

She parted her lips, likely to hurl more barbs, but I wanted only moans from that mouth. My hand delved beneath her dress. A thong tonight—simple to nudge the flimsy lace aside. She was drenched.

I spun her around, clamping a hand over her mouth before she could protest, and aligned myself.

"Look at this city," I whispered in her ear. "It's my domain. And you're my woman. No matter what schemes brew in that head of yours, you belong to me alone."

I brushed off her muffled curses—labeling me a pervert, a freak, all that. One hand kneaded her breast, pinching and rolling the rigid peak, while the other ventured lower, stroking her slick, swollen folds. "Gonna fuck you right here," I growled. "You like that, Noelle? Getting railed out in the open, exposed for anyone to see?"

She shot me a glare over her shoulder, eyes blazing. But they were edged with red, her body quivering under my caresses, fresh waves of arousal slicking my fingers. I knew she was aroused, secretly thrilled. Satisfaction flooded me.

"Want it?" I teased, circling her clit with deliberate pressure. "Be honest, and I'll give you what you need."

Stubborn as ever, she refused to speak. So I persisted, teasing her relentlessly, then gripped the icy railing to cool my hand before plunging my fingers inside her. The frosty shock made her gasp and arch.

"I want it," she finally breathed, her voice fracturing.

"Good girl," I murmured approvingly, withdrawing my hand. Without delay, I freed myself and drove into her from behind, sinking deep in one powerful thrust.

I pounded hard, each stroke merciless, shattering her fragmented curses into breathless gasps. "Fucking... pervert..." she stuttered, but my relentless rhythm splintered her words into moans.

"You dare let them ogle you like that again?" I demanded, hips slamming forward. "This filthy, dripping side of you—begging for it— is mine alone to witness. Admit it." I plunged deeper. "Who owns this greedy little cunt? Who turns you into such a soaked mess?"

She couldn't form a response, just whimpered, her inner walls gripping me tight.

I seized her breast, guiding the taut nipple to graze the cold railing. "Like that? The freeze tormenting your sensitive tip while I fuck you raw?"

Her moans flowed endlessly, but the way she clenched around me revealed her delight. It fueled my excitement, my thrusts growing fiercer, slamming her against the barrier.

Noelle tossed out broken curses—"You bastard... so damn rough..."—the kind that teased and tempted, only heightening my arousal. I spanked her ass, the crack echoing in the night. "Louder, sweetheart. Let me hear you scream."

She clamped her teeth together, resisting. I pressed her forward, her entire chest flush against the railing, the cool metal abrading her nipples with every punishing drive.

At last, she shattered—piercing cries and moans erupting. "Okay, I love it! Please... Kholod, it's overwhelming!"

Only then did I relent, but not before the dress became a nuisance, bunching up and hindering my access. With a snarl, I gripped the fabric and ripped it savagely down the seam, tearing it apart to spread her legs wider, allowing me to bury myself even deeper.

Her body trembled with each brutal thrust, the bridge's lights casting flickering shadows over us as I claimed her utterly. The city stretched out below, indifferent, but this moment was ours—raw, vulnerable, entirely mine.

I kept the filthy whispers coming, reminding her she'd never invite another man's gaze. "Feel me stretching you? Every thick inch owning you. You're mine to fuck, mine to brand. Pull that stunt again, and I'll bend you over right in front of them—prove exactly who you belong to."

Noelle's retorts dissolved into panting pleas, her defiance crumbling under the onslaught of pleasure. I clutched her hips, angling to strike that perfect spot, making her back bow and her cries intensify. The railing's chill against her skin heightened it all, her nipples scraping the metal in sync with my rhythm, sending electric shivers through her that I could feel pulsing around me.

"You adore being my filthy little secret, don't you? Bent over here, stuffed full of my cock like the eager slut you are." I delivered another sharp smack to her ass, demanding more. "Scream my name, Noelle. Let the entire bridge know how desperately you crave this."

She tried to hold back, jaw tight, but I ground her harder against the rail, the unyielding friction on her peaks merciless. Her moans built to outright screams, her body spasming as she pleaded, "Yes, Kholod! I love it... don't stop!"

That capitulation sent me spiraling, but I prolonged it, relishing every plunge, every gasp. The tattered dress dangled uselessly now, leaving her bare to the night breeze. I savored her exposure, her heat clamping down with each lewd query. "Still fantasizing about those stares? Or is my cock the only thing that gets you this wet?" She couldn't speak, just nodded wildly, adrift in ecstasy.

I shifted tempos—slow, grinding depths to torment, then rapid, punishing slams—her curses morphing into affectionate taunts: "You animal... give it to me harder..." It spurred me on. Another firm spank to her flushing cheeks, and she yelped even louder, the noise blending with the far-off city drone.

Finally, as she quivered on the brink, I unleashed fully, propelling us both to climax. Her orgasm crashed first, her walls milking me in rhythmic waves, drawing out my own release amid her echoing screams across the bridge.

Once it was over, Noelle practically melted in my arms. The dress was in ruins, and she had no energy left for fighting or swearing. At last, she could actually hear me.

I slipped off my jacket and draped it around her, holding her snugly.

I recognized my loss of control. It happened every time with Noelle. In that game, she'd simply spotted the cheat with her keen eye and warned me—there was nothing wrong with that.

I replayed the evening in detail. Her gaze had stayed fixed on me, tracking every subtle shift in my expression. Only when I furrowed my brow did she turn to the table, then immediately signaled me.

She was looking out for me. That inner light wasn't performative; it was innate, radiant no matter how I tried to dim it.

Then Isabella's line resurfaced—"If I had half your smarts, all the guys here would be falling over me!" That had ignited my explosion. She delivered it with innocent flair, but if it wasn't deliberate, why had it provoked me so intensely?

Connecting it to my prior doubts about Isabella, my eyes narrowed. Tonight's true danger might not have been at the card table at all.

This so-called "savior" was far from straightforward.

"Noelle, I didn't mean..." I wanted to apologize for my heated outburst. But my pride sealed my lips.

"Fine, fine, I get it. Kholod, can we head back? I'm freezing." Noelle rolled her eyes.

"Right away." I lifted her carefully, carrying her to the car without a thought for my own state.

I bundled her in a blanket, activated the seat warmer, and secured her belt. Seeing her relaxed and content against the cushion eased me. I straightened myself, stowed the shredded dress, then settled into the driver's seat and steered us toward the manor.

CHAPTER TWENTY-SIX

Noelle

"Noelle, are you free today? There's this amazing antique shop on South Street that just got in a collection of Victorian picture frames. You'd absolutely love them!"

Zoe's energetic voice bubbled through my phone. I sat on the edge of my bed, gazing out at the manor's gardens, hesitating.

A week had passed since that poker game. Kholod had been... different. Still unpredictable as ever, but that suffocating need to control everything seemed to have eased up. Yesterday, he'd even asked if I wanted to join the family hiking trip. If it hadn't been for my period, I might've actually said yes.

"I'm not sure," I said quietly. "I'd need to ask—"

"Ask Kholod?" Zoe's voice carried a note of concern. "Noelle, you can always be honest with me. If something's wrong..."

"Nothing's wrong." I cut her off. "It's just... protocol."

After hanging up, I stood there for a moment. This would be my second outing this week. Would Kholod even agree?

Finally, I worked up the courage to go downstairs and find him. He was in his study with Dmitri, discussing business. When he saw me, he gestured for Dmitri to leave.

"What is it?" He looked up, those amber eyes settling on me.

"Zoe asked me to go shopping today. If you don't want me to—"

"Go." He cut me off, his tone flat but decisive. "Dmitri will arrange a car and security. Be back by six for dinner."

I stared at him, certain I'd misheard.

"You're saying yes?"

"Stay safe." He was already looking back at his papers.

* * *

SOUTH STREET WAS one of Philadelphia's most artistic neighborhoods. Narrow streets lined with every kind of shop imaginable—tattoo parlors, vintage stores, independent bookshops, coffee shops... The air was thick with the aroma of coffee and the sound of street music.

Zoe was already waiting by the antique shop, wearing ripped jeans and a T-shirt with some abstract design, her hair thrown up in a messy ponytail. Her smile was as bright as sunshine.

"You made it!" She rushed over and enveloped me in a huge hug. "God, I was starting to think you'd be trapped in that big manor forever."

"I was starting to think that too."

She pulled me into the shop. "Look at these frames! The owner says he got them from an estate auction in England. All hand-carved —the details are so exquisite they'll make you weep."

The little shop was crammed with antiques—old typewriters, phonographs, paintings, china... Every piece carried the patina of years.

The elderly man with round glasses brightened when he saw Zoe. "Miss Harper, brought a friend?"

"This is Noelle, the one I told you about." Zoe introduced me enthusiastically.

The old man studied me appraisingly. "Does look like an artist. Come on, the frames are in the back."

We followed him to the rear of the shop. Against the wall stood about a dozen picture frames, each one beautifully carved—some with elaborate Baroque flourishes, others with cleaner neoclassical lines.

"Wow!" I couldn't help but gasp.

"Right?" Zoe leaned in close. "I knew you'd love them. Look at this one—see how detailed the roses are? You can even make out the texture of the petals."

I reached out to trace the carvings, feeling the warmth and grain of the wood beneath my fingertips. How many years had these frames witnessed? What paintings had they once displayed? Who had cherished them?

"Noelle, what are you thinking about?" Zoe asked.

"I'm wondering where all the paintings that used to be in these frames are now."

Zoe blinked, then laughed. "You always think of things no one else does. That's the artist's soul, I suppose."

"Maybe."

"Oh, Noelle, guess what!" Zoe picked up an old palette, practically vibrating with excitement. "I just landed this incredible project—painting a mural on a wall down by Fisherman's Wharf! Five whole stories tall!"

"God, how long will that take?"

"At least three months." She shrugged. "But the pay's fantastic, and I get complete creative freedom. The client just wants something ocean-themed. Everything else is up to me."

"That sounds incredible!"

"It really is," Zoe grinned. "Though I had an epic battle with the gallery owner about the exhibition layout. That old codger insisted on hanging my paintings in the corner, muttering something about 'maintaining overall aesthetic harmony.' I told him straight up—either display them prominently, or I withdraw. Guess what happened?"

"He caved?"

"Of course!" Zoe lifted her chin proudly. "Artists need backbone, or people will steamroll right over you."

"Speaking of which, how's Lily doing? Last time you mentioned she was sick." Lily was Zoe's orange tabby cat.

"She's completely recovered, but she caused absolute chaos."

"What happened?"

"That little demon punctured a whole tube of my brand-new cadmium yellow paint while I wasn't looking, then tore through the house like a maniac. Now there are yellow paw prints on every surface imaginable." Zoe looked simultaneously exasperated and amused. "It took me an entire day to clean up the mess."

"Did you scold her?" I asked, laughing.

"Of course not, I couldn't bear to." Zoe sighed. "I've had her for three years. No matter how mischievous she gets, she's still my baby."

Her words made me laugh, and I felt unusually lighthearted.

"You mentioned wanting to see landscapes from around the world, right?"

"Yes."

"I have a photographer friend who's traveled to nearly every continent. She has thousands of photos. I should introduce you two sometime. She says every location has its own unique quality of light—completely distinctive."

"That would be wonderful! If I could see the photos, even better." My eyes lit up.

"Absolutely!" Zoe patted my shoulder. "We could organize a little gathering—coffee, photos, art talk. You could bring your paintings too, and we could all share ideas."

"I can hardly wait!"

"Slow down there, Noelle. She's currently communing with penguins in Antarctica. Won't be back until later this year."

"What a shame."

Zoe shrugged, and we wandered through several more shops, collecting art supplies and small treasures. When we grew tired, we ducked into a corner café.

The café was intimate, maybe six or seven tables, with walls covered in local artists' work. We ordered coffee and pastries, claiming a table by the window.

"Noelle," Zoe stirred her coffee thoughtfully, "have you ever considered... starting fresh?"

"What do you mean?"

"I mean the travel blog, the painting—the things you're actually passionate about." She looked at me earnestly. "I can see this isn't the life you want. Why not change it?"

"Change..." I smiled ruefully. "It's not that simple."

"Why isn't it?" Zoe challenged. "Noelle, you're still young. You're two years younger than me, for crying out loud. You have plenty of time to pursue the life you actually want."

"I'll think about it," I said softly.

Just then, my phone rang. Isabella.

I stared at the name on the screen, hesitated for several seconds, then answered.

"Noelle!" Isabella's voice was honey-sweet and effusive. "Are you free today? There's this gorgeous new boutique that opened near Rittenhouse Square. Want to explore it together? We haven't had a proper girls' day in ages. I miss you so much."

I opened my mouth to respond, but scenes from that poker night flashed through my mind—how her seemingly innocent comments had twisted my kindness into calculated manipulation, ultimately sparking that explosive confrontation between Kholod and me. Suddenly, the thought of spending time with her felt exhausting.

"Sorry, Isabella." I tried to keep my voice natural. "I already have plans today. Perhaps another time."

Silence stretched across the line.

"Oh... I see." Isabella's voice deflated noticeably. "All right then, another time. Are you with Zoe? You two have grown quite close."

"Yes."

"Well, I won't keep you then." Her voice grew smaller. "Goodbye."

"Goodbye."

I hung up and found Zoe watching me intently.

"Friend of yours?" she asked.

"Yes, we've known each other since childhood." I felt a complex mix of emotions.

"You don't really want to see her?" Zoe's intuition was sharp.

After a moment's silence, I nodded. "She's... changed recently."

Zoe didn't press for details, simply squeezed my hand. "Then trust your instincts."

Looking into her genuine eyes, I felt my throat tighten with emotion.

"Thank you, Zoe," I said quietly. "Thank you for being my friend."

"Don't be silly," she smiled warmly. "We are friends. The lasting kind. Now, try this cake—they make it absolutely divine here."

I returned to the manor at four o'clock. Walking into the foyer with my shopping bags, Darya informed me dinner would be at six and suggested I rest in my room first.

I took a long shower and changed into a simple dress—Kholod had finally abandoned his silk fixation. The dresses he'd been selecting lately were all cotton, exactly as I preferred.

Standing before the mirror, arranging my hair, I noticed the color in my cheeks and the brightness in my eyes. I felt genuinely happy. When I was with Zoe, I could temporarily forget all the oppression and pain, simply be an ordinary girl who loved painting and traveling.

Perhaps this was what true friendship meant—no need for defensiveness or second-guessing, just being together naturally, sharing happiness and sorrow.

And Isabella...

Thinking about that brief silence on the phone stirred complicated feelings. We'd been friends since childhood—she'd been there for me through the darkest period after Father's death. But since my marriage to Kholod, everything had been subtly shifting. I understood her love of luxury, but I'd never imagined it would transform her into someone so... unfamiliar.

Maybe this, too, was part of growing up—learning to distinguish who was truly worth trusting.

"Ma'am, dinner is served," Darya announced from my doorway.

"I'll be right there."

Today, Kholod had miraculously arrived punctually for dinner. The staff filed in, presenting course after course of elegant dishes. The first was French onion soup, its aroma filling the air.

I politely tasted a spoonful, then grimaced slightly. Far too much thyme—that overpowering herb made my stomach turn. But I said nothing, simply set down my spoon and waited for the next course.

"Replace her soup." Kholod's voice cut through the quiet, calm but brooking no argument.

Everyone froze.

The staff exchanged bewildered glances, unclear about what had transpired.

"Sir, is there an issue with the soup?" the chef inquired cautiously.

"She doesn't like it." Kholod didn't even glance at the offending bowl, stating matter-of-factly, "Bring her a clear broth instead."

I gaped at him in astonishment. How could he possibly know I disliked the flavor? I hadn't uttered a word.

Anya's spoon remained suspended mid-air as she stared at us in disbelief, then silently resumed eating. Anastasia lowered her napkin, the ghost of a smile playing at her lips.

Within five minutes, a bowl of simple chicken broth seasoned only with salt and pepper appeared before me. Its clean, delicate fragrance was exactly what I loved.

"Thank you," I murmured.

Kholod made no response, simply continued with his meal as if what had just occurred was perfectly routine.

Dinner proceeded in a peculiar atmosphere. Kholod maintained his impassive expression, but I noticed he barely touched his own food, spending most of the time observing whether I was eating properly.

The second course was pan-seared cod with asparagus, the third roasted lamb, the fourth dessert—raspberry mousse. Each dish was exquisite and delicious. For once, I had a genuine appetite and ate more than usual. I caught the corner of Kholod's mouth twitching upward almost imperceptibly.

After dinner, Kholod departed first.

"Noelle," Anastasia called to me. "Walk with me a moment."

I followed her to her private sitting room. Though I'd been here before, I was still struck by the refined décor. Classical oil paintings adorned the walls, while the shelves held leather-bound volumes. A fire crackled in the fireplace, and the air carried hints of sandalwood.

She gestured for me to sit, then settled gracefully on the opposite sofa with her tea.

"Your work in the collection room has been exemplary," she began. "Far exceeding my expectations. You're both patient and meticulous. The cataloging of those pieces is flawless—I couldn't find fault if I tried."

"Thank you."

"I've been considering," she set down her teacup, her gaze gentle, "perhaps it's time you became involved in family affairs. Kholod carries an enormous burden, and many responsibilities require our support. You must fully understand how this family functions and what protocols govern us."

I was stunned. "You mean..."

"Naturally, this will require preparation time. You may ready yourself accordingly."

"I'll prepare thoroughly."

She nodded approvingly, then her tone warmed. "Do visit me more often for conversation. Anya is constantly occupied with her design company. You could share discoveries from organizing the collection, or discuss your artistic insights. I was passionate about art in my youth, though I was forced to abandon it later."

A flicker of wistfulness crossed her features before quickly fading.

"I will," I said sincerely. "Thank you... Mother?"

"Oh, maybe just Ana." My form of address brought a soft smile to her face. "Go now, rest well."

In the hallway, I encountered Anya heading upstairs. Seeing me, she paused mid-step.

"Anya," I called out.

She turned, eyebrows drawing together slightly. "What?"

I approached quickly, withdrawing a folded paper from my dress pocket.

"This is for you." I felt nervous butterflies. "I often see you browsing jewelry magazines. While cataloging the collection, I noticed the iris pattern on the Faberge egg was stunning, so I sketched out a design. Perhaps it might inspire you."

Anya unfolded the paper with suspicion. I'd merged classical iris motifs with contemporary lines, creating a brooch design with careful notations about petal layering and gemstone placement.

She studied it for so long I was certain she'd tear it up and fling it back at me.

"It's... okay, I suppose." Her tone remained frigid.

But I noticed her fingertips delicately tracing the paper's edges, the gesture almost reverent.

"If you don't care for it—"

"Who said I don't care for it?" She interrupted sharply, turning away with obvious discomfort. "I didn't say it was terrible."

She carefully refolded the paper and tucked it into her handbag, securing the zipper.

"Well... thanks." Her voice was barely audible.

"You're welcome." I smiled warmly.

Anya regarded me with a complex expression, seeming about to speak, but ultimately just turned and ascended the stairs.

Back in my room behind closed doors, I leaned against the wood and exhaled deeply. The warmth blooming in my chest told me this house was gradually opening its arms to embrace me.

CHAPTER TWENTY-SEVEN

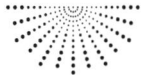

Kholod

"Boss, there's a meeting at three this afternoon about the East Coast collaboration—"

"Reschedule it." I cut Dmitri off, snapping the file shut in front of me. "They're still being evasive. We don't need to push."

"Understood."

"That's all for today." I grabbed my coat. "Contact me only if it's an emergency."

"Yes, sir."

I stepped out of the dock's control room and got into the car.

"Home."

The car wound through Philadelphia's streets. I gazed out the window, but my mind kept replaying one scene—Noelle last night at the dinner table, sipping her soup in small, delicate bites. She cradled the bowl of clear broth I'd specially requested from the kitchen, her lashes casting faint shadows on her eyelids, a subtle smile playing at the corners of her mouth.

It was a faint smile, so subtle you'd miss it if you weren't paying attention. But I noticed.

I found myself paying more attention to these little details about her—what she liked, what she disliked, what made her smile, what made her frown.

This kind of fixation felt utterly alien to me.

The car pulled into the manor. I got out and entered the hall. The maid bowed respectfully, and I casually asked, "Where's Noelle?"

"Boss, she's in the library."

I headed toward the library, but paused at the doorway.

Noelle was curled up on the sofa, lying on her side, hands pillowed under her cheek, fast asleep. Her legs were slightly bent, a thin blanket draped over her, her slender ankle exposed.

A thick art book lay open on her lap, titled Wonders of the World. It was turned to a page featuring photos of Norway's fjords—deep blue waters, sheer cliffs rising on either side, distant snow-capped mountains.

The light bathed her hair in a soft golden halo. Her sleeping face was serene and vulnerable, long lashes casting shadows on her cheeks, lips slightly parted, her breathing steady and gentle.

I stood there, watching her, suddenly unsure of what to do next.

This woman—the one I'd imprisoned, tormented, and hurt—now appeared heartbreakingly beautiful in my eyes.

I approached quietly and sat on the armrest beside her.

She didn't stir, just shifted slightly into a more comfortable position. The book nearly slipped from her knee. I caught it and flipped through a few pages.

Each page had small sticky notes attached, filled with her elegant handwriting—"Norway, Lofoten Islands, best viewing March-April," "New Zealand, glowworm caves, advance booking required," "Morocco, Chefchaouen blue town, perfect for photos"...

She'd annotated every location meticulously, planning trips that might never come to pass.

My fingers lingered on the Norway page, reminding me of the necklace—the compass pendant I'd given her.

She still wore it. Even after that brutal night on the bridge, she kept it on.

My hand rose involuntarily, yearning to touch her cheek. My

fingertips hovered just above her skin, sensing the faint warmth of her breath.

But at the last moment, I pulled back. These hands had harmed her, tortured her, caused her endless tears.

I leaned back on the sofa, simply watching her in silence. I lost track of time—maybe ten minutes, maybe half an hour. I just observed, listening to her even breathing, basking in this rare moment of tranquility.

It felt strange.

In my world, peace always carried an undercurrent of vigilance. Every lull was merely the prelude to the next storm. But watching her now, I experienced genuine calm.

I began to examine my own emotions.

Initially, my obsession had been with pursuing the phantom savior from my memories, believing she could fill the void inside me. Only now did I realize I'd never truly known Noelle—not as my rescuer, not as the Bellucci daughter, not as my captive or wife.

She was simply a soul passionate about painting and distant horizons, resilient yet fragile, clinging to hope even in despair. And I'd responded to that purity with confinement, suspicion, and pain.

Noelle shifted, letting out a soft murmur. I froze, thinking she was waking.

But she merely rolled over, facing me, and continued sleeping.

Her cheek bore a faint red imprint from resting against her arm. A few strands of hair clung to her face, quivering lightly with each breath.

I raised my hand again and gently tucked those strands behind her ear.

Her skin was warm and soft, the contact making my heart skip a beat.

"Noelle," I whispered her name.

Her lashes fluttered, and she slowly opened her eyes. Those brown eyes were still hazy with sleep, gazing at me in confusion.

"Kholod?" Her voice was raspy from slumber. "When did you get back?"

"Just now," I replied. "You were asleep."

"Sorry, I..." She sat up, hastily smoothing her hair and skirt. "I was reading and got tired, and I just..."

"No need to apologize," I interrupted. "This is your home. You can rest wherever you like."

She paused, a flash of disbelief in her eyes.

I picked up the art book from her lap and turned to a page. "You want to visit these places?"

She followed my finger to the photo of Iceland's blue ice cave. Her eyes immediately sparkled.

"Yes," she said softly. "I've always wanted to see them."

"Then let's go."

"What?"

"I said, let's go." I closed the book, locking eyes with her. "Wherever you want, I'll take you."

Her eyes widened, as if she couldn't believe her ears. "Are... are you serious?"

"I don't joke about this." I stood up. "Pack your things. We leave tomorrow."

She stared at me, the light in her eyes growing brighter. Then, before I could react, she leaped from the sofa and flung herself into my arms.

"Really? We can actually go?" Her voice trembled with excitement.

My body stiffened for a moment. She hugged me tightly, her face buried in my chest, her warm breath seeping through my shirt onto my skin.

"Really," I said, slowly wrapping my arms around her waist. "I never break a promise."

She looked up at me, those brown eyes brimming with joy and something else I didn't dare identify.

Then, she rose on her tiptoes and brushed a light kiss across my lips.

It was brief, like a dragonfly skimming water, tentative and shy.

But in that instant, my heart seemed to stop.

She pulled back quickly, cheeks flushing, head lowering. "Sorry, I got carried away..."

"Don't apologize," I said, my voice rough.

I cupped the back of her head with my hand, leaned down, and kissed her again. When we parted, her face was as red as a ripe apple, her breathing rapid.

"Go pack," I said, gently stroking her cheek. "I'll have Dmitri arrange everything."

"Okay." She nodded, that glow in her eyes captivating me.

The next morning, we boarded my private jet.

Noelle stood at the cabin entrance, staring at the Gulfstream G650, eyes wide with astonishment.

"This is yours?"

"Yes." I took her hand and led her inside. "From now on, you can use it anytime you want to travel."

"Oh my God..." she whispered. "I've never seen a plane this luxurious."

I glanced around—the cream leather seats, the solid wood coffee table, a small bar. At the rear, a private bedroom with a large bed.

"Just the basics," I said, guiding her to a window seat. "Once we're airborne, you can watch the sea of clouds."

She sat obediently, fastening her seatbelt. I settled beside her, watching her eyes shine with excitement, my lips curving into a smile without effort.

The plane taxied, accelerated, and soared into the sky.

Noelle pressed against the window, watching the ground structures give way to clouds, then an endless expanse of white, her wonder never fading.

"It's so beautiful..." she murmured. "It's been ages since I've seen anything like this..."

"I'm glad you like it."

She turned to me, eyes glistening with emotion. "Thank you, Kholod. Really... thank you."

"No problem," I said, taking her hand. "It's what I should have done." Should have done much sooner.

The plane reached cruising altitude, the flight steadying. The flight attendant brought champagne and snacks, then tactfully withdrew to the front cabin.

Noelle unbuckled her seatbelt and returned to gazing at the clouds. Sunlight poured through the window, making her entire being seem to glow.

I watched her intently—the excited flush on her cheeks, her slightly parted lips, those eyes overflowing with delight.

A scorching impulse began eroding my self-control.

"Noelle," I said, my voice already husky.

"Yes?"

I didn't say anything. Instead, I stood, wrapped my arm around her waist, and drew her into my embrace.

"Kholod?" She looked up at me, puzzled.

I bent down and lifted her into my arms, bridal style.

"Kholod!" she exclaimed, her arms instinctively looping around my neck.

I said nothing, carrying her toward the rear bedroom.

"Wait, we're on a plane—"

"I know." I pushed open the door and laid her on the large bed with its silk sheets. "But I want you right now."

Her face turned scarlet. "But..."

"They won't interrupt." I anticipated her concern, reassuring her as I shrugged off my jacket and tossed it aside. "It's soundproof. No need to worry."

I leaned over her, bracing my hands on either side of her body, trapping her in my shadow.

"Noelle," I murmured. "Right now. Right here, high above the clouds."

Her breathing quickened, her eyes flickering with nervousness, shyness, and a concealed spark of anticipation.

"I..." She bit her lower lip.

I didn't wait for her to finish. I lowered my head and claimed her lips.

As I kissed her, I pulled down the zipper of her dress. Her body quivered beneath my hands, but her arms rose to my shoulders, returning the kiss.

"Kholod..." she whispered against my lips.

"Yeah?"

"I... I'm a little scared..."

"Scared of what?" I paused, meeting her gaze.

"I don't know..." Her eyes were dazed. "This all feels like a dream. You're suddenly so kind to me, taking me on trips, treating me gently... I'm afraid I'll wake up and it'll all disappear."

Her words twisted like a knife in my chest.

I cradled her face, my thumb softly caressing her cheek. "It's not a dream, Noelle. This is real. I'm real. You're real."

I leaned down and placed a tender kiss on her forehead.

"I'll take you to all the places you dream of seeing. I'll protect you, treasure you, and never hurt you again."

She wrapped her arms around my neck, burying her face in the crook of my shoulder. "Then prove it to me right now."

Those words shattered the last of my restraint.

I captured her lips again, deeper this time, my hands moving swiftly to strip away her dress. The fabric slipped from her shoulders, pooling at her waist, and I tugged it off completely, leaving her in just her lacy bra and panties. She shivered under my touch but didn't pull away—instead, her fingers fumbled with my shirt buttons, undoing them one by one until she could push the fabric off my shoulders.

I kicked off my shoes, discarded my pants, and soon we were both naked, skin pressed to skin. Her body was a masterpiece—soft curves, warm and inviting, her breath coming in shallow pants as I trailed kisses down her neck. I lingered at her collarbone, nipping gently, savoring the salty taste of her skin. My mouth descended lower, over the curve of her breast, and I took one nipple between my lips, sucking softly, my tongue swirling around the hardened peak.

She arched toward me, a soft moan escaping. "Kholod..."

I lavished attention on her breast, then switched to the other, my hand kneading the first as I licked and teased. My gaze fell on the tattoo there—the mark I'd once imposed on her, now a symbol of our complicated history. But I handled it tenderly, kissing the inked skin, tracing it with my tongue as if it were something cherished, not a scar.

Her hands tangled in my hair, pulling me closer. I moved lower, planting open-mouthed kisses along her stomach, but I didn't hurry. Instead, I positioned myself between her thighs, parting them gently. She was already slick and ready, glistening, and I groaned at the sight. I leaned in, my breath hot against her core, and began to grind against her slowly, my erection sliding along her wet folds without penetrating, teasing her entrance with deliberate, torturous slowness.

"Noelle," I murmured, my voice low and gravelly, "tell me what you want."

She whimpered, her hips bucking up toward me, craving more contact. "Please..."

I maintained the steady rhythm, grinding just enough to drive her mad, my tip brushing her clit with every stroke. Her body trembled, her inner walls clenching emptily, desperate for more. "Say it," I urged, nipping at her inner thigh. "Tell me you want me inside you."

"I... I want you," she gasped, fingers clutching the sheets. "Kholod, please... I want you inside me."

That was all I needed. I aligned myself and pushed in slowly, inch by inch, relishing the tight heat that enveloped me. She was like velvet, gripping me perfectly, and I groaned deeply as I sank fully inside her.

We moved together, starting slow, building a rhythm. Her legs wrapped around my waist, drawing me deeper with each thrust. Then the plane hit turbulence, a sudden drop creating a fleeting sense of weightlessness. Noelle gasped, her body clamping down around me like a vise, squeezing so intensely it nearly sent me over the edge.

"Fuck, Noelle," I growled, a half-laugh escaping through the fog of pleasure. "You trying to strangle my cock with that tight pussy? Keep squeezing like that and you'll make me come before I'm done with you."

She flushed even deeper, but the turbulence made her grip tighter, her nails digging into my back. The momentary loss of gravity heightened every sensation, her walls fluttering wildly around me. I was right on the precipice, that sudden clench almost too much—damn, she was going to unravel me right there.

Screw it. I pulled out briefly, ignoring her protesting whine, and scooped her up into my arms. "Wrap your legs around me," I commanded, my voice thick with lust.

She complied, locking her ankles behind my back, her arms around my neck. I slid back into her seamlessly, the new angle allowing me to hit even deeper, eliciting a cry from her lips. Holding her like that, I began to walk—slow, leisurely steps around the compact lounge room, as if we were taking a casual stroll, not fucking thousands of feet in the air.

Each step bounced her on my length, gravity and movement driving me deeper. Noelle clung tighter, her breath ragged, body tensing with every motion. The way she squeezed me—nervous, thrilled, impossibly tight from the tension—ignited me further, desire surging. "God, you're holding on like you never want to let go," I murmured in her ear. "Feel that? Every step buries me deeper inside you. Up here in the clouds, you're completely mine—no escaping, just taking me over and over."

She moaned, her head falling back, baring her neck for me to kiss and suck. But the extra tightness from her nerves, the way she clenched with every shift, pushed me to my limits. I couldn't hold back anymore. I backed her against the wall, pinning her there with my body, and thrust hard, unrelenting.

"Yeah, just like that," I groaned, pounding into her with raw force. "Scream for me, Noelle. Let the fucking sky hear how good I'm owning you. We're miles high, baby—no one but the heavens to see how soaked you are, how you're dripping for my cock."

Her cries filled the space, raw and desperate, absorbed by the soundproof walls. I gripped her thighs, spreading her wider, slamming in with thrusts that rocked us both. The plane stabilized, but I didn't ease up, driving deeper and faster, whispering filthy words in her ear. "You feel incredible, clenching around me like a vice. High above the world, like gods—me claiming every inch of you, you swallowing me whole. Come for me up here, Noelle. Shatter and soak my cock, let me feel you milk me dry in the clouds."

The turbulence returned briefly, another dip that made her tighten even more, her body arching against the wall as I hammered into her. "Fuck, that's it—squeeze me harder, like you're trying to keep me forever. Up in this private heaven, I'm going to fill you up until you're overflowing." I reached between us, my thumb circling her clit, adding to the frenzy. She bucked against me, moans turning to pleas, her nails raking down my back.

I shifted angles, hitting that spot inside her that made her gasp louder. "Look at you, Noelle, falling apart for me at thirty thousand feet. No one else gets this—you're my sky-high secret, wet and begging." My pace quickened, hips snapping forward with bruising intensity, the slap of skin echoing in the room. She was so responsive, every thrust drawing out whimpers, her walls fluttering in anticipation.

"Keep moaning like that, and I'll fuck you through every cloud," I rasped, nipping her earlobe. "Imagine it—me buried deep while the world rushes by below. You're mine, all mine, clenching so perfectly." The pressure built, her body trembling on the edge, and I didn't hold back, pounding relentlessly, one hand bracing the wall, the other holding her hip to pull her down onto me harder.

She shattered first, her climax crashing over her like a wave, body convulsing, walls pulsing in rhythmic waves that dragged me right along. I followed with a guttural groan, spilling deep inside her, holding her pinned against the wall as we rode the aftershocks, our bodies slick with sweat and satisfaction.

We stayed entwined for a long moment, breaths mingling, hearts racing in unison. Slowly, I eased her down, my kisses turning soft—on her forehead, her cheeks, her lips—tender now, reverent. "See?" I whispered. "It's real. All of it."

She smiled up at me, exhausted but radiant, and I knew this was only the beginning.

CHAPTER TWENTY-EIGHT

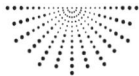

Noelle

The plane touched down at Keflavik International Airport as evening fell. Stepping out of the cabin, a chilling wind laced with the salty tang of the Atlantic hit me full force.

I shivered, instinctively hugging my arms tight.

A heavy coat suddenly draped over my shoulders. Kholod's movement was a bit stiff, like he wasn't used to gestures like this. "Put it on," he said, his tone still carrying that commanding edge, but his eyes betrayed an awkward hint of concern.

"Thanks." I pulled it close, a warmth blooming in my chest.

His coat was massive, practically swallowing me whole. The sleeves dangled way past my hands—I had to roll them up to free my fingers. It still carried his scent, that familiar mix of cedar and tobacco.

"Let's go." He reached out as if to take my hand but hesitated midair, then just strode ahead. "The car's waiting outside."

Watching that rigid gesture, I couldn't help but find it oddly amusing. This man who called the shots in Philadelphia, fumbling over something as simple as holding hands.

We checked into a boutique hotel near Vik Town—the spot I'd

highlighted in my guide, right by the black sand beach, ideal for catching the northern lights and exploring nearby attractions.

Kholod flipped through my thick guidebook, a subtle note of surprise in his voice. "You've planned out daily itineraries, opening hours, even the best angles for photos."

"Of course." I unpacked my camera and tripod from the suitcase. "I take my planning seriously. It was all just armchair dreaming before, but now it's finally happening."

"Where to tomorrow?" he asked.

"Skogafoss and Seljalandsfoss." I pointed to the photos in the guide. "Those south coast waterfalls are stunning. Then the black sand beach for the Basalt Columns—maybe puffins if we're lucky."

"They're ugly."

"No way!" My eyes widened as I shoved my phone with pictures right under his nose. "Look, they're adorable."

He glanced at it, his lips twitching slightly. "If you say so... then fine, they're not."

"You're such a liar." I picked up on his half-hearted tone. "Just wait till you see them. Oh, and if the weather cooperates, we can chase the aurora tonight. The forecast looks perfect for it these next few days."

Kholod watched me enthusiastically break down the itinerary, his gaze softening.

"Alright, it's your show," he said. "You lead, I'll follow."

That made me pause. Kholod Morozov, the ultimate control freak, saying he'd let me take the reins?

"You won't change your mind halfway?" I probed.

"I won't." He took the guide from my hands and pored over it carefully. "This is your trip. You decide. I'm just here to keep you company."

The way he said "keep you company" sounded a little forced, like he wasn't quite used to the phrase.

But it sent a warm flutter through my heart all the same.

The next day unfolded exactly as I'd planned.

Skogafoss's mist refracted rainbows in the sunlight, and the trail behind Seljalandsfoss let us slip right inside the cascade, gazing up at water thundering down like a galaxy in freefall.

"Watch your step," Kholod called from ahead, glancing back often. "It's slippery here."

"Got it." I carefully lifted my skirt hem, navigating the slick rocks.

Suddenly, my foot slid out from under me, and I lost my balance.

"Noelle!" Kholod spun around, grabbing my arm and pulling me straight into his chest.

I collided with his solid frame, my heart racing.

"You okay?" He held me tightly, his voice laced with clear tension.

"I'm fine..." I looked up, catching the worry in his eyes, and couldn't help but laugh. "I just almost slipped. No need to panic."

"You..." He frowned. "Alright, from here on, I'm holding your hand."

"No need—"

"This isn't up for discussion." He intertwined our fingers, gripping firmly. "You slip again, and we're heading back to the hotel."

I glanced at our clasped hands, feeling the heat from his palm spread all the way to my heart.

"Fine," I conceded.

We continued on, hands linked. His was large and warm, holding on tight, as if he feared I'd vanish at any moment.

By the time we reached the black sand beach, the wind had picked up fiercely. My hair whipped around chaotically, and my skirt fluttered up.

"Wait." Kholod stopped, pulling a hair tie from his backpack.

"You brought that?" I asked, surprised.

"Yeah." He looked a bit uncomfortable. "Saw it when you were packing last night and grabbed one."

He stepped behind me and clumsily gathered my hair, tying it up. It took him two attempts, and it ended up a little lopsided.

"Sorry, I'm not great at this."

I rose on my tiptoes and kissed his cheek. "It's perfect."

He stiffened for a moment, his ears flushing red. Seeing this normally stoic man like that made me smile even more.

On the black sand beach, the Basalt Columns stood like organ pipes, waves crashing against the dark shore with a deep, rumbling roar.

"Incredible..." I raised my camera and snapped away furiously.

Kholod stood quietly nearby, not rushing me, just watching with a content expression as I got excited.

"Kholod, let's get a photo together!" I set up the tripod on timer and ran over to him.

"Smile."

"I don't do smiles."

"Then just be yourself."

Click.

I hurried over to check—him with his usual blank expression, me grinning brightly, the black beach and surging waves as our backdrop.

"One more," I said. "Different pose this time."

"Again?"

"Absolutely!" I grabbed his hand. "This is a once-in-a-lifetime thing —we need plenty of memories."

He sighed but went along with it, striking various poses. His face stayed serious, but I could tell he wasn't actually annoyed.

On the fifth shot, inspiration struck—I tiptoed up and kissed his cheek just as the timer went off.

Click.

The photo captured me mid-kiss, with him staring wide-eyed at the lens, looking completely stunned—no trace of his typical cool demeanor.

I laughed so hard I could barely stand. "Your expression is priceless."

"Delete it." He moved to grab the camera.

"No way!" I dodged nimbly. "This is my favorite!"

"Noelle—"

"Absolutely not!" I clutched the camera and ran, with him chasing after me.

He finally caught up, wrapping his arms around me from behind. We collapsed in laughter on the black sand, like the most ordinary couple in the world.

In that moment, I almost forgot everything about Philadelphia. It was just us and this vast, free landscape.

That night, we staked out a spot in a clearing near the hotel to wait for the aurora. Iceland's chill pierced even through my thick down jacket, and I started shivering.

"Cold?" Kholod asked.

"A little." I rubbed my hands together, breathing on them for warmth.

He stepped closer, took my hands, and tucked them into his coat pockets.

"That should help," he said.

Warmers were already inside, radiating heat. I looked at him in surprise. "When did you prepare these?"

"Had Dmitri pick them up before we left." He averted his gaze. "I checked—nights here get brutally cold."

My nose tingled with emotion.

"Thanks," I said softly.

"Yeah."

We stood there in the darkness, waiting for the lights to appear.

About half an hour later, a faint green glow streaked across the sky.

"Look!" I grabbed his hand excitedly. "The aurora! It's starting!"

The green intensified, swirling and dancing through the night sky, blended with shades of purple and pink, painting the darkness like a living canvas.

"It's so beautiful..." I tilted my head back in awe.

"Beautiful indeed," his voice came from beside me.

I turned and realized he was staring at me, not the sky.

"I'm talking about the aurora."

"And I'm talking about you."

His gaze was so intense it made my cheeks burn.

"You... what are you even saying..." I looked away. "We should enjoy this rare sight properly."

"I'm enjoying what I want to see." He pulled me into his arms. "Noelle, you're more captivating than any aurora."

My heart pounded wildly.

I turned and wrapped my arms around his waist, burying my face in his chest. His steady heartbeat echoed in my ear.

"Kholod."

"Yeah?"

"I'm really happy."

He tightened his embrace, pulling me closer.

"Me too," he whispered into my hair.

Over the following days, we explored the south coast's highlights —the dreamy blues of the ice caves, the floating icebergs of Jokulsar-lon, the explosive geysers of the Golden Circle. Each place left me in awe.

And Kholod was always right there with me.

He'd hold my hand firmly during glacier treks, carry my gear when I was busy photographing, and suggest rests whenever I seemed tired.

He even figured out how to use my camera, though his compositions were still a bit rigid and documentary-like—I cherished every shot anyway.

On the third afternoon, we strolled the streets of Vik Town. The tiny village, with its cobblestone paths and colorful houses, felt like something out of a fairy tale.

"This place is so charming," I said, admiring the buildings. "Like a storybook come to life."

"You like it here?" Kholod asked.

"I do." I nodded. "It's small, but so cozy."

We popped into a souvenir shop, shelves brimming with Icelandic specialties—wool items, volcanic rock jewelry, handmade soaps, postcards...

"Get whatever you want," Kholod said. "Don't worry about the price."

"I want to pick up some gifts." I selected a handmade wool scarf. "Mother would like this."

"Yeah."

Then a bracelet made from volcanic rock. "This one's for Anya— she loves things with a unique design edge."

Kholod stood beside me, watching as I carefully chose each item.

"Nothing for yourself?"

"Me?" I pondered. "How about this Iceland map fridge magnet? I can stick it in my room as a keepsake."

"That's all?"

"Yeah." I smiled. "The memories are what matter most."

He picked up a silver bracelet with an abstract aurora-shaped pendant, sleek and artistic. "Wrap this up," he told the shopkeeper.

"It's for you," he said, handing it to me. "Put it on."

The silver chain gleamed softly in my palm, the pendant simple yet dynamic.

"It's gorgeous. Thank you."

He fastened it around my wrist, and I kissed his cheek. "I really love it."

That flush crept up his ears again.

We got back to the hotel around ten.

"You rest first; I'll take a shower," Kholod said.

"Okay." I nodded. "I want to run back to the gift shop quick—I forgot postcards."

"Don't stay out too long," he cautioned. "It's freezing at night."

"I know."

I bundled up in a thick coat and headed down. The hotel shop was small but stocked with quality items. I grabbed a few postcards with aurora and glacier themes, plus some chocolates and handmade cookies.

At the counter, a plump polar bear plushie caught my eye.

"How much for this?" I asked the clerk.

"Three thousand krónur."

"Wrap it up, please."

I wanted to give it to Kholod. It might seem childish, but I didn't care.

Back in the room, the shower was still running. He was taking his time.

I set the shopping bag on the table and pulled out the little bear, studying it for a moment.

A bold idea popped into my head.

I took a deep breath and walked to the bathroom. My hand touched the doorknob, heart pounding like it might burst from my chest.

Noelle, are you sure?

Yes, I'm sure.

I pushed the door open.

Steam filled the bathroom, swirling around the large round tub that brimmed with water. Kholod leaned against the edge, eyes closed, seemingly relaxed.

The mist blurred his form, but I could still make out his broad shoulders, defined abs, and what lay beneath the water...

My face flushed hot.

He heard the noise and opened his eyes, surprise flickering as he saw me in the doorway.

"Noelle?" His voice was husky, dampened by the steam. "You..."

I didn't respond. Instead, I unbuttoned my coat and let it fall to the floor. Then the sweater, the skirt, the underwear... My fingers trembled with nerves, but I steadily removed every layer.

Kholod's gaze grew hotter, his amber eyes igniting with that familiar fire.

When I stood before him completely bare, his breathing deepened noticeably.

"Come here," he commanded, extending a hand, his voice a low, beastly growl.

I stepped into the tub, the warm water enveloping my skin, and he immediately pulled me into his embrace.

"You know what you're doing?" He gripped my waist, guiding me to straddle his lap. "Offering yourself up like this?"

I wrapped my arms around his neck.

"So... how are you going to handle this willing prey?"

His eyes darkened further. "Prove it to me."

I leaned in and kissed his lips. My tentative initiative was quickly overtaken as his tongue took control, guiding me, teaching me how to respond. His hands slid down my spine to my hips, alternating between light caresses and firm grips that sent shivers racing through me.

"Kholod..." I murmured against his lips.

His kisses trailed to my neck, fingers inching toward the softest spot between my thighs.

He slipped a finger inside me, thrusting slowly at first, then adding another, curling them perfectly to hit that sensitive spot. I moaned, rocking against his hand as heat built rapidly. The water sloshed with his movements, his thumb circling my clit, driving me to the edge. My breaths came in ragged pants, my body clenching around his fingers, chasing release.

Then, abruptly, he withdrew, his fingers sliding out, leaving me empty and throbbing with need.

I blinked in confusion, my hips still twitching involuntarily. "What... why did you stop?"

He smirked, leaning back against the tub's edge, his eyes locked on mine with a predatory glint. "You said you were taking the initiative. So show me. Touch yourself for me. Put on a good show."

I froze, a wave of heat flooding my cheeks—not from the steam. "You... you want me to... what?"

"You heard me." His voice dropped to a commanding rumble. "Play with that pretty little pussy of yours. Make yourself come while I watch. Or I won't lay a finger on you. No getting you off, no making you feel good. Your choice, Noelle."

My heart hammered, shame twisting with the insistent ache between my legs. I'd never done anything like this before, not with someone watching so intently. But his hungry, unyielding stare ignited something reckless in me. If I refused, he'd follow through and leave me hanging, frustrated. Fine. I'd do it.

Biting my lip, I shifted back in the water, parting my knees. One hand trailed down my stomach, fingers hesitant as they reached my slick folds. I started with slow circles over my clit, gasping at the immediate spark of pleasure. It felt so exposed, so vulnerable, but the need was too strong to ignore.

Kholod's eyes darkened even more, his own hand dipping below the water to wrap around his thick cock. He stroked himself lazily at first, matching my pace, his length hardening visibly under his grip. The sight of him like that—watching me while pleasuring himself—sent a fresh thrill through me. "That's it, baby. But go slower. Tease yourself. I want to see you squirm and beg for it."

I whimpered, dragging out the circles, my fingers growing slicker with arousal. The steam made everything feel hazy and intimate, the water lapping gently around us as I built the tension.

"Not enough," he growled, his strokes picking up speed, fist pumping with deliberate slowness. "Use your other hand. Grab those perfect tits. Pinch your nipples—hard. Show me how desperate you are, how much you need to come."

Humiliation burned through me, but so did the fire in my core, making my body ache for more. I obeyed, my free hand cupping one breast, thumb rolling over the hardened nipple before pinching it sharply. The jolt shot straight down to my clit, making me arch and gasp. "Like this?"

"Fuck yeah, just like that," he rasped, his voice rough with lust, hand working his cock faster now, veins standing out along its length. "Twist it harder. Make it hurt a little—shit, look at you, all flushed and needy. Now finger yourself. Slide them in deep, Noelle. Pretend it's my cock filling you up, stretching that tight hole."

I dipped two fingers inside, thrusting shallowly at first, then deeper, curling to press against that sweet spot. Moans spilled from my lips, my body rocking with each movement, water splashing softly. His gaze was locked on my every action, his own hand stroking harder, breath coming in heavy grunts. The sight of him jerking off to me like this only heightened the intensity, making me wetter.

"Good girl," he muttered, eyes glued to my hands. "Faster now. Fuck that dripping pussy for me. Let me hear those dirty little sounds —yeah, that's it. Rub your clit while you do it. Harder, baby. I want to see you lose control."

I sped up, fingers plunging in and out, my thumb grinding relentlessly against my clit. The other hand twisted my nipple again, the mix of pain and pleasure coiling everything tighter inside me. "Kholod... oh God, it feels so good..."

"Shit, you're fucking soaked," he groaned, his fist pumping furiously now, pre-cum beading at the tip of his cock above the water. "Look at you, all desperate and.wet for me. Rub it harder—yeah, fuck, just like that. Add another finger. Stretch yourself wide. Come on, make yourself come screaming my name, you little tease."

The pressure built unbearably, every nerve alight. I followed his commands, slipping in a third finger, thrusting deep and fast, my body trembling. The water churned around my movements, steam thickening the air with our shared heat. His dirty words pushed me further, his hand a blur on his cock as he watched, utterly transfixed.

"Don't stop," he ordered, voice strained. "Pinch that nipple again— harder. Fuck, you're close, aren't you? Let me see it. Come for me, Noelle. Scream my name like the good slut you are."

The coil snapped. I cried out, fingers buried deep as ecstasy crashed over me in waves, my body shuddering and pulsing around my own touch. "Kholod! Oh, fuck, Kholod!"

Before I could even catch my breath, he surged forward, grabbing my hips and yanking me onto his lap. His cock pressed insistently against me, thick and rock-hard. "My turn," he snarled, positioning himself at my entrance and thrusting up hard, burying every inch inside me in one brutal stroke.

I screamed, my body still hypersensitive from the orgasm, the sudden stretch and fullness sending shockwaves through me. It was overwhelming, every nerve ending firing as he filled me completely.

"Fuck, you're so damn tight," he groaned, hands digging into my ass as he started pounding upward relentlessly, hips slamming with raw power. Water erupted around us, splashing over the tub's edges and flooding the floor in chaotic waves. "Take it all, baby. This what you wanted? My cock owning that greedy pussy, making you scream?"

"Yes... Kholod, harder!" I gasped, nails raking down his shoulders, riding him through the frenzy. He growled, one hand sliding up to capture my breast, pinching the nipple with just enough force to sting, amplifying every thrust. He drove deeper, water churning into frothy waves that soaked the tiles, the bathroom echoing with the wet slaps of skin on skin.

"Shit, you feel incredible clenching around me like that," he panted, his pace turning savage, hips snapping up with brutal force. "Gonna fuck you senseless, fill you up until you're dripping with me. You're mine, Noelle—every fucking inch of this body belongs to me. Say it."

"Yours... all yours," I moaned, lost in the rhythm, the pleasure bordering on pain as he hit that perfect spot over and over. Water flew everywhere, pooling on the floor, but I couldn't care less. I clung to him, chasing the building edge, words rising in my throat—I wanted to say it, "I love you," but they caught there, unspoken, as the ecstasy mounted higher.

He must have sensed my nearness, his thrusts faltering just a fraction before redoubling in intensity, eyes locking onto mine with raw hunger. "Let go for me," he demanded, his thumb finding my clit and rubbing frantic circles that synced with his punishing rhythm. "Come on my cock, baby. Milk me dry—fuck, squeeze me like that. You're gonna make me come so hard inside you."

I shattered again, my body convulsing in overwhelming bliss, walls gripping him like a vice as the orgasm tore through me, louder this time, my cries bouncing off the steamy walls. "Kholod! Yes, oh God!"

He followed seconds later, thrusting deep one final time with a guttural roar, spilling hot and thick inside me, holding me down firmly as if he'd never let go. His cock pulsed, filling me completely, the sensation drawing out my aftershocks.

We collapsed against each other, panting heavily, the water settling into gentle ripples around us. His arms remained wrapped around me, possessive yet tender, as the intensity faded into a warm glow. I buried my face in his neck, my heart still racing, those unspoken words lingering like a secret between us.

He pressed a kiss to my temple, his voice rough but gentle. "You okay?"

"Yeah," I whispered, tracing lazy patterns on his chest. "Better than okay."

The night melted into more languid touches, our bodies exploring each other slowly in the cooling water. He eventually lifted me out, drying me off with that same clumsy care he'd shown earlier, handling me like something fragile and precious. We tumbled into bed, his body curling protectively around mine, and for once, the outside world—Iceland, Philadelphia, everything—felt far away and insignificant.

CHAPTER TWENTY-NINE

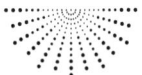

Kholod

"Boss, this is the hotel information for the South Island of New Zealand that you requested." Dmitri placed a folder on my desk. "As per your instructions, I've booked the best lake-view suite in Queenstown for ten days."

"Good." I opened the folder, studying the stunning photos—impossibly blue water, snow-capped peaks reflected in its surface. "Noelle will love this."

Three days since we'd returned from Iceland, and my mood remained unusually light. Faced with mountains of paperwork, I felt no irritation. I'd even started browsing through Noelle's travel albums, planning our next destination—New Zealand, Norway, Scotland. Every place she'd marked, I wanted to take her to.

"Any other arrangements?" Dmitri asked.

"Look into Norwegian fjord cruise routes," I instructed. "The best company."

"Yes, sir." Dmitri nodded, a flicker of surprise crossing his eyes.

He'd worked for me for years—probably never seen me care this much about a woman's preferences.

"Oh, and," I remembered something. "Those Nordic handicrafts I sent yesterday—did she receive them?"

"She did. Mrs. Morozov loved them, especially the wool blankets. Darya said she's been reading while wrapped in one of them."

My lips curved slightly. I was eager to see her surprised expression.

I headed to the library. Seeing me, Noelle's face lit up with delight.

"Kholod, you're here!"

"Yeah."

"I'm picking our next destination!" She held up her album, showing me. "There are so many places I want to go, I can't decide."

"How about the Norwegian fjords?" I flipped to the Sognefjord page. "Good for hiking."

"Great idea!" She practically bounced with excitement.

"I remember this place from your itinerary."

"You actually remember!" She leaned closer, her hair falling forward to brush my cheek, carrying that faint orange blossom scent.

"Of course I remember. And I've already made plans."

"What?" Her voice held disbelief.

I pulled her down beside me. "Since Iceland made you so happy, we can visit every place you've marked."

"All of them?" Her eyes widened.

"All of them," I confirmed. "Wherever you want to go."

She suddenly threw herself into my arms, hugging my waist tightly.

"What's wrong?" I wrapped my arms around her.

"Nothing." Her voice was muffled. "You've just... changed."

"For better or worse?"

"You've become..." She looked up at me, tears shimmering in her eyes. "You've become like a normal person."

I paused, then laughed. "I wasn't normal before?"

"No." She was brutally honest. "Before, you were more like a breathing iceberg."

"And now?"

"Now..." She tilted her head, thinking. "Now it's like the iceberg is starting to melt. Still cold, but at least... at least there's warmth."

I cupped her face, thumb brushing her cheek. "Noelle, I—"

"Boss."

Dmitri's voice cut through from the doorway, interrupting what I was about to say.

I frowned, looking toward the entrance. Dmitri stood there, his expression grave.

"What is it?" My tone carried displeasure. Being interrupted felt awful.

"Urgent matter to report." He glanced at Noelle. "About... that matter."

I understood his meaning. That situation—the ambush three years ago that nearly killed me.

"I see." I released Noelle and stood. "Go back to your room. I need to handle something."

"Okay." She nodded obediently, taking her sketchbook as she left the library.

At the doorway, she looked back with concern. "Don't work too hard."

"Alright."

Once she was gone, my expression turned cold.

"Boss." Dmitri's voice was unusually hoarse. "We need to talk."

I looked up, seeing his expression, and felt an ominous premonition.

"Speak."

"About the firefight that left you critically injured three years ago." He paused. "We've made some new discoveries."

Dmitri pulled an encrypted file envelope from his briefcase, placing it before me.

"This came from our source inside Kieran O'Connell's operation. We caught one of Kieran's old crew members—he'd just been used as cannon fodder by Kieran last week and spilled some information."

I opened the envelope, extracting the documents.

The first page was a handwritten statement, scrawled but clear.

"...That winter, Kieran approached Marco Bellucci. Marco owed gambling debts he couldn't pay. Kieran said he could help with the money, but Marco had to do a favor—provide Morozov's whereabouts. Marco hesitated for a long time, but finally agreed..."

My breathing stopped.

I continued reading.

"...On Christmas Eve, using Marco's information, we set up an ambush in South District. Didn't expect Morozov to fight so hard—lost several brothers... Afterward, Kieran was pissed, said Marco's intel wasn't accurate enough. Two months later, Marco jumped off a building..."

The document slipped from my hands, fluttering down to the desk.

"There's more." Dmitri's voice was quiet. "These are financial records between Marco Bellucci and Kieran. The timeline matches perfectly."

He handed me more pages of bank transfer records.

I stared at those numbers, each transaction like a knife driving into my heart.

"Confirmed?" My voice was hoarse.

"We cross-referenced this testimony. Look here." Dmitri pointed to one transaction. "Three days before your attack, five million dollars was transferred to his account. The source was a shell company, controlled by Kieran O'Connell."

Five million dollars. Marco Bellucci sold my life for that money.

"More evidence?" My voice was terrifyingly calm.

"Yes." Dmitri produced more documents. "Phone records from that period. Marco Bellucci was in frequent contact with Kieran's men. And this—"

He handed me a blurry surveillance screenshot. "This was taken two hours before your attack that night, at a South District bar. Look at this person—"

I stared at the photo. The image was fuzzy, but I recognized that hunched silhouette.

Marco Bellucci.

He sat at the bar, across from a man in a baseball cap. They leaned close together, apparently in deep conversation.

"The man in the cap is Sean Donovan, one of Kieran's lieutenants," Dmitri said. "Died in a gang firefight three years ago. But before he died, he bragged while drunk about personally orchestrating the ambush on Morozov."

"We found three independent sources for cross-verification, including two others who participated in the operation. Their accounts are highly consistent. Boss, this... appears to be true."

I shot to my feet, the chair toppling backward with a loud crash.

"What about Noelle..."

"Mrs. Morozov shouldn't know," Dmitri spoke quickly. "From the timeline, when Marco Bellucci did these things, Mrs. Morozov was only eleven. And the official story has always been that your pressure drove Marco to suicide—Mrs. Morozov likely believes that too."

I gripped the desk edge, feeling the world spin.

That ambush years ago—Bellucci had betrayed me.

What bitter irony.

"And..." Dmitri hesitated, as if there was worse news.

"Speak."

"About your request to investigate who leaked the manor information..."

"Didn't we already deal with that mole?"

"According to the latest intelligence..." Dmitri took a deep breath. "That person revealed they'd planted a deep sleeper. We interrogated him extensively—he only said it was a woman. I had him identify everyone at the manor... he pointed to Mrs. Morozov, Isabella, and three maids, said he'd seen one of them once, that these people looked similar."

"We already interrogated the maids," Dmitri closed his eyes. "They're all dead. Said nothing."

My heart turned to ice.

"Boss, are you alright?" Dmitri asked with concern.

"I'm fine." I forced myself to breathe, to stay calm. "Leave me alone."

"Yes, sir."

I leaned back in my chair, closing my eyes.

Noelle's face appeared in my mind—her excited smile under the Icelandic aurora, her shy expression when she'd actively embraced me in the bathtub, her soft voice when she'd whispered "very happy" against my shoulder...

These images now became blades, cutting into my heart one by one.

I'd fallen in love with my enemy's daughter. She might very well be the sleeper Kieran had planted beside me.

I picked up the file again, reading page by page. Every detail, every piece of evidence, so perfect, so airtight.

Marco Bellucci, controlled by Kieran because of gambling debts.

He'd leaked my whereabouts.

He'd taken five million dollars in blood money.

Then, six months after I controlled Philadelphia, he "committed suicide." Guilt-driven suicide, or Kieran silencing him?

It no longer mattered. What mattered was that Noelle's father had tried to kill me.

And Noelle—did she know? If she did, then her mother selling her to me could only be premeditated. Her becoming Kieran's sleeper would make perfect sense.

Her father was my enemy. She might be the mole.

Vodka burned my throat but couldn't drive away the chill in my heart.

Just moments ago, I'd been planning our next trip, wanting to show her more of the world. I'd even had people prepare the Norwegian fjord itinerary, wanting to surprise her.

Now, it was all a joke. An absurd and cruel joke.

I poured another glass, downing it harshly.

Noelle's smile lingered in my mind. Every smile, every word, every spontaneous embrace...

Was any of it real?

I gripped the glass tightly, knuckles white.

No.

I couldn't continue like this.

I had to stay calm. Stay rational.

I pulled out my phone, calling Dmitri.

"Initiate the final plan. Under the pretense of 'debt collection,' seize all restaurants and companies under the Bellucci family name. Cut off all their food import channels."

"Boss..." Dmitri's tone was hesitant. "If we do this, the Bellucci family will be completely finished. Sofia Bellucci will..."

"I want her to become truly penniless before dawn."

"Yes, Boss."

I hung up and walked to the floor-to-ceiling windows, looking out at Gladwyn Manor's night landscape. Moonlight bathed the snow-covered forest, everything so peaceful, so beautiful.

Like a carefully woven lie.

I didn't go find Noelle.

I waited.

Like a hunter waiting for prey to enter the trap.

I'd wait for her to receive the news, to come running to me in panic, to watch her shatter piece by piece before me.

Just like her father had once tried to do to me.

CHAPTER THIRTY

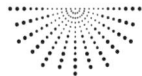

Noelle

"Noelle! Noelle! You finally picked up!"

My mother's hysterical voice exploded through the receiver, so sharp it pierced my eardrums. I jolted upright in bed, checking the time—three a.m.

"Mom? What's wrong?"

"It's over! Everything's over!" Her voice trembled, laced with sobs. "The restaurants have been sealed shut, all of them! The company, the bank accounts—everything's frozen! Noelle, what on earth happened?"

My mind snapped into focus.

"What? What got sealed?"

"All of it! The Ninth Street restaurant, the Bellavista cafe, the food import company!" She was practically screaming. "They said it's for debt repayment! But we don't owe a thing... Noelle, go ask Kholod! This has to be a mistake! It must be some mix-up!"

My hands began to shake.

"Mom, calm down..."

"How can I calm down?!" She shattered. "Noelle, I have nothing left! They're even taking the house! I... what am I supposed to do..."

"Mom, listen to me—"

"Go beg Kholod!" She interrupted, her voice raw with desperation. "You're his wife! You can make this right! Noelle, please, save your mom..."

I closed my eyes, tears sliding down my cheeks.

"Alright. I'll ask him."

After hanging up, I slumped on the edge of the bed.

The screen showed over thirty missed calls, all from her.

And the texts—

"Noelle, they're kicking me out!"

"Please, beg Kholod!"

"I'm your mom! You can't just abandon me!"

My fingers gripped the phone tightly, knuckles turning white.

This had to be a mistake. Something must have gone wrong somewhere.

I had to ask him.

I snatched a robe at random and rushed out of the room barefoot.

The hallway was eerily quiet, my footsteps echoing sharply on the marble floor, frantic and uneven.

Kholod's study door was slightly ajar, warm yellow light seeping through.

He wasn't asleep.

I pushed it open and burst inside.

"Kholod!"

He was seated behind the desk, cradling a glass of liquor, gazing out the window. At the sound of my voice, he turned slowly.

Those amber eyes were now as cold as ice.

"Mom said..." I panted, my voice quivering. "She said the family businesses have all been sealed... This... what's going on? Is it some kind of mistake?"

He stared at me in silence.

"Please..." I approached him, tears streaming down. "Help her, okay? It has to be a mix-up..."

"There's no mistake, Noelle." He finally spoke, his voice calm in a way that chilled me to the bone.

My heart plummeted.

"What do you mean?"

He rose and walked toward me. I instinctively backed away. He reached out, his thumb gently wiping a tear from my cheek. The touch was soft, but his eyes remained frozen.

"This is the price you and your family," he leaned in close, whispering in a devilish tone only we could hear, "should have paid long ago."

"I don't understand." I shook my head. "Kholod, what are you talking about..."

He didn't respond. Instead, he returned to the desk, picked up a file, and tossed it at my feet.

"Read it yourself."

With trembling hands, I picked it up and flipped through the pages.

Each line made my heart sink further.

Confessions. Bank transfer records. Call logs. Surveillance screenshots.

All of it pointed to one damning truth: My father, Marco Bellucci, ensnared by gambling debts to Kieran, had sold out Kholod's whereabouts, leading to that nearly fatal ambush.

"No... this can't be..." My voice shook. "It's fabricated... Dad wouldn't... he couldn't..."

"The evidence is ironclad." Kholod's voice sliced like a knife. "Noelle, this is the truth."

"It's not!" I shook my head frantically. "Kholod, it has to be fake! Dad would never do something like that!"

"Then how do you explain the five million dollars?" He pointed sharply at the bank record. "Just appeared out of nowhere?"

"I... I don't know..." My voice grew faint. "Maybe he really did owe Kieran..."

"Maybe?" Kholod sneered. "Noelle, you don't even believe that crap yourself, do you?"

"Kholod, please believe me..." I clutched his arm. "I had no idea about any of this! If I'd known what Dad did, I never would have saved you that night!"

"Still lying to my face?" He shook off my hand violently, his eyes blazing with rage. "Noelle, Isabella was the one who saved me—you know that. Or was that just another piece of your elaborate scheme?"

"No!" I nearly shouted. "Kholod, it was me that night! I remember your face, every detail—"

"Enough. I'm done with your fairy tales."

"I'm not lying! If the Morozovs hadn't driven my father to suicide, I never would have..."

"What? Out of excuses, so now you're trying to pin the blame on me?"

"I don't know how any of this happened!" I sobbed. "But Mom and I are innocent! We..."

"You're a Bellucci." His voice was devoid of any warmth. "His sins are your sins."

"That's not fair!"

"Fair?" He let out a cold laugh. "Noelle, that word doesn't exist in my world."

He turned and picked up the phone. "Dmitri, proceed as planned."

"No!" I lunged to grab it. "Kholod, please... spare my mom—she's innocent!"

He shoved me back with force, sending me stumbling.

"And what about me?" I screamed in despair. "I married you, got imprisoned by you, tormented by you, branded like some object—isn't that enough?!"

"Not enough." His voice was like ice as he advanced. "Far from it."

I retreated until my back hit the wall.

He planted his hands on either side of me, caging me in.

"When you were moaning beneath me, were you secretly laughing at what a fool I was? The Belluccis used your pretty face, your body, to earn my trust, to secure my protection for your family—did you think that was a good deal?"

"I didn't!"

"Still denying it!" He seized my arm with bruising force, making me cry out in pain. "Your entire family is full of liars! Your father betrayed me, your mother exploited you, and you..."

His gaze darkened further. "You used your body, your tears, your feigned innocence to wear down my defenses, even plotting to sell out the Morozovs. Noelle Bellucci, you're a master manipulator."

"It's not..." Tears flooded my face. "Kholod, I never... how could I... I'm..."

"What?" He sneered. "You're in love with me? Don't make me laugh."

"Take her down."

At his command, two maids surged forward and restrained me. They pressed something against me—my body went limp, unable to move, my mouth muffled so tightly I couldn't even whimper.

Kholod led the way, opening a hidden door behind the storeroom. He entered a code, and the door slid open, revealing a descending staircase.

The stairs were narrow, flanked by cold concrete walls, illuminated by dim lights.

They dragged me down. The air grew colder, my heartbeat pounding faster.

It was a small room with thick soundproof walls. In the center stood a torture chair, and in the corner, cabinets and racks displayed an array of tools, gleaming with menacing silver light.

My legs turned to jelly. The maids forced me into the chair and shackled my wrists and ankles.

"Kholod, please..." My voice trembled. "Let's just talk this through..."

"No need for talk now." He approached, his eyes colder than I'd ever seen. "Noelle, you had countless opportunities to come clean."

"I didn't know anything!"

"You didn't know your father was a gambler? That he owed massive debts? That he received huge payments right around the time of my ambush?"

"I..."

I did know about the gambling and the debts. But I never knew who was behind them. Mom always kept me out of those matters.

"What? Cat got your tongue?"

He snatched a remote, and the chair suddenly reclined, spreading my legs apart. The abrupt shift caused the metal cuffs to scrape harshly against my skin. He grabbed a fistful of my hair—

"Ah—!" I cried out in pain.

Without a shred of pity, he ripped off my robe and tore open my nightgown, leaving me in nothing but panties.

"Kholod... don't..."

"Don't?" He bent over me. "When your father sold me out and your mother basked in the protection I provided, did they ever think 'don't'?"

"I didn't deceive you!" I cried. "Kholod, please..."

He sneered, his fingers clamping my chin, forcing me to meet his gaze. "Noelle Bellucci, thinking back, every glance, every word, every act of submission was just mocking me."

"It's not..."

"When you initiated that kiss, were you celebrating how your performance had fooled me? When you said you wanted me, were you scheming to extract even more?"

"No! Kholod, that's not it! I like you! I love you, Kholod!"

"Noelle, you really think I'll believe that now?!"

My mouth opened, but no words emerged.

"Kholod..." I choked out. "Let me explain... I always thought... you were the one who killed my dad... that's why I..."

He seemed to have had enough, turning to the cabinet and yanking open a drawer. Inside were neatly arranged whips, candles, and other tools I'd never laid eyes on.

Fear surged through me like a tidal wave.

"Kholod... not like this..."

"I'll make you understand," he said, selecting a black leather whip and weighing it in his hand, "the cost of betraying me."

He pressed the whip against my collarbone, sliding it downward slowly.

"See this?"

I shook my head desperately, terror rendering me nearly speechless.

"Answer my questions honestly," he murmured, "or you'll regret it."

"I'll tell... anything..."

"Good." He smiled, a grin more terrifying than any scowl. "First question—what exactly was your father's plan?"

"What plan? I don't know—"

The whip lashed down across my chest, slicing precisely over the right peak. It wasn't like any whip I'd imagined—this one seemed specially made, not excruciatingly painful, but delivering a sharp sting laced with a tingling numbness that rippled through me.

I screamed, the bizarre sensation tearing a cry from my lips.

Kholod leaned in closer, his voice a menacing growl. "Tell me what your family's been plotting, Noelle. All the schemes, the betrayals —spill it."

Tears poured down my face. "I don't know! I swear, I have no idea!"

"You're lying." He swung again, this time striking the left peak. That same odd blend—pain buzzing into an electric thrill, making my body arch against the restraints.

I yelped, gasping for air. "I'm not lying!"

"Bullshit," he snarled. "If you're so innocent, explain the connections between Kieran and your father. The calls, the money—it's all documented."

My heart twisted in agony. He didn't believe me. After everything we'd shared, he saw me as part of this nightmare.

"You can't say that about me," I blurted out through sobs. "I didn't do anything!"

He stepped forward, eyes burning with fury, and pressed the whip's handle against my core, rubbing it slowly, teasingly. A few deliberate strokes, and when he withdrew it, the handle glistened with my slick arousal, betraying me completely.

"Look at this," he sneered, his voice laced with venom. "You filthy little slut. No matter how I treat you, you're always soaking wet, your greedy cunt begging for my cock like the cheap, desperate whore you are. Pathetic, Noelle—your body's a lying bitch, just like you."

Shame scorched through me, but the friction ignited sparks of unwanted heat. Then he ground the handle mercilessly against that most sensitive spot, crushing it with brutal pressure.

I screamed, the intensity amplified—pain and an itchy ache blending into something overpowering.

Not content, he thrust the handle inside me abruptly, the rough invasion stretching me painfully, sending shockwaves through my core.

"Ahh!" I cried out, my body clenching around it in protest.

"Look at you," he taunted, pulling it out and shoving it back in with a vicious rhythm. "Writhing like a bitch in heat, your dripping hole sucking this in. This is what you are, Noelle—a deceitful, scheming cunt who gets off on her own lies."

Rage boiled over, mixing with the humiliation. "You bastard!" I spat. "You're the real monster here, Kholod! Twisting everything to suit your paranoia!"

That only inflamed his anger further. "Your family nearly got me killed, and you—you were plotting to betray me too. Clearly, this punishment isn't harsh enough."

He discarded the whip and grabbed a few candles from the drawer. It released a faint, intoxicating scent as he lit them.

He yanked my hair back, forcing my head up. "Last chance, Noelle. Confess the Bellucci conspiracy. Every detail."

Sobs racked my body. "There's no conspiracy! I swear, there isn't!"

"I don't believe a word." He tilted the candle, letting warm wax drip onto my most intimate area. A mild burn, but the sensitive flesh erupted in itchy tingles, drawing an involuntary moan from me.

"Tell the truth," he demanded.

"I really don't know!"

Another drop fell in the exact same spot, heightening the sensation. I moaned louder, my hips bucking against my will.

"Still not talking?" He pressed.

"That's the truth!" I shouted.

"You just don't learn." With a sadistic edge, he used his fingers to part my folds, dripping wax inside—one precise drop after another, each landing on the most sensitive nerves, sending waves of hot, itchy pleasure-pain coursing through me.

My moans echoed through the soundproof room, my body writhing as I begged, "Kholod... stop... please..."

"This is only the beginning," he murmured, his eyes dark with determination.

Then he set the candles aside, freed himself, and plunged into me with forceful abandon, his body taking over where the tools had tormented. As he thrust deeply, he seized a candle again, dripping wax onto my chest—warm beads splattering across my peaks, making them throb with exquisite sensitivity.

The dual assault was overwhelming—his relentless pounding below, the heated drips above—igniting every nerve in my body. I couldn't string together coherent words, reduced to gasps and cries as he drove into me, interspersing his movements with questions.

"Who else was involved? Your mother? Kieran? Confess!"

"I... don't... know..." I stammered, my voice fracturing.

He didn't relent, maintaining the punishing rhythm while continuing the interrogation, his hips snapping forward with unyielding force. The wax cooled on my skin, forming teasing crusts that cracked with each impact, heightening the friction.

Eventually, he uncuffed me roughly, flipping me face-down on the chair and rebinding me securely. From behind, he entered me again, deeper and more possessively, while the whip cracked across my ass, each lash delivering that custom sting—a buzzing numbness that left welts but stirred a twisted craving.

"Feel that, you backstabbing bitch?" he growled, swinging again with precision. "This ass belongs to me, just like every inch of your traitorous body. Beg all you want—your slutty hole is clenching around me, loving the abuse, isn't it? You're nothing but a cum-hungry whore, Noelle, dripping for more."

I had no sense of time anymore. The whip's specialized leather kissed my skin repeatedly, not tearing but electrifying nerves in a haze where pain melted into aching desire. He'd alternate with wax, dripping scented drops down my back, letting them pool in the curve of my spine or trail lower, seeping into sensitive crevices as his thrusts grew more savage.

"You're mine to shatter," he'd rasp harshly, pulling my hair to arch my back further, exposing fresh skin for the lash. One vicious crack landed on my inner thigh, perilously close to where we connected, the vibration surging straight through me, forcing an involuntary clench around his length.

"Admit it," he commanded, slowing to agonizing, drawn-out strokes, using the whip's handle to tease my entrance before slamming back in himself. "Your family's scheme—confess!"

But I had nothing to admit, only sobs and pleas as he accelerated, faster and fiercer. The candles dwindled, wax building in sticky layers —hardening into tantalizing weights on my nipples that tugged with every jolt; tracing paths down my abdomen, cooling and fracturing under his gripping hands.

He flipped me once more, facing up, splaying me wide on the chair. The whip now teased with lighter flicks over my peaks, each one jolting me into writhing ecstasy. "See how you arch for it," he mocked, his voice roughened by lust and fury. "Greedy little whore— bet you'd come just from the lash if I allowed it, your body betraying you like the filthy liar you are."

But he edged me mercilessly, denying release. More wax followed, dripped in deliberate designs—circling my navel, then venturing lower, sealing over our joined bodies. The heat blossomed within, a peculiar, stimulating burn that rendered every inch hypersensitive, amplifying his every movement.

How long it lasted, I couldn't tell—minutes blurring into hours. He'd pull out only to substitute the whip's handle, twisting it deep while wax cascaded over my exposed form. My cries grew hoarse, my body a throbbing nexus of sensation—pain, pleasure, and degradation intertwining into an unrelenting tempest.

At last, he buried himself one final time, releasing deep inside with a guttural groan. I had no energy left for tears, lying limp and utterly spent beneath him.

"Ready to tell the truth now?" he asked, his voice still laced with frost.

I gazed into those amber eyes that had once made my heart flutter, summoning my final ounce of strength, and whispered, "Kholod, I wish you... burn in hell forever."

CHAPTER THIRTY-ONE

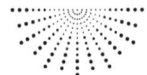

Noelle

"Ma'am, you need to eat something."

Darya's voice sounded distant, as if coming from underwater.

I opened my eyes and stared at the ceiling. A blank expanse, just like my heart.

"Ma'am?" She called again, worry threading through her voice.

I didn't respond. Not because I wouldn't, but because I'd lost the strength to speak.

How long had it been? Three days? Five? A week? I'd lost count. Time had ceased to matter.

"Ma'am, the doctor is here to examine you," Darya said softly.

I remained silent, just lying there.

Emily entered, carrying her medical bag.

"Ma'am." She sat beside the bed, her tone gentle. "I need to check your condition."

I turned my head toward the window.

"Ma'am?" She tried again.

Darya explained quietly. "Doctor, she's been like this for days... won't speak, won't eat anything."

"I understand." Emily nodded. "Let me begin the examination."

She took out her stethoscope and placed it on my chest.

The cold metal touched my skin. Then came the blood pressure cuff, thermometer—one instrument after another.

I let her do whatever she needed, like a soulless puppet.

"Vitals are normal," she finally said, "but she's severely malnourished. She must eat, or it will become dangerous."

"But she refuses everything..." Darya's voice was strained.

"I'll start her on IV nutrition," Emily said, packing up. "Also, her mental state is very concerning. I recommend psychological intervention."

"I'll inform the boss."

After Emily left, silence settled over the room again.

Darya sat on the edge of the bed and gently took my hand. "Ma'am..." her voice broke, "You can't continue like this... You need to eat something..."

I slowly turned to look at her. Her eyes were red and swollen—she'd been crying.

"Darya." I finally spoke, my voice hoarse and unrecognizable.

"Ma'am!" She gripped my hand tightly. "You're willing to talk!"

"Help me..."

"Tell me what! I'll do anything!"

"Close the curtains..." I whispered. "Too bright."

She paused, then nodded. "Of course."

The heavy curtains drew shut, plunging the room into darkness.

I closed my eyes again.

In the days that followed, I maintained my silence.

Doctors came daily for examinations, and nurses administered IV nutrition.

I cooperated with all treatments but refused to speak again.

Kholod occasionally appeared in the doorway. He would stand there, expressionless, watching me for a moment before turning away.

I watched his retreating figure with dead eyes. That man who had taken me to Iceland to see the aurora, who had clumsily braided my hair...

He was gone. What remained was a monster I never wanted to see again.

"Noelle."

Anastasia's voice pulled me back to reality. She and Anya had returned from their business trip to discover what had happened.

She stood beside the bed, holding a bowl of soup.

"Sit up," she commanded.

I didn't move.

"Noelle." She called again. "Sit up and drink this."

I slowly sat up and accepted the bowl.

The soup wasn't hot—cooled to the perfect temperature. A faint warmth stirred in my chest.

I slowly brought the spoon to my lips, sip by careful sip.

"Good." Anastasia sat on the bed. "You must live, Noelle."

I looked at her with hollow eyes.

"Why?" My voice was barely a whisper. "Why should I live?"

"Because you're young," she said gently. "Life continues."

"But I feel like I'm already dead."

Anastasia fell silent for a moment.

"Kholod went too far," suppressed anger colored her voice. "Acting so impulsively before all the facts were established."

"It doesn't matter anymore, Mother."

"Noelle—"

"Mother, I want to rest." I pleaded softly.

She studied me, complex emotions flickering in her eyes. Finally, she stood and left the room.

That evening, Anya came.

She entered while I sat by the window, staring into space.

"Noelle," she called.

I turned. She looked unwell too.

"Are you... all right?" Her tone held unusual concern.

"I'm fine," I said, my voice frighteningly calm.

"You're not fine at all." She approached and sat across from me. "Noelle, you can't go on like this."

"Then what should I do?" I asked quietly. "Continue playing the perfect Mrs. Morozov?"

"I..." She opened her mouth but found no words.

"Anya, thank you for visiting me."

She remained silent for several seconds before standing. At the door, she turned back. "If you need anything, tell Mother and me anytime. As for Kholod... I'll make sure he doesn't disturb you as much."

"Thank you."

After the door closed, I gazed out the window again. The sky was overcast—it looked like rain.

Sudden nausea struck. I covered my mouth and rushed to the bathroom, retching over the toilet.

My stomach was empty—only the bitter taste of bile.

"Ma'am!" Darya hurried in to steady me. "What's wrong?"

"Nothing..." I leaned weakly against the wall. "Probably caught a cold."

"I'll call the doctor—"

"No." I stopped her. "I just need rest."

This wasn't the first time.

This wasn't the first time. I'd been experiencing nausea, fatigue, and loss of appetite recently. I'd managed to suppress it before, but today I couldn't control it.

I'd assumed it was a lingering effect from that terrible ordeal. But now...

I slowly stood and walked to the sink. My reflection showed a pale face and empty eyes.

A thought suddenly flashed through my mind.

I hurried back to the bedroom and grabbed the calendar from the nightstand—my hands began trembling. My period was nearly two months overdue.

"No..." I whispered. "That's impossible..."

But every symptom pointed to the same possibility. I was pregnant.

Tears streamed down my face. "No... this can't be real..."

I couldn't be pregnant. Not now, not under these circumstances.

I needed to stay calm. I grabbed my phone, hands shaking as I tried to dial Zoe's number—no, all communications were monitored. That would be like telling Kholod directly.

I sat in a daze for a long time until my gaze fell on the sketchpad, and finally I had an idea.

The next afternoon, Darya knocked and entered.

"Ma'am, your friend sent a package." She held an elegant gift box. "From Zoe Harper."

My heart raced.

"Thank you." I took the box, struggling to appear calm. "Put it here. You may go."

"Yes, ma'am."

The moment the door closed, I tore open the box. Inside were beautiful crafts and a box of chocolates. I found a long chocolate bar— trust Zoe to think of this method. I cracked open the chocolate, and there was the pregnancy test, carefully wrapped in plastic film.

My hands shook as I held the test.

I went into the bathroom and followed the instructions.

Three minutes. They felt like three centuries.

When I finally found the courage to look—two clear red lines.

I was pregnant.

"No..." I covered my mouth as tears poured out. "No..."

My trembling hand moved to my abdomen. There was a tiny life growing inside—innocent, mine.

My world turned upside down again, but an unprecedented strength rose from within.

I would never allow my child to be born in this cold prison. Never let Kholod harm them.

I had to escape. Leave this suffocating place.

From that day forward, I forced myself to eat, despite the persistent nausea. I suppressed it through sheer willpower.

I began refusing Emily's examinations, but seeing my life gradually return to normal, she reluctantly agreed.

Perhaps the baby sensed my situation—as my diet improved, the morning sickness actually decreased, helping me conceal this secret.

I became compliant and quiet, like a truly subdued wife.

"Noelle, are you really better now?" Anastasia asked me every day.

"Mother, I'm fine." I even managed a relaxed smile. "For you and Anya, I must live well."

"That's good to hear." Anastasia smiled back.

Kholod's attitude also softened somewhat.

The guards at the master bedroom door were reduced by half. I could walk in the garden again and visit the library. But he still forbade me from leaving the manor and monitored all my communications.

"Noelle..." We encountered each other in the garden.

"Yes?"

He paused, studying my eyes as if searching for something.

"About that incident—I'm conducting a new investigation. But regarding your father's actions..."

"I understand." I interrupted him. "The Bellucci family should pay for my father's crimes. I accept that."

He remained silent for a long time.

"Is there anything else?"

"No."

A week later, Kholod finally permitted me weekly phone calls with Zoe.

"Fifteen minutes," he said. "On speakerphone."

"All right." I nodded obediently.

During the first call, Zoe's voice came through. "Noelle! Are you okay? I couldn't reach you and was so worried!"

"I'm fine. Just family matters—Morozov family rules, you understand."

"I do! By the way, what subject are you planning for the Association Exhibition painting?"

"Landscapes, mainly Icelandic glaciers. I'm practicing cold blue tones."

"Which blue? Prussian blue or ultramarine?"

"Primarily ultramarine. I want to capture the profound depths of the glacier's core."

A second of silence on the other end—Zoe was surely shocked. But she quickly recovered. "Very challenging! When do you plan to finish?"

"In three weeks. I want to work quickly."

"Excellent! You must show me when it's done. Do you need any special art supplies? I can help you get them."

"Thank you. I'll send you a list."

"Perfect! I'm looking forward to your work!"

"Goodbye."

After hanging up, I noticed Kholod standing in the bedroom, watching me.

"What were you discussing?"

"The Association Exhibition. We talked about my artistic concept."

He scrutinized me for a long time before finally nodding. "You can call her again next week."

"Thank you."

He turned and left. I returned to my seat by the window.

My hand gently touched my belly. Wait a little longer, baby. Mama will get us out of here.

Zoe worked quickly.

During the second call, she told me, "I found a wonderful partner. She has friends who are willing to help you find rare blue pigments."

"Really? When can they deliver?"

"Next week. She's holding an art exhibition in town—we need to wait for her return."

"I wish I could go see it too."

"She would definitely welcome you. You could sell paintings there too—with your skill level, the income would be quite good."

"That sounds wonderful! I'll definitely go if I have the chance. I should continue preparing my artwork now."

"Keep it up!"

The third call came a week later.

"Noelle, I found an excellent frame supplier who offers custom services and can handle shipping for you."

"Perfect! I've been too busy lately to leave the manor."

"You focus on completing your painting. He'll come directly to pick it up."

"Thank you so much, Zoe!"

"No need for thanks between us."

After hanging up, I looked out the window. Late May—storm season was approaching.

I had to start preparing.

Every day, I secretly gathered essentials—a few changes of clothes, cash, documents—hiding them under the mattress, waiting for the right moment.

At the same time, I began writing divorce papers. Word by word, carefully crafted. I wanted none of his money, none of his property, nothing belonging to the Morozov family. I only wanted freedom and my child's future. After finishing, I hid the papers deep in the closet.

Tonight, Kholod wasn't home—probably handling business matters again.

Lying in bed, listening to thunder rumbling outside, I waited quietly.

Countless images flashed through my mind—Kholod taking me to Iceland, clumsily braiding my hair, his awkward expression when he said "whatever you want," his warmth as he held me in the bathtub... But he had destroyed all of that with his own hands.

Hearing commotion outside the manor, I got out of bed barefoot, retrieved the clothes and documents I'd hidden in the closet, took the divorce papers from the drawer, and changed into the maid's uniform I'd secretly altered.

Everything was ready. Taking a deep breath, I walked to the door.

With my hand on the doorknob, I took one last look around this room—it held too much joy and pain.

Goodbye, Kholod Morozov.

The door opened silently. The corridor was dim, with only emergency lights flickering faintly.

The Morozov manor's electrical system was indeed robust, but the thunderstorm arrived as expected. During my recent walks, I had studied the electrical system and secretly placed a metal rod near the transformer. Although there were backup generators, full startup would take several minutes—exactly the chaos I needed.

I hurried through the corridor, down the stairs, past the main hall. The servants were all dealing with the power outage—no one noticed this "hurried maid."

I pushed open the side door, threw on a rain poncho, and rushed into the storm. The rain was freezing, but I couldn't stop.

I ran desperately toward the manor gates. Zoe had said the contact would wait on the side road at midnight. I had already passed the manor's layout to her through scattered paintings.

Rain blurred my vision, and the muddy ground nearly made me fall several times. But I couldn't stop.

Finally, I saw the manor gates. I hid behind a sculpture to observe. A patrol team had just passed, and the guardhouse was empty—they must have gone to handle other situations.

I seized the moment to slip through the gates. A black sedan was parked by the roadside, its headlights flashing twice.

The contact.

I rushed over and yanked open the door.

"Go!"

The car started immediately and sped into the rainy night.

"Are you all right?" He turned around, the scar on his face particularly stark in the dim light.

"Lorenzo?"

CHAPTER THIRTY-TWO

Kholod

"Andre spilled everything, boss."

Dmitri's voice came through the phone, heavy with post-interrogation exhaustion.

"Clean it up." I crushed out my cigarette.

"Yes, sir."

I hung up and checked my watch—3:45 AM.

Another traitor eliminated.

Since the last incident, we'd been purging the manor's inner circle. Intelligence confirmed Andre had been our leak all along. But according to his confession, there was still a high-level mole buried deeper—someone who'd gone dark these past months, leaving no trace.

I didn't want to suspect anyone close to me, but silence was crucial now. No point in spooking our target.

I stood up, rolling the stiffness from my shoulders. Time to head back.

Strangely, I found myself wanting to see Noelle. I'd taken my anger over her father's betrayal out on her, but looking back now, she was innocent in all this.

Maybe I should tell her the truth about Marco Bellucci's death. Put this to rest. As for the mole situation—until we found them, she was safer at the manor. I was sick of all the constant suspicion.

The car cut through Philadelphia's empty streets, windshield wipers beating a steady rhythm. The storm had hit suddenly, rain hammering the roof like gunfire.

"Boss, the manor's electrical system had a brief failure. Backup generator's running, but we might have a few minutes of surveillance gaps."

I wasn't concerned. The manor's security was solid enough. A short outage posed no threat.

We pulled up to the main house. I pushed open the car door, rain hitting my face, washing away some of the day's irritation.

The power was back on inside, everything quiet. I headed straight for the stairs, but noticed light seeping from under the study door.

Something was off.

I walked over and pushed it open—

The moment I opened the door, I froze.

The study's main lights blazed, illuminating a scene on the oak desk—a silver dagger driven deep into the wood, its sapphire pommel catching the cold light. It was the souvenir Noelle had bought in Iceland, always kept on her vanity.

Papers were pinned beneath the blade.

My heart hammered, legs suddenly heavy as lead.

One step. Two steps. I reached the desk and gripped the handle, yanking hard—the cut was deep. How much force had she used?

I set down the dagger and grabbed the papers.

The top page read: Divorce Agreement.

Those words hit like knives straight to the heart. My hands started shaking, barely able to hold the paper. I forced myself to keep reading—

Party A: Noelle Bellucci

Party B: Kholod Morozov

Both parties voluntarily divorce, property division as follows...

At the bottom was her signature—neat and delicate, but carrying unshakable resolve. Dated tonight.

"No..." The sound that escaped my throat was barely human.

I flipped to the second page. Just one line.

"From this day forward, Noelle Bellucci and Kholod Morozov have no relationship whatsoever."

No relationship whatsoever. She wouldn't even keep the Morozov name.

"Noelle..."

I clutched the agreement and bolted from the room, grasping at straws.

"Noelle!"

Stairs, hallway, master bedroom—I nearly smashed through the door.

"Noelle!"

Empty.

The room was vacant. The fire still burned in the fireplace, the bed made with military precision.

In the walk-in closet, all her gowns hung organized by color. The jewelry box on her vanity held every necklace, earring, and bracelet.

"No... impossible..."

I rushed to the library. Darkness. I shoved open the door—her art supplies sat neatly on the table. Sketchbooks, charcoal pencils, paints.

I opened the sketchbook. Inside were her drawings. Iceland's glaciers, the black sand beach's basalt columns, and... me.

Me sleeping on the plane. Me smiling in front of the blue ice cave. Us embracing under the aurora. Every stroke was tender and detailed.

"Noelle..." My voice cracked. "Why... why..."

If you hate me, why leave these behind? If you wanted to go, why not take everything?

I carried the sketchbook back to the master bedroom and collapsed to my knees.

The polar bear plushie from Iceland sat on the windowsill, the unfinished Norway travel book lay beside the bed, and her orange blossom scent still lingered in the air.

Everything was unchanged, as if she'd just stepped out.

"AHHH—!!"

A roar tore through the night's silence, like a wounded animal's wail. I pounded my fists against the floor, knuckles splitting, blood staining the carpet, but I felt nothing.

"Boss!" Dmitri burst through the door.

"Find her!" I looked up, eyes bloodshot. "Use everything we have. Turn over every stone if you have to, but bring her back!"

"Yes! I'll immediately—"

"Check Zoe, Isabella, Sofia, Lorenzo," my voice was ice-cold. "I want every movement and communication record they have."

"Understood!"

Dmitri rushed out.

I stood in the empty room, taking in the traces she'd left behind.

Only now did I realize—somewhere along the way, this supposed prisoner had become the only queen of my frozen kingdom. Her presence had seeped into every corner, her laughter echoed in every room, her image was burned into every inch of ground I'd walked.

And now she was gone.

"Noelle..." I whispered. "What have I done..."

Savior, family vendettas, betrayals—losing her, it all seemed so ridiculous, so meaningless.

Why had I taken my rage out on her? Why had I hurt her?

"Because you're a bastard," I told my reflection. "Kholod Morozov, you're a complete bastard."

In the days that followed, I barely slept. Two or three hours, maybe. The rest were buried in family business and chasing leads.

"Boss, you need rest," Dmitri said for the tenth time.

"Did you find her?"

"Still searching..."

"Then keep searching. Expand the range to the entire East Coast."

"Yes..."

A week passed. Nothing.

Two weeks. Still nothing.

A month later, Noelle had vanished without a trace.

My condition deteriorated daily. Stubble unkempt, eyes sunken, I'd lost weight—my suits hung loose on my frame.

"Kholod," My mother's face was etched with worry.

"Yes," I responded mechanically.

"You need to eat." Her tone was stern. "You haven't had a proper meal in three days."

"I'm not hungry."

"I'm not asking," she said. "Kholod Morozov, you're the head of this family. We need a clear-minded leader, not a self-destructive madman."

"I know..."

"You know nothing." She cut me off. "All you know is how to wallow in your own misery. But Kholod, that accomplishes nothing."

"Then what should I do?" I looked up, eyes full of exhaustion and despair. "Tell me, what else can I do?"

"First, take care of yourself." She said. "Only if you stay rational and healthy will you have a chance to find her, a chance to make things right."

She was right.

I took a deep breath, picked up my knife and fork, and forced myself to take a bite of steak.

It tasted like cardboard, but I swallowed it. One bite, two, three...

My mother watched me, her stern gaze gradually softening.

"Also," she continued, "you need to reorganize your thoughts. Start over, go through everything again."

"I've been thinking..."

"Not deeply enough." She shook her head. "Kholod, you need to think from Noelle's perspective. What did she see, what did she experience, why did she make that choice?"

From Noelle's perspective...

I set down my utensils and closed my eyes. In her eyes, I was the killer of her father, the monster who forced her into marriage, the jailer who imprisoned her freedom.

"I hurt her, Mother." I opened my eyes. "I hurt her deeply."

On the fifth night, still with no appetite, I downed two bottles of vodka and continued reviewing new leads.

The study door suddenly burst open.

Anya stormed in, fury written across her face.

"Kholod Morozov!"

"What?" I looked up.

"Look at yourself!" She stepped in front of me, jabbing her finger at my forehead. "Are you planning to destroy yourself like this?"

"Anya..."

"Shut up!" Her eyes were red. "You're going insane over that woman! A whole month! Do you know what you look like right now?"

"I..."

"You don't know anything!" Tears streamed down her face. "All you care about is finding her! But have you thought about me and Mom? If you collapse, what happens to us?"

"I..."

"Have you considered that your investigation has been wrong from the start?"

That stopped me cold.

"What do you mean?"

"Isabella Vance!" Anya was practically screaming. "Kholod, wake up! Ever since she showed up, haven't you and Noelle been having constant misunderstandings?"

"You're saying..."

"I'm saying Isabella has been manipulating you both all along!" She grabbed my shoulders, shaking me hard. "She always acts so innocent, drops those ambiguous hints! And you, you idiot, believed every word!"

I shot to my feet. I'd always felt Isabella was trouble, but that "savior" filter kept me from seeing her true nature.

"Dmitri!"

Seconds later, he appeared in the doorway. "Boss."

"Boss, we're processing it, but it's been so long. Some of the hospital recordings are corrupted—we need data recovery."

"I don't care what it takes!" I cut him off, my voice more urgent than ever. "Double the manpower. I want to hear that recording ASAP!"

"Yes!"

He turned and rushed out.

Anya looked at me, wiping away her tears.

"Kholod, there's something else. When you were investigating the manor's information leaks, I went through the records—have you noticed the leaks started after Isabella arrived? When she left, they stopped." She gave me a meaningful look.

It hit me like lightning—why had I never considered this?

"Kholod, I never liked Noelle before, but I know she's not a bad person."

"I know."

"So you have to find her," Anya said. "And then treat her right."

"I will."

Three days later.

When Dmitri pushed through the door, he clutched an old recording device in his hands.

"Boss, we recovered the data." His voice trembled slightly. "This is the emergency call recording from back then."

My hands shook as I reached for the device.

"Boss," Dmitri pressed down on my hand. "You... should prepare yourself."

"Play it."

He released my hand. I hit play.

After a burst of interference—

"Hello? Hello? Is this emergency services? I'm at... South District, near the narrow alley behind Seventh Street. Someone's been shot."

A young girl's voice came through the speaker.

My breathing stopped.

That was Noelle's voice.

Seventh Street.

That alley.

The exact place where I'd been attacked all those years ago.

"Yes, miss, the ambulance is on its way. Please stay calm and don't hang up. You confirmed the location is Seventh Street? Can you tell me about the injured person's condition?"

"Yes, he's badly hurt... please hurry!"

"Alright, miss. Please stay on the line with me. The ambulance will be there in about five minutes..."

"Over here!"

The recording ended.

I sat frozen, finger still on the play button.

It was her.

Really her.

With trembling hands, I hit replay.

That voice came again.

Young, frightened, but incredibly determined.

For a bleeding stranger, she'd risked staying behind.

Called for help.

Wouldn't abandon him.

That person was Noelle. The "savior" I'd searched for three years, obsessed over for three years. It was Noelle—the one I'd personally dragged to hell, the one I'd hurt the most.

And I'd so easily believed Isabella's false information.

"No..."

My voice shattered.

"No... no..."

The recording kept looping.

"Please hurry..."

"Please hurry..."

...

That was her voice. She'd cried for me, begged for my rescue. And I'd believed Isabella's lies, torturing her again and again, even punishing her in the most brutal ways in that basement.

"Fuck!"

I swept everything off the desk.

Papers scattered, the lamp shattered, glass flying.

"Fuck! Fuck! Fuck!"

I destroyed everything in the study. Books tumbled from shelves, the liquor cabinet's glass doors smashed, picture frames, vases—anything breakable turned to pieces.

"Boss!" Dmitri rushed in. "Please calm down—"

"Get out!" I roared. "Everyone get the hell out!"

He retreated to the doorway, not daring to approach.

I stood among the wreckage, hands braced against the desk, breathing hard.

Glass shards cut my palms, blood dripping onto the wood, but I felt nothing.

"Noelle..." My voice was raw. "What have I done..."

I'd destroyed the only person who truly cared about me, personally shoved that guiding light into the abyss.

The truth was a blade, and in this moment, it carved me to pieces.

CHAPTER THIRTY-THREE

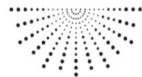

Noelle

"Leo, baby, no more crying."

I held my son, pacing gently around the shop, my palm stroking his tiny back. He'd just woken up and was fussing restlessly.

"Oh, my sweet boy... Mommy's here..."

The little one gradually quieted, his soft cheek pressed against my shoulder. He'd just learned to crawl and always babbled happily, reaching out his little hands for me to hold him.

The doorbell chimed softly as a customer pushed inside.

"Welcome." I greeted them while continuing to pat Leo gently.

"Tara, how much for this ceramic pot?" It was Mrs. Yoki, a regular.

"Twenty dollars."

"I'll take it. This child is absolutely adorable!" She moved closer to examine Leo. "He looks more like you every day."

"Thank you."

After the customer left, I placed Leo in the baby cradle in the shop. He played happily with his stuffed toys, giggling from time to time.

Watching him, my heart grew extraordinarily tender.

Two years now. I'd settled in Niaube under a false identity, built a wooden house facing the ocean, and opened this little shop called "Faraway Handicrafts."

All of this thanks to Lorenzo—if he hadn't known friends among the Maka people, I never would have been accepted here.

I painted the landscapes from my travels—Iceland's aurora, Norway's fjords, New Zealand's glowworm caves—onto ceramics and wove them into tapestries, creating various handicrafts.

Business wasn't booming, but it was enough to support Leo and me.

My successful escape was thanks to a code system Zoe and I had established during her obsession with murder mystery games. During the days when Kholod had relaxed his guard, I gradually transmitted distress signals through paintings and paint colors.

She contacted the Women's Aid Organization through a friend, and this place was provided by sisters in the organization. The paintings I sent out were indeed handled by a professional framing shop. Zoe had thought everything through carefully, even venturing deep into the mountains beforehand to paint landscapes—according to her, even hunting dogs couldn't find tracks there.

Now I lived here under the false identity "Tara," with no one knowing my past. I could finally be myself again.

"Knock, knock, knock."

The knocking came, and before I could respond, Lorenzo pushed the door open.

"Tara, I bought..." He saw Leo in the cradle and immediately lowered his voice. "Is he sleeping?"

"No, he's playing. What did you buy?"

"Roofing materials." He set down his bag. "It leaked again last night during the rain. While the weather's good today, I'll help you fix it."

"You're always going to so much trouble..."

"Don't say that." He cut me off, walking to the cradle. "Hey, little guy!"

Seeing him, Leo immediately babbled excitedly, his hands and feet dancing with joy.

"Come here, let me hold you." Lorenzo carefully lifted the child. "Tara, I'll take him to my place to play while you work."

"Okay, thank you."

Watching Lorenzo carry Leo toward the back door, complex emotions surged in my chest.

After that incident, Lorenzo had moved here too. His public identity had long since left Philadelphia, and now he lived in a wooden house not far away.

This past year, he'd constantly helped me—fixing the roof, unclogging pipes, moving heavy things, watching Leo...

He was like a reliable older brother, always appearing when I needed him. The obsession and fanaticism had faded from his eyes, leaving only quiet tenderness.

That evening, I went to pick up Leo.

"Thank you for watching him today."

"You're welcome." He handed the sleeping Leo to me. "Tara, I want to tell you something."

"What is it?"

"About that incident at the café." His expression grew serious. "I've always wanted to tell you the truth."

"The truth?"

"Yes." He nodded. "That day I got a call from Isabella saying you wanted to see me. She said you were waiting for me at Rittenhouse Palm Pavilion, that you had something important to tell me, and specifically asked me to bring flowers."

My heart sank.

"She... really said that?"

"Yes." Lorenzo's face darkened. "I was so happy at the time, I didn't think twice. Just bought flowers and rushed over."

"But the call I received," my voice began to tremble, "was her inviting me for tea, saying she had a surprise for me..."

Lorenzo's fists clenched tight, veins bulging.

"So..." he gritted his teeth, "she deceived both of us. Made me think you were asking to meet, and made you think I arranged the meeting..."

"Then had Kholod show up at just the right moment." I finished his thought, a chill running down my spine. "Making him think we were..."

"Having a secret affair," Lorenzo growled. "It was all Isabella's trap!"

We stared at each other in silence, feeling only bone-deep cold.

"She was lying to us from the very beginning," I murmured. "From the very beginning..."

"Tara, I'm sorry." Lorenzo was full of guilt. "If I could have stayed calm then, confirmed with you first..."

"It's not your fault."

"Why would she do this?" Lorenzo was bewildered. "Weren't you childhood friends who grew up together?"

"I don't understand either. Maybe jealousy? Maybe ambition? I don't know."

We fell silent for a long time.

"Forget it, let's not talk about that." Lorenzo finally broke the silence. "That's all in the past. Tara, you're safe now. I'll protect you both."

"Thank you, Lorenzo."

"Stop thanking me all the time." He smiled slightly. "We're friends, aren't we?"

"Yes, friends."

He turned to leave, then looked back at the door.

"Tara, get some good rest. See you tomorrow."

"See you tomorrow."

Days flowed by quietly. Every morning, I carried Leo to the shop to tend to business. At noon, Lorenzo would bring lunch, and in the evening, he'd help me close the shop before we went shopping together. Sometimes we'd share dinner, and afterward he'd play with Leo until night fell deep before saying goodbye.

This simple, warm routine almost made me forget that completely different life I'd once lived.

That day, Lorenzo finally finished fixing the roof. He climbed down the ladder, sweat beading on his forehead. "This should last a long time."

"You worked so hard." I handed him a towel. "Stay for dinner?"

"I'm actually hungry." He wiped his sweat, readily agreeing.

I prepared dinner in the kitchen while sounds of him playing with Leo came from the living room.

"Leo, come on, give me the blocks."

"Ya ya..." Leo clutched the blocks and wouldn't let go.

"Little rascal." Lorenzo laughed. "How about I trade you? This ball for your blocks?"

"Ya!" Seeing the ball, Leo immediately released the blocks and grabbed for the ball.

"What a little smarty."

Hearing their happy interaction, my chopping motions unconsciously became lighter.

At dinner, the three of us sat around the table. I fed Leo pumpkin puree while Lorenzo tasted the pasta I'd made.

"It's really good." He praised sincerely. "Your cooking keeps getting better."

"Just home cooking."

"Home cooking is the warmest." He smiled. "More comforting than fancy restaurants."

I laughed.

During our chat, I mentioned plans to set up a stall at Sequim Market next week, and he immediately offered to help watch Leo and carry merchandise.

"That's too much trouble for you..."

"Not at all." He looked at me seriously. "Tara, I'm happy to help."

Looking at him, warmth surged in my chest.

"Thank you, Lorenzo."

After dinner, Lorenzo insisted on washing dishes.

"You go spend time with Leo." He said. "I'll clean up."

"That doesn't seem right..."

"Go on, go on." He pushed me out of the kitchen. "You're tired already."

I had to go to the living room to play with Leo.

The little guy was full of energy, wanting this one moment and that the next. He reached out his little hands, grabbing at my hair.

"Ow, gentle, gentle." I laughed, moving his little hands away. "Leo, you can't pull Mommy's hair."

"Ya ya..." He giggled and reached for it again.

"You little troublemaker."

Lorenzo finished the dishes and came out, seeing us with a tender smile on his face.

"Is he bullying you again?"

"Yes," I said with mock helplessness. "This little guy has quite the grip."

"Then I'll help you." Lorenzo came over and picked up Leo. "Come on, Leo, gentlemen protect their mommies."

"Ya..." Leo squirmed in his arms.

"Good boy, let's play with this." Lorenzo picked up a stuffed animal. "Look, it's a little bear."

Leo was immediately attracted, reaching for the stuffed bear.

I sat on the couch, watching them.

Lorenzo holding Leo looked so natural, so gentle. As if Leo really was his son.

Kholod Morozov was the past. And Lorenzo—maybe he could be my future.

"Tara, it's getting late. I should go." Lorenzo handed Leo back to me. "Get some rest."

"Okay." I held Leo and walked him to the door. "Lorenzo, you get some rest too."

The next day at noon, I closed the shop and went to the backyard to see Lorenzo playing with Leo.

Lorenzo was sitting on the grass holding Leo, telling him a story.

"Once upon a time there was a little rabbit who lived in the forest..."

Leo listened intently, his little eyes fixed on him without blinking.

"What happened next?" I walked over and sat beside them.

"Then the little rabbit met a big bad wolf." Lorenzo continued. "But the little rabbit was very clever. It hid in a tree hole where the big bad wolf couldn't catch it..."

"Ee ya!" Leo clapped his little hands, seeming very happy.

Watching this scene, I suddenly felt moved. If I hadn't married Kholod back then, Lorenzo and I might really have formed a family. He would patiently play with Leo, tell him stories, be gentle and considerate with me—he'd definitely make a good father.

"Tara?" Lorenzo's voice interrupted my thoughts. "What are you thinking about?"

"Nothing." I shook my head. "Just thinking how good you are to Leo."

"He's a lovely child." Lorenzo smiled. "Besides, I like children."

"Tara," he suddenly grew serious, "have you thought about it?"

"About what?"

"What I told you last time." He looked at me. "About us."

I stayed silent as he continued gently. "I know I shouldn't rush you, but I want you to know—I truly want to marry you, want to give Leo a complete family."

"Lorenzo..."

"You don't have to answer me now." He gazed at me. "I can wait, until the day you're ready."

His eyes were so sincere, completely different from Kholod's burning possessive gaze—full of respect and acceptance.

"Lorenzo," I took a deep breath, "you know my past. You know about Leo's parentage... you really don't mind?"

"What I mind is the suffering you endured." He said firmly. "Tara, none of that matters. What matters is that I love you and am willing to accept everything about you."

His words made my eyes well up.

"But I..."

"You don't love me, I know." He interrupted. "But love can grow. As long as you're willing to give me a chance, I'll spend my whole life making you fall in love with me."

I looked at him, at this man with scars on his face but gentle eyes.

"Give me a little more time."

"We have all the time in the world." He smiled. "Take it slow, no rush."

Leo crawled onto my lap then, his little hands grabbing at my clothes.

"Ya... ah..."

"What is it, baby?"

He pointed at the swing in the distance.

"Want to play on that?" Lorenzo asked.

"Ya!" Leo waved his little hands excitedly.

Lorenzo picked him up. "Tara, you rest. I'll take him to play."

"Okay."

I watched Lorenzo carry Leo toward the swing, their silhouettes stretching long in the sunlight.

Lorenzo carefully placed Leo in the baby swing, fastened the safety belt, then gently pushed.

Leo giggled, his little hands waving. The scene was so heart-warming it made me want to cry.

I looked down at the aurora bracelet on my wrist. Sunlight hit it, making the silver chain gleam softly. I raised my hand, wanting to take it off. But when my fingers touched the clasp, I couldn't undo it.

"Forget it." I lowered my hand. "I'll try again another day."

CHAPTER THIRTY-FOUR

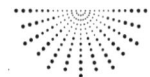

Kholod

"Speak."

My voice cut through the air like ice, the gun barrel pressed against the forehead of the man kneeling before me.

Allen McBride, Kieran's right-hand man. This bastard had been lying low until last night, when my men dragged him out of some run-down apartment in Newark.

"I'll tell you... I'll tell you everything..." He was trembling like a leaf, urine staining his pants. "Mr. Morozov... please spare my life..."

"Then start talking." I tapped his skull with the gun barrel. "Marco Bellucci. What really happened back then?"

"It was... it was Kieran who forced him..." Allen's voice shook. "Marco owed Kieran gambling debts, couldn't pay up. Kieran threatened to go after his daughter... he had no choice."

My finger tightened on the trigger.

"His daughter?"

"Yeah... that girl Noelle... Kieran knew Marco loved his daughter most, so he used her as leverage."

"What information did he leak?"

"Some... some trivial stuff..." Allen swallowed hard. "Places you frequented, your license plate numbers, and that you'd be passing through South District that night... but he didn't know Kieran had set up an ambush!"

"And his death?"

"That was Kieran..." Allen was shaking all over. "He silenced him, made it look like suicide... then spread rumors that you drove him to it..."

My breathing suddenly grew heavy.

So Marco Bellucci never wanted to kill me. Everything was just to protect Noelle.

"Who else was involved in this scheme?"

"No... no one else."

"Ah—" I snapped one of his fingers.

"Really! Really, no one else!"

"Tell me everything you know."

"There's Isabella Vance... she was Kieran's informant, responsible for passing along your information. Kieran helped her fabricate evidence to make you suspect Miss Noelle..."

"Why?"

"Because... Isabella wanted to marry you, wanted to become Mrs. Morozov..."

My hand began to tremble.

Isabella. Of course it was her. That seemingly innocent woman had actually conspired with Kieran to orchestrate such an elaborate scheme.

Bang!

The gunshot rang out. Allen collapsed in a pool of blood.

"Boss." Dmitri stepped forward.

"Dump him in the Delaware River."

"Yes, sir."

I walked out of the warehouse into the deepest darkness before dawn. Standing at the dock, watching the churning waters—the truth was finally clear.

Noelle was innocent. And I had destroyed the most innocent person of all.

"Where's Isabella Vance?"

"At her apartment."

"Bring her to me."

Half an hour later, Isabella was brought to an abandoned factory in Kensington.

When she was pushed in, she was still wearing a silk robe, her hair disheveled, makeup smeared.

"Kholod?" She saw me, terror flashing in her eyes. "What is this? Why did you bring me here?"

I sat quietly in my chair, watching her coldly.

"Kholod, say something!" Her voice began to tremble. "What did I do wrong?"

"You know exactly what you did wrong."

"I... I don't understand..."

"Don't understand?" I stood up, walking toward her step by step. "Let me help you remember. Three years ago, on Christmas Eve, the person who saved me—was that you?"

Her face instantly turned deathly pale.

"It was... it was me... I saved you..."

"Liar." I grabbed her chin. "You worked with Kieran, drove a wedge between me and Noelle, fabricated evidence, set one trap after another..."

"No... I didn't..."

"Still lying." I released her and turned to Dmitri. "Proceed as planned."

"No!" She screamed. "Kholod! Listen to me! I love you! I did all this because I love you!"

I laughed coldly. "You call this love?"

"Yes!" She sobbed. "I've loved you since the first time I saw you! But you only had eyes for Noelle! I was jealous of her! Hated her! Why should she get everything from you without lifting a finger?"

"Because she deserves it."

I leaned down and whispered in her ear.

"And you're nothing but a greedy fraud."

"No!"

"Take her away."

Isabella's screams gradually faded beyond the door.

I lit a cigar, standing in the empty factory. I'd originally planned to use every interrogation method to torture her, but now I felt only exhaustion, too drained even for anger.

Since escaping death and controlling Philadelphia—hell, half of America—I'd been confident everything was under my control. Only when it came to Noelle had I repeatedly lost my mind to suspicion and jealousy, easily believing fabricated evidence, forgetting the most basic Morozov family rule—evidence must be verified three times.

I'd even needed Anya to point out the obvious flaws.

Killing Allen, disposing of Isabella—it was just putting an end to this farce. Meaningless. Noelle had already left me, abandoned everything connected to me, vanished without a trace.

Now I didn't even know who to hate, except myself.

Back at the manor, I didn't enter the bedroom but went to the library instead. Her landscape paintings still hung on the walls, her art supplies sat by the fireplace. I picked up a charcoal pencil—so light, still bearing traces of her grip.

"Noelle..." I whispered.

Leaving the library, I pushed open the master bedroom door. Her scent hit me immediately—faint orange blossom mixed with something uniquely hers. I lay on the side where she used to sleep, her fragrance still lingering on the pillow.

Eyes closed, face buried in the pillow, suffocating regret completely overwhelmed me. Tears fell silently.

The next morning, Dmitri was already waiting in the study.

"Boss."

"Report."

"Kieran's remaining forces have been eliminated, all Philadelphia strongholds destroyed, key members confirmed dead, but Kieran escaped."

"Find him. Kill him."

"Our men are closing in. He headed northwest. Isabella has been dealt with as ordered."

I nodded.

"Next, except for those hunting Kieran, use every resource to find my wife. Remember—we're asking her to come back. No disturbance, no harm. Confirm her safety first. I'll see her myself."

"Yes, boss."

He turned to leave.

I walked to the window.

Noelle, where are you?

Are you safe?

* * *

"BOSS, WE HAVE A LEAD!" Dmitri practically burst into the study, excitement in his voice for the first time in ages.

I immediately stood and took the photograph from his hand. The image showed Iceland's blue ice cave, signed "T.C."—but that distinctive brushwork and signature made me catch my breath instantly.

"Give me details!"

"We found this painting at an auction house in Boston. After comparison by multiple experts, the brushwork is confirmed to match your wife's exactly. This is the most reliable lead we've had in two years."

Two years. She'd vanished without a trace. Zoe had gone into the mountains early to paint, Isabella was handled, and Lorenzo had disappeared, too. Only now, from these carefully designed disguises, could I glimpse her trail—both annoyed by her cleverness and proud of that quick thinking.

My fingertips traced the signature in the photo, as if I could see her standing at an easel, lost in her work.

"Any other leads?"

"We only found that the artist goes by Tara Coleman. We suspect it's Mrs. Morozov's alias. But the painting's origin isn't clear—they just said it changed hands several times."

"Tara Coleman..." I repeated the name, the style feeling strangely familiar.

"Continue investigating the painting's source."

"Yes, sir."

"Tara Coleman..." I muttered the name, unconsciously walking to the library.

I went in, pacing before the bookshelves, thinking about possible origins for this name. Casually, I caught sight of a book about Native Americans.

"Of course! The Indians!"

I rushed to the map, finding the Maka tribal lands in Washington State.

I immediately dialed. "Dmitri, send people to Washington. Focus on searching for 'Tara Coleman' who appeared suddenly two years ago."

"Yes, sir."

Found you, Noelle.

This time, I won't let you leave.

* * *

"Boss, are you really going to live here?"

Dmitri stood before a modest little building, brow furrowed.

"Yes." I pushed open the door. "You head back to Philadelphia."

"But boss—"

"The family needs someone in charge." I cut him off. "Don't contact me unless it's urgent."

Dmitri was silent for a few seconds, then finally nodded.

"Yes, boss. But Nick and the others will stay with you."

"Fine."

Niaube was a tiny seaside town with fewer than a thousand residents. Noelle's little shop was on the coastal street. This was primarily a fishing town, over 4,000 miles from Philadelphia.

Sea breeze carried the salt-tinged air. The streets were narrow, lined with colorful little houses. My place was close to Noelle's, around the corner where she couldn't easily spot me.

I positioned myself behind a wood carving near her shop, keeping hidden while watching her through the storefront window. Noelle was talking with a customer, smiling.

She wore a beige knit sweater and jeans, hair casually pulled into a ponytail. Simple, plain, yet beautiful enough to capture my complete attention.

After the customer left, I was about to approach when I saw a familiar figure emerge from the back door.

Lorenzo Conti. He was actually here! So he had helped her escape.

He was carrying a child. My breathing stopped.

The child wore a soft green onesie, curly hair framing his forehead, giggling happily.

Noelle walked over, naturally taking the child from his arms as the three of them left the shop.

"Tara, he just woke up." Lorenzo's tone was gentle and familiar.

"Thank you, Lorenzo." She kissed the child's forehead. "Hey, baby, did you miss mommy?"

The child giggled, little hands patting her cheek. Finally, I could see those eyes clearly—clear brown, identical to Noelle's.

"He's a good boy. Went right to sleep after his bottle."

"Thank you for this."

"I enjoy taking care of him."

The harmony of their scene together stabbed at my eyes. Rage boiled in my chest, my fingertips unconsciously moving to the gun at my waist.

I wanted to charge in.

I wanted to demand answers.

I wanted to—

Just as impulse peaked, memory crashed down like ice water— Noelle bound and wounded, those dead eyes looking at me saying, "Kholod, I wish you burn in hell forever."

"Kholod, I wish you burn in hell forever."

My hand slowly dropped from the gun. What right did I have to be angry? I had pushed her away with my own hands, driven her off in the most brutal way possible. This scene was nothing but the consequence of my own actions.

After the rage died, only bone-deep cold remained. I stepped back, silently watching that warm picture.

That figure who once belonged to me, that family that would never be mine.

I had lost her forever.

CHAPTER THIRTY-FIVE

Noelle

"Tara, those two guys are back."

Shahruk from the grocery store next door poked his head in, worry etched across his weathered face. He was a local, his words thick with accent.

I looked up and, sure enough, there were the same two thugs from last week standing by my door, cigarettes dangling from their lips as they surveyed my shop with obvious malice.

"I know. Thanks, Shahruk." I nodded at him.

"Want me to get the chief? Chadon will be here quick with his men." He lowered his voice. "He'll deal with these punks for sure."

"No need. I've troubled him enough already. I'll handle this myself."

Shahruk gave me a dubious look but eventually shook his head and left. He never hid his wariness of outsiders—including me, the "Tara Coleman" who'd appeared out of nowhere two years ago.

I took a deep breath and walked to the door, watching the wooden shop sign sway gently in the sea breeze.

"Can I help you?" I kept my voice steady.

"Hey there, gorgeous." The blonde thug blew smoke rings. "Seems like last time wasn't clear enough."

"This street's our territory. You know the rules?" The one with the nose ring sneered, his scar looking particularly menacing.

"Niaube doesn't have those kinds of rules."

"We're not locals." The blonde grinned and stepped inside, reaching for a painting in the window display. "We're here to teach you the rules."

He walked in and reached for one of the paintings in the window display.

"Don't touch!" I blocked him.

"Oh, feisty." He shoved me aside. "Be smart about this. Pay up. Otherwise... these crappy paintings look pretty expensive."

"Otherwise what?"

Lorenzo's voice came from the doorway, his expression dark.

"Lorenzo!" I sighed with relief.

"Scarface again." The blonde scoffed. "Want another beating?"

"I suggest you leave now." Lorenzo cracked his knuckles as he stepped inside. "Or you won't like what comes next."

"What comes next?" The nose ring guy laughed. "Just you against both of us?"

Lorenzo didn't waste words. His fist connected squarely with the blonde's face.

"Shit!"

Both thugs rushed him immediately.

I ducked behind the counter, clutching Leo tight. The baby's cries were drowned out by the sounds of fighting—fists hitting flesh, furniture crashing, and curses flying.

"Get lost!" Lorenzo roared. "Let me see you again, and you're going straight to lockup!"

The two thugs stumbled out, clutching their wounds in defeat.

"Tara, are you okay?" Lorenzo walked over, fresh scratches on his face and a split lip.

"I'm fine..." I looked at his injuries. "You're hurt..."

"Just scratches." He wiped away the blood dismissively. "They shouldn't bother you again."

"Thank you, Lorenzo."

To my surprise, not only did those two thugs never return, but all the other troublemakers in town mysteriously vanished as well.

"Shahruk," I couldn't help asking one day, "where did those thugs go?"

"No idea," he scratched his head. "Heard they left town."

"Just like that?"

"Who knows." He shrugged. "Maybe Chadon warned them off."

"Maybe."

But something still felt off.

A few days later, during a torrential downpour, water started leaking through the roof cracks again.

"Damn it..." I grabbed a pot to catch the drips. "Leaking again..."

After inspecting it the next day, Lorenzo's expression was grim. "The crack's too big. You need a professional team to redo the water-proofing."

"But..." I hesitated. "Professional repairs are so expensive..."

"About three thousand dollars. I've got some work lined up, money's decent right now. I can cover it for you."

"No." I shook my head firmly. "Lorenzo, you've already done enough for me. I'll figure it out myself."

"But Tara—"

"Really, no." I insisted. "I'll save up some money and fix it later."

Lorenzo sighed in resignation.

However, the next afternoon, a truck marked "Bay Roofing" pulled up in front of my house.

"Excuse me, is this Ms. Coleman's residence?" the lead worker called out loudly.

"Yes... that's me."

"Perfect." He pulled out a crumpled flyer. "Ma'am, we're running a raffle promotion. Your house was randomly selected for free repair service."

"A raffle?" I didn't remember entering any raffle.

"Yes, we randomly selected ten households. Here's the company documentation, take a look."

I examined it. The company documents he showed looked legitimate enough.

"Well, thank you then."

"Our pleasure!"

The repair crew was professional and efficient, completely solving the problem in just one afternoon.

Before leaving, the lead worker said, "Ms. Coleman, this roof should stay good for at least three years."

"I really can't thank you enough..."

"Just doing our job!"

Watching the truck drive away, I couldn't help but wonder. Could luck really be this convenient?

Strange things kept happening over the following days.

Every morning, a fresh bouquet of roses appeared at my shop door —no card, no sign of who left them. The gallery's door lock broke, and the next day a self-proclaimed "new locksmith in town" showed up offering free replacement. Even the usually cold supermarket owner suddenly greeted me with smiles, calling me a "special customer" and giving me fifty percent off.

"Here's your discount, Ms. Coleman." She handed me the receipt with an unsettlingly genuine smile.

"Thanks... but I don't remember signing up for membership."

"It's the boss's promotion," she said vaguely. "You're lucky."

Walking home with my shopping bags, unease spread through my chest.

Back home, I closed the shop early and started organizing a new shipment of handmade ceramics. These were custom pieces from an artist friend in Portland—each one delicate and requiring careful placement.

Leo slept peacefully in his cradle, cheeks rosy.

As I unpacked, the dust that stirred up triggered a familiar tightness in my chest.

"Cough, cough..." I gripped the shelf as breathing became difficult.

My asthma was flaring up. I instinctively reached for the inhaler in my pocket—empty.

"No..."

I frantically searched all my pockets—jacket pocket, pants pockets, apron pocket...

Nothing.

The inhaler was gone.

It must be in the bedroom.

My vision started blurring. Through the ringing in my ears, I stumbled toward the bedroom. Three steps in, my knees buckled and I crashed hard to the floor.

The loud crash woke Leo. The baby's cries mixed with my suffocation, tearing at my consciousness.

"Baby..." I reached helplessly toward the cradle, but my arm wouldn't respond.

Breathing became harder and harder.

Was I going to die?

"Leo..."

I stretched out my hand toward the cradle.

If I died, how could Lorenzo take care of him alone?

Just as consciousness began slipping away, a familiar voice cut through the fog.

"Noelle!"

Was I hallucinating?

"Fuck! Noelle!"

The glass door shattered with a tremendous crash, and I was enveloped by that familiar scent of cedar and tobacco.

"Kholod..." I struggled to open my eyes.

Kholod's pale face came into blurry focus—stubble disheveled, eyes sunken, but those amber eyes still burning bright.

"Don't talk!" His voice was trembling with a panic and terror I'd never heard before. "Damn it, where's your inhaler?"

"Bedroom... drawer..."

He carried me toward the back rest room, kicking the door open.

"Where? Which drawer?"

"...Left side..."

He set me on the couch and rushed to the drawer, ransacking it. Things scattered everywhere.

Finally, he found the blue inhaler.

"Found it!" He rushed back, dropping to his knees before me. "Open your mouth!"

I weakly parted my lips. He inserted the inhaler and pressed the spray button.

"Deep breaths! Follow my rhythm!" One hand supported the back of my neck, the other controlled the inhaler. "Breathe in... breathe out... that's right..."

The medication entered my lungs and the suffocation finally began to ease.

Once, twice, three times...

I gasped deeply, feeling my lungs finally working normally again.

"Better?" Kholod knelt before me, cupping my face in his hands, thumbs gently wiping the cold sweat from my cheeks. "Noelle, look at me. Are you okay?"

I nodded weakly.

"I'm taking you to the hospital." He moved to lift me.

"No..." I tried to push him away, my voice weak. "Why are you here..."

"Now's not the time!" He scooped me up horizontally. "You need to get checked!"

"Leo..." I struggled, turning toward the cradle by the door. "My baby..."

Leo was still crying, his little face flushed red.

"I'll have someone watch him!" Kholod strode out of the rest room carrying me.

"Nick!" he shouted toward the door. A strange man entered immediately. "Take care of the child!"

"Yes, boss!"

As he carried me out of the gallery, I heard passersby whispering. A black sedan sat conspicuously out of place on the street. Kholod settled me in the back seat, gripping my hand tightly and repeating over and over, "Don't be afraid. We'll be at the hospital soon. Hold on, please hold on..."

His palm was damp, his voice choked. He was shrouded in uncontrolled fear. I'd never seen Kholod like this—the man who always controlled everything was now trembling for me.

"Kholod..."

"I'm here." He leaned close. "Always here."

The ER lights were blinding. A nurse stopped Kholod. "You can't go in."

"No! I need to stay with her!"

"Please don't worry, sir. Your wife will be fine..."

An oxygen mask covered my face. The last thing I saw was him being held back by medical staff, eyes bloodshot, lips moving in words I couldn't hear.

CHAPTER THIRTY-SIX

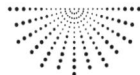

Kholod

"Did you do this?"

Lorenzo's voice echoed from the end of the hallway, thick with barely restrained fury.

I leaned against the wall outside the emergency room, my gaze fixed on that sealed door. The red light above it blazed harsh and unforgiving.

Hearing his accusation, I didn't turn around.

"Kholod Morozov!" Footsteps approached rapidly. "Answer me! Did you hurt her again?"

I slowly turned. Lorenzo stood several steps away, his face ashen, fists clenched. The light fell across the scar on his face—my handiwork.

"No." My voice came out hoarse.

"Then how the hell were you in Niaube? And just 'happened' to be there when she collapsed? You think I'd believe such a coincidence?"

"Believe what you want." I turned back to stare at that door. "But I would never hurt her."

"Bullshit!" He lunged forward, grabbing my collar. "You imprisoned her, tortured her, drove her to flee across the country! Now you're stalking her again—"

"Let go." My voice turned ice-cold.

"Like hell!" His grip tightened. "Get out of here, Kholod Morozov! Stay away from Noelle!"

I seized his wrist and twisted hard, forcing him to release me.

"Listen, Lorenzo. I'm not in the mood to fight you right now."

"You think I am?" He rubbed his reddened wrist. "I just want you gone! Noelle finally started a new life. What gives you the right to destroy it again?"

"I'm not trying to destroy anything."

"Then what are you here for?"

I fell silent. Was I supposed to admit I just wanted to watch over her from afar? To ensure she was safe, to see that she was well? Those thoughts of forcing her back had long since died. Now I only wanted to protect her in silence.

"Well?" He pressed closer. "What's your real purpose?"

"I just wanted to know she was doing well."

"And then what? Drag her back?"

"No, I—"

"Your promises are worthless."

I had no response. He was right. Where Noelle was concerned, my credibility was destroyed.

"Kholod Morozov, I'm warning you. If you hurt her again, I'll make you pay with my life if necessary."

"You won't need to." I met his eyes. "If I hurt her again, even slightly, I'll end it myself."

Lorenzo froze, clearly not expecting those words.

The emergency room doors opened. A doctor emerged, pulling off his mask. We both rushed forward.

"Doctor, how is she?" My voice trembled with tension.

"She's out of danger." The doctor said. "Acute asthma attack. Good thing you brought her in when you did. A few minutes later and..."

He didn't finish, but we understood. My legs nearly gave out.

"How is she now?" Lorenzo asked.

"Still unconscious, but her vital signs are stable. She should wake up soon."

"I need to see her."

"She still needs observation. Once she's awake, ten minutes visiting time each."

I sank back onto the bench to wait.

"Kholod."

"What?"

"These past two years... Noelle's had it rough." He took a deep breath. "Raising a child alone, running that little shop. She barely sleeps, cries constantly..."

"I know."

"You know nothing!" He grew agitated. "Do you know she trembles when she sees black cars? That she cries and begs for mercy in her nightmares? How terrified she is of seeing you again?"

Every word cut like a blade.

"Lorenzo, she's still my wife."

"You never acted like a husband."

"I love her."

That stopped him cold.

"What?"

"I said I love her." I looked him straight in the eye. "Lorenzo Conti, I know I have no right to say that. I know I hurt her beyond measure. But I need you to know—I love Noelle."

"Your love only destroys her."

"I understand," I admitted. "That's why I won't force her to come back."

"And about Leo..."

"I'll wait for Noelle to tell me herself. I respect her choice."

Lorenzo studied me carefully, shock written across his features.

"Kholod Morozov," he finally said, "I don't trust you. But I'll be watching."

"As you wish."

Noelle woke the next morning.

"The patient is awake." A nurse opened the door. "You may go in now."

Lorenzo and I both stood.

"I'm going in first."

"Says who?"

"I'm her husband."

"Bullshit!" Lorenzo snapped. "You're divorced! I'm the one who—"

"You're what?" I turned to face him.

He clenched his jaw, remaining silent.

"Lorenzo, I never signed those divorce papers."

Ignoring him, I pushed through the door.

Noelle sat propped up in bed, pale as death, the oxygen mask removed. The moment she saw me, her body went rigid, fear flashing in her eyes.

"Don't be afraid." I stopped at the doorway. "I won't hurt you."

She didn't speak, just watched me warily.

"Why are you here?" Her voice was weak.

"I arrived a month ago."

"What?"

"I bought a house near yours," I confessed. "I've been living there."

"You... you've been watching me?" Her face grew even paler.

"Protecting." I corrected. "I just wanted to ensure you were safe."

"Please leave."

"I will." I took several steps closer, stopping beside her bed. "But first, you need to know the truth."

She closed her eyes. "I don't want to hear it."

"Noelle, listen to me." I moved closer, stopping at her bedside. "I uncovered everything."

She opened her eyes, looking puzzled.

"About the attempted murder—Kieran threatened your safety to force your father into leaking some trivial information."

Her breathing quickened.

"Your father's death wasn't suicide either. Kieran killed him and staged the scene to frame me."

"No..." Tears slid down her cheeks.

"And Isabella. She was colluding with Kieran, orchestrating every deception. That day at the café—she tricked both you and Lorenzo into meeting there, then led me to witness it."

"I already know all this." She turned away. "If there's nothing else, please leave."

"Noelle, I was wrong about everything."

"Too late!" Her emotions erupted. "What gives you the right to say you were wrong after destroying everything?"

"I understand." I took a deep breath. "I know no apology can heal your pain. But I must tell you—"

I dropped to my knees.

Noelle stared in shock, eyes wide.

"Kholod! You—"

"I'm sorry." I bowed my head, voice breaking. "Noelle, I'm sorry."

"Get up." Noelle stammered.

"I shouldn't have doubted you." I raised my reddened eyes. "Shouldn't have believed Isabella's lies, shouldn't have been deceived by fabricated evidence, and I never should have... hurt you like that."

"Kholod, get up..."

"No." I shook my head. "Noelle, I must apologize on my knees."

"Kholod Morozov!" She raised her voice. "Get up!"

"Not unless you forgive me."

"Never!" She pounded the bed rail in fury. "You think kneeling erases what you did? I would never—"

She stopped mid-sentence, her face flushing red, breathing becoming rapid again.

"Kholod! You promised you wouldn't hurt her anymore!"

Lorenzo burst in, shoving me aside and quickly placing the oxygen mask over Noelle's face. He glared at me with blazing eyes.

I'd messed up again. My fists clenched until my knuckles went white. Once again, I'd hurt her.

Lorenzo hauled me to my feet and drove his fist into my face. The impact sent me staggering backward, my lower back hitting the wall.

"You bastard!" He landed another punch to my stomach. "You promised you wouldn't hurt her again!"

Nausea churned through me. Instinctively, I raised my fist to retaliate—

But seeing Noelle struggling to breathe on the bed, all fight drained from me.

It was me.

I did this to her again.

I unclenched my fist, dropping all resistance.

Lorenzo hesitated momentarily, then unleashed even more violent punches.

One, two, three...

My lip split, blood poured from my nose, my eye socket swelled. Each blow carried his hatred. I didn't dodge or defend, just let him vent his rage.

"You know how much she's suffered!" He roared. "And now you do this to her again! She's lying in a hospital bed, you bastard!"

Another punch struck my face.

"Do you know what she—"

"Enough."

Noelle's weak voice interrupted him. She removed the oxygen mask, struggling to sit up.

"Noelle!" Lorenzo rushed over. "Don't move, you need to rest—"

"Stop, Lorenzo."

She looked at me, eyes cold as frost. "Kholod, please leave."

I wiped blood from my mouth. "I still have things to say—"

"No need." She cut me off, voice weak but firm. "Kholod Morozov, I never want to see you again."

"Noelle..."

"Leave." Tears streamed down her face. "For saving my life, I'm begging you to disappear from my world forever."

"I..."

"If you don't go," she took a shaky breath, voice trembling, "I'll jump from that window. Kholod, I'd rather die than see you again."

Those words extinguished all hope like ice water. Seeing the finality in her eyes, I finally understood—

"Alright." My voice was hollow. "I'll go."

Step by step, I backed toward the door, each movement tearing through me like agony.

At the threshold, I stopped, my back to her. "Take care, Noelle."

I pushed open that door that would forever separate our futures. Nick's subordinates waited in the hallway.

"Boss, you—"

"We're leaving."

"But—"

"Now."

"Yes, sir."

One final glance at that closed door, and I knew this was the ending I deserved.

CHAPTER THIRTY-SEVEN

Noelle

"Tara, more stuff for you," Shahruk called from outside the shop.

I pushed open the door and picked up the blue gift box with the Tiffany logo, irritation surging through me.

"Did you tick someone off?"

"Just some stalker I can't shake."

"Want me to call Chief Chadon?"

"No." I hefted the heavy box in my hands. "He's just a nutcase. Let him waste his time."

I opened the box. A diamond necklace sparkled in the sunlight.

"Jesus..." Shahruk sucked in a breath. "How much is that thing worth..."

"Doesn't matter how expensive it is. It's still garbage." Without hesitation, I tossed the box into the trash can by the door.

Clang.

A few locals walking by stopped dead in their tracks, staring at me in disbelief.

"Outsiders are so weird..."

"But those were diamonds..."

I ignored the murmurs and headed back into the shop, Shahruk following close behind. "Even if you don't want it, you could sell it."

"I don't need the money. You want it? Everything that comes after this is yours."

"I wouldn't dare touch anything that shady." He waved his hands frantically. "What if that psycho comes after me..."

This was the fifth day since I'd been discharged from the hospital. The expensive gifts had been arriving nonstop since I came back. Did Kholod Morozov think he could buy forgiveness with this junk?

Dream on.

As I said this, my eyes drifted toward the window. That shadowy figure lurking behind the wooden sculpture was still there, watching.

He was watching.

Perfect. I wanted him to understand that his money meant absolutely nothing to me.

That afternoon, another box arrived—half my height. I had someone carry it straight to the garbage pile out back.

"Don't you want to see what's inside?" the delivery guy asked.

"No point."

These annoying gifts kept coming, only making me despise him more.

I went out to collect some tapestries. When I returned, there was another box waiting.

I opened it. Baby clothes, toys, and various high-end baby supplies scattered everywhere. Every piece was from a top brand, every piece worth a fortune.

I gritted my teeth, crouched down, and started picking everything up piece by piece, shoving it all back into the box.

Just as I stuffed the last piece of clothing back in, a voice came from behind me.

"Tara, did he send more stuff?"

It was Lorenzo. He walked over, glanced at the box contents, and his face immediately darkened.

"Damn it." He picked up the box, headed upstairs, pushed open the window, and hurled the entire thing onto the street without hesitation.

The box tumbled through the air and crashed down hard—Kholod should have seen every bit of it.

"Like a bloody ghost." Lorenzo turned back to me. "Maybe you should consider moving?"

"Where could I go?" I laughed bitterly. "He found me all the way out here."

Lorenzo fell silent, too.

"Don't worry, you still have me." He took my hand. "I'll always take care of you and Leo."

Looking at him, warmth filled my chest. Thank God I still had Lorenzo by my side.

That evening, Lorenzo came to help me give Leo a bath.

"How's the water temperature? Too hot?"

"Just right." I lowered Leo into the baby tub. "Bath time, sweetheart."

"Gah gah!" Leo happily splashed the water, sending droplets flying everywhere.

"Whoa!" Lorenzo got splashed in the face. "You little rascal!"

I couldn't help laughing. "Leo, stop playing with the water."

"Gah!" Leo completely ignored me, his little hands continuing to splash.

"Watch this." Lorenzo held up a rubber duck to catch Leo's attention. "When you're bigger, I'll teach you how to swim."

"He's still too young."

"He'll grow up fast." He gently wiped the baby's arm. "Tara, when Leo's older, we can take him traveling."

Just then, Leo splashed again, this time soaking my face.

Lorenzo couldn't help but laugh. "Nice shot, little guy!"

"Don't encourage him!" I pretended to be annoyed and splashed water back at him.

The impromptu water fight filled the bathroom with laughter, Leo giggling delightedly in his tub.

"Truce! Truce!" I laughed, surrendering.

"You started it." Lorenzo's eyes sparkled with mischief. "Giving up?"

"I surrender!"

After wrapping Leo in a towel, I nudged the soaked Lorenzo toward the door. "Go change your clothes before you catch a cold."

"See you tomorrow." He left reluctantly.

After seeing Lorenzo off, I carried Leo back to the bedroom.

I changed him into clean pajamas and placed him in his crib.

"Sleep tight, okay?" I kissed his forehead.

"Gah gah..." He yawned, his little eyes slowly closing.

I sat beside the bed, watching him sleep. This kind of peaceful, warm routine—this was what real life should be.

The next day at noon, Leo babbled and pointed at the window. I followed his gaze—the figure behind the wooden sculpture was still there.

"Don't look that way, baby." I turned to block his view. "There's a bad man over there."

Leo blinked, seeming to half-understand.

The shop bell chimed. Lorenzo walked in carrying lunch. "Brought your favorite seafood chowder."

"Thank you for always being so thoughtful."

He reached out to take Leo, and the baby immediately threw himself into Lorenzo's arms with delight.

Watching their closeness, I suddenly thought of that voyeur. Since Kholod insisted on watching, I'd give him something worth seeing.

I walked over to Lorenzo and deliberately slipped my arm through his.

"Lorenzo." I looked up at him.

"Yeah?" He seemed surprised—this was the first time I'd been so forward.

"I've made up my mind," I said. "About what you asked me before."

"Really?" His eyes lit up. "You mean..."

"I'm willing to try." I deliberately raised my voice. "To give Leo a complete family."

Lorenzo was speechless with joy.

"Tara..." He held Leo with one arm, wanting to embrace me with the other. "You... you really mean it?"

I didn't answer with words. Instead, I stood on my tiptoes and kissed his cheek.

Lorenzo's face turned crimson instantly. "Tara, you..."

"What, I can't do that?" I asked teasingly.

"No! Of course you can!" He pulled me close excitedly. "I... I'm so happy! Tara, I'll be good to you, I'll take care of you and Leo, I swear—"

"I know." I cut him off. "I trust you."

We stood there in the shop, sunlight streaming through the window. The scene probably looked heartwarming, like genuine lovers.

But only I knew how frantically my heart was beating, how cold my palms were.

Though I wasn't completely ready, I really didn't want to face Kholod anymore.

"The weather's lovely today. Want to take Leo to the beach?" Lorenzo suggested the next morning while helping me hang tapestries.

We strolled slowly along the boardwalk. Lorenzo pushed the stroller while seagulls circled overhead, crying out.

"Tara," he suddenly stopped walking. "Do you really want to be with me?"

"Yes," I nodded. "I want to give Leo a stable home."

"Just for the baby?" He studied my face. "Do you have feelings for me?"

I was quiet for several seconds. How should I answer? Say yes? That would be lying to him. Say no? That would be too cruel.

"I'll try my best." I finally said. "Lorenzo, I'll try to love you. At least right now, being with you makes me feel safe."

"That's enough for me." He smiled. "I just want you to be happy."

He gently took my hand. I didn't pull away, allowing that warmth to flow between us. Leo slept peacefully in his stroller. This moment of tranquility made me think that maybe life could continue like this forever.

Out of the corner of my eye, I caught sight of a figure standing on the distant rocks. Kholod stood there, the sea breeze lifting his coat, his silhouette isolated and forlorn.

I deliberately moved closer to Lorenzo.

"Getting cold?" he asked with concern.

"Let's walk a bit more. It's such beautiful weather."

When we passed in front of Kholod, Lorenzo naturally put his arm around my shoulders. "Watch out for the rocks."

I could feel that burning gaze following us until his figure gradually blurred in the distance.

That evening, I was feeding Leo when the doorbell rang.

"Who is it?" I called out.

"It's me."

Kholod's voice made my hand tremble slightly, and I nearly dropped the bottle.

"I don't want to see you," I said. "Go away."

"Noelle, I want to talk to you."

"We have nothing to talk about."

"Just five minutes." His voice sounded almost pleading from outside the door.

I bit my lip, then finally stood up, carrying Leo to the door.

After a moment's hesitation, I opened it while still holding Leo.

Kholod stood outside, his face still bearing bruises from his altercation with Lorenzo.

"Five minutes only." I stepped aside to let him in.

He walked in, his gaze immediately falling on Leo in my arms.

"He..."

"Has nothing to do with you." I cut him off. "Kholod, say what you came to say."

He held out a first aid kit in his hands. "I noticed your inhaler is nearly empty. This is a new one."

"I don't need it."

"Noelle, this is about your safety." He insisted. "You can hate me,

319

you can refuse to forgive me, but please don't gamble with your own life."

I bit my lip, then finally accepted the first aid kit.

"Is there anything else?"

"Yes." He took a deep breath. "Noelle, give me a chance to make amends."

"No."

"Please." His voice was almost humble. "Let me do something for you."

Looking at this man who had once been so arrogant now humbling himself before me, complex emotions churned in my chest. I should have refused outright, but instead I heard myself saying:

"You really want to make amends?"

"Yes."

"Fine." I lifted my chin with a cold smile. "Do one thing for me. If you succeed, I'll give you that chance."

CHAPTER THIRTY-EIGHT

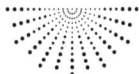

Kholod

"Raw lazurite?"

I stared at the data on screen, frowning. Noelle wanted ultramarine ground from top-grade lazurite from Afghanistan's Sar-e-Sang mines.

"What?" Nick was stunned. "Boss, you can't go! It's not just the altitude—the whole region's a war zone! Taliban controls most areas, mining's all done by hand on steep cliffs, cave-ins and falls happen constantly..."

"I don't care." I kept scrolling through the files. "She wants it, I'm getting it for her."

"But boss, we could send our people—"

"No." I cut him off. "Has to be me."

"What?" Nick looked shocked. "Boss, have you lost your mind? That place is a war zone!"

"I know." I closed the laptop. "But this has to be personal to mean anything."

"Boss—"

"Nick, set it up." I stood. "Fastest route, local guides, security detail."

"Boss, you're really doing this?" He was still trying to talk me out of it. "The danger level... Dmitri will never approve..."

"Nick, that's an order."

Nick fell silent, then finally nodded. "I'll put together the best team."

Two days later, I boarded a private jet bound for Kabul.

"Boss, this is Abdullah, our local contact." Nick made introductions. "He knows the Badakhshan mining region inside out."

A bearded Afghan man stepped forward and bowed. "Mr. Morozov, honored to serve you."

"Can you find the best veins?"

"Yes, sir. But the mines are dangerous now, frequent firefights..."

"I only care about results."

"We'll need armed escorts, bribes for all factions, professional climbing gear..."

"Money's not an issue."

As the plane took off, I closed my eyes and recalled Noelle's words —the masters used ultramarine that had to be ground from lazurite. That deep blue couldn't be replicated with synthetic pigments.

No matter how dangerous, I'd get it for her.

Kabul airport was chaos.

Armed soldiers everywhere, tension thick in the air.

"Sir, stay close to me."

We got into a battered SUV, part of a three-vehicle convoy, each loaded with armed men.

"Kabul to the Sar-e-Sang Mining Area in Badakhshan takes about two days," Abdullah said. "We'll hit several checkpoints, but I've greased the right palms. Just..."

"Speak."

"Mountain conditions change fast." He said. "Sir, are you absolutely sure? I could send my most trusted men instead—"

"No." I said. "Has to be me."

"Alright." He sighed. "Then we go. God willing."

The convoy left Kabul and entered the mountains.

Roads were rough as hell, the vehicle lurching violently.

At checkpoints, Abdullah smoothly handed over cash.

"In Afghanistan, money solves a lot of problems," he said. "But not all of them."

The next day at noon, the convoy reached the mountain base. Looking up at snow peaks piercing the clouds, Abdullah handed me climbing gear. "From here we walk. The mines are at seventeen thousand four hundred feet."

"How long?"

"If we're lucky, eight to ten hours. You have high-altitude experience?"

"No."

"It's going to be hell."

The climb was brutal. Past thirteen thousand feet, splitting headaches and breathing problems forced me to use an oxygen mask.

"Sir, your lips are turning blue."

"Keep moving."

When we finally saw the mine entrance, I was running on fumes. The opening in the cliff face looked ready to collapse.

"The mine runs deep, could cave in anytime." Abdullah handed me a hard hat. "Any trouble, we evacuate immediately."

I nodded and put on the gear. The mine entrance was narrow, barely wide enough to crawl through. We got on our bellies and started in. The rock was ice-cold and sharp, tearing my clothes.

"Sir, watch those jagged stones!" Abdullah called from behind.

Breathing got harder, my head felt like it would explode.

"Damn it..."

I stopped, gasping.

No, I couldn't stop.

I kept crawling forward.

Finally, the tunnel opened up some.

I managed to stand, and by headlamp light, saw the surrounding rock walls.

Deep blue lazurite veins threaded through the stone.

"Abdullah," I called back, "where's the best stuff?"

"Further in!" his voice echoed from outside the tunnel. "But sir, it's more dangerous! The walls aren't stable!"

"Got it!"

I continued deeper.

Loose stones under my feet kept sliding, making scraping sounds.

About fifty meters in, I saw it.

A perfect piece of lazurite, embedded in the wall.

Fist-sized, deep blue throughout, with evenly distributed golden pyrite flecks that glittered under my headlamp.

"That's it..."

I pulled out chisel and hammer, carefully starting to chip away.

One strike, two, three...

Each hit had to be controlled—too light wouldn't work, too hard might crack the stone.

Sweat ran down my face. In this freezing mine, I was burning up like I was in a furnace.

"Crack—"

The stone finally loosened.

Just then—

A massive explosion, the whole tunnel shaking violently.

"What the hell?"

"No!" Abdullah's face went white. "That's blasting! Must be the next tunnel over! Get out!"

Before he finished speaking, rocks started falling from the ceiling.

"Run!"

I spun around, but it was too late.

A huge boulder slammed down right in front of me, blocking the exit.

"Shit!"

Dust filled the air, choking me.

"Sir! Sir!" Abdullah's voice came from the other side. "Are you okay?"

"I'm fine!" I shouted back.

"I'm outside!" he said. "Sir, don't move! I'll get help!"

Footsteps faded away, leaving me alone in the tunnel. Dark, cold, dead silent. I leaned against the wall, gasping. The thin air made my head spin again.

"Damn it!" My oxygen tank had been punctured by falling rocks. Was I going to die here? In some foreign mine shaft?

"No..."

I couldn't die. I hadn't earned Noelle's forgiveness yet. I hadn't made it up to her. I couldn't die.

I felt around and stood up, using the weak light from my torch to look for a way out.

Rocks piled like mountains, completely blocking the way back.

"Fuck..."

I started clawing at the stones with my hands. One, two... my fingers were soon raw and bleeding, blood mixing with dirt.

But I couldn't stop.

"Noelle..." I mumbled. "Wait for me..."

I don't know how long passed—could've been an hour, could've been three—when I finally heard voices outside.

"Sir! Sir!"

"Still alive!" I called back.

"Hang on! We're getting you out!"

The sound of drilling started, deafening. Rocks cleared bit by bit. Finally, light broke through.

"Sir! Quick!" Abdullah's face appeared in the crack. "Grab my hand!"

I reached out, and he yanked me through.

The moment I saw daylight again, I gulped down fresh air.

"Sir, you're hurt!" Abdullah stared at my mangled hands.

"I'm fine." I stood up, swaying as I headed back toward the mine. "The lazurite... I didn't get it..."

"Sir! You can't go back in!"

"I have to!" I broke free from him. "I promised her... I have to deliver..."

"Sir!"

Ignoring his protests, I went back into the mine. This time, I was more careful, moving slowly along the walls. Finally, I saw that piece of stone again.

I carefully chiseled out the lazurite. When I held the cold stone in my palm, I finally breathed easy.

"Noelle... I found it."

The descent was even harder. The shoulder wound kept bleeding, every step pulling at torn flesh. Blood loss made the altitude sickness worse, dizziness hitting in waves. I nearly fell several times.

The convoy was ambushed on the way down, bullets whining as they struck the vehicles.

"Get down!" Abdullah yelled.

I ducked, protecting the wooden box with the lazurite, gunfire thundering around us. Ten minutes later, the attackers finally withdrew.

"Sir, you okay?" Abdullah looked back at me.

"Fine," I said, though my ears were still ringing.

"Too dangerous." He said. "We need to get out of here fast."

The convoy sped up, finally leaving the mountain region before dark.

When we reached Kabul, I was barely conscious.

"Boss, you need rest," Nick said. "You look like hell."

"No need," I said. "Back to America."

"But your hands..."

My mangled hands had lost several fingernails completely.

"Deal with it on the plane."

"Boss—"

"Leave now."

Nick sighed helplessly. "Yes, boss."

During the flight, exhaustion, altitude sickness, and infection finally knocked me out. The last thing I heard in the darkness was Nick's panicked shouting.

When I came to, the smell of hospital disinfectant hit me.

"You were out for two days." Nick was keeping watch by the bed.

"Where's the lazurite?" I struggled to sit up.

"Right here." He quickly handed over the wooden box. "Boss, lie back down, the doctor wants you under observation..."

"No." I threw off the covers. "I'm going to see Noelle."

"Boss!"

"Pull out these tubes."

"But—"

"Now."

Knowing how stubborn I was, Nick complied.

"At least let me bandage your wounds..."

"You can do it on the plane."

We landed in Washington, then drove straight to Niaube.

"Boss, you sure you don't need more rest?" Nick looked at me worriedly. "You look terrible..."

"I'm fine."

The car finally entered the small town.

"Stop here," I said.

"Yes."

I pushed open the door and got out with the box.

"Let me help you." Nick came around to support my arm.

"No need. I'll go myself."

Sea wind carrying salt spray hit my face. I walked toward that familiar shop, clutching the wooden box, the sign swaying gently in the breeze.

I pushed open the door. The bell chimed.

"Welcome—"

Noelle's voice cut off. She stood frozen with her paintbrush, staring at me in disbelief.

"Kholod? You..."

"I found it." I walked over and set the box on the counter. "The lazurite you wanted."

She stared blankly at the box.

"Open it," I said.

She hesitantly lifted the lid, her breath catching.

"This... this is..."

"Top-grade lazurite," I said. "I dug it out myself."

"You went to Afghanistan?" Her voice trembled. "There's a war going on!"

"I know."

"Why risk it?"

"Because it's what you wanted." I looked into her eyes. "Noelle, whatever you want, I'll get it for you."

Her gaze fell on my bandaged hands.

"Your hands..."

"Nothing, just scratches," I said, though my fingers were still throbbing. "Noelle, I did it. That chance to make things right—does it still count?"

CHAPTER THIRTY-NINE

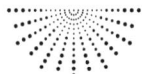

Noelle

"Tara, you're really going to let him stay?"

Lorenzo stood at my front door, his face dark with anger, eyes fixed on Kholod, who sat awkwardly in my living room, looking completely out of place.

"I made a promise." I kept my voice calm. "Lorenzo, he did bring back the lazurite. I can't go back on my word."

That condition was meant to make him back down. I never thought he'd actually risk his life to bring back the mineral, returning covered in cuts and bruises. Right now, I couldn't bring myself to keep being harsh.

"But—"

"He wants to make amends, so I'll let him." I shrugged. "What's wrong with free labor?"

Lorenzo stared at me in disbelief. "Tara, are you serious?"

"Of course." I nodded. "Lorenzo, think about it. We're both busy, and taking care of Leo is exhausting enough. Now someone's helping —doesn't that make things easier?"

"But he's Kholod Morozov!" Lorenzo lowered his voice. "Have you forgotten what he did to you?"

"Of course I haven't forgotten." My voice turned cold. "Lorenzo, I'll never forget. But that's exactly why I want him to pay. Making him work his ass off to compensate me—isn't that perfect?"

Lorenzo froze, studying me carefully.

"You... you really see him as just labor?"

"What else?" I shot back. "Lorenzo, do you think I'd forgive him?"

He fell quiet for a few seconds, then finally nodded.

"Fine." He said. "But Tara, I'll be watching him. If he crosses any line, I won't hold back."

A few days later, my asthma flared up again.

Not as severe as last time, but it left me miserable for an entire day.

"Noelle, you need proper rest," Kholod said. "I have a mountaintop villa outside Washington—beautiful environment, fresh air. I thought..."

"No need." I cut him off.

"Noelle, let me finish." He persisted. "There's a professional medical team there, plus a nutritionist. You could really recover..."

"I said no." My tone grew cold. "Kholod, I'm not going anywhere that belongs to you."

"But your health—"

"I know my own body," I said. "I don't need any villa or medical team. I'm fine here."

"But—"

"No buts." I stood up. "Kholod, if you really want to make amends, stop making these requests."

He fell silent.

"Fine, I won't bring it up again," he said. "Then... could I move in to take care of you?"

"What?"

"I mean, move in here," he said. "That way I could look after you and Leo whenever needed..."

"Don't even think about it," I said firmly. "Kholod Morozov, if you dare move in, I'm moving out immediately."

"Okay, okay, I won't move in," he said quickly. "Can I come by every day then?"

"Whatever."

"I'll be here on time tomorrow."

"Fine."

* * *

"HOW DOES THIS... STICK..." Kholod held the diaper, completely lost.

"You put it on backwards." I pointed out coldly. "The velcro goes on the outside."

He fumbled to adjust it, his movements so clumsy that Leo started crying in discomfort.

"Let me." I stepped forward and took the baby. "You're just making it worse."

"Sorry." He stepped back like a student who'd made a mistake.

I changed the diaper efficiently, gently patting Leo to calm him. Kholod asked carefully, "Could you teach me how to change diapers?"

"Why should I teach you?" I sat on the couch with the baby. "The all-powerful Kholod Morozov doesn't know how to change diapers?"

"I really don't know how to take care of children." He said quietly. "But I want to learn."

"Then figure it out yourself."

The next morning, he showed up on time with breakfast ingredients.

"You actually cook?" I raised an eyebrow.

"You barely ate anything yesterday." He insisted. "For Leo's sake, you need to take care of yourself."

I considered it, then finally let him in.

"Put it in the kitchen."

"Okay."

He went into the kitchen and started clumsily preparing breakfast.

I sat in the living room with Leo, listening to the sounds from the kitchen.

"Noelle, how do you like your eggs?" He poked his head out.

"Whatever."

"Should I fry one for you?"

"Sure."

Soon, the kitchen filled with sizzling sounds and the aroma of eggs.

But then—

"Shit!"

A curse, followed by the smoke alarm's piercing shriek.

I carried Leo to the kitchen doorway and saw Kholod frantically waving a towel, trying to clear the smoke.

The eggs in the pan were burnt black.

"What are you doing?"

"I..." He looked at me sheepishly. "The heat was too high..."

"So you turned the eggs into charcoal?"

"Sorry..."

I walked over, turned off the exhaust fan, and opened the window.

"Forget it. I'll do it myself."

"No, let me." He insisted. "Noelle, I'll get it right."

"You sure?" I looked at the charred eggs.

"I'm sure."

"Suit yourself." I returned to the living room with Leo.

Ten minutes later, Kholod emerged carrying a plate.

"Noelle, it's ready."

I glanced at it—

The eggs were scrambled into pieces, the bacon half-burnt, the toast hard as rocks.

"This is what you call 'ready'?"

"I..." His face reddened. "I really tried my best..."

"This is your best? You can't even make breakfast, and you want to make amends?"

"Sorry..." He hung his head. "I... I'll keep trying..."

"Forget it." I stood up and handed Leo to him. "Hold him. I'll cook."

"Okay..." He carefully took Leo.

I went into the kitchen and surveyed the disaster zone, sighing deeply.

I cracked two fresh eggs and fried them quickly.

Cooked new bacon, toasted fresh bread.

When I came out with the plate, I saw Kholod holding Leo stiffly, his posture so awkward it was almost comical.

"Holding him like that makes him uncomfortable."

"Then... how should I hold him?"

"Support his head, steady his bottom." I demonstrated. "Like this. Got it?"

"Let me try..."

He adjusted his position but still looked stiff.

Leo squirmed in his arms, clearly uncomfortable.

"Forget it, give him back." I took Leo back.

"Noelle..."

"What?"

"Thank you for teaching me," he said earnestly.

After that, he showed up every day. Despite constant mishaps—pasta turned to mush, formula powder spilled everywhere—he was slowly improving.

A month later, he could finally handle basic tasks like making bottles and changing diapers independently.

"Noelle, look, I did it!" He held Leo, beaming with pride. "He's not crying!"

"Wow," I responded flatly. "That's nice."

"Maybe I deserve some praise?" Kholod suddenly asked tentatively.

I looked up, surprised.

"It's what you're supposed to do." I looked back down at my ledger. "Nothing worth praising."

The light in his eyes dimmed momentarily, then he nodded. "You're right."

Seeing him look so earnest yet dejected, I felt an unexpected pang of sympathy.

"I hope you maintain today's standard."

His eyes lit up.

"I will! Noelle, I'll definitely do better!"

I turned away, not wanting him to see the slight smile tugging at my lips.

That afternoon, Kholod played with Leo's blocks in the living room.

He sat stiffly on the carpet, letting Leo stack blocks on his head one by one.

"Leo, don't mess around..."

Leo giggled and picked up another block.

"Fine, fine..." Kholod surrendered. "Stack away if you want..."

I sat on the couch, organizing accounts while secretly watching them. Leo placed the final block on Kholod's head, then clapped and cheered.

"Ya ya!"

"Pretty impressive, right?" Kholod carefully maintained his balance, afraid the blocks would topple. "Leo's so smart."

I couldn't help but laugh.

Kholod turned his head, and all the blocks crashed down at once.

"Ah—" Leo froze for a second, his little mouth pouting, about to cry.

"Don't cry, don't cry!" Kholod quickly soothed him. "I'll stack them with you again, okay?"

Leo broke into a smile.

Watching them, a strange feeling welled up inside me, and I found myself smiling unconsciously.

"You smiled." Kholod suddenly looked up, his eyes bright with surprise.

"You're seeing things."

"I saw it." He insisted, his voice carrying a lightness I hadn't heard in ages. "You finally smiled at me."

"I was just laughing at Leo."

He didn't argue further, but joy was written across his entire face.

I turned back to my work, feeling my heartbeat skip.

That evening, Lorenzo returned. He'd gone to Portland for a major job, renovating an entire villa, and had been gone almost two weeks.

"Tara!" He burst through the door, dusty from travel. "I'm back!"

"Lorenzo!" I stood up. "You're back? Work finished?"

"Yeah, finished ahead of schedule." He set down his suitcase, eyes scanning the room. "Where's Kholod?"

"He just left," I said. "Went to buy groceries for dinner."

"He's still here?" Lorenzo's brow furrowed. "How long has it been? Isn't that enough?"

"He's helping me," I said. "Lorenzo, taking care of Leo alone is truly exhausting."

"Well, I'm back now," he interrupted. "Time for him to go, right?"

I was momentarily speechless.

"What?" Lorenzo caught my hesitation. "You don't want him to leave?"

"It's not that I don't want him to leave," I said. "It's just that he finally learned how to take care of Leo..."

"So what if he learned?" Lorenzo cut me off. "Tara, he's Kholod Morozov! Have you forgotten?"

"Of course I haven't forgotten..."

"Then why are you..." He stared at me. "Tara, you smiled when you mentioned him just now."

I froze.

"I didn't..."

"You did." Lorenzo stepped closer. "When you said he finally learned, your voice was gentle, and you were smiling. Tara, you've softened toward him, haven't you?"

"I haven't softened."

"You have!" His voice rose. "Tara, have you forgotten? Have you forgotten how he treated you?"

"No, I haven't!"

"Then why are you so gentle with him?" Lorenzo demanded. He suddenly rolled up his sleeve, revealing several ugly scars on his arm —remnants from when Kholod's men had kidnapped him.

"You see this?" He pointed to the permanent scar on his face, his voice trembling with emotion. "These are all from him! Tara, have you forgotten what he really is? He's a monster!"

"I remember!" Tears spilled from my eyes. "I've never forgotten that pain!"

"Then why keep him around?"

"Because he's Leo's father! It's not that simple!"

The room fell dead silent. Lorenzo stood frozen, his face draining of color.

"So..." He looked at me, eyes filled with hurt. "You're choosing him?"

"No," I said. "Lorenzo, I don't know what to do either. But blood ties can't be erased."

"Blood ties?" His voice turned sharp. "A man who nearly destroyed you deserves to be Leo's father?"

"Lorenzo..." That familiar suffocating feeling gripped me. "Let go of me!"

"You promised to be with me..."

"But my life should be my choice!" I broke free from his grip. "Lorenzo, I'm grateful for your care, but you don't get to choose for me."

"But—"

"No buts!" I cut him off.

"I'm just worried about you." His voice dropped. "I'm afraid he'll hurt you again."

"I know you mean well, Lorenzo," my tone softened slightly. "I need time. I need time to sort through all of this."

"You still love him, don't you?" He asked, voice trembling. "You never really let go."

I fell silent. Watching Kholod clumsily learn to change diapers, carefully prepare breakfast—that ice seemed to be quietly melting.

"I'm sorry. I'm so confused right now."

"Then what am I?" His eyes filled with pain. "Did you agree to be with me just to spite him?"

"It's not like that..."

"Enough." He smiled bitterly as he headed for the door. "I need some air."

"Lorenzo..."

"Don't follow me."

I stood there as tears streamed down my face. I'd hurt Lorenzo, and I didn't know how to face Kholod either. I didn't want to forgive Kholod—or rather, I didn't want to forgive him easily.

Leo started crying in his crib, frightened by the argument.

"Don't cry, sweetheart..." I picked him up and whispered soothingly. "Mommy's here."

CHAPTER FORTY

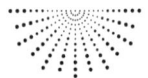

Noelle

"Did your heart run off with him?"

Kholod's voice came from the doorway, low and dangerous.

I lounged on the sofa with my eyes closed, resting. At his words, I opened them and shot him a cold glare. "Kholod Morozov, don't start acting crazy here."

"I just want to know," he said, stepping closer, "are you in love with him?"

"None of your business."

"How is it not?" He sat across from me. "You're my wife."

"Ex-wife," I corrected. "I signed the divorce papers."

"But I didn't." His voice dropped low. "Noelle, you smile for him, you're gentle with him, but with me, you're always ice cold. I get jealous too... Can't you smile at me a little more?"

"You deserve it." I stood up. "If it weren't for you, I could've had a peaceful life with Lorenzo, no nightmares, no painful memories every time I see you—"

Before I finished, I caught the flicker of hurt in his eyes. Those reddening rims sparked a twisted thrill in me. I stepped forward, tilting my head up to stare down this towering man who looked utterly wrecked right now.

"So, what gives you the right to be jealous?"

His Adam's apple bobbed, like he wanted to say something, but my sharp gaze shut him down.

"I don't want to hear your excuses." My voice stayed soft. "Right now, you don't get to question me. Only to obey."

I eased back onto the sofa, like he was the one under scrutiny.

"Look me in the eyes."

He lifted his head as told.

"Remember this feeling, Kholod." I hammered each word into his heart. "Insecurity, jealousy, that gnawing fear... That's everything you put me through. Now it's your turn to taste it."

I leaned forward a bit, my gaze burning into him.

"You want my attention? Want me to smile at you like I do for Lorenzo?" I chuckled softly. "Fine. But not by throwing tantrums, making threats, or that pathetic possessiveness."

My eyes roamed his face, forcing him to face the rules.

"Earn it with loyalty, regret, and proving yourself day after day. Got it?"

His breathing came rough, and finally, he ground out through clenched teeth, "...Got it."

"Then go. I don't want to hear another word about Lorenzo tonight."

I got up to pour some water, ignoring him.

Suddenly, he wrapped his arms around me from behind, burying his face in the crook of my neck. His voice muffled, laced with a barely hidden plea. "Noelle... Don't leave me..."

I felt the strength in his hold, didn't pull away, didn't respond. The glass clinked crisply as I set it down in the silence.

"Kholod, is this your idea of regret? Forcing a hug against my will to beg for comfort?"

He froze, slowly released me, and stepped back. I turned, seeing the aggrieved unease on his face, and that thrill bubbled up again.

Fun.

"Looks like you didn't really get it. Fine, tomorrow night, I'm hosting Zoe. You'll handle dinner prep and serving."

Yeah, Zoe was back from the woods, knew I was here, and wanted to visit.

His pupils flickered—making the Morozov boss play waiter? Pure humiliation.

"Not willing?" I arched a brow. "That's how regretful you are?"

"...No." He lowered his eyes. "I'll do it."

The next evening, Kholod stood in the corner of the dining room, dressed in a perfectly tailored black suit. When Zoe glanced at him curiously, his jaw tightened, but he still stepped forward to pour our wine, just like I demanded.

"This is Kholod," I said casually. "Helping out tonight."

Zoe clearly recognized him and knocked over her glass in shock. Kholod's temple vein throbbed, but he silently righted it and refilled.

All through dinner, I deliberately ignored him, chatting and laughing with Zoe. Only when dessert came did I glance his way.

"This wine's bland." I swirled my glass. "What do you think?"

He paused, then said low, "My oversight. I'll replace it right away."

As he turned toward the kitchen, Zoe leaned in, whispering. "God, do you know what you're doing? That's Kholod Morozov!"

I just smiled without a word. That's the point—I wanted to crush that arrogant Kholod Morozov.

After seeing Zoe off, I headed back to the living room.

"Today... Did I do good enough?" Kholod's voice rasped, with a hint of hidden hope.

I walked up to him, reached out to untie his apron, moving slowly. My fingers brushed his neck skin by accident, feeling his muscles tense instantly.

"Barely passable." I met his tired amber eyes. "But it's nowhere near enough, Kholod. Your past work was too masterful; it'll take a lot more to fix it."

A spark flickered in his eyes, hardening into resolve.

For days, Kholod stuck to my demands, burying that restlessness under a calm facade. But I sensed the undercurrents churning beneath.

Until that rainy night.

He'd just finished reading me a passage about the Icelandic Aurora, his voice hoarse from the long session. I stared at the rain-streaked window and murmured, "Read like it has no soul. You don't get freedom, Kholod. You only know how to cage things."

The book slammed shut, shattering the quiet.

I turned calmly, watching him rise slowly. His massive frame cast an oppressive shadow in the light. All that earlier restraint vanished from his eyes, replaced by a cornered sharpness.

"I don't get it?" He advanced step by step, voice low and dangerous. "Yeah, I don't get the freedom you crave. But I'm starting to get other things..."

He stopped right in front of me, close enough to feel the heat radiating off him.

"You enjoy this, don't you?" His hand hovered, tracing the air along my cheek, sending a shiver through me. "Enjoy watching me grovel, enjoy stomping on my dignity, enjoy carving up my pride with words like a dull knife..."

His piercing gaze locked on mine, like it could strip away every mask.

"Tell me, Noelle," he leaned in close to my ear. "Treating me like this, are you really as cool as you seem? Or is this just your twisted kind of thrill?"

I backed up instinctively, but he anticipated, grabbing my wrist. Firm enough to hold me, not to hurt.

"Game's over. Or should we switch to something we're more 'familiar' with?"

I turned my face away from his stare.

"Look at me."

"I won't."

He gripped my chin, forcing my head up. Our eyes met, and fire blazed in his.

"Noelle," his voice husked, "you remember this?"

His fingers slid to my collarbone, then lower, pressing lightly over my clothes right on that tattoo spot.

"H.M."

His initials. Etched into me, impossible to erase.

"This brand isn't for me—it's for you." His breath ghosted my ear. "We're bound, Noelle. You can't run."

"Let go..."

"No." His voice stayed low, unyielding. "From the moment you saved me, from the second I marked you, you're mine."

Before the words faded, his lips crashed onto mine. I tried to shove him off, but he pinned my wrists to the wall. In that deep kiss, my struggles weakened.

Damn it. My body still remembered him—his scent, his touch, everything.

"Don't push me away..." He pulled back slightly, voice ragged.

"I..."

Before I could answer, he scooped me up in his arms.

"Leo's still—"

"He's asleep." He glanced at the crib. "This'll be quick."

"Kholod Morozov! Don't push it!"

"You're my wife. This isn't pushing it."

He carried me into the bedroom, kicking the door shut.

He set me on the bed, fingers slipping under my hem. "Your body remembers me, Noelle. You can't deny it."

"Stop..."

"Really want me to?" His fingers lingered at my waist. "Then why are you shaking?"

I bit my lip, refusing to answer, but he was right—that damn familiarity betrayed me.

"Why are you always like this..." My voice caught with a sob.

"Because I want you so bad it's driving me insane."

As he undid my buttons, I tried futilely to stop him, my hands weak.

"Tell me you want me too."

"I don't..."

He sealed my unfinished denial with another kiss. Clothes peeled away, cool air hitting my skin, followed by his scorching palms and heated breath.

"Noelle..." he panted, "my Noelle..."

Kholod's grip tightened as he hovered over me, his eyes dark with raw hunger. "God, I've been holding back so long I'm about to lose it," he growled, his voice thick with frustration. His hand trailed down my body, fingers parting my thighs with deliberate slowness. He dipped in, exploring, and a low chuckle escaped him when he felt the slick warmth there. "You're soaked, Noelle. Admit it—you've been wanting this too. Been craving me just as bad."

I glared up at him, fire in my eyes, refusing to give him the satisfaction. "Fuck you," I spat, lunging forward to bite his shoulder, hard enough to make him hiss. "Get off me, you bastard. Roll away and leave me the hell alone."

But he was faster, grabbing my chin and tilting my head back. Before I could clamp down again, his thumb pressed against my lips, prying them open. "Oh no you don't," he murmured, his tone laced with dark amusement. He slipped his fingers into my mouth, toying with my tongue, stroking it slowly, teasingly. "Bite me? That's cute. But let's see how you like this." His fingers danced, curling around my tongue, pulling it gently, making me gasp around them. "Suck on them, Noelle. Show me how much you hate me."

I tried to pull away, mumbling curses around his intrusion. "Stop... you asshole... get out..." But the words came out garbled, and damn it, the way he played with me sent unwanted sparks through my core. He leaned in, his breath hot on my neck. "What was that? Can't hear you with your mouth full. Try again—tell me to stop. Or is this turning you on more?" He withdrew slightly, only to plunge back in, mimicking a rhythm that had my body clenching involuntarily. "Yeah, that's it. Fight me all you want, but your tongue's betraying you. So eager, wrapping around me like it misses this."

"Bastard," I managed, my voice muffled, but the fight was draining as heat pooled lower. He kept at it, his free hand roaming my breasts, pinching my nipples just enough to make me arch. "Come on, Noelle, say it. Tell me you want my fingers deeper. Or should I replace them with something else?" His eyes locked on mine, challenging, as he finally pulled out, strings of saliva connecting us. I panted, glaring, but my body softened, melting under his touch despite myself.

Satisfied with my pliancy, Kholod positioned himself between my legs, his hard length pressing against my entrance. Without another word, he thrust in, filling me in one swift motion. I gasped, a sharp twinge of pain mixing with the stretch. "Ouch... back off, Kholod, it hurts," I whimpered, pushing at his chest, my nails digging in.

He stilled for a moment, but didn't pull back. Instead, his hands moved to my most sensitive spots—thumb circling my clit with expert pressure, while his other hand kneaded my breast, rolling the nipple between his fingers. "Shh, relax for me," he coaxed, his voice a husky whisper. "Let go, Noelle. Feel how good this can be. I've got you." The rhythmic rubbing eased the discomfort, turning it into waves of pleasure that had me unclenching, my body yielding despite my resolve.

Once I relaxed, he started moving, slow at first, deep thrusts that built a torturous rhythm. His mouth found the tattoo on my chest, lips pressing reverent kisses to the "H.M." etched there. "Don't leave me, Noelle," he murmured against my skin, his voice breaking with need. "Please... stay with me. I can't lose you." He kissed it again, tongue tracing the letters as he picked up pace, driving harder. "Promise me. Say you won't leave me."

I bit my lip harder, refusing to respond, even as he pounded into me relentlessly, each thrust sending jolts of ecstasy through my veins. No way I'd give in, not after everything. He groaned, sensing my silence, and shifted tactics. "Not satisfied? Guess I'm not trying hard enough." With a wicked grin, he flipped us so I was on top, his hands gripping my hips as he guided me down onto him. "Ride me, then. Take what you want—but don't think you can ignore me."

I tried to hold back, but he bucked up, hitting that perfect spot inside, making stars burst behind my eyes. Still, I stayed silent, clenching around him in defiance. He growled, pulling me down for a bruising kiss, then trailed his mouth lower, sucking on my nipples while his fingers worked my clit in tight circles. "Come on, scream for me. Let it out." But I wouldn't—until he angled just right, adding a twist of his hips that had me crying out despite myself, body shuddering in release.

Not done, he rolled us again, pinning me beneath him. "Still holding out? Let's fix that." He slowed, teasing the edge, pulling almost out before slamming back in, over and over. His hand slipped between us, fingers vibrating against my swollen bud as he whispered filthy promises. "Feel that? This is me owning you, Noelle. Every inch." He kissed the tattoo obsessively, begging between thrusts. "Don't leave... I need you... say it, please."

I arched, screams tearing from my throat as wave after wave crashed over me, my body betraying me with clenching spasms. But I clamped my mouth shut on any words, refusing to surrender, even as pleasure ripped through me like fire. He kept going, inventive now—switching positions, bending me over the edge of the bed, taking me from behind with slaps to my ass that stung deliciously, then pulling my hair to arch my back while he drove deep. "Like that? Or this?" He'd alternate speeds, fast and furious, then agonizingly slow, edging me until I was a trembling mess, screams echoing off the walls.

By the end, I was a wreck, body spent from multiple peaks, screams raw in my throat, but I never gave him the words he craved. No promises, no admissions. He finally spilled inside me with a guttural roar, collapsing over me, still murmuring pleas against my skin. But I stayed silent, my defiance intact, even in the afterglow.

Kholod's arms locked me tight against him. His heartbeat thrummed steadily in my ear, stark in the quiet.

I stared blankly at the ceiling, everything from before feeling like a storm I'd lost control of.

CHAPTER FORTY-ONE

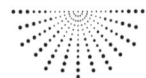

Noelle

Kholod set the carefully prepared lasagna in front of me, his eyes bright with anticipation.

"Try it. I made it the way you taught me."

I took a bite. The cheese and tomato melded perfectly on my tongue. "Better," I said objectively. "But you still used too much cheese."

He immediately pulled out his phone to record my feedback, his serious expression making me smile despite myself.

His transformation over these past weeks was undeniable.

From kitchen disaster to decent cook. From fumbling with a crying Leo to expertly changing diapers and getting him to sleep. Even when I remained cold toward him, he stayed patient.

That night, Leo was particularly fussy, squirming in my arms, refusing to settle.

"Come on, baby..." I patted his back gently. "Close your eyes..."

Kholod looked up from his paperwork. "Need help?"

"No," I said. "He's almost asleep."

I carried Leo to the window, gazing out at Niaube's peaceful night. The distant sound of waves drifted in. Lorenzo suddenly crossed my mind, and I murmured without thinking, "Wonder how Lorenzo's doing..."

The temperature in the room plummeted.

"You're still thinking about him." Kholod's voice could have frozen hell.

I turned to face his dangerous stare. "I'm just worried about a friend," I said wearily. "Don't be ridiculously jealous."

"Friend?" He moved closer, step by predatory step. "Noelle, are you sure he only thinks of you as a friend?"

"What else would it be?"

"I think he wants a hell of a lot more than that." His voice turned acidic. "And you... you enjoy his attention."

"Kholod Morozov," I took a deep breath. "Stop being paranoid."

"I'm not." He stopped in front of me. "I just want to know how much longer you're going to keep giving him pieces of your heart."

"Kholod!"

"I watch you smile at him, accept his help, live like a family..." His voice dropped, wounded. "Do you know how much that hurts?"

I stayed silent.

"I'm here, trying everything to make you happy. Learning to cook, taking care of Leo..." His voice cracked. "But he's still in your heart."

"You deserve it," I said. "Think about what you did to me."

"I know." His voice shook. "I know I deserve it. But Noelle, I'm human too. I get jealous. I hurt..."

Leo stirred in my arms, making soft little sounds.

Finally getting sleepy.

"Let me put him down first."

Kholod stood frozen, watching me. I gently placed Leo in his crib and tucked him in.

"Sleep tight," I whispered.

When I turned around, Kholod was still there.

"Noelle," he said suddenly. "I've made a decision."

"What decision?"

"I'm moving in here."

"Kholod, don't push your luck!"

"How is this pushing my luck?" He stepped closer. "I need everyone to see exactly who you belong to."

"You're insane! I'll never agree to that!"

"Why not?" He kept advancing. "I'm your husband. I have every right to live here."

"You—"

"I know you don't accept me yet, but I can wait. Noelle, I can't stand watching you and Lorenzo be so close anymore."

He trapped me between the wall and his body, hands braced on either side of me.

"Don't worry," he leaned down, his breath brushing my cheek. "I'll just take even better care of you."

"Impossible!"

"Say yes." His eyes pleaded. "Let me stay. I promise I won't bother you. I can sleep on the couch, do whatever you want..."

"No..."

"Why?" Panic flashed in his eyes. "Noelle, are you waiting for him to come back?"

"I'm not..."

"Then let me stay." His voice turned stubborn. "Noelle, please..."

His tone was demanding, his movements possessive, but the vulnerability and fear in his eyes were crystal clear. Even after all these days together, he still lived in constant terror—afraid of losing me, afraid Lorenzo would return, afraid I'd choose someone else.

Seeing him like this made my heart soften. Then I hated myself for that softness. Just like I hated this body that he could always so easily bewitch.

Fine.

One more month. If he behaved himself for one more month, maybe... maybe I could consider telling him the truth about Leo.

"All right," I finally gave in. "But you sleep on the couch."

"Yes! The couch is perfect!"

"No going in the bedroom."

"Fine."

"And absolutely no watching me sleep."

"I swear—"

Before he could finish, chaos erupted outside.

Glass shattered, followed by screams and shouts.

"What the hell?" I tensed.

Kholod's face darkened as he yanked me behind him. "Stay put." It was an order.

"But—"

The door exploded open.

A crowd surrounded the entrance. Lorenzo stood in the doorway, eyes blood-red, hair wild, radiating pure madness.

"Noelle!" he roared, reaching out. "Come with me! Now!"

"Lorenzo?" I stared in shock. "How did you—"

"Come with me!" he repeated. "Get away from this monster!"

"Lorenzo Conti." Kholod's voice was ice-cold as he shielded Leo and me. "Do you know what you're doing?"

"Of course I know!" Lorenzo bellowed. "I'm taking Noelle! Taking her away from you!"

"She won't go with you."

"That's not up to her!" Lorenzo pulled a gun from his waistband, the black barrel pointed straight at Kholod. "Kholod Morozov, let her go!"

My heart stopped.

"Lorenzo!" I screamed. "What are you doing? Put the gun down!"

"I won't!" His hand shook. "Noelle, come with me! I'll take you somewhere he'll never find you!"

"Lorenzo, calm down..."

"I am calm!" he roared, madness blazing brighter in his eyes. "Noelle, he destroyed you! You can't forgive him! You can't be with him!"

"Put down the gun." Kholod's voice was arctic. "Lorenzo, last warning. Put it down."

"No!" Lorenzo's finger tightened on the trigger. "Unless you let Noelle go!"

"Never."

"Then die!"

The gunshot rang out.

I instinctively shielded Leo, then felt strong arms wrap around me.

"Ugh..." Kholod grunted.

I looked up—

Blood. Pouring from his back, staining his white shirt red.

He'd been shot.

"Kholod!" I screamed.

Kholod staggered but stubbornly stayed standing, using his body as a shield between Lorenzo and me.

"You... you still won't let her go?" Lorenzo held the smoking gun, voice shaking.

"No." Kholod's voice was weak but steady. "Lorenzo, kill me if you want. But you'll never take her. And you sure as hell won't hurt her."

"Kholod..." Tears streamed down my face.

He turned back to me and smiled.

That smile—weak but tender.

"Don't be scared..." he said. "I won't let anyone hurt you... including myself..."

Before he finished speaking, his body swayed and crashed to the floor.

"Kholod!"

I rushed to him, dropping to my knees.

Blood kept pouring from the wound, soaking the carpet.

"Kholod! Kholod!" I pressed my hands to the wound, trying to stop the bleeding. "Don't die! You're not allowed to die!"

"Noelle..." he whispered weakly. "Is Leo... is he okay..."

"He's fine!" I sobbed. "Don't talk! I'm calling an ambulance..."

"Noelle..." He gripped my hand. "Sorry... didn't mean to scare you..."

"Shut up!" I yelled. "Kholod Morozov, I forbid you to die! You hear me!"

He smiled—satisfied and peaceful.

"Noelle..." His voice grew fainter. "I love you..."

"I know! I know!" Tears fell on his face. "Kholod, hold on..."

I turned toward Lorenzo. He stood there dazed, the gun fallen from his hands while his men started to advance.

"I... I killed him..." Lorenzo mumbled, walking toward me, even trying to take my hand. "I killed him... Noelle... come with me..."

"Get away!" I dodged his touch, voice fierce. "Lorenzo Conti, get out! Now!"

"Noelle..."

"GET OUT!"

He stumbled backward as Nick arrived with backup to restrain him. His accomplices were captured too.

"Boss! How bad is it? The doctor's coming!" Nick shouted.

"Get... everyone... out..." Kholod whispered.

"Boss—"

"That's... an order..."

"Yes..."

After Nick left with the others, only Kholod, Leo, and I remained. Leo was crying in his crib.

"Kholod..." I leaned down, pressing my forehead to his. "Hold on... please hold on..."

"Noelle..." His hand touched my cheek. "Don't cry..."

"I don't care!" I cried harder. "Kholod, you can't die... Leo needs you... He's your son! Yes! He's your son! You can't abandon us... I..."

I haven't forgiven you yet.

Light flickered in Kholod's eyes, then faded.

"Noelle..." His voice was barely audible. "Tell Leo... Daddy loves him..."

"You tell him yourself!" I yelled. "Kholod Morozov! You stay alive!"

His hand fell limp.

His eyes slowly closed.

"NO—!" My scream tore through the room.

Something ripped apart in my chest at that moment. The wall I'd spent over a year building crumbled to pieces.

CHAPTER FORTY-TWO

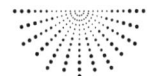

Kholod

When I opened my eyes again, the first thing I saw was Noelle's bloodshot eyes.

She was leaning over the bedside, her hair disheveled, tear tracks still fresh on her cheeks. When she saw me wake up, she froze for a moment before intense joy flooded her eyes.

"You're awake..." Her voice was hoarse and thick with tears.

"Noelle..." I tried to reach for her, but my arm was tethered to an IV line. My throat felt raw and my voice came out raspy, but I had to confirm what I'd heard before losing consciousness. "Leo... he's my child, isn't he? Not Lorenzo's, right?"

Her body went rigid. She lowered her gaze as fresh tears fell, then gave a barely perceptible nod.

"Yes."

That single word seized my heart like a vice, squeezing until it nearly spasmed.

"Really?" My voice trembled. "You're not lying to me?"

"I'm not lying to you." She lifted her head, tears blurring her vision. "Kholod, Leo is your son."

Heat flooded my eyes.

I had a son.

I really had a son.

"...I have a son."

Tears spilled uncontrollably, sliding down my temples. I didn't bother wiping them away, just gripped her hand tightly.

"But I missed his birth..." I choked out. "Missed all these months... I didn't even know he existed..."

"You deserved that." Her voice cracked, though tears still shimmered in her eyes. "If you hadn't treated me the way you did back then..."

"I know..." I closed my eyes and let the tears flow freely. "I'm sorry... it's all my fault."

She said nothing more, just gently withdrew her hand and clumsily wiped my tears with a tissue.

"Stop crying. You just woke up—you can't get agitated. The doctor said you need complete rest."

"I'm just... so happy." I opened my eyes and caught her hand again. "Noelle, thank you... thank you for giving me a son."

"You shouldn't thank me," she said. "Thank yourself for surviving. If you had died, Leo would never have known who his father was."

"I won't die." I looked directly into her eyes. "For you, for Leo—I'll never die."

She turned away, but I could clearly see her shoulders trembling.

She was crying.

Crying for me.

Over the following days, Noelle barely left my side.

"Lift your arm."

The warm washcloth moved gently across my skin, carefully avoiding the wounds on my back.

"Does it hurt?"

"No."

"You're lying. I saw you wince."

"It really doesn't hurt." I smiled. "With you taking care of me, even pain doesn't matter."

"Smooth talker." She chided softly, though the corners of her mouth lifted slightly.

"Ma'am, the boss's lunch is ready." Nick entered with a tray.

"The doctor said you can only have liquids for now." She picked up the porridge bowl and sat down. "I simmered this for two hours. It should be soft enough."

"You made it yourself?"

"Who else would?" She ladled up a spoonful. "Open your mouth."

"I can feed myself..."

"You have an IV in your hand. Don't move—I'll feed you."

"Alright."

She fed me patiently, one spoonful at a time.

"Is it too hot?"

"Perfect."

"Then eat more. You lost a lot of blood and need to rebuild your strength."

"Noelle."

"What?"

"You're so good to me. These past few days have been happier than my entire lifetime."

"Don't say that," she murmured. "Just eat."

But I noticed her ears turning pink.

At night, the pain from my wounds made sleep impossible. Strangely, I'd endured worse injuries before without complaint, but in front of her, I found the discomfort unbearable.

"Noelle, are you asleep?"

"No." She sat up from the cot beside my bed. "Is the pain bothering you again? I'll call the doctor."

"No need," I caught her hand. "Just stay and talk to me."

"About what?"

"Anything... I just want to hear your voice."

She was quiet for a moment before finally settling on the edge of my bed.

"How about I tell you about Leo?"

"Yes."

"When he was born," her voice was soft, "he only weighed five pounds. The doctor said it was because I was too exhausted during pregnancy and didn't get proper nutrition."

My heart clenched.

"I'm sorry..."

"Don't interrupt me."

"Sorry."

"When he first came into the world, he cried so loudly. The nurse said he had excellent lung capacity."

"Like me. I was the same as a baby."

"Really?" She glanced at me. "Then that's definitely like you."

"What else does he take after me?"

"Well... his nose and chin resemble yours. But his eyes are like mine—brown."

"I want to see him."

"Of course."

She pulled out her phone and showed me photos one by one. I studied each image intently, wanting to burn every detail into my memory.

"Noelle, I've missed so much of him."

"Yes."

"I'll make up for it," I said earnestly. "I swear I'll be a good father."

She studied me, complex emotions flickering in her eyes.

"You'll have your work cut out for you," she finally said. "Kholod, being a father isn't easy."

"I know." I squeezed her hand. "But for you and Leo, I'm willing to do anything, no matter how difficult."

A month later, I was finally able to use a wheelchair. Noelle pushed me out to the garden for some fresh air. Since my injuries were too severe to return to Philadelphia immediately, we remained at the Washington estate.

The early winter sunlight felt warm against my skin.

"Such beautiful weather." I gazed up at the sky.

"Yeah." She settled on a nearby bench.

"Noelle."

"Yes?"

"I have something I want to tell you."

"What is it?" She turned to face me.

I tilted my head back to meet her gaze. The sunlight cast a soft halo around her.

"Noelle," I took a deep breath, "will you marry me again?"

She went completely still, shock filling her eyes.

"What... did you say?"

"I said, marry me." I gripped her hand with my functional arm. My palm was cold and clammy with nerves, but my hold was steady and firm.

"Kholod, you..."

"I know I have no right to ask this of you. I destroyed our beginning, gave you a wedding filled with terror and humiliation. I forced you at that altar, shamed you in front of everyone."

"Kholod..."

"I hurt you and claimed you in the most despicable way possible, subjecting you to every kind of degradation." I continued. "I imprisoned you, tormented you, branded you as my property. I refused to trust you, doubted you, even locked you away in that basement..."

"Enough," she interrupted. "Stop talking."

"No, I have to say this." I stared directly into her eyes. "Noelle, you need to know how deeply I regret everything. Every single day and night, I'm consumed with regret."

"But what good does regret do?" Tears streamed down her face. "Those wounds don't heal just because you're sorry."

"I know," I said. "That's why I'm not asking for your forgiveness. Noelle, all I'm asking is..."

"Please give me one more chance. Not as the head of the Morozov family, but as Leo's father—as a man who wants to spend the rest of his life loving you and making amends."

Her tears fell faster.

"I want to give you a real wedding," I continued, my voice thick with emotion. "On Christmas Eve, at the Cathedral Basilica of Saints Peter and Paul. I want to place a ring on your finger in front of everyone and tell them you're my one and only beloved wife. I want to erase all those nightmares and give you the fresh start you deserve. Noelle, marry me. Let me spend my lifetime proving that you and our child can depend on me."

She stared at me as tears continued streaming down her cheeks.

"I'll give you everything you've ever wanted. Wherever you wish to go, I'll take you there. Whatever freedom you desire, I'll provide it. Just please give me one more chance..."

"Enough," she interrupted again, wiping her tears. "Kholod, stop."

"Noelle..."

"I..." She took a shaky breath. "I need time to think about this."

My heart sank slightly. Not a rejection, but not acceptance either.

"Of course." I nodded. "Take all the time you need. Whatever your answer may be," I looked deep into her eyes, "I won't give up."

She didn't respond, just silently turned and pushed the wheelchair back toward the house.

But I noticed her hands trembling on the handles.

Noelle still hadn't given me her answer, but she continued caring for me as devotedly as before—bathing me, feeding me, keeping me company.

"Noelle, I'm missing Leo."

"Should we video call him?"

"Yes."

She pulled out her phone and connected with Darya. I'd assigned Darya to Niaube along with several nannies to care for Leo. Initially, Leo would cry whenever he saw strangers, but the moment he spotted Noelle on video, he would calm down.

Soon, my son's tiny face appeared on the screen.

"Leo!" Noelle called to him.

"Ma...ma..." The little boy broke into a grin. He could already say "mama."

"Do you miss mommy?"

"Ya ya!"

"Good boy, mommy will be home soon..."

Watching this scene filled me with unprecedented contentment.

"Leo," I couldn't help calling out.

The little one turned toward me on the screen.

"This is..." Noelle hesitated. "This is daddy."

My heart lurched.

"Da...da..." Leo tilted his head, seeming to understand but not quite.

"Yes, that's Daddy." My voice caught. "Leo, Daddy will come see you very soon."

"Ya!"

Seeing my son's smile brought tears to my eyes again.

"Kholod," Noelle sighed softly. "Why do you cry so often now?"

"Sorry," I wiped away the tears. "I'm just... so overwhelmed."

"Alright, alright," she said gently. "Stop crying now. Leo, wave bye-bye to daddy."

"Ah ah!" Leo flailed his tiny hands.

"Goodbye, my son." I waved back. "Daddy will be there soon."

After the call ended, I continued staring at the darkened screen, lost in thought.

Three weeks later, the doctor finally cleared me for discharge.

"Noelle, shall we return to Niaube?" I asked from my wheelchair.

"Yes, Leo is still there."

"I can hardly wait to see him."

"Neither can I."

The car finally arrived.

Noelle helped me from the vehicle and pushed the wheelchair toward the small building. The instant the door opened—

"Ma...ma..."

A tiny figure came toddling over unsteadily. He could already walk.

"Leo!" Noelle knelt down and opened her arms wide.

Leo tumbled into her embrace, giggling with delight.

I sat in my wheelchair watching them, my chest filled with warmth.

"Leo," Noelle held him and turned toward me. "Look, this is daddy."

Leo looked at me, tilting his little head as he glanced between me and Noelle.

"Go ahead," Noelle encouraged softly. "That's your daddy."

Leo slowly extended his small hand. I carefully lifted him onto my lap.

His body was soft and warm, carrying the faint scent of milk.

"Leo..." My voice trembled. "Daddy's Leo..."

"Ya!" He patted my cheek.

"Does that hurt?" Noelle asked.

"Not at all," I laughed through my tears. "It doesn't hurt one bit."

Leo stared curiously at my tears and reached out to touch them.

"Da...da..." he called in his sweet, babbling voice.

My heart melted completely.

"Yes, daddy's here." I held him close. "Daddy will always be here."

Another two weeks passed before the doctor said I could abandon the wheelchair.

"But you still can't overexert yourself," the doctor cautioned. "The wounds need more time to fully heal."

"I understand."

The moment I stood up from that wheelchair, I felt reborn.

"Noelle, look," I took a few careful steps. "I can walk."

"Be careful," she steadied me. "Don't fall."

"I won't."

I walked over to Leo's crib and gazed down at my sleeping son.

"Noelle, I want to take you both back to Philadelphia."

"Why? Isn't it nice here?" Resistance colored her tone.

"I know you don't want to go back." I took her hand. "There are too many painful memories there. But Noelle, I want to show you—everything has changed."

"What do you mean?"

"Before I came to find you, I had the entire place renovated," I explained. "All those cold colors you despised are gone. Everything is warm tones now—very cozy and inviting. I also replaced all the clothes in your wardrobe with styles you actually like."

"Kholod, did you plan this from the beginning?"

"No. But I kept hoping that maybe, just maybe, you'd be willing to come back. I wanted everything to be ready if you did."

She remained silent.

"I know it takes courage. But Noelle, that place is our home."

"Let me think about it," she finally said.

"Of course," I nodded. "Take your time."

That evening, Noelle came to my room.

"Kholod, are you asleep?"

"Not yet," I sat up. "What is it?"

"I've made my decision," she sat on the edge of the bed. "About returning to Philadelphia."

"Oh?" I couldn't help tensing.

"I'm willing to go back," she said. "But I have conditions."

"What conditions? Tell me."

"First, I want my own space. I don't want to be monitored or have my freedom restricted."

"Absolutely," I agreed immediately. "You can go anywhere you want."

"Second, I want to continue pursuing my own interests. I refuse to be some idle trophy wife."

"I completely support whatever you want to do."

"Third," she met my eyes. "About the wedding..."

"Yes?"

"I accept," she said. "Kholod, I'm willing to marry you again."

I froze, hardly daring to believe what I'd heard.

"You... what did you say?"

"I said I will marry you," she repeated. "Kholod, I'm willing to give you another chance."

"Noelle!" I started to rise excitedly, but she gently pressed me back down.

"Don't move!" she said. "Your injuries aren't completely healed yet."

"But..."

"Let me finish first." Her tone was measured. "Kholod, I'm willing to remarry you for Leo's sake, but that doesn't mean I've forgiven you. Those wounds and that pain—I still need time to process everything."

She paused before continuing. "We'll... take things slowly. Start from the beginning."

"Yes," I gripped her hand tightly. "Noelle, thank you... thank you for giving me a chance..."

"Don't celebrate too early," she warned. "Kholod, if you ever make the same mistakes again, I'll leave immediately—and this time, you'll never find me."

"I won't," I vowed solemnly. "Noelle, I swear I'll never hurt you again."

She looked at me, uncertainty still lingering in her eyes, but finally —slowly and resolutely—she squeezed my hand in return.

In that moment, I felt like I possessed the entire world.

CHAPTER FORTY-THREE

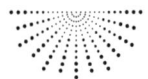

Noelle

"Ma'am, here's the revised guest list."

Dmitri placed a file on the coffee table. I sat beside Kholod, flipping through it. The pages were packed with the most powerful names from Philadelphia and the entire East Coast.

"Isn't this too many people?" I frowned slightly.

"This is the trimmed version," Kholod explained gently. "Noelle, you're the lady of the Morozov family. This wedding isn't just about family honor—it's our fresh start. It has to be grand enough."

"But..."

"I want everyone to see," he looked at me with determination, "that you're the only wife I treasure."

I sighed softly and continued reading through the list. Ever since I'd agreed to come back with him, he'd been announcing to everyone that I was his wife.

"Boss, there's something else to report."

"Go ahead."

"About that night's attack—it was Kieran with his remaining forces who planned it."

"Kieran?" I looked up in surprise.

"Yes." Dmitri nodded. "Boss should have mentioned Isabella's situation to you. After that incident, we've been hunting him down, but he managed to slip away and hide. This attack was his revenge."

"And now he's..."

"Dead." Kholod's tone was calm. "This time we're certain."

I'd just started to relax when my heart clenched again.

"What about Lorenzo? How is he?"

Dmitri and Kholod exchanged a glance.

"Ma'am," Dmitri chose his words carefully, "Lorenzo Conti went completely insane after the attack."

"What?" My voice trembled slightly.

"The Bellucci family took him in. But he couldn't accept that you chose Boss... He wanders the Philadelphia streets all day with a bundle of withered roses, telling anyone who'll listen that he needs to bring his bride home."

"He's lost his mind?" I couldn't believe it.

"Yes, ma'am. Completely."

My hands started shaking, tears welling up instantly.

"Lorenzo..."

"Noelle." Kholod pulled me into his arms. "Don't be sad."

"But it's because of me..."

"Not entirely," he said softly. "Kieran exploited his feelings, and he chose this path himself."

"But..."

"I won't destroy him completely." Kholod sighed. "There's no point with a madman, especially one who helped you before. This is more about his own obsession."

I leaned against him, tears sliding down silently. Lorenzo, who had helped me, protected me—how had he ended up like this?

"Stop crying." He patted my back gently. "All the old grudges and entanglements should be let go. We need to look forward."

I wiped my tears and nodded.

"Dmitri," Kholod instructed, "arrange for someone to regularly send Lorenzo necessities. Make sure he has food and shelter."

"Yes, boss."

"Also, how's the Bellucci family asset transfer progressing? Have our people assist with it—all of that will be Noelle's from now on."

"Everything's been returned. By the way, ma'am, since you've been back, Madam Sofia has requested to see you six times. Would you like to meet with her?"

I sighed softly. I resented my mother, but I couldn't blame her for everything. During my three years away, except for Zoe, I'd cut contact with almost all my relatives.

"Arrange the meeting."

"Understood."

After Dmitri left, Kholod held me tighter.

"Noelle," he whispered in my ear, "it's all over. From now on, we can truly start our new life."

I closed my eyes, settling safely into his embrace.

* * *

Christmas Eve arrived as planned.

I stood outside the Cathedral Basilica of Saints Peter and Paul, staring at the building that had once witnessed my humiliation.

"Nervous?" Zoe walked over—today she was my maid of honor.

"A little," I admitted honestly.

"Don't worry," she squeezed my hand, "I'll be right here with you."

"Thank you, Zoe."

She smiled. "We don't need to say things like that between us."

"Noelle." Anya's voice came from behind me. She and Anastasia had just returned after handling business in Russia.

"Long time no see." Anya looked me up and down. "Nice dress. Much better than the last one."

"Thank you."

"Who said I was complimenting you?" She turned away, ears slightly red. "I'm just stating facts."

"You're right." I couldn't help but smile.

"Also," she pulled an elegant jewelry box from her bag, "this is for you."

Inside was a bracelet with a simple yet exquisite design.

"This is..."

"Wedding gift." Her tone was awkward. "That design sketch you gave me last time—I had someone make it into the real thing. Mother and I each have one, and this is yours."

"Anya..." My eyes grew hot.

"Don't cry!" She said quickly. "This is just returning the favor! Don't read too much into it!"

"Okay, I won't read into it. Thank you, Anya."

"You talk too much." She turned around. "The ceremony's about to start. Get inside. Can't keep Kholod waiting too long."

The church doors slowly opened, and the pipe organ began its solemn melody. I walked into the church on my mother's arm, the red carpet lined with guests on both sides, all eyes focused on me.

But in my eyes, there was only that figure at the altar—Kholod.

He wore a black suit, standing tall and straight. When he saw me, his eyes instantly lit up.

I walked toward him step by step, heart pounding like a drum. But this time, it wasn't forced—it was my choice.

"You look beautiful," he said softly when I reached him.

The priest began the ceremony.

"Kholod Morozov, do you take Noelle Bellucci to be your wife, through good times and bad, wealth and poverty, sickness and health, to love her, honor her, and stay by her side for life?"

"I do." His voice was firm and strong.

"Noelle Bellucci, do you take Kholod Morozov to be your husband, through good times and bad, wealth and poverty, sickness and health, to love him, honor him, and stay by his side for life?"

I took a deep breath.

"I do."

Kholod's eyes grew slightly misty.

"Now, groom, please place the ring on your bride's finger."

He pulled a diamond ring from his jacket—simple yet elegant design with a brilliant center stone.

"Noelle," he took my hand, slowly sliding the ring onto my ring finger, "this time, I want to marry you the right way."

"I now pronounce," the priest smiled, "you husband and wife. Groom, you may kiss your bride."

Kholod cupped my face and leaned down tenderly.

The kiss was reverent and deep.

Applause echoed through the church.

I closed my eyes, letting tears of happiness fall.

After the wedding, we returned to Gladwyn Manor.

"Noelle, close your eyes," Kholod said at the door. "I have a surprise for you."

"Okay." I obediently closed my eyes.

He took my hand, leading me down the long hallway.

"You can open them now."

I opened my eyes and froze in place.

On the desk sat a brand new laptop and a set of professional camera equipment.

"This is..."

"For you," he said. "Noelle, you've been writing a blog all along, haven't you?"

"But that account was deleted..."

"I had it restored." He walked to the desk and picked up a document. "This is the ownership papers for the 'Vagabond Dreams' domain. Now this blog belongs completely to you."

I took the document, hands trembling slightly.

"You... you restored all the data?"

"Every article, every photo," he said with certainty. "All of it's back."

"Kholod..." Tears filled my eyes.

"Don't cry." He gently wiped away my tears with his fingertips. "I once destroyed your dreams with my own hands. Now, let me help you pick them up again."

"Thank you..."

"No need to thank me." He kissed my forehead lightly. "This is what I should do."

He walked to the bookshelf and took down a large scroll.

"What's this?"

"Look."

He slowly unrolled the scroll on the floor.

It was a detailed world map, marked with countless locations.

"These," he pointed to the map, "are all the places you once wanted to visit, right?"

I crouched down, staring at those familiar place names. Iceland, Norway, New Zealand, Morocco... all the dream destinations I'd recorded in my blog.

"Yes."

"Then let's go." He crouched beside me. "From now on, anywhere you want to go, we'll go together."

"Really?"

"Really." He pulled a black card from his pocket and handed it to me. "This card has no limit. Wherever you want to go, whatever you want to buy, you can use it."

I took the card, looking at the name "Noelle Morozov" on it.

"Kholod..."

"Your world," he gripped my hand tightly, his gaze gentle yet determined, "shouldn't be trapped in any manor. Noelle, I promise—from now on, I won't be your cage anymore. I'll be the companion who explores the world with you."

I looked at the sincere light in his eyes and couldn't help throwing myself into his arms.

"Thank you..." I choked up. "Kholod, really, thank you..."

"No, I'm the one who should say thank you." He held me tightly. "Noelle, thank you for giving me a second chance. I'll spend my whole life treasuring you, loving you."

We embraced in front of this map filled with dreams.

Outside the window, snow began to fall again.

But this time, I only found the scene breathtakingly beautiful. Because I knew that no matter where the future took us, he'd be by my side. And I could finally spread my wings and fly free.

Printed in Dunstable, United Kingdom

79351536R00210